The SISTER ACT

By Helena Harte

2025

Butterworth Books is a different breed of publishing house. It's a home for Indies, for independent authors who take great pride in their work and produce top quality books for readers who deserve the best. Professional editing, professional cover design, professional proof reading, professional book production—you get the idea. As Individual as the Indie authors we're proud to work with, we're Butterworths and we're *different*.

Authors currently publishing with us:

E.V. Bancroft
Valden Bush
Addison M Conley
Jo Fletcher
Helena Harte
Lee Haven
Karen Klyne
Sydney Lear
AJ Mason
Ally McGuire
James Merrick
JP Preston
Robyn Nyx (RJ Nyx)
Simon Smalley
Brey Willows

For more information visit www.butterworthbooks.co.uk

This trade paperback is published by Butterworth Books, UK

CATALOGING INFORMATION
ISBN: 978-1-915009-91-3
CREDITS
Editor: Victoria Villaseñor
Cover Design: Nicci Robinson
Production Design: Global Wordsmiths

Acknowledgements

Ally and I talk about book ideas all the time. When we were talking about a fake-romance book, I ran with it and had a fully formed story within ten minutes of the initial spark. That made it mine to write, which—yippee—was great, because the story practically poured out of me, and I wrote it in less than two months! So my first thank you is to my wife. I love how we share this creative journey we're on!

Thank you as always to Margaret Burris, who combs my manuscripts for Britishisms and errors everyone else has missed. You're a great proof reader, and I'm so glad we're working together.

My final thank you is to my readers, old and new. Thank you for buying my books and sharing my love of all things romance.

Your support means so much to me. And for those of you waiting "patiently" for book three in the Windy City Romance series, the wait will soon be over. I'm already back in the writing chair, crafting Solo and Janie's second-chance story!

Dedication

To my wife,
If the world is a stage,
you're my leading lady.

Chapter One

Leoni York twirled the pen between her fingers and smiled at the fluffy purple creature flopping about on its end, googly eyes rolling wildly. "We have ten packages to suit all budgets running from standard all the way through to stellar, Mr. Stephens," she said, no longer needing the script she'd learned within two days of working at Perfect Fit. *All budgets* was a bit misleading since the standard package started at $2,000, but that was pocket change for most of the people who used this company.

"I just need someone for one night on the Fourth of July. Four hours max," he said. "Which level is that?"

"That would be our silver tier, Mr. Stephens. We'll send you a secure link to access the available companions for that time and date once you've made the initial deposit. Then you choose your perfect fit." She looked across the open-plan office when the boss's door opened. Ruth waved a pink and gold folder in her direction and beckoned Leoni to join her. Leoni tapped her ear to show she was on a call, and Ruth drew her finger across her throat before pointing to Sissy at the adjacent cubicle. She nodded and rolled back on her chair to tap Sissy on the shoulder. She made their transfer code sign and tilted her head to Ruth's office.

Sissy gave her the thumbs up. "Whenever you're ready."

Leoni passed her the notes she'd made on the potential client. "I'm so sorry, Mr. Stephens, but would you mind if I transferred you to my colleague, Sissy? She's fully up to speed on your requirements and will be able to assist you." She switched the call without waiting for a response and headed over to Ruth, who was already sitting behind the giant oak desk that made her look like a kid at the adults' table.

"Leoni, we have a problem, and only you can fix it." Ruth gestured for her to sit on the couch by the window, where the pink folder waited for her attention.

"I haven't had a stellar file for a while." She picked it up and placed it on her knee but didn't open it; Ruth liked a bit of drama, and Leoni was always happy to play along.

Ruth raised her eyebrow. "Incorrect. You had the gig in Austin three weeks ago."

Leoni smiled. "I mean a pink stellar instead of a green one. Too many straight guys need perfect women."

"Whereas all the queer girls have got it figured out? Remind me...are you still single?"

Leoni huffed. "You keep me too busy going on fake dates to have time for real ones. And I don't need to be in a couple to be complete, thank you very much."

"Well, anyway, you have universal appeal, and you're in demand. What can I say?" She glanced away briefly. "But this one's a little different."

Leoni's fingers twitched around the folder. Ruth never avoided eye contact; what the hell was in her hands that would make her so squirrelly? "Different in what way?"

Ruth stood and came around her desk to sit beside Leoni. "You're our only college-educated, trained actor, Leoni, and you're going to need your chameleon skills even more than usual."

Like she needed to be reminded of the degree being wasted. Ruth's gentle pat on Leoni's knee caused her to narrow her eyes. Ruth was never this nice unless she wanted something *very* special. "Different, *how*?" She prayed there hadn't been a sudden change in company policy, and this was Ruth's way of conveying that to the troops. Leoni wasn't about to be the messenger everyone would want to shoot before they all hung up their heels and tuxes and deserted the place.

Ruth placed her hand on the file, her expression super serious.

"Tyler has COVID. Her wife just called to tell me that she's in the hospital."

"Jesus, it's that bad?"

Ruth pressed her lips together and wrinkled her nose again. "I hope not. Tyler isn't exactly a weakling now, is she? I'm sure she'll be fine."

Leoni bit her lip at the exceptionally pleasant memory of how Tyler was precisely the opposite of a weakling in the stamina department. She still hadn't forgiven her for getting married, really, but Tyler better beat that damn virus. Then the penny dropped, and Leoni's jaw did the same. "Wait. Is this the gig Tyler's been bragging about for the past month? The gig that starts *tomorrow*?"

Ruth nodded slowly. "A week in the Hamptons with one of the Hartwell family daughters."

Leoni gestured to herself. "How am I supposed to turn all this femme swish into...that." She pointed to the full-length photo of Tyler on the wall opposite Ruth's desk. Short back and sides, impeccably tailored tuxedo, all that swagger...pretty much everything Leoni looked for in a one-night stand.

"You're the trained actor. *Act*. This could be the best role of your life. Think Charlize Theron in *Monster*."

Leoni frowned. "Tyler's hardly a monster; she's the most handsome person on your roster."

Ruth waved the observation away. "I didn't mean literally, dear. I meant, be a method actor. Transform yourself into the complete opposite of all that feminine loveliness. Become a masc dreamboi."

Leoni instinctively touched her hair. "There is no amount of money you can offer me that would convince me to cut off my hair."

Ruth twirled her fingers in Leoni's locks and shook her head. "Pah, as if I'd ask you to do that for one job. Do the thing all the younger lesbians are doing: pull it up into a ponytail and wear a ball cap." She took Leoni's hand. "Get rid of the polish and trim the nails." Then she ran her finger along the collar of Leoni's silk blouse. "Buy some flannel and some Converse. That's what your company credit card is for. Just do your research and do it quick. You're booked on an early morning flight to Newark tomorrow. The daughter wants you to make a grand entrance, so Jonn will meet you at Newark with a brand-new G-class."

Jonn? Leoni racked her brain. Ah, he was their car guy on the East Coast, though she had no idea why Ruth had paused so dramatically, as if that little piece of information should make her drop to her knees and kiss Ruth's feet for this poop-covered opportunity. Acting like the world's best girlfriend was one thing, but transforming herself into a butch woman as strong and smooth as Tyler would be more than a stretch. She didn't know the first thing about chivalry other than she liked very much to be on the receiving end of it.

Ruth rolled her eyes. "Mercedes-Benz *G-class.*"

The emphasis on the repetition didn't help but pointing that out might get her fired. She glanced at the file in her hand; this might get her fired anyway... "And that's a nice car?"

Ruth snatched the folder from Leoni's knee, flipped through it, and gave it back to her at a full-page color photo of something that looked like it belonged on a battlefield. The brief image of Tyler behind the wheel made her a little twitchy though. If only Tyler's wife was open to a little polyamory, Leoni would be happy being the secondary. All the fun and none of the boring relationship responsibility sounded just about perfect to her.

"It's not a car," Ruth said. "It's a luxury SUV that you can take off-road."

Leoni grimaced. "Why would I want to go off-road? I'm not a big fan of driving *on* the road."

Ruth flipped the file closed. "Tyler was *very* excited about it."

"Duh, of course she was." Leoni treated herself to another glance at Tyler's picture. "I'm sure she had plans to zip up and down the beach on it..." Dressed in nothing but a white tank top and cut-off jean shorts, with all her tan muscly hardness on show. "But I'm not Tyler, am I? Is there really no one else who can step in?

What about Blair or Harper?"

Ruth shook her head. "Both on several different jobs all week."

"Jesse?"

Ruth clasped Leoni's hand firmly. "There's no one else."

"But I have gigs next week too. Four of them." Even before she said it, she heard the whininess.

"Sissy and Katie will cover those." Ruth released Leoni's hand and returned to the stately position behind her desk.

Discussion over. Not that there was ever any question that Ruth's proposal was up for debate. Leoni ran her hand across the embossed gold stripe on the folder. Stellar files *did* pay well.

"Ginny has all your travel arrangements, and the Hartwell daughter has been given your contact details. We've shortened your name to Leo, so at least you don't have to remember to answer to a different name all week," Ruth said.

A different moniker would be the least of her worries with this job. She deliberately exaggerated a sashayed walk to Ruth's door. God, she was going to miss heels. The last time she'd gone a whole week out of high heels was when she'd been forced to go to a ridiculous summer camp. "No one has *ever* shortened my name to Leo and escaped with their tongue. A different name would've been preferable."

"You know I love your fiery side, darling, but suck it up. Pull this one off without a hitch, and we can talk bonuses."

That was the one thing that could make this job worthwhile. It might be just the right amount to finally make that move... She chided herself silently. Who was she kidding? She'd settled, and she loved the lifestyle this job afforded her. Dreams were meant to fade. That was just part of growing up and realizing not everyone was meant to be something special, wasn't it?

Chapter Two

Aspen Hartwell glanced at her watch sitting on the drafting table beside the beginnings of her fifth draft for a particularly picky client. The lead in her mechanical pencil snapped again as she pressed it harder on the tracing paper. Just thinking about the guy ramped up her tension.

She clicked out another few millimeters of lead, then checked the route to LAX again. She only had ten minutes before she had to get on the road, so she rolled up the design and slid it into a blueprint tube. Aspen looked out the floor-to-ceiling windows of her temporary office and sighed. The night sky glowed with the city's light pollution. That was one thing she wouldn't miss for the next week. The stars at the beach house would be spectacular, even if the rest of it was fraught and exhausting. If only her parents would let go of this annual ritual or at least allow her a hall pass occasionally. Well, they were going to have to be okay with her working a lot of the time, because Henry Mancharlson, or Mancub as she'd taken to calling him, wasn't going to wait much longer for yet another design draft. And this was her last chance to give him whatever the heck it was he wanted, or he'd take his considerable business elsewhere.

She put her watch on, packed up the rest of her gear into her soft leather messenger bag, and slung it and the drawing tube over her shoulder. Then she switched off her desk lamp and headed to the elevator to the building's underground parking. Once there, Aspen placed her gear alongside her luggage in the trunk. Her mom had wanted, as usual, to send an executive driver to pick her up and take her to the airport. And as usual, Aspen had declined.

It was dark at nearly four in the morning, but she still didn't want anyone to see her being chauffeured around in a limo.

She got behind the wheel of the Niro and pushed the start button. The electric whirr was barely audible, and she smiled. Betty, her much sexier and much louder Bronco Raptor, was in the beach house garage, and if it was the only fun thing Aspen did all week, she would definitely be carving out some time for an off-roading adventure. As if she'd sent that message out into the Universe, her cell vibrated in her pants' pocket and her watch display identified the caller as her long-time buddy and business partner.

She tapped answer on the watch screen. "Hey, Flynn."

"Asp, I've got a problem."

She pulled out into the night traffic and headed down West Jefferson. "You'd better not be pulling out. The only way I can survive this week is if you're by my side."

Flynn laughed. "As if I'd miss the Hartwell Independence family vacation, bro. And also, that's so not true. I bet you're planning to spend the whole week in Betty."

"That sounds all kinds of wrong, and you know it's more fun with both of us in the cab," Aspen said. "But that's not to be. I've got our new client breathing down my neck, changing all the specs after commission. I'll have to work some of the time."

"So you'd survive just fine without me, huddled up in the tower away from everyone."

"No way. I need my buddy there to remind me real people exist *outside* that bubble." She turned left on South La Brea, loving how empty the roads were. The sun wouldn't rise for another couple of hours, and then the mayhem would begin on the 405 and every road surrounding it. But Aspen didn't have to worry about that for now; she'd be settled in the airport lounge eating breakfast by then. "Anyway, what's your issue? You almost sound serious."

"It's a plaid problem... You didn't tell me which colors you were packing, and I don't want to end up looking like two butch bookends, especially at the big party."

Aspen chuckled. "I just slung some shirts into the suitcase. I didn't pay much attention to the color."

"You lie. When did you last sling anything anywhere? Don't play with me. I've got to look my best for your brother's bi bestie."

"You been working on that alliteration for a while?"

"A whole week, bro."

"No doubt. One second," Aspen said and stopped at the lights. The woman she'd seen there every day for the month she'd been in LA sidled up to the car with an armful of flower bouquets. She rolled the window down and exchanged a twenty for a bunch of yellow tulips, just like she'd done every couple of days when the lights stopped her. "Don't you ever sleep, Millie?"

Millie shook her head. "People need flowers. People need beauty. Especially here. Are you on your way *to* or *from* the lucky girl with these?"

"Neither. I'm on my way to the airport to go home for a week." Though she really would prefer to be on her way to a hot date.

Millie smiled, and the streetlights reflected in her gold front tooth. "Fourth of July?" She whistled through her teeth when Aspen nodded. "Better celebrate while you can. Who knows when the civil war will start?" She patted the roof of the car and stepped back onto the sidewalk when the light changed to go. "Enjoy, pretty boy."

"Yes, ma'am," Aspen said, slightly perturbed by the civil war comment, mostly because it really was a concern.

"Pretty boy?" Flynn asked after Aspen had pulled away.

"Yup. I don't know if she actually thinks I'm a guy or not, and I don't—"

"You don't ask because you like being called a pretty boy!" Flynn snort-laughed. "Pretty boy, pretty boy," she sing-songed.

"I'm gonna kick your ass if you keep that up."

"So scared. Anyway, back to me and my clothing issue. We both look great in blue—it brings out the color in our eyes—but you don't need any help in the romance department, and I've decided to finally make my move with Kelly. I'm hoping there won't just be fireworks in the sky on the Fourth of July."

"Nice rhyme. You're working it hard tonight," Aspen said as she merged onto La Cienega. "Bring whatever you want, but I've got some shirts in my closet at the beach house too. If all else fails, you can wear something of mine to impress Kelly, and I'll put on a trash bag."

"Cool, cool, cool. You know how much I covet your Ralph collection."

A public address announcement came over the cell from Flynn's side, and Aspen shook her head. "Busted. You're already at the airport. Have you packed *any* clothes?"

"Gotta go," Flynn said. "That's my flight, and my best buddy will *not* be happy if I'm not there when she lands. She can be so clingy and gets so lonely, you know?"

"You're a butthead."

"You're a pretty boy."

Flynn laughed and hung up before Aspen could threaten her with more bodily harm. "You'll keep," Aspen said to the dead line and pulled into the valet parking. She grabbed the flowers and her stuff from the trunk and a tired-looking, barely-an-adult yawned his way through the drop-off process before issuing her a receipt from the machine hung around his neck.

He gestured toward the bus outside the office. "Shuttle'll take you to the terminal. Just tell the driver which one you need," he muttered, then loped off.

Aspen boarded the empty shuttle, and a woman who looked older than her mom emerged from the office.

"Morning, hun. Where you headed?" she asked as she climbed into the driver's seat.

"Terminal five, please." Aspen leaned over the middle console and offered the woman the tulips. "Any chance you could give these a good home? I'm pretty sure they won't survive the plane ride."

The woman took them, smiling widely, and placed them on the passenger seat. "There's every chance, hun. I won't tell my husband if you don't," she said and winked in the rearview mirror.

"I'll make sure to avoid that." Aspen sat back in her seat and checked the messages from her mom again. So many messages. And one from her sister that she hadn't read, but she didn't want to get involved in whatever drama that would entail until she had to.

When they'd been driving for a few minutes, the woman caught Aspen's eye in the mirror again. "Not too many flower shops open at this time. Did your night not go like you expected?"

Aspen frowned momentarily at the intrusive question but decided to roll with it. Once she was back in New York, there'd be no conversations with total strangers. She had a feeling that she'd miss Millie a little too. "Not many of my nights have gone according to plan this past month," she said. In fact, every time she'd gone out with the other architects from the office she was sharing, she'd ended up in Silver Lake at the brand-new sapphic hangout her temporary co-workers were eager to show off. The place was reliably packed to the rafters with women who looked like they'd just stepped off a sound stage at any one of the twenty-plus nearby studios. But that was finely balanced with regular people, making the place not too daunting or too pretentious for its own good, something Aspen really appreciated. And every night she'd been there, she'd gone back to her hotel with someone new.

But that wasn't information she was about to share.

"Don't you worry, hun," the woman said. "We all strike out sometimes. Love could be just around the corner." She pointed to the terminal as she pulled up. "Or it could be waiting in the seat next to you on the plane. Someone's sure to snap up a hunk like you soon enough."

Aspen bit her lip to prevent a laugh escaping; she couldn't recall ever being called a hunk before. "You never know, I guess." Though she did know, because her mom had booked her ticket and insisted on Aspen flying first-class, so there'd be no seat next to her at all, let alone the great love of her life sitting in it waiting for her. And after her last experience of love, she was in no rush to go there again anyway.

Chapter Three

"THANKS FOR DOING THIS, Jesse." Leoni ran her fingers along one of a hundred or so ties on the table display and tried not to pout. "I like taking these *off* a hot butch woman; I really don't want to wear one."

"You've never worn a tie?"

Leoni arched her eyebrow at Jesse. "Honestly, Jesse, do you even need to ask? Have you ever seen me in anything other than dresses, skirts, and heels? What would I do with a tie?"

Jesse wiggled her eyebrows and gave a deep, low laugh. "You don't really want me to answer that. It'd spoil our friendship and our professional relationship."

Leoni licked her lips and blew Jesse a kiss. "Would it though?" She hadn't gone there with Jesse, but she certainly wasn't averse to the notion. In fact, she'd often daydreamed about being the soft filling in a Jesse and Tyler butch sandwich. Now that Tyler was off the menu, maybe she should follow that possibility through to its natural conclusion. "Or would it enhance our friendship and make our professional relationship stronger?" She took one of the ties, placed it around Jesse's neck, and began to knot it.

Jesse nodded slowly. "Like it did with you and Tyler?"

Leoni completed the Windsor knot—she knew them all, of course—and ran her finger along it firmly, making sure Jesse *felt* her. "Exactly like that, yes."

A cough from behind her made her grin. She enjoyed few things more than making uptight straight people uncomfortable by shopping for a butch woman in the so-called "men's department." Her grin fell away when she remembered *she* was the butch woman she was shopping for.

She sighed and turned around. "Have you tested for COVID recently? That's a nasty cough."

"Apologies, miss." The young man swallowed hard against his too-tight shirt collar though the rest of his suit was perfect. "I just wanted to get your attention to let you know that everything in the store has an extra twenty percent off in our early Fourth of July sale."

She waited for his gaze to drift over her shoulder and settle on Jesse, but he didn't seem to react, which she very much appreciated and so, decided to cut him some slack. "I need a more masc look for a job I've been commissioned for. I need a whole new wardrobe for casual, smart casual, and semi-formal, and enough to see me through a whole week. And a big butch bag to carry it all in." She handed him her Black Card AmEx and smiled at the way his eyes lit up when he took it from her. It reminded her of a scene from her mom's favorite old movie, and she half-wished her mom was there with her so they could giggle at it together.

When Jesse said, "I think we're going to need a few more people helping us out," Leoni almost laughed out loud and *really* wanted to FaceTime her mom. It wasn't the exact line from the movie, but it was close enough.

"You're right." The young man looked her up and down as he tapped the card. "One moment," he said and left them alone.

"My mom loves that movie." Leoni turned back to Jesse to remove the tie.

"What movie?"

Leoni rolled her eyes and tossed the tie back on the table. "Never mind."

Five minutes later, the young man returned with several other assistants, all of whom had armfuls of clothes. The one holding up the rear couldn't be seen above the stack of shoe boxes they were holding.

"Follow me, please, miss."

He led the way to the dressing rooms, and Jesse dropped into one of the numerous chunky leather armchairs edging the wall.

"Seating for the show," Jesse said.

"Well, if it's a show you want..." Leoni turned away with an exaggerated swirl of her skirt and entered the cubicle where one of the assistants seemed to be struggling to hold back the heavyweight drapes.

The following two hours would usually have been the stuff of her dreams *if* she'd gotten to choose the many, *many* items of clothes she tried on. But tight sports bras that squished the girls into a band across her chest, T-shirts three sizes too big, and flat Converse that did nothing to show off her calves were not her idea of sexy. And when one of the assistants proffered a multi-colored plaid shirt, the thought of telling Ruth where to shove her pink and gold folder jumped into her mind. Briefly. The bonus Ruth had dangled like a rolled-up wad of cash carrot won out...a little too quickly for her integrity to be completely comfortable, but she was getting used to that feeling, and it wasn't so bad.

On the positive side, Jesse seemed to get more and more interested in exploring an intimate relationship with her the more outfits Leoni modeled.

"This is the best version of a guilty pleasure," Jesse whispered when Leoni emerged from the cubicle in jeans, shirt, tie, and a vest. "It's all hot butch-on-butch, but underneath the shirts and jeans, there is *nothing* masc about you at all."

"We're almost done here." Leoni tugged on her tie and opened the top button of her shirt. "Maybe you should choose your favorite outfit on me, then we can go to my place, and you can take me out of it...*very, very* slowly."

Jesse sighed deeply. "I'll take everything off but the tie."

Leoni smiled and walked back to the cubicle, only slightly irritated that the sneakers she was wearing made sashaying away all but impossible. She was already focused on *other* uses for the tie around her neck...

***

"It's not just about the clothes." Jesse folded the shirt in exactly the same way the shop assistants had when they filled the eight bags of Leoni's purchases. "It's the walk. The swagger. The attitude. Clothes are just dressing. Manners and attitude maketh the butch, as someone from Downton Abbey would say. But you know that; it's why you love us so much."

"It's hard to concentrate on the words coming out of your mouth when you're swaggering around in your tank and boxers, but yes, those are some of the very appealing things about your type." Leoni tilted her head slightly to get a better view of Jesse's ass. Tighty-whities were made for a butt like hers. "There's a difference between loving those things and *being* those things though, right?"

"Of course." Jesse pulled her own shirt on and sat on the edge of Leoni's bed. "Does that help?"

Leoni shook her head. "I'm afraid not. I see what you were going for, and it's sound logic. In principle, you *should* be less sexy to me with less skin showing…" She sighed. "But a short-sleeved denim shirt *over* a tank top," she fanned herself, "is as hot, if not hotter."

Jesse tapped her watch. "Unfortunately, we don't have time for another round."

Leoni pouted, and Jesse covered her eyes.

"Doing that isn't fair," Jesse said, still refusing to look at her. "You've got a plane to catch in a few hours."

"Fine." Leoni swung her legs off the bed and went to her closet without stopping to put underwear—or any item of clothing—on.

"And *that* definitely isn't fair."

Leoni grinned and got on her tiptoes to pull her suitcase from the top shelf. The divine-smelling leather carryall the clerk had sold her was never going to fit everything in it, but he'd added it free of charge after she'd spent so much of her company's money. "I'd apologize, but it wouldn't be sincere." She flopped the bag onto her bed and opened it. "So I can call you any time if I need help butching it up?"

"Absolutely." Jesse handed the shirt she'd folded to Leoni. "Remember you'll be three hours ahead of me though. I get up at five, but—"

"What? Why?" Leoni turned one of the shopping bags upside down and emptied it into the bottom of her case.

"You think a body like this doesn't take work?"

Leoni allowed herself a long, sweeping look over said body and exhaled happily. "It's appreciated immensely. But five a.m.? Yuck. The only thing getting me out of bed that early would be a flight to Paris."

Jesse tapped her watch again. "It's getting close to that now."

"Yes, but I haven't been to sleep—for a very good reason. And the Hamptons isn't Paris, but a week of luxury living has its draw." Leoni emptied another couple of bags into her case and shuffled the items around to make them fit. "Anyway, I can call you, right?"

"Sure, but you're a great actress. You can pull this off." Jesse put Leoni's new Varvatos Converse into the cotton bag they came with and laid them beside her carryall. "All you really need to remember in any situation is how you would like *your* butch to act. If you'd want them to open your door for you, zip your ass around the truck pronto and open her door. If you wake up wanting fresh-cut flowers with your breakfast, drive to the nearest market and buy her a bunch. Think about everything you'd want your perfect gentlebutch to do, and then do it before she asks or even realizes that's what she wants." Jesse shrugged. "Being butch is all about anticipating anything and everything your girl might need or want, and then delivering those things with a rakish smile."

"Like the one you're giving me now?" Leoni asked.

Jesse inclined her head. "No, this is my smile. You'll have your own. Practice in the mirror."

Leoni frowned. "You can't be serious?"

Jesse held up her hands. "It won't come naturally to you, so you'll need to dig deep into your classical training," she said and grinned.

Leoni balled up a shopping bag and threw it at Jesse's head. "You're making fun of me."

Jesse dodged the missile. "I'm being serious. You've got a whole armory of smiles from super cute to super sexy and everything in between, and they get you whatever you want. But this smile," she pointed to her own lips, "has a totally different motivation. *This* smile comes from me wanting to make sure you're the happiest woman on the planet."

Leoni hummed. "Well, you achieved that in the past couple of hours."

Jesse half-bowed. "Happy to be of service, miss. Any time."

"Anytime?" Leoni dumped the last bag into the other side of her suitcase and ignored the fact that it looked like an elephant would have to sit on it to get it closed. She positioned herself between Jesse's legs and wrapped her hand around the back of Jesse's head. Her buzzcut tickled Leoni's fingers as she pressed Jesse's face to her naked stomach.

Jesse put her hands on Leoni's hips and gently eased her away, emitting a low growl as she did so. "I'm not made of stone, woman, and I honestly hate turning you down, but you really do have a plane to catch, and I need to repack all your stuff into the carryall instead of that ridiculous bright pink suitcase."

"The case can wait." Leoni pushed Jesse onto her back and straddled her. "And there won't be much traffic to the airport at this time in the morning. Just one more." She pushed out her bottom lip and fluttered her eyelashes. "I won't be getting any action for a whole week. You'll be doing me a favor."

Jesse brushed Leoni's hair over her ear and smiled mischievously. "And you'll owe me one?" she whispered.

"I'll owe you more than one, and you can collect on that *anytime* when I get back." Leoni retrieved the tie they'd played with earlier and draped it around her neck. "And I'll wear your new favorite outfit."

Jesse growled again, this time louder. "You're *wearing* my new favorite outfit."

Leoni pressed herself against the length of Jesse's body. "Showing me what I can do with a tie really *has* enhanced our friendship," she said and kissed her hard.

Chapter Four

"Flynn's not family, but she gets to come here every year," whined Willow.

She really didn't say the words: she actually whined the whole sentence. Aspen's sister seemed to have spent most of her adult life whining about something, despite having *everything* placed in her lap. Maybe that was part of the problem. She glanced at Flynn and shook her head. *And so it begins.*

"Flynn *is* family, Willow," their mom said, "and we've known her for nearly two decades. She's Aspen's best friend and her business partner." Their mom smiled apologetically toward Flynn. "And you're being quite rude considering Flynn is right here."

"Whatever." Willow flicked her long hair from her face and then waved dismissively in Flynn's direction. "Shouldn't you celebrate with your *own* family?"

"Flynn's presence isn't up for discussion, Willow," their mom said before Flynn could respond. "Your new friend is the issue."

"She's not my friend, Mom." Willow shot a look at Aspen that conveyed nothing good, and there might even have been a smirk lurking beneath the general contempt. "I wasn't going to tell you until after you'd met her." A pause for another dramatic flick of her hair. "She's my girlfriend."

Aspen spluttered her beer back into the glass, and Flynn slapped her on the back as she chuckled.

"Oh." Their mom's gaze shifted back and forth between Aspen and Willow, until she rested on Willow, her expression dumbfounded.

"It's not funny, *Flynn*. Why are you laughing? Newsflash—Aspen and Oakley don't have the queer market locked down. And we don't all have to *look* like stereotypical lesbians, you know?"

Aspen clenched her jaw. "And what do stereotypical lesbians look like, Willow? Enlighten us."

Willow pointed toward Aspen and then Flynn. "You two. A lesbian can have long hair and...and style."

Flynn put her hand on Aspen's shoulder and squeezed, not so gently. It was her way of cautioning Aspen not to react to her sister's constant *Willowness*. "Our matching plaid shirts are *very* stylish, actually. And we know lesbians with long hair exist too. In fact, in case you hadn't noticed, we're big fans of exactly those kind of lesbians."

"Huh." Willow snorted and narrowed her eyes. "And what about bi-girls with long hair, Flynn? Are you a big fan of those too?"

Flynn raised her hands. "You're on your own, Asp," she said.

"No problem, buddy." Aspen was almost impressed that Willow had registered Flynn's adoration of their brother's best friend. She was usually so self-absorbed that anything not revolving around her went unnoticed or was dismissed as irrelevant. God, Aspen hoped Willow would grow out of this childish behavior before she hit her thirties; she wasn't sure she could handle another five years of this without strangling her or just completely avoiding family get-togethers.

"Now you've made Flynn uncomfortable, Willow," their mom said. "We've taught you better than that. Apologize right now, or you can call your girlfriend and tell her not to come at all."

Willow scowled. "Sorry."

"And again like you mean it, please, Willow."

Willow huffed then seemed to actually take a moment to think about the next words that might otherwise just have tumbled out of her mouth.

"I'm sorry, Flynn," Willow said, sounding pretty genuine. "I just want..."

What could she possibly want that she hadn't already been

given? Willow had everything she could ask for; their parents indulged every crazy idea she came to them with for investment, especially their dad, and still, she acted like a petulant teenager. It was like she hit fourteen and stayed there.

"What, honey?" their mom asked.

"I want my family to support my choices." Willow's moment of maturity slipped away without a trace, and she glared at Aspen. "I don't see why everyone's making a big deal out of me bringing someone to this stupid week. She's got Flynn. Oakley has Kelly. It stinks."

Their mom sighed. "You remember that the family has a net worth of $2.6 billion, Willow? That kind of money attracts a lot of attention, most of it negative. We ran background checks on Flynn and Kelly before they were allowed anywhere near your siblings."

"Is that true?" Flynn whispered.

"Which part?" Aspen asked. "The net worth or the invasion of your privacy?"

"The privacy one! You know I never want to know anything about your money."

"You and me both, but it's news to me." Aspen bumped Flynn's shoulder. "Anyway, no one could've stopped us being buddies. Not even my insanely paranoid family."

Flynn punched Aspen's arm. "That better be true."

"It is, but I'm not challenging Mom about it right now; it'll give Willow more ammunition."

"Do you even hear yourself, Mom? How am I supposed to get into a normal relationship when you get the CIA poking around everyone I've ever been interested in? It scared them all off, you know? That's why I've never been in a long-term relationship."

Their mom sighed deeply. "The CIA doesn't work for individual families. We just have a detective agency on retainer, Willow."

"And I really don't think that's what scared them off," Aspen said, then wished she'd kept her mouth shut. This kind of futile, circular argument was exactly why she hadn't wanted to come this year.

Willow whirled around to face her. "What's *that* supposed to mean?"

"This. You." Aspen waved her hand at Willow. "When are you going to grow up? And also, when did you start liking women?"

"I am grown-up. You don't get to patronize me just because you're old. And I've always liked girls," Willow said and looked back at their mom briefly. "No one ever asked. Everybody *assumed* I was straight, because there couldn't possibly be three interesting queers in the family."

Aspen laughed. "I think the assumption came through observing every relationship you've had since the fourth grade, starting with your teacher catching you and Tommy getting creative in the art supply closet."

Flynn stifled a laugh beside her.

"Aspen's right, dear. There's never been a whiff of a woman."

Flynn nudged Aspen. "You might want to tell your mom that was a poor choice of words," she whispered.

"And I might not. I don't want to be in the same room as this conversation, let alone be part of it." And yet, she hadn't been able to keep from getting involved. "I'm going upstairs. I've got work to do."

"Work? This week?" their mom asked.

Aspen nodded. "I've gotten behind on the Mancharlson proj—"

"Gotten behind?" Their mom tilted her head. "That's not like you at all; you always clear your desk for our Fourth of July celebrations."

Willow widened her eyes and pulled an unflattering face. "Yeah, Aspen, that's not like you and your perfect self at all."

"It would've been complete, but he keeps changing spec every time we submit a draft. This is our fifth and final attempt, so we've got to make it work. He's worth a lot of money to the company."

Their mom smiled. "*Your* company, dear. Never be ashamed of your success and how hard you've worked." She touched Flynn's arm. "How hard you've both worked."

Over their mom's shoulder, Willow rolled her eyes before she stomped out of the room without another word. *Thank God.*

Their mom turned and shook her head. "Willow," she called and then started after her, "we weren't finished talking. At the very least, I need a name and an address for Philip."

When she'd left the room, Flynn jutted her chin. "Does everyone know I've got a thing for Kelly?"

"I don't think so. I reckon it was just a lucky guess. Willow doesn't see anything unless it's going to affect her in some way. You know that." Aspen slapped Flynn on the back. "And I'm sorry she was such an ass to you. Maybe one day I'll be able to stop apologizing for my little sister's childish behavior, but it doesn't look like that's going to happen anytime soon."

"I'm used to it." Flynn shrugged. "And she might be a giant pain in your ass, but isn't that on the little sister job description?" She rubbed her hand over her buzzcut. "She'll find her way soon enough."

"Will she?" Aspen took out a couple of bottles of water from the fridge and tossed one to Flynn. "How many crazy schemes has Dad invested in now? It must be reaching double figures." She pressed the chilled bottle to her forehead to stave off the dull throbbing, the one she always had following any interaction with Willow.

"It keeps them both happy and out of your mom's hair most of the time, doesn't it? What's the harm?"

Aspen shook her head. "I don't get why you're always defending her."

Flynn smiled. "Yeah, you do. I never had a little sister, did I? I barely had parents."

Her words hit Aspen like a gut punch. Flynn was so far removed from the Bronx River projects' kid she was when they met that Aspen sometimes forgot her difficult history. "I'm sorry. I'm being an insensitive butthole. I should always remember who you are."

"Well, I won't ever forget." Flynn rolled the water bottle in her hands. "But that community raised me, not my parents, and they made me the woman I am today too. There are plenty of people with bigger problems than I ever had. I've got nothing to be sad about."

Aspen pulled Flynn into a bro hug that lasted just long enough not to make either of them uncomfortable. She liked to think that she was aware of how her privileged upbringing wasn't the burden some of her more ridiculous peers made it out to be, but sometimes it took her best bud to remind her that she was still part of a family in the top one percent of the country.

They both took unnecessarily long drinks of their water until the throaty roar of an engine caught Aspen's attention.

Flynn's eyes lit up. "Is that Kelly and Oakley?"

Aspen caught hold of Flynn's shoulder and half-shoved her toward the front door. "Let's go find out."

She hadn't really had the time to think about who she'd expected to climb out of the brand-new Mercedes Benz G-Class that pulled to a halt in the gravel driveway behind their house. And she definitely hadn't considered how she might feel about the woman who pulled Willow into her arms and lifted her off her feet, though that part looked like it took some effort.

"That's the new south sea blue magno and obsidian black paint job." Flynn gave a low whistle. "My dream car *and* color."

"For this season, maybe. Your dream car changes every year, and it has for every one of the seventeen years I've known you." Aspen chuckled, and though there was plenty to admire about one of the most expensive SUVs money could buy, she was too busy admiring its driver. Hair like that shouldn't be held captive under a ball cap.

"What's with you?" Flynn pushed her finger under Aspen's chin as if she was closing her mouth. "She's got way too much swagger to be your type."

Aspen shoved her hands in her cargo shorts. "What're you talking about? I'm just interested in seeing who my little sister's first girlfriend is, that's all."

Flynn narrowed her eyes then studied Willow's visitor. "That better be all it is. The last thing you and your sister need is one more thing to fight about."

Aspen didn't respond. Flynn was right. Of course she was. So Aspen should stop staring at Willow's girlfriend. She should stop appreciating how nicely Willow's *girlfriend* filled out those cargo pants. And she should definitely stop imagining *Willow's girlfriend* freeing that gorgeous blond hair from under its cotton cage and shaking it out like she was in a car commercial.

And yet...

Chapter Five

"Oh my God, did you see their faces?" Willow closed the bedroom door behind them and jumped onto her bed.

Leoni placed her carryall and suit bag onto an ornate cream chair and tried not to judge when Willow began to bounce up and down on her bed like an excitable child. She mentally scanned the file again; yep, Willow was twenty-five. Using her giant bed as a trampoline didn't seem like the behavior of a billionaire heiress. "They looked surprised, that's for sure." Were they as surprised as Leoni had been when she'd discovered that her client was the younger and up-to-now *heterosexual* sister and not the super-hot and famously out masc sister? She doubted it. And she bet they weren't disappointed like Leoni was either.

Willow stopped bouncing and looked at Leoni from tip to toe. Her upper lip curled at the edge, almost into a junior snarl. "You're not what I asked for though. I can't believe they got my order wrong."

I'm a person, not take-out. "I know, and we're really sorry about that." Leoni offered Willow one of her killer smiles then realized it was likely wasted on her since she was a self-identified straight girl. The folder said this whole ruse was just about trying to get one up on the sister. The hot sister. Not that Willow didn't have a *certain appeal*, but Leoni was *certain* Willow didn't *appeal* to her at all. "I believe Ruth has offered you a partial refund," she said, not really wanting to get into the business side but also needing to get beyond the hiccup, so she could just get on with the gig.

Willow scoffed. "Like that makes any difference. Look around: the money doesn't matter. I would've happily paid four times what your top package cost. I just wanted someone who was a better lesbian than my stupid sister."

Leoni bit her tongue, literally and pretty hard, to keep from laughing. She blinked away her creeping judgment and focused on the task at hand. There was plenty of stuff the file didn't cover, like the deeper motivation behind Willow's decision to go this route, and Leoni had to discover what that was so she could better deliver on her end. "I understand." She gestured to the array of beanbags at the foot of the floor-to-ceiling windows in front of the perfect ocean view. "Can I sit?" She would've loved to have sat out on the balcony, caught some evening sun, and watched it set. But if they were outside, there was a chance someone could overhear the conversation. There'd be no more talk of bonuses if Leoni was sent home because she'd blown her cover.

"Sure."

Leoni dropped onto the enormous squishy cushion, thinking how impractical it was and that she could never enjoy seating like this in any of her usual outfits, but cargo pants gave a girl a certain freedom she didn't get to experience in pencil skirts. She'd already taken full advantage of that when she'd had to climb into that giant SUV-trucky thing. She didn't know how she would've managed it in her usual attire.

Anyway... "Tell me how you want me to be a better lesbian than your sister."

"Jesus, you're not gay as well as not being super masc?" Willow flopped back onto her bed dramatically. "This week is going to be a disaster."

"I *am* gay. Why would you think that I'm not?"

Willow propped herself up on her elbows and frowned. "Because you asked me how to be a better lesbian that my sister. If you're gay, shouldn't you just *know* how?"

Wow. So living around a lesbian all your life hasn't given you an understanding of queer people? "I see. Well, I don't know your sister outside of the info in the file and the stuff I found on the internet. Maybe you can tell me more about what *kind* of lesbian she is, so I can figure out how to be better." What Leoni wanted was to spend the next few hours educating the little Hartwell honey on alternative sexualities, but she suspected Willow's ignorance ran to more than this particular topic. She was nearly a decade younger than Aspen. Since she didn't have the same facial structure as her mom or Aspen, maybe she was the result of a naughty little fling on her dad's part. That might explain the lack of sharp intellect that seemed to be the signature of the other two women, if her Google research was to be believed.

Willow pouted. "She's great at everything she tries her hand at. Top five percent of her class all the way through high school and college; great at sports; supports non-profits and works at a soup kitchen instead of going on vacation. Everyone thinks the sun shines out of her butt."

Now little sister's jealousy was beginning to make sense. "So she's some sort of angel sent down from heaven to make us mere mortals feel bad about our lack of...*everything*?" Leoni asked.

Willow sat up on her bed, and her shoulders slumped. "Exactly."

"So maybe we should make this week more about showing everyone how great *you* are."

Willow snorted. "That would be impossible."

For a brief moment, the permanently petulant pout slipped from Willow's expression, and Leoni thought she saw a whisper of sorrow, but then Willow jumped up from the bed and grabbed her phone from the top of one of the many dressers in the room. Leoni decided not to pull on that thread; she was here to play pretend, not try her hand at therapy. And, she reminded herself, she wasn't being paid to actually *care* about the clients either.

"Look." Willow thrust her cell into Leoni's face. "Her last girlfriend was a model."

Leoni raised her eyebrows at the image of the long-haired beauty hooked onto Aspen's arm. "She's far too skinny."

Willow frowned. "There's no such thing." She looked at Leoni again with the same almost-snarl as before. "But you would say that because you're a bit chunky."

Leoni blinked away her disbelief at the lack of filter on almost everything that came out of Willow's mouth. Not quite skinny enough. Not quite tall enough. Not quite…*enough*. Ugh, Willow was like every casting director she'd ever met. Leoni could've told Willow that she was a healthy weight and size for her height, but just like she wasn't being paid to care about the client, she shouldn't care about what the client thought about her outside her performance in the role.

That was easy to say. Her clients usually hand-picked her and thought she was perfect. But in this case, she was a poor substitute for super butch Tyler…whom Leoni needed to call and check up on as soon as she had a minute to herself. Earlier at the airport, when she'd called Tyler's wife, Penny, it'd gone straight to machine, and Leoni had only been able to leave a message.

"Leo?"

Leoni looked up, aware she'd drifted away. Willow's phone was still in Leoni's face, but now it showed CCTV footage of a car pulling alongside her SUV-trucky thing. "Sorry, I was thinking about Tyler, the woman you actually booked for this week. I need to—"

"I don't care what you need right now." Willow slipped her phone into the band of her high-waisted and super-snug leggings. "My dad and the grands have just arrived, and *I* need you to meet them."

Leoni stood and glanced back at the beanbag collection. With the right arrangement, she supposed they'd make for a comfortable bed for the next six nights. She'd slept in worse. "You don't want to talk some more about how you want me to outshine your sister?"

"We don't have time." Willow checked herself in the mirror and applied some lipstick on her already made-up lips. "You read everything in the file, right?"

"Of course." Leoni tapped the side of her head. "It's all in here."

"It better be. And I'm going to need some sort of physical contact at all times. I want them to think you adore me."

"Touching is fine, but no kissing, okay?" She waited until she'd received a nod and an inevitable eye roll then asked, "Adore or love? The notes in the file didn't specify."

Willow snickered. "Oh, of course, the U-Haul cliché! We've been seeing each other for two months, so I guess we should already be thinking about marriage, right?" She flicked her hair over her shoulder and flounced to the door, holding out her hand. "I'm not pretending to be *that* kind of lesbian. Just adoration is good, but you better sell it."

Leoni took Willow's hand and squeezed. "Don't worry. This is the part I'm really good at." She accompanied Willow along the hall and down the semi-circular staircase that opened into a giant hexagonal hallway. The flagstone floor was arranged in a random and captivating design that would've driven Tyler's OCD to distraction, and Leoni could imagine her jumping from stone to stone to avoid the cracks just like she did in the parking lot back at the office. It was the only vaguely quirky thing Tyler ever did, and it was adorable. No matter what, she'd make time to call Penny before she went to bed tonight.

The oak double doors opened as they approached, and Willow loosed her hand from Leoni's to run into the old guy's arms.

"Gramps!"

Leoni stopped and waited to be introduced as everyone else entered the house. She hadn't expected that level of enthusiasm nor the child-like glee in Willow's voice. Everything Leoni had read and everything Willow had told her indicated that Willow was the black sheep of the family. Or certainly, Willow believed that to be the case, and she was snarking about, playing up to that role... hence Leoni's presence. But this looked like a positive relationship.

"Peanut!" Willow's grandad wrapped her up in a big hug. "How's our favorite granddaughter?"

He released her, and from Leoni's position, it looked like he pinched Willow's cheeks, or at the very least, gave them a good rub. No doubt she'd be running back up to her room to fix her makeup soon enough. Leoni instinctively touched her own face, which was void of any makeup at all. God, she felt weirdly naked and couldn't really remember the last time she'd gone out in public without her mask. She'd definitely never gone to work this way. That train of thought led her to the memory of tracing her fingers over the soft skin covering Jesse's chiseled jaw. She likely hadn't ever let a lick of cosmetic product touch her face.

Willow grabbed Leoni's wrist and tugged her forward. "Gramps and Grammy, this is Leo." Then she looked toward the younger man in the trio. "And this is my dad."

Leoni shook each of their hands firmly, remembering it as one of the top tips Jesse imparted when she dropped Leoni at the airport: *No floppy wrists when you meet someone, and don't offer your hand like you want your ring kissed. That's a femme thing, and for the next seven days, you are the exact opposite of the core you, okay?*

"Leo, huh?" Willow's gramps said. "Like the lion. You better protect my little peanut like you're the king of the jungle, or you'll have me to answer to."

Willow's dad patted Gramps' chest. "Stand down, colonel. I'm sure she comes in peace." He smiled at Leoni. "Do you prefer she or they? Willow didn't say."

Leoni nodded, impressed and already liking him more than his daughter. "That's right, sir." Another top tip checked off; Jesse would be proud.

"Oh God, I've never been a sir, and I'm not about to start now. Please call me Jim, and my parents are Thomas and Margaret."

"If you really want to call someone sir, that'd be Catherine." Willow's gramps guffawed, and Willow laughed.

His wife swatted his arm but barely stifled her own giggle. "Thomas!"

Willow's dad tilted his head and looked around. "Dad!" Jim said.

The old man grunted dismissively and patted Leoni's shoulder. "You'll see, Leo, you'll see."

"It's lovely to meet you all," Leoni said, eager to avoid any family conflict. This was already a complicated situation, and she didn't want to get in the middle of anything that wasn't absolutely necessary as part of her duties to Willow.

"See if you think that at the end of the week, Leo," Thomas said.

When Thomas grinned widely, Leoni was slightly perturbed by his crooked, tobacco-stained teeth. They were a puzzling sight given the family's wealth.

Willow hooked her arm into his. "Beer and wings on the deck, Gramps?"

Leoni spotted the opportunity to get away and make her phone call to Penny. "I'm just going to use the bathroom. I'll join you in a few minutes. Is that okay?"

Willow glanced back over her shoulder as she and her gramps headed toward the back of the house. "Sure."

Leoni was already getting used to Willow's dismissive tone, but this was different, like she'd forgotten who Leoni was and why she was there. Whatever. She wasn't here to analyze the family. She turned and took the stairs two at a time, another tip from Jesse and another thing she could do in these mascy outfits that she couldn't in her usual attire. Not that she'd want to. It all seemed so unnecessary, and she was never in that much of a hurry to get anywhere.

She closed Willow's bedroom door behind her and settled back onto the bean bags to make the call to Tyler's wife.

"Hi, Leoni." Penny picked up the call just as Leoni was about to give up. "Sorry I haven't called you back. We've just gotten home from the hospital, and I've put Tyler to bed."

"Oh, hey, no problem." The weight of worry in her chest eased up a little. "That's great news. Are you isolating?"

"Yeah, I work from home most days anyway, so that's not a

problem," Penny said. "And even though I've been around so many who've had it, I haven't caught it once." She groaned. "I should probably knock on wood or something."

Leoni tapped the wood-paneled wall. "I've done it for you."

"I'll tell Tyler you called. Jesse said you just got to the Hamptons; Ruth got you to cover her?"

Leoni only bristled a little at the implication she wasn't a perfect replacement, but she knew that just as well as anyone else. "Generation Z has more flexible opinions on what butch and masc are, Pen." She sighed and let her defenses ebb away. "But yeah, it's not a great fit. I'm doing my best." Which she figured would be fine. Willow wanted her to be a "better lesbian" than her sister and that didn't necessarily mean having to out-butch her. Leoni had only seen Aspen for a few minutes before Willow had dragged her upstairs to the bedroom, but it was clear that she'd lose that battle in seconds. Aspen hadn't even had to move or "swagger," as Jesse had called it. She simply exuded everything butch that Leoni had a soft spot for. Damn, she was playing fake girlfriend with the wrong sister.

"Jesse thinks you'll do great," Penny said.

There was something about the way she delivered that line that included a whole level of sub-text, and Leoni knew exactly what Penny *wasn't* saying. "Did Jesse tell everyone in the office we had sex, or just you and Tyler?"

"Come on, Leoni, you know Jesse isn't like that. You're not just another notch on the bedpost for her, and she's always been discreet—just like Tyler was."

Leoni didn't know—nor did she really *want* to know—Penny that well, and in this instance, she didn't need to. Penny wasn't even trying to disguise the implicit brag that she'd put lipstick on Tyler's right cheek and taken her off the market. While Penny knew Leoni and Tyler had been intimate, she didn't know that Tyler had asked Leoni for a commitment just before Penny came on the scene, and Leoni had turned her down. Leoni *did* miss her fuck buddy, but Jesse had shown herself to be more than capable of filling that position.

"Good," Leoni eventually said.

"Jesse might be interested in settling down, you know?"

"Well, it won't be with me," she said, eager to nip that nonsense gossip in the bud before Penny watered it in her next conversation with Jesse. "It's just sex. We can do that too, you know? Just have sex without it getting all emotional and complicated." In fact, she'd generally found it was the other way around, and butch women fell an awful lot faster than she ever could.

Leoni glanced at her watch and realized she'd been up here far longer than the time a quick pee break took. "I have to go. I'm glad Tyler's okay. Would you just let her know I was thinking about her?" She hung up without waiting for a response. Her parting shot was immature, of course, but she hadn't been able to resist. Penny had just been a little too *Penny*, and she'd struck a nerve. Leoni couldn't contemplate getting into a relationship where she'd have to connect deeply with another person. She needed to connect deeply with herself first, and she was too busy working all the time to think about that can of worms.

Chapter Six

Aspen tapped Flynn's thigh under the table. "How many times do I have to tell you? It's rude to stare," she whispered.

Flynn leaned her head back and sighed deeply. "I'm trying not to. Is it that obvious?"

"It would be if you didn't have your shades on. They hide your puppy dog eyes." She pushed her chair away from the table and got up to get more meat from the grill, but before she left, she whispered in Flynn's ear, "But the sun's about to set, and you're going to have to take them off, so get a grip."

Flynn joined her at the grill a few feet from the giant outdoor dining table and the extended Hartwell family. "Do you think this is a bad idea?"

Aspen wafted a half rack of ribs under Flynn's nose. "What? More food? That's never a bad idea," she said and grinned.

"You know what I mean, butt-face. Kelly. Me. Kelly and me."

Aspen dropped the ribs onto Flynn's empty plate and turned back to the grill. "What I think doesn't matter, does it? Do *you* think it's a bad idea?" When Flynn's expression went into hangdog mode, Aspen softened. "I think that you need to tell Kelly how you feel, for the sake of your sanity if nothing else." She grasped Flynn's shoulder with her free hand and squeezed. "If she wants to explore things with you, that'll be fantastic. But if she doesn't, then she'll be missing out. Either way, you'll know how she feels, and then you can stop driving yourself crazy. She'd be the luckiest woman alive if she opens her heart to you."

Flynn swallowed, though it sounded more like a comedy gulp. "It's good I've kept these glasses on, because now I'm all teared up."

Aspen gave her a hard shove. "You say that like it's a joke, but I *know* you're being real, buddy. If I tore those shades off right now, everyone'd see you blubbering."

"Yeah, well, so what? 'Bois don't cry' is bullcrap."

"Damn right. Come here." Aspen tossed the grill tongs back on the marble countertop and bro-hugged Flynn. The loud scoff Aspen heard could only have come from one person, and she glanced up to see her little sister putting some salad on her plate.

"Get a room," Willow said.

She accompanied the words with her trademark look of disgust and superiority. Aspen couldn't put her finger on the exact time when her little sister lost her cuteness, but the good memories of her running around in just her underpants while Aspen and Oakley pretended she was too fast for them to catch were fading like the painted wood of next door's old back porch.

Neither she nor Flynn commented. Aspen had long ago discovered that continuing the behavior Willow so desperately disapproved of was a far more effective response than engaging her in a battle of words. Sometimes it made her feel as immature as her sister, but most of the time, it was simply a case of ignoring she was there and just trying to get through the day without another tantrum.

"You're embarrassing Leo and yourselves."

So apparently Willow wasn't quite done yet. Aspen half turned to look Leo's way; she was engaged in animated conversation with Gramps. Unsurprising. He was inexplicably tolerant of Willow's childishness, so of course the new squeeze would be trying to impress him. "She looks too busy with Gramps to be concerned with what we're doing."

"She's just not staring at you because she's polite...unlike some people," Willow said and glared at Flynn.

Aspen stepped between the two of them. "Give it a rest, Willow. Go and play with your new toy—unless you're already bored?"

Willow flicked her hair dramatically. "What's that supposed to mean?"

She shrugged. "Seems like Leo is just a plaything for you to get Mom's attention. Or am I wrong, and you really are a lesbian trapped in a straight girl socialite's body?"

Flynn nudged Aspen's arm. "Ease up, bud."

She turned away from Willow and continued to load up her plate, thankful for Flynn's timely intervention as usual.

"You don't have the monopoly on being queer in this family, Aspen," Willow said. "Other people can be interesting too."

Aspen clenched her jaw. If Willow was under the impression that being interesting was the primary facet of being gay, she was in for an eye-opening journey. "You know what? You're right, Willow. I should be more supportive."

Willow's eyes narrowed. "Yeah. You should," she said and flounced away.

Aspen put her plate back on the table, grabbed her beer, and wandered to the edge of the deck. Flynn did the same and stood beside her. "I hate when she turns me into that person."

Flynn laughed. "You weren't Mr. Hyde for long, but did you mean it about being supportive?"

Aspen took a long drink of her beer then placed it on the balustrade with more force than was necessary.

Flynn smirked. "No then."

Aspen shook her head. "I want to be, I really do. Especially if this isn't just another one of her—"

"Oh my God, you were gonna say phase, weren't you?"

"Gimmicks," Aspen said. "I want to be there for her if this isn't a gimmick." She looked out over the ocean and avoided Flynn's knowing stare.

"But you don't think it's real?"

"Do you?" She glanced back at Willow and Leo. They made a cute couple, to be fair. Perhaps her negativity was rooted in a little envy; Leo was handsome *and* somehow beautiful at the same time. Aspen had always gravitated toward high femmes, but there was definitely something about Leo that was appealing. "I don't know. Willow's life has been like the boy who cried wolf on repeat, except she's been insulated from the real wolf so far."

"We've talked about this before, buddy. She's not like you and Oakley; you both knew what you wanted to do from an early age, and you went for it. Maybe Willow's just trying to find out who she is. Most of us just have to figure out who we are in the world, but she has to figure out how she fits into the Hartwell family on top of that."

Aspen inclined her head and sighed. She and Flynn *had* talked about it. Repeatedly. And each time, Aspen had decided she was being too judgmental and that she should have more patience. But then Willow would be *Willow*, and so the cycle went on.

"I hope you two are plotting how we can get away to the lake tomorrow." Oakley clapped them both on the back, jolting them forward with the force.

Aspen smiled. "What did you have in mind?"

He frowned. "Kayak polo and camping, dummy. Mom's already got Monday locked down for the family golf tournament at West Sayville. And I don't want the week disappearing without some," he raised his hand and started ticking off his fingers, "off-roading, mountain biking, night fishing, horseback riding, and some one-on-one basketball."

"You remember we're only here for a week, right, little brother?" Aspen asked, but then she saw the way Flynn's eyes lit up at the potential of all the time with Kelly those activities would afford. If that meant filling every hour of the next seven days to help Flynn, she'd do it. Though she did have to fit her work in there somewhere too. She could do that while everyone slept, she supposed.

"Exactly! We've got to cram everything in before time runs out, and I barely see you again 'til Thanksgiving."

She punched his arm lightly. "You're too busy building on the family empire to miss me."

"Not true. I can be insanely busy *and* miss my little sister." He grinned as he evaded her punch.

"Hey, I'll always be your big sister, squirt."

He stood shoulder-to-shoulder with her and indicated the slight difference in their heights as if it were huge. "See? I'm the big brother now."

"You're an inch taller than me, tops."

"An inch matters," he said and stole her beer for a quick swig. "What would happen if you got one of your plans wrong by one inch somewhere? Disaster. An inch can be the difference between success and failure." He wiggled his eyebrows.

Aspen gagged and snatched her bottle back from him. "Don't be gross."

"Or impressive," Flynn said, laughing. "Your segue from architecture to sex was seamless."

Oakley nodded and grinned, wrapping his arm around Flynn's shoulders. "See? My little brother gets it."

"Bro!" Flynn said and fist-bumped Oakley.

The low evening sun was still providing some heat, but that was nothing to the warmth Aspen experienced from the exchange between two of her favorite people. She glanced at Willow again, wishing their connection could be as strong. Her little sister was clearly capable of maintaining a positive relationship, given the one she shared with Gramps. Was that just because he gave her unconditional acceptance and showed endless patience? Maybe Aspen should try the same thing.

"You three look as thick as thieves," Kelly said as she approached them. "What are you all up to?"

Flynn pulled down the front of her shirt and straightened her shoulders. "Wouldn't *you* like to know?"

"Well, yeah," Kelly said, sounding unusually serious. "That's why I asked."

Flynn's clever grin disappeared. "Uh, nothing. I'm sorry. I was just—"

Kelly smiled widely and touched Flynn's forearm. "Relax, silly. I'm messing with you."

Flynn's cheeks flushed the color of the receding sun on the horizon. "Uh, sure. Okay."

Oakley frowned and looked at Flynn with a puzzled expression. "What's your deal?"

"Ignore her; she's had a rough week." Aspen nudged Flynn and gave her the side-eye. "Haven't you?"

"Yeah, that's it." Flynn raised her beer bottle. "Another couple of these and more time in your dazzling company, and I'll forget all about it."

Aspen winked at Flynn. "Oakley wants to go kayaking tomorrow in the hope that he'll tire me out so he can win the Cardboard Cup on Monday."

Kelly discreetly thumbed toward Willow and Leo. "What if Willow's friend is a ringer? Has anyone claimed her for their team yet?"

Flynn leaned in conspiratorially. "That's not her friend. It's her girlfriend, and they've been seeing each other for two months."

"Really?" Kelly wrinkled her nose. "I thought they were just friends."

"Do friends touch each other all the time like they've been doing all through dinner?" Flynn asked.

Kelly shrugged slightly. "I touch you like that."

Flynn gulped. "Uh, yeah, I guess you do."

Aspen bit her tongue. *And it's been driving her crazy for about three years now.*

Kelly stuck out her bottom lip. "My gaydar must have a blind spot for this family. Did either of you have suspicions that Willow might be queer?"

Aspen shook her head. "If sexuality is a spectrum from super-straight to gloriously gay, I would've put Willow on the farthest end of the scale."

Flynn grumbled. "I don't think there's a time limit to people coming to realizations about themselves and their feelings." She toe-ended the deck, not making eye contact with anyone. "That's why you get people coming out in their fifties and even later."

"I guess," Kelly said. "But Willow's witnessed nothing but positive reinforcement around Aspen's and Oakley's sexuality, so it's not like she's been scared to come out."

"I don't think it's always about that though," Flynn said. "Sometimes it takes people longer to understand themselves and what they want. Willow's not really settled in any aspect of her life, and she's still young."

Kelly giggled. "Listen to the old voice of reason. Anyone would think you were sixty-five."

Aspen shook her empty bottle in the air. "This conversation is getting way too intense, and I need another beer. Anyone else?"

There were nods all around. Aspen tugged on Flynn's arm. "Give me a hand."

"Sure."

Flynn's words were nonchalant, but her eyes screamed gratitude for the rescue.

When they got back into the beach kitchen, Aspen leaned against the counter and laughed lightly. "That was painful to watch."

Flynn scoffed. "Take that pain and multiply it by ten. Then you've got about a fifth of what I'm feeling." She smacked her palm to her forehead. "I don't know how to act around her."

"Why don't you act like you would around any other woman? I've seen you in action. You can be ultra smooth and majorly charming. Be *that* Flynn."

"I can't." Flynn helped herself to a beer and popped the top on one for Aspen. "She's not any other woman: she's *Kelly*."

"So try to act like you used to before you realized you were in love with her," Aspen said and took a long pull on her beer.

Flynn sighed loudly. "That won't work either. She won't be able to see me as anything other than a friend. Or worse yet, family."

"Okay." Aspen nodded slowly. Figuring this out had to be her new priority for the week, or Flynn was going to spin out. "If acting like you used to won't work, and you don't want to act like you do around other women, then you've got to come up with a whole new approach to showcase the Flynn that Kelly doesn't know."

"Easy to say, but I don't know where to start."

"I promise we'll figure it out. By the end of this vacation, everything will change for you both." Aspen had to figure some things out too, like why her relationship with her little sister was so broken. She glanced across at Willow, but her gaze soon drifted to Leo; she was even more attractive when she laughed. That sparkle in her eyes really elevated her presence in the space, and everyone's attention focused on her like they were powerless to resist.

Aspen looked away. She couldn't let herself be drawn in by those stunning eyes. Falling for Willow's new girlfriend definitely *wasn't* the way to go about repairing their sisterly bond.

Chapter Seven

LEONI CLOSED THE BEDROOM door behind them and blew out a long breath. "How are you doing?"

Willow stopped at the edge of her bed and turned around. It was hard to tell if she was frowning since she was too young to have any lines yet, but Leoni had spent the evening studying Willow's expressions and physical reactions, and *that* face meant she was puzzled. Leoni might go as far as to say that Willow was bamboozled.

"What?" Willow asked.

"How are you doing? How do you feel?"

Willow's eyes narrowed. "What do you care?"

"Just checking in."

Willow's expression softened slightly before her top lip curled into the sneer Leoni was becoming familiar with, though Willow seemed to reserve the really beastly version of it for her hot sister and her similarly sexy friend.

Willow pushed open the bathroom door. "You mean you want to know how well you're doing, and if you're making up for the fact that you're not really anything like the woman I ordered?"

First she was takeout, now she was a mail-order bride. "No, but we can do that too."

"We'll talk about it when I've taken a shower..." Willow gave Leoni the once-over again, looking like there was a bad smell under her nose. "Or maybe after *you've* taken a shower too," she said and closed the door.

Leoni stared at the door and took three deep, cleansing breaths. She was going to need a boatload of meditation time to get through this week if Willow didn't chill out some. She sighed and set about unpacking. She unzipped her carryall and peered inside; she had no idea how Jesse had worked this witchcraft. After their final round of sex, Jesse had done as she'd promised, folding and rolling everything into tiny tubes, and then she'd Jenga'd them into a bag that really wasn't big enough to hold Leoni's shoes for a weekend break.

She placed the neatly prepared clothes on the top of a dresser, not wanting to search for an empty drawer. Jesse had said the shirts had to be hung up too. There was a whole wall of closets, but Leoni doubted there'd be any space for a few items of her clothing. Again, she decided to wait until Willow emerged from the bathroom to find a place for everything. The thought of all her clothes being on show for the next week gave her the squeebies. From the end pocket of the carryall, she withdrew her wash bag and didn't stifle her laugh. It was made from a rugged leather and part of the carryall set, but it was the tiniest thing she'd ever seen for the purpose. It certainly wouldn't be fit for her usual toiletries. Jesse assured her that the average butch needed only deodorant, a toothbrush and paste, hair product, shower gel, and cologne, so that's what Leoni had. But she'd also squeezed in tiny travel-size containers for her face and body regime. What she did in the privacy of the bathroom was no one's business but her own, and there was no way she was neglecting her skin for seven days, especially when that time included two plane flights and, if Willow was to be believed, a ridiculous number of outdoor pursuits Leoni was in no way interested in participating in.

Think of the bonus. In college, she'd been pretty sporty, and she was confident she could dredge that enthusiasm back. She'd had to lose her acrylic nails, so she might as well make that worth it. Leoni doubted that she could out-sport Aspen like Willow wanted her to, but looks could be deceptive. Aspen might well be packing an athlete's body underneath her baggy cargo shorts and oversized T-shirt, but that didn't mean she could use it to win at everything.

God, it'd been a while since Leoni had to be competitive in anything other than auditions. She chose to ignore the irritatingly squeaky voice at the back of her mind reminding her that hadn't gone so well either, and she slouched onto the beanbag mountain to enjoy the deep blue sky dotted with stars and illuminated with a low-hanging quarter moon.

The slight squeak on the bathroom door hinge woke Leoni. She hadn't intended to drift off but given that she'd only had about two hours' sleep since Friday morning, she shouldn't have been surprised.

"Shower's all yours," Willow said before she slipped into her bed.

"Thanks," Leoni murmured, grateful for the lack of snark. She pushed herself up from her beanie nest and picked up her wash bag and a clean tank and briefs from her pile of clothes. The bathroom was like a steam room, awesome for her pores and the slight all-over muscle ache from the travel. She pulled her ponytail out and inspected her hair in the mirror. *Yuck*. Wearing a ball cap for the past fourteen hours had made her hair greasy; if she was going to have to keep it on, she'd have to wash her hair every day. *That's going to be tedious.*

Leoni stepped under the shower to enjoy the liquid caress of the hot water on her skin. She inhaled and exhaled several times, wishing she could stay under here for the rest of this gig, then she quickly showered and washed her hair. She had to find a way to connect with Willow, or the next seven days were going to be horrendous. Though she got the impression that Willow's mere presence was uncomfortable for everyone in the family other than her dad and his parents. That was her way in. She'd spent the hours over dinner fostering a relationship with Tom, since he was clearly someone Willow really adored, and it'd gone well. Now she had to cement her appreciation of Tom into Willow's mind, because if they couldn't find some way to work together nicely, this whole charade was doomed. She'd worked with all kinds of clients over the past three years, but none had been quite as difficult and generally miserable as Willow had been thus far.

Leoni wrapped herself in a towel that enveloped her like a fluffy cloud and used a smaller one to dry her hair. She did as quick a job as she could with her creams without neglecting the process, redressed, and steeled herself for the next round of *Willowness*. Could that even be a state of being?

When she came out of the bathroom, she saw the top of the dresser was cleared, and her clothes were nowhere to be seen.

"I've hung your shirts in there," Willow said, pointing to the end closet. "And everything else is in the bottom drawer of the dresser closest to the bedroom door."

"Oh, thank you." *That* was unexpected. This girl really was a conundrum. Willow must be exhausted trying to keep up with herself and her various moods. Leoni rearranged her beanbag throne and noticed a blanket and one of Willow's pillows had been added to the pile. "And thank you for these." She looked across at Willow, who just made a little grunting sound from behind the wall of her phone. "So you're the favorite granddaughter?"

Willow lowered her cell, and her responding smile looked genuine. "That's what he tells me."

Surprisingly, her words weren't accompanied with any kind of dismissive or disbelieving expression.

"I really enjoyed getting to know him a little tonight. I can see why you love him so much; he's got a sharp wit."

Willow nodded. "He makes me laugh even when I feel like... even when I don't want to."

Leoni wished Willow hadn't self-censored. If she could be honest, it would make this week a whole lot easier for Leoni—for them both. "He said that by the end of the week, I'd think differently about it being lovely to meet your family. Does your gramps not like anyone but you?"

Willow put her phone down on the bed and moved farther down it. "There's a bit of a divide between Dad's side and Mom's side." She looked at Leoni seriously, as if deciding what she should share or what Leoni should know about their family. "Look, I'm… you know… I shouldn't have been such a bitch to you. You're not the person I thought I'd get, but you seem, you know, more than qualified." She fiddled with her phone and didn't look up. "And besides, Gramps likes you, and he's an awesome judge of character, so that's good enough for me."

Leoni smiled. A breakthrough and probably the closest thing anyone ever got to a Willow apology: she considered that a success after the rocky start. "That's like the presidential seal of approval—Obama administration, obviously. I'll take it."

Willow giggled. Another surprise and another step forward. Leoni thought politics would hold no interest for her. She reprimanded herself for being so judgmental and smiled. "You seemed really happy around your gramps until your mom, sister, and her friend came to the table."

Willow's lip curled, and she pushed back up the bed slightly. "Flynn is the second daughter my mom wishes she had."

In a normal, everyday conversation, Leoni would be quick to ask Willow to elaborate, but the way she physically retreated told Leoni to back off a little. "I'm sorry. That must suck."

Willow moved forward on the bed. "It *does* suck. But she's been around the family almost as long as I've been alive, and she doesn't have any real family of her own." She turned her cell around and around on the comforter and glanced away. "But that's not my fault, is it?"

"Definitely not," Leoni said, starting to see more of the vulnerable kid beneath Willow's harsh, defensive veneer, and the reason for it. "Do you mind me asking what the story is between Flynn and your sister?"

"Why?"

The slight edge of mistrust had crept back in, so Leoni smiled. "Understanding everyone here will help me be a better lesbian than your sister." Maybe she shouldn't reinforce Willow's characterization, but this was about her doing the best job she could for the client. And it *wasn't* about getting involved in the deeper family dynamics and things she couldn't hope to change and, honestly, were none of her business anyway.

Willow nodded slowly. "I get it. Do you want the whole story or the short version?"

Tiredness tugged at Leoni's eyelids, reminding her that sleep would be a good thing, and the short version was preferable. *But* this wasn't a nine-month run on Broadway, and she didn't have six weeks of prep time. She needed all the information she could gather as quickly as possible. "Always the whole story," she said and winked, channeling the gesture she'd received too many times to count. It felt more like she had a weird tick; how did Tyler and Jesse and every other butch or masc she'd entertained pull it off without being so self-conscious?

"They met at Columbia when they were both studying architecture," Willow said. "Flynn was on a full scholarship because of her financial situation."

Her reference to Flynn's position told Leoni more about Willow than it did about Flynn, but she didn't react. And she really didn't want to know if Willow harbored *that* kind of social prejudice.

"Aspen had to pay for everything, obviously, because of the family name." Willow shook her head and sighed dramatically. "But because she's Aspen, she wouldn't use a penny of family money to finance her education."

Leoni's eyes might as well've jumped out of their sockets. "Really?" The stellar file had informed her that the Hartwell Media family was worth billions. A college education would be less than the interest they likely earned on that fortune in a month.

Willow raised her hands then let them fall. "That's what I'm competing with. I mean, who puts themselves into hundreds of thousands of dollars' worth of debt when they have access to the kind of money our parents have?"

"Wow." Leoni couldn't stop her admiration. She'd found, in her own quick research, that Aspen had chosen architecture and had built her own company instead of getting into the family business, but she'd still assumed that Aspen's parents had bankrolled the whole endeavor. This was a woman who put her money where her principles were.

Willow flopped onto her back. "Exactly. *Everyone's* impressed with big sis. Which is why her and Mom are always looking down their nose at me when Gramps funds my little business ideas." She bolted upright and wagged her finger at Leoni. "But if anything turned out to be successful, I was always going to pay his investment back." She stuck out her bottom lip and looked at the bed. "But nothing's taken off yet."

"That's a shame." Leoni's shallow Google dive had also yielded info on Willow's many endeavors...and their spectacular failures, most of which were chronicled on her social media platforms as well as in the press. "You just haven't found your passion yet. Those things probably didn't do well because your heart wasn't really in them, you know? When you find something that you really believe in, I bet you'll succeed." She hoped that sounded less phony than it did in her head, as she realized her words applied to her own career too. That was a bit harsh though. She was doing well enough, earning good money that paid for a nice lifestyle. From the outside looking in, she'd be considered successful.

Willow inclined her head slightly. "Is this your passion?"

Leoni chuckled. "I'm afraid not. But I don't have the resources you do, and you should damn well use them, no matter what some people think. You should keep trying everything that might inspire you until you get to the one thing that does."

Willow smiled widely. "You really think so?"

"I really do." Leoni suddenly succumbed to a giant yawn that almost broke her jaw.

Willow giggled and flicked her hair back. "I suppose you should get some beauty sleep...or do you call it handsome sleep when you're masc?"

Leoni shrugged. "I've never thought of that actually, but you're right. I haven't slept since Thursday night, and it sounded like your brother and sister have big plans for tomorrow."

Willow huffed. "I hope you've got good balance. They like to play a weird version of water polo on kayaks. Someone *always* ends up wet."

"Do you play?" She expected Willow to scoff but asked anyway.

"Yeah," Willow said as she shuffled down under her covers. "But Aspen can be super competitive sometimes, and that sucks the fun out of it." She switched the lights off with a voice command. "I'm usually the top scorer after her," she said quietly.

"Cool. I'm looking forward to seeing you in action." Leoni realized they'd gone off topic, and her information-mining had gone astray, but she had enough to play with, and more importantly, she'd managed to break through Willow's defenses a little. That alone would make the next week go far more smoothly than she'd thought it would when they'd met a few short hours ago.

She burrowed into her giant beanbag and closed her eyes. Willow wasn't really the one Leoni was looking forward to seeing getting hot and sweaty on the water, obviously, and all the more fun if Aspen was the one who ended up wet. She could surreptitiously ogle the sexy sister while she worked. There'd be no harm in that, right?

Chapter Eight

"Make sure no one breaks anything today, Aspen," their mom said.

Aspen frowned. "Oakley was twelve when he broke his arm, Mom."

Oakley shoved her from behind. "You mean when *you* broke my arm?"

Their mom swatted his shoulder. "Just be careful, please. Everything's set for the golf tournament tomorrow."

Willow smirked. "Are you spending the day polishing the Cardboard Cup?"

Their mom sighed. "Yes, Willow. I have nothing better to do, obviously," she said and went back inside.

Aspen shook her head. Willow wasn't even trying to be on her best behavior or make any kind of good family impression on Leo. If Aspen ever went to a girlfriend's house and she acted like Willow, there'd be red flags and alarms going off everywhere. But Leo didn't seem to react and took everything in her stride. Maybe that's why she'd survived longer than any of Willow's previous flings; she didn't let it affect her.

"That's a sweet ride, Leo." Flynn ran her fingers over the hood of Leo's Merc and whistled. "Does it drive as good as it looks?"

Leo held up the electronic key. "Do you want to see for yourself?"

Flynn's jaw dropped open, and her eyes widened. "For real?"

Leo shrugged, like the offer was nothing. "Why not?"

Aspen glanced at Kelly and Oakley heading for his Wrangler and was caught between the choice of the two vehicles on Flynn's behalf. The car or the girl? She tapped on Flynn's shoulder and tilted her head in Kelly's direction. "I thought you wanted to ride with them. Your wet bag is already in Oakley's trunk."

Willow pressed her lips together tightly and narrowed her eyes. "What did you say, Aspen? You'd rather ride with little bro than little sis?"

Flynn looked between the two options like a kid caught between an all-you-can-eat ice cream station and a car full of adorable kittens. Aspen might've laughed if it hadn't been for the presence of her irritating sister. "No, Willow," she said. "I was just wondering about insurance, and if she'd be covered if there was an accident."

Leo waved. "You don't have to worry about that. It's a company car, and it's fully insured for anyone to drive." She pulled her cell from her pocket. "All Flynn has to do is give me her full name and drivers' license, and she'd be set."

"What kind of business has $200k cars for its people?" Aspen whispered.

"The kind of business I'd like to be in," Flynn said and headed toward Leo.

"Hey! We get to build stuff. Ours is pretty damn cool." She followed Flynn, because there was no way she'd subject her to Willow's caustic company alone.

Oakley hung out of his Jeep. "It's like that? Someone comes along with a flashy German automobile, and you jump ship? Ruby's offended."

"Don't pretend you wouldn't do the same," Flynn shouted before she started tapping her details into Leo's phone.

"So fickle, Flynn," Kelly said, shaking her head and patting the Jeep's hood. "She still loves you, Ruby. Don't worry."

Flynn looked down at Leo's phone as if it were the most interesting thing on the East Coast. It might be harder to see Flynn blush, but Aspen would bet money on it that she was. Kelly frowned, perhaps at the lack of response, then climbed into Ruby, Daisy Duke-style. Aspen inclined her head; Flynn would be sorry she missed that.

"You should ride up front." Leo strode around the front of her SUV, opened the passenger door, and motioned for Aspen to jump in. "I'll take the back with Willow."

Aspen had an adverse, almost physical reaction to the chivalrous gesture but managed to keep it inside. Or maybe she didn't manage it, because Leo arched her eyebrow and looked like she was trying to suppress a laugh. At her expense? Was Leo trying to out-butch her? *Like that's going to happen.* "Thanks. That's nice of you." She gave her ridiculous reaction a hard shove back into her subconscious, and no, she wouldn't analyze it later, because it didn't deserve another moment's thought. She slipped into the passenger seat at the same time as Flynn hopped into the driver's side.

Flynn handed Leo her cell back. "Thanks, bro."

Aspen clenched her jaw then almost kicked herself. What the hell was wrong with her? Now she was jealous of Flynn being friendly? Maybe that was better than the reaction she'd had when Leo had joined Aspen in her dreams last night... To distract herself, she inhaled the sweet smell of fresh leather upholstery and studied the SUV's dashboard. Everything looked like it was top of the range, with any and all available extras, including fancy blue interior lighting that featured in the A/C fans in addition to the footwells. It probably flashed in time to the music too. This was the kind of car her dad would think nothing of dropping cash on. "What did you say you did for work?" she asked, catching Leo's gaze in the rearview mirror as Flynn turned the car around and headed down the driveway.

Leo raised her eyebrow and gave her a mischievous smile. "I didn't."

Aspen waited for Leo to say more, but the silence filled up the space between them instead. She saw Willow place her hand on Leo's thigh and squeeze, which seemed like an uncharacteristically reassuring gesture from her sister. She couldn't recall ever seeing her show that kind of affection to any of the men she'd seen Willow with.

Flynn gave her the side-eye, and Aspen forced her gaze forward. Flynn passed the entrance to the village beach, and the parking lot already looked busy. No doubt Indian Island would be the same, but they had their own boats in storage there, so that shouldn't be a problem.

She flicked her gaze to the backseat again, unable to resist. "Where did you fly in from, Leo?"

"Jeez, Aspen. What's with all the questions?" Willow pushed the back of the passenger seat with some force.

"Two questions, Willow. I've asked *two* questions. It's called trying to have a conversation so you can get to know someone better." She looked in the mirror again, and again it was Leo she locked eyes with. God, she had nice eyes. They seemed to change color depending on the light. *Stop it.*

"Whatever." Willow leaned across the center of the backseat and glared at the mirror.

Aspen focused on the houses they were passing instead of her exasperating sister *or* her very attractive girlfriend. She'd always loved all the different styles of architecture on show around there. If she really thought about it, spending so much time here as a kid probably inspired her career. She switched her attention to the gray tarmac that stretched out in front of them. The rain from last night's downpour hadn't dried out yet, and it looked brown and dirty at the point where driveways met the road. Even some of the grass verges were flooded, and the pools of water were so large, the few morning clouds reflected in them.

"Did you know this G-Wagen goes from zero to sixty-two in less than 5.8 seconds?" Flynn asked. "We should go off-roading and compare it to your Bronco. This thing's got a real-time off-roading cockpit that includes a transparent hood, so you can see obstacles under the vehicle while you're driving."

Willow groaned. "Or you could have a contest to see who could pee the farthest and get it over with."

"You wouldn't have to come," Aspen said, though spending time with Leo without Willow was equal parts appealing and ill-advised. Willow probably had another money-pit scheme she could pitch to Gramps instead, but Aspen didn't say that. She didn't want Leo thinking she enjoyed childish banter with her sister.

"Don't you have a work project to finish this week? Haven't you 'gotten behind'?" Willow asked, mimicking their mom and still hogging the mirror. "How are you going to have time to play with the boys *and* get that done? Mom's not impressed."

"I'm going to help with that." Flynn nudged Aspen's arm. "It's widely accepted I'm the brains of the outfit," she said and gave a raucous laugh. "And the beauty too, actually."

"You guys work together?" Leo asked.

"Yeah." Aspen half-turned in her seat so she they could converse face to face. "Even after six years of college, Flynn couldn't bear to be parted from me, so we started our own architecture firm."

Leo raised her eyebrows, and her frown lines disappeared under the bill of her ballcap. "Six years?"

Aspen nodded and ignored Willow's dramatic eye roll and relatively quiet sigh. She wanted to get to know Leo better, whether Willow approved or not, especially if Leo might end up sticking around for longer than her sister's usual love interests. "Four years as an undergrad and two more for the master's so we could be officially licensed."

Leo smiled. "I managed four years, just, and I couldn't wait to get out into the world and...really start my life. Do you know what I mean?"

Aspen nodded again. She didn't miss the micro pause, like Leo was holding something back. She glanced at Flynn, but she didn't react. Aspen couldn't decide if Leo was deliberately building up the suspense around her career, or if she just didn't like talking about it for some reason. But that simply created more intrigue; *why* wouldn't she want to talk about what she did for a living? Aspen acknowledged that the Hartwell family was intimidating, but whatever Leo did, and whoever she worked for, she was clearly bossing it if her wardrobe and vehicle were anything to go by. "What did you study?"

Leo wrinkled her nose. "Nothing that I'm making full use of in real life."

Again with the cryptic instead of a straight answer. Willow was going to have to do more than send dagger-eyes Aspen's way to deter her from digging. "Philosophy?" she asked and grinned.

"I was going to guess Dance Major," Flynn said. "You can't play, because you must already know."

Willow glanced out the window, like the idea of the game was beneath her. "I *don't* know, actually, so I'll say psychology."

Aspen frowned. "You've been talking for two months, and you don't know what degree Leo has?"

Willow locked eyes with Aspen, and her nostrils flared. "Formal education isn't the cornerstone of intimacy. I don't need Leo to have a fancy degree to be attracted to her or to know she's worthy of my attention. *I'm* not an elitist."

Aspen didn't like Willow's inference, but more importantly, she didn't want Leo thinking she was some sort of privileged, rich asshole. She didn't retort and pulled back a little, realizing she might've hit a nerve. Willow had tried a number of undergrad courses, including medicine, and none of them had stuck. But that was Willow's overall problem: *nothing* stuck.

"Are any of us close?" Flynn asked.

Leo inclined her head. "You were closest, Flynn, so you get the points."

Leo didn't disappoint since Aspen had half-expected her to evade answering again. "Close only counts in horseshoes and hand grenades," Aspen said. "Come on, I promise we won't laugh."

Leo shook her head and arched her eyebrow. "Said everyone who's ever burst into laughter following a revelation."

Aspen swallowed. There was something about a beautiful woman arching her eyebrow that sent signals to places she didn't want to think about, especially when it came from her sister's girlfriend.

"Why can't you just leave it, Aspen?" Willow glared at her. "Maybe she doesn't want to tell you, and she's too polite to ask you to butt out."

Aspen sighed and held up her hand. "Okay, no worries." She decided to give up—for now—and began to turn around.

"It's not that, Willow," Leo said. "I'm not ashamed of it. If anything, I sometimes wish I *was* using it." She shrugged. "But my life took a different path, and everything's worked out pretty great." She edged forward. "I studied Musical Theater Performance. Go ahead and laugh if you want."

Aspen shook her head. "Not at all. That's really cool," she said and turned back to face the road. Because far from laugh, she was ready to swoon—in a butch way, obviously—and she didn't want Willow picking up on it like she somehow had with Flynn's attraction to Kelly.

But what was sexier than a woman who could sing? Instantly, she was running through songs she wanted to hear Leo take on. What kind of voice did she have? And how could Aspen engineer the situation to get Leo to let loose with it? She was already imagining a sing-along around the campfire. When she was putting their bags into Oakley's Jeep, she'd had to shift Kelly's guitar, and Flynn said she loved to watch her play. She glanced at Flynn, who didn't look at her, but she was grinning widely. *Definitely* on the same wavelength. It was a win-win for both of them. Except...

Except Aspen shouldn't be thinking of Leo in those terms at all. Not only was Leo already in a relationship, but that relationship was with Aspen's little sister. Her newly queer little sister, apparently, which she was still trying to wrap her head around. Leo seemed to adore Willow, so Aspen hoped for her sake that it wasn't some youthful experiment that would end with Leo getting dumped.

Though maybe that wouldn't be the *worst* outcome. How long was a polite amount of time to wait before she could contact

Leo and suggest they meet for dinner? Before she could see if Leo might be attracted to her too? Aspen was, after all, the more mature, more masc version of Willow.

It might make for some awkward family vacation time. Not for the first time on the drive, Aspen demanded of herself that she put the brakes on any train of thought that deviated from seeing Leo as her sister's girlfriend. Searching for distraction, Aspen prodded the infotainment screen, torn between wanting to find out and needing to leave it the hell alone.

Chapter Nine

Leoni got out of the car and wandered across the parking lot, grateful for the lack of conversation on the remainder of the journey to Indian Island. She'd been doing gigs like this one for a few years now, but she'd never had one this fraught, especially so early on.

She'd been enjoying playing with Aspen, whose unusual interest in discovering Leoni's background just made her hide it more. Usually, she'd trot out the cover story Ginny had created, secure in the knowledge that all the relevant subterfuge would be in place: fake social media accounts, bogus website, and possible calls for whatever company she was supposed to work for or own routed to Ginny. Leoni was under no illusions about why she hadn't done that; she was having too much fun being the focus of Aspen's attention.

And that was dangerous. She couldn't kid herself that she was doing it to frustrate Aspen, and in doing so, please Willow, who clearly liked nothing more than to constantly bitch and jab at her sister. Willow was already hyper-sensitive to Aspen being the star of the show. It wouldn't take her long to figure out that Leoni was starting to fall into Aspen's orbit too. If Leoni messed this up, she could kiss that bonus goodbye. All she had to do was remember why Ruth had faith in her. Remember her training. And remember she was damned good at this job.

But God, why did she tell the truth about her undergrad degree?

"What was that all about?" Willow whispered when she came alongside Leoni.

Ah, crap. Willow was more astute than people gave her credit for. "What do you mean?"

"That. In the car. You were flirting with my sister."

"I was, but not for the reason you might think," Leoni said, scrambling to cover her attraction. "You've told me that Aspen gets everything she wants, right?"

Willow frowned and nodded slowly. "So?"

Leoni grinned. "But she can't have me, can she?" she asked and gave Willow time to work it out for herself.

Willow's eyes lit up. "Oh! You mean, your plan is to get her *interested* interested in you, so she's jealous of me?"

Leoni gave her the thumbs up. "Exactly. Good plan or not?" she asked, as if that had been the idea all along.

Willow clasped her hands together and smiled widely. "I *love* it! For once in her life, she'll want something that I've got, and she won't be able to have it."

"Yep." Leoni didn't much *want* to feed the monster inside Willow, but this way would work for both of them.

Willow tapped the bill of Leoni's ballcap. "You might have to take this off occasionally though. I've never seen Aspen with or interested in anyone other than super feminine model-type women."

Leoni suppressed a grin at the new knowledge that her regular self was exactly Aspen's type. "I can do that, but I can't do much with the clothes I've brought with me."

Willow shrugged. "From the way she's already asking you loads of questions, maybe the long hair will be enough." She looked back toward where the others were unloading their bags, then she grasped Leoni's hand, suddenly looking serious. "Oh God, we've got a problem."

Leoni glanced over her shoulder and couldn't see the cause of Willow's concern. "What?"

"Kelly's brought her guitar. They're going to make you sing."

Leoni laughed lightly. "*Make me*?"

Willow tugged on Leoni's hand. "Yes. Later, around the *perfect* fire that Aspen will build, they'll all start singing like we're at some hippie commune, and they'll expect you to be Taylor Swift." She began to pick at her nails and huffed. "God, I'm stupid. I can't remember what the file said about your education at all. Were you telling the truth about your degree?"

"Yes, but don't call yourself that." Leoni put her hands on Willow's upper arms and pulled her in a little closer, but Willow wouldn't look at her. "It doesn't matter what the file said. It's just some guidance so we have our stories straight, but it can change if we need it to." She placed a finger under Willow's chin and tipped it up gently. "Okay?"

Willow finally looked up. "Okay."

"Good. And stupid is such a horrible word. You're *not* stupid, right?"

Willow nodded slowly.

With her slightly trembling bottom lip and almost glassy eyes, Willow once again looked like the vulnerable kid trying too hard to find herself. A rush of protectiveness overwhelmed Leoni, and she drew Willow into a hug. She almost told her that everything was going to be okay, but who was she to promise that, especially when she'd be gone in six days? Instead, she held Willow tightly for a little longer.

Across the parking lot, she locked eyes with Aspen, who gave her a quick smile before disappearing back behind Oakley's Jeep. God, this was getting complicated. She released Willow and put her arm around her shoulder. "Ready to kick some ass?"

Willow's familiar half-sneer fell back into place like a veil covering her real self. "Let's do it."

Leoni followed Willow to a row of trailers chock-full of sit-on-top kayaks and canoes, and Aspen jogged up beside them.

"Do you have the key?" Aspen asked, as if she expected the answer to be no.

"Duh." Willow pulled a keychain from her pocket and dangled it. "Of course I do. You don't get to control everything, you know?"

Leoni watched the way Aspen closed her eyes, took a deep breath, and exhaled it slowly. She was an only child—sort of—so she'd never had to deal with sibling squabbles. As well as making her extremely uncomfortable, it also made Leoni want to thank her mom for not having another kid. Growing up the way she did had been enough of a challenge; it would've been another level of hell with this kind of rivalry. Although maybe it was inflated because of their top one percent status. From what Leoni could tell, Willow hadn't faced any genuine obstacles yet, so her conflict with her sister existed in a bubble of privilege the real world had yet to pop.

Willow opened a padlock and began to pull at one end of the chain, but it didn't move much. Jesse's voice popped into Leoni's head, reminding her that this was one of those chivalry moments where she'd need to step up. "Do you want me to help with that?" she asked at exactly the same time Aspen reached for the chain without saying anything.

Willow yanked it away from Aspen and handed it to Leoni. "Yes, please."

Leoni fed the chain backward through the security loops rather than attempting to tug it Wonder Woman-style, and everyone else helped unload six sit-on kayaks. Aspen and Oakley laid paddles, life preservers, and a water bag onto them, and then they took everything to the lake's edge in pairs.

"Has Willow explained the rules, Leo?" Oakley asked as he tossed a ball from one hand to the other.

"From the videos I watched this morning, it doesn't look like there *are* any rules." In fact, the videos Leoni had watched on Willow's phone scared the crap out of her, but she couldn't admit that. Jesse hadn't mentioned anything called butch bravado, but Leoni was certain she had to exhibit something like that for this situation. Maybe butches admitted fears when they felt safe in long-term relationships, but since Leoni didn't have experiences longer than forty-eight hours to draw on, she stuck with her gut on the issue and concentrated on exuding supreme confidence.

Flynn grinned. "Don't worry. We don't play hard like that."

"She wasn't worried," Willow said.

Clearly, Willow had been scrolling the same "How butches act and feel" websites as Leoni. That didn't seem right, like Leoni should turn in her LGBTQ card for lack of knowledge. She resolved to talk to Jesse and Tyler about it when she got back so she could be better prepared if Ruth threw her into something like this again.

Aspen dug her paddle into the sand in front of her and leaned on it. "Let's make the teams. Leo and Kelly can choose. Leo should go first because this is her debut game with us." She smiled at Leoni and quirked her eyebrow slightly.

Was that a challenge? *Perfect.* Choose to win, or choose to keep the peace? "Willow," Leoni said and grasped Willow's hand.

Kelly tugged Oakley's shirt and pulled him closer. "I want Oakley."

"Yes!" Oakley yelled. "Ten dollars on us to win by at least three clear points."

Aspen shook her head. "Do you have to bet on everything?"

"Scared you'll lose?" Oakley asked.

"That's never going to happen," Aspen said.

Leoni hadn't gotten around to finding out Kelly and Oakley's story from Willow yet, and she didn't want to assume they were a couple. Although the way Flynn flinched when Kelly made her choice indicated there might be something floating around there. Envy maybe? It could be anything with this family.

That left the hot sister and her cute best friend. Did Leoni want to play with or against Aspen? In a different game, her answer to that would be instant. "Aspen," she said, deciding it would be easier to control her attraction if they were cooperating rather than facing off. Leoni had already spotted Aspen's solid-looking arms pushing against her T-shirt; when she started paddling, they'd be stretching them to busting point, and that would be incredibly distracting.

Willow scoffed beside her. "*Great.*"

"It's going to be fine," Leoni said and pulled on a life preserver.

"With the two top scorers on the team, we're going to smash this." She'd heard a similar refrain from Tyler once in relation to her baseball team, and she matched her conviction. She wrapped her hand around the paddle and was instantly relieved she'd had her acrylics removed. Though she couldn't remember the last time she'd been inclined to clench her fist, and her nails usually made that action impossible.

Everyone got into their boats and shuffled into the water. Aspen strapped a bag onto one kayak, then she and Oakley put hoops with cork floats around their waists and led the way. Leoni had played lacrosse in college and hoped her long-neglected defensive skills might return once they started playing. Willow came alongside her, and they started to make progress across the lake. She was a little wobbly to begin with, but Willow told her to put her feet on closer footrests, so her knees were bent, and that helped a lot.

When Leoni was relatively confident she wasn't about to fall in with every stroke, she took the time to look around. The clear bluebird sky reflected on the lake's surface, which was edged by giant evergreens, and it would've made a perfect photo had she not left her cell in the car. The iPhone might be company property, but that didn't mean Leoni didn't look after it, and there was no way she was risking dunking the phone in the lake. She wasn't eager to be dumped herself either. She'd look like a wet rat if her hair got wet—not a winning look to attract Aspen. Not that anything could come of it even if her off-the-cuff plan worked, though from the looks Aspen kept trying to disguise every time she glanced Leoni's way, it seemed like the goal might already have been achieved.

She focused on Aspen paddling, her arm muscles straining hard. She and Oakley were pulling ahead, as if they were participating in a race no one else had been informed of. Leoni suspected their sibling rivalry was only slightly less destructive than Aspen and Willow's.

"Are they always competing like that?" Leoni matched Willow's slow, steady strokes, making sure her paddle didn't slap the water.

Willow rolled her eyes. "You noticed?"

She smiled. "Hard not to. They set off at the same time as us, but they're pretty far ahead. Looks like Aspen has the edge though."

"She usually does." Willow stopped paddling, and her kayak glided effortlessly across the water. "Oakley is less than three years younger than her, but they're well-matched physically. I don't even try to keep up." She held out her arms. "This is a Pilates and yoga body. I've never wanted to be stocky like Aspen. What do you do? You're in decent shape."

Leoni laughed lightly. "Wow, 'decent' is high praise."

Willow smiled, and her face softened. When she smiled like that, she was so much more attractive than when she was pouting, but Leoni couldn't really tell her that.

"Sorry," Willow said. "I should have said that you've got a beautiful body."

Leoni nudged Willow's kayak with her paddle. "I think you said that I was chunky."

Willow covered her mouth, and her face flushed. "I know. I wasn't very nice to you yesterday. I wanted this week to go a certain way, and I had an idea of the woman I needed to make that happen, and then your boss called..." She sighed deeply and shook her head.

She looked like she might want to say something more, but she fell silent. They'd spent less than twenty-four hours together, but Willow was beginning to show Leoni a very different side from the initial impression she'd made.

"It's okay." She reached across the water and squeezed Willow's hand. "I don't get to show the real me to many people either."

Willow opened her mouth as if to protest, but then she shrugged. "I don't have a lot of friends... Well, any, really. With all the family money, it's hard to know when someone is *actually* interested in you and not what you can buy them, y'know?"

Leoni didn't know, obviously, but she nodded. "I don't have

many friends either."

Willow gave a half-smile and looked ahead. "Maybe after this... Ignore that. I know this is just business for you."

Yep, that's what it was supposed to be. And yet, the women in this family were starting to get under Leoni's skin. "If you promise never to call me chunky again, we can be friends."

Willow's smile widened. "Cool." She picked up her paddle again and dug it into the lake. "Come on, we're way behind."

Leoni followed suit, trying not to read too much into her unprofessional offer. Nothing would likely come of it anyway. When this week was over, Willow would return to New York and do more of the nothing she did, and Leoni would fly back to Las Vegas and move on to the next fake relationship, leaving the chance of a real one far behind.

Chapter Ten

ASPEN HURTLED TOWARD THE ball at full pace, sure that she'd gotten the drop on Oakley. "Too slow, bro!" She reached it just before he did, scooped the ball from the water, and hurled it back over her head toward Willow. Then she dug her paddle into the lake at the rear of her kayak and pushed it forward with all her strength to spin around to the left.

"I've got it!" Willow yelled. She grabbed the ball and threw it in front of Leo's path.

"You're toast, Flynn!" Leo shouted.

Her progress toward the ball was more sedate than Aspen would've wanted in an ideal world, but it had become clear from the moment Leo got on her kayak that the water and she weren't well-acquainted. It had been a series of early Christmas miracles that Leo hadn't managed to dunk herself yet, like some higher power had her back.

"Don't bet on it," Flynn said, as she paddled hard to where the ball had landed.

Well, hard for Flynn but barely faster than Leo even though Flynn had been playing this game with them for well over a decade. "Don't paddle too fast, or you'll get your hair wet!"

Leo got to the ball first and threw it into the space Willow was headed.

"You're lucky I just got these done," Flynn gestured to her cornrows. "I'm going easy on you all."

Kelly glided alongside Flynn and prodded the front of Flynn's kayak with her paddle. "That's what you say every time we play."

"And it's *true* every time we play." Flynn stuck out her tongue.

Aspen scooted past both of them and winked at Flynn. Her hair wasn't the only thing distracting Flynn from her game, and Aspen was more than happy to take advantage of the situation.

Oakley powered up alongside Aspen a few feet away, clearly gunning to defend their goal. Willow collected the ball and had a clean shot on goal, but Oakley would probably be able to toss his paddle and cut it off.

"Aspen's open," Leo yelled.

Aspen held back the laugh that wanted to explode from her mouth. As if her little sister would ever pass to her when she had even the tiniest chance of scoring.

When the ball came sailing toward Aspen, she was almost too dumbstruck to react. But she swiped at it with her paddle. Oakley had anticipated Willow shooting, and he'd already sped past Aspen to put a barrier between Willow and the goal, leaving it completely open. Aspen connected with the ball and sent it powering into the center of the ring, putting their team at ten points and winning the game. Leo and Willow punched the air, then they both paddled toward her, crunching either side of her to make an Aspen sandwich.

"Losers collect the rings and the firewood," Willow said, with more than a hint of glee as she threw her arms around Aspen.

Aspen frowned. When had she slipped into an alternate universe? And when had her sister reverted to the Willow she used to be when she was a teenager? Leo smiled at Aspen as if she knew what she was thinking, and Aspen inclined her head, puzzled beyond belief. Sure, she hadn't seen Willow since Christmas, but she'd been her usual unfriendly self last night and in the car. Could this glimpse of the old Willow be part of a *Leo effect* in just a couple of months? Aspen hadn't stopped to consider that her sister's general malaise and bad attitude might be a reflection of her unhappiness, and that all she had to do was find herself a hot, slightly older woman. Maybe Aspen could learn something from her little sister after all.

Willow loosed her arms from around Aspen. "God, Aspen, don't get clingy. It's not like we just won the Olympics." She wrinkled her nose as if the lake were covered in stinky green algae. Then she pushed away from Aspen's boat and began to paddle for the shore.

And there she is again.

"Are we not heading back to the parking lot?" Leo turned her kayak to follow Willow.

Aspen pointed over her shoulder to the bag strapped down tight on the rear of her kayak. "We've got what we need for now in there. Oakley will hike to the trucks and bring everything else back in the beach wagon." She smiled. "I hope you're not shy."

Leo arched her eyebrow. "About what? I didn't get wet, so I don't need to change."

Aspen swallowed and looked away, hoping that might obliterate the instant image of Leo getting naked from her mind.

It didn't.

"About singing," Aspen said, sufficiently pulled together to continue the conversation...for now, at least.

Leo chuckled and began to paddle away in pursuit of Willow. "I get stage fright. Why else do you think I'm not taking Broadway by storm?"

Aspen dug in and followed Leo stroke for stroke. "Why don't I believe that?"

Leo shrugged. "Because you're obviously a very mistrusting person."

Aspen tapped her paddle on Leo's boat. "How'd you figure that out in the two short conversations we've had?"

Leo's grin smacked of mischief. "Are you counting?"

"Yeah." And she wanted that number to increase exponentially—purely on a friend level, obviously.

"Are you saying it's true? You don't trust people?"

Aspen shook her head. "I didn't say that."

"Then you'll have to wait until conversation number four for the answer to your question." Leo pressed her lips together, clearly trying not to laugh.

"Why do I get the feeling you're playing with me?"

Leo pulled at the peak of her ballcap. "I thought we were all playing together?"

Aspen shook her head, unable to get a grasp of Leo's banter but enjoying it all the more because of that. Few people surprised her, but Leo didn't seem to match any initial judgments Aspen had made about her. "That game's over."

Leo inclined her head but didn't look at Aspen as she continued to catch up with Willow. "Isn't life one big game? It's not over until you check out, is it?"

Aspen laughed. "Wow, that's a bit deep and philosophical for me."

Leo scoffed and glanced at her briefly. "So you're shallow and don't go deep? That's disappointing."

Aspen misjudged the placement of her paddle and almost followed it into the lake as she dug in. Jesus, what game *was* Leo playing?

And why, oh, why, did Aspen want to play too?

"Incoming!"

She turned just as Flynn drove her kayak into Aspen's. She bounced, almost losing her balance, and had to slap the water with her paddle to stay upright. As Leo's laughter rang out, Aspen grabbed the end of Flynn's boat and wiggled it from side to side.

Flynn's wide grin disappeared, and she abandoned her paddle to grasp both sides of her kayak. "Don't do it. I'm begging you."

"You shouldn't play rough if you can't take it," Aspen said, looking over at Leo, but she was already paddling away to Willow. She released the boat and handed Flynn her escaping paddle that had begun to float away.

"What are you doing?"

Aspen looked at Flynn and frowned at her unusually serious tone. "Saving you from getting stranded."

Flynn came alongside Aspen's boat, so she laid her paddle across it to connect them, and Flynn did the same.

"That's not what I'm talking about." Flynn jutted her chin in Leo's direction. "What are you doing with Leo?"

"Getting to know her," she said, maybe too vehemently. "She's the longest relationship Willow's been in, outside the family, so I figured I'd better make an effort and start building a connection."

Flynn narrowed her eyes. "That's not it, and you know it."

Kelly and Oakley came up alongside them. "What are you guys up to? You've got to help me collect firewood, Flynn."

"Uh-huh," Flynn said and slapped the side of her boat. "I'll follow your lead in. I just wanted to chat with Asp about something."

"Oh, yeah? Anything I can help with?" Kelly asked.

Her firebrand smile practically melted Flynn into a puddle of want, and Aspen fought to suppress a laugh. It was *everything* Kelly could help Flynn with. Why didn't Kelly see what was right in front of her? *Crap.* Unless she *did* see it and was ignoring it because she didn't feel the same way. Flynn had been in a few relationships, but Aspen had never seen her this messed up and wobbly about a woman. If Kelly didn't reciprocate Flynn's feelings, it'd take more than a few beers over a basket of chicken wings to pick up the pieces and put her back together again. And future family events would be drop-your-pants-in-front-of-the-doctor awkward if Flynn offered her heart and Kelly let it fall to the floor.

"It's about work," Aspen said after Flynn failed to respond for way too long to be comfortable. "Sorry. I know we're supposed to leave the office at the city limits, but we've got a real butthole of a client, and we're on a tight deadline."

Oakley tsked loudly. "I bet Mom loves that."

Aspen shrugged. "You know her well."

"Don't take too long," Oakley said. "You're the firebug, and I'm hungry."

Aspen shooed him off. "Go get the beer and food then. I'll have the fire roaring before you get back."

Oakley and Kelly paddled off, and Aspen laughed lightly. "So you're no closer to a strategy with Kelly then?"

"Don't change the subject."

"Oh, you found your voice again," Aspen said.

"And it looks like you've found your mojo again." Flynn motioned again toward Leo.

Aspen saw that Leo had reached the shoreline and was helping Willow pull up her kayak. She must've lost her grip, because she fell back on her butt in the sand, and both she and Willow laughed so loud, Aspen could hear them. "Doesn't look like she's done that before, does it?"

Flynn shoved her. "Mojo. Leo. What's the deal?"

Aspen let out a short sigh. "There is no deal. She's cute, and she's my sister's girlfriend."

"And she's the first woman I've seen you look at *that* way since Sarah."

Aspen briefly closed her eyes and wrapped her hands around her paddle. "I'm ready to move on. That's a good thing, isn't it?"

"Not if you're trying to move on to Willow's girl, it isn't. And I thought you weren't into mascs."

"She's still got long hair, and I keep getting hits of that fiery femme attitude too. I swear it." She couldn't describe how Leo was different, but there was something about the way a really feminine woman arched their eyebrows that was just... Well, it defied definition, but it existed, for sure. "Also, I don't discriminate; I'm equal opportunities for all sapphics—"

"With long hair."

"With long hair." Aspen grinned. "But it doesn't matter. She's with Willow, and I respect that."

Flynn retrieved her paddle and pushed away from Aspen's boat. "You make sure you do that. I've got enough going on this week with Kelly. I can't micromanage your inappropriate attractions like I usually do."

Aspen laughed. "That's a two-way street, buddy, and you know it."

Flynn slapped Aspen's back and grinned. "I do. So now would be a good time for you to shower me with your wisdom on how to turn my friend into my lover."

"First, we need to find out if she's seeing anyone," Aspen said as she headed to join the others. "I haven't seen anything from Kelly in our group chat, but it's not like she's ever shared that part of her with either of us, is it?"

"I guess not. Should we ask Oakley?"

"No, definitely not. If he figures out you like his best friend, he'll spill it before you get the chance to do it your way." Aspen smiled. "He's never been able to keep a secret, and Kelly's his ride-or-die. He tells her everything."

"And you're sure he doesn't like her that way."

"Ew, gross." Aspen gagged a little at the notion. "They've known each other since kindergarten."

"What does that matter? I've only just realized that I have feelings for her."

"Not true," Aspen said. "You've only just realized that you have to do something about it. You've always carried a flickering torch for Kelly, but now you've let the gasoline flow, and it's burning bright."

Flynn grinned. "I might use that line... Do you think her family will be okay with me—y'know, if Kelly does want to explore a relationship?"

Aspen clenched her jaw and dug her paddle in harder. Flynn had suffered prejudice because of her skin color and upbringing too many times before, and Kelly's family were card-carrying, hardline Republicans from the Deep South as well as being top one percenters. "Kelly isn't that close to her family, so you shouldn't worry about that."

"Maybe I could talk to her tonight," Flynn said. "It doesn't get much more romantic than a fire at night by the lake."

"Except you've got four other people intruding on your special moment. No, that's not going to work." Aspen chewed on her lip, searching for inspiration. "I think you could engineer a late-night walk on the beach after dinner sometime this week. I can run interference with Oakley, and you can sweep Kelly off her feet."

"Okay, okay. I like the sound of that. Should I wait until the Fourth of July party?"

Aspen frowned. "Why wait?"

"Because if I strike out, I'm leaving the next morning anyway, so it doesn't have to be awkward and weird for either of us."

Aspen picked up the pace as they got closer to the shore to beach the kayaks. "That's a good idea. And hopefully, Mom's annual pyro display won't be the only fireworks that night." She powered up to the water's edge and glided to a stop on the dusty soil, with the rear end of her boat just in the lake.

"Want me to pull you in?" Leo asked as she approached Aspen's kayak.

I'm already in too far. "Like you pulled Willow in? I'm good." Aspen winked and laughed, then jumped off and tugged the boat in herself. She glanced across at Willow, who glared at her. Did she know Aspen was crushing hard on her girlfriend? Or was that just her usual level of contempt? Whatever it was, the glimpse of old Willow had disappeared as rapidly as Aspen's residual sadness for her failed relationship with Sarah had since she'd set eyes on Leo.

Damn it, she had to stop thinking about Leo, or this was going to be the longest week of her life.

Chapter Eleven

By the time Oakley returned, pulling a beach wagon loaded up with a giant Yeti cooler, the guitar, and a bundle of blankets, Flynn and Kelly had collected enough firewood to keep Aspen's fire going until the autumn.

"Are we camping?" Leoni whispered to Willow. "I don't do camping."

"God, no. We'll paddle back around and head home when I've had enough." Willow looked up from her phone briefly and inspected her nails as if the lake had melted her acrylics. "I haven't camped out here with them since I was nine."

Leoni chose to ignore Willow's return to selfish form and did the math. "Before Aspen went to college for her first semester?"

Willow shrugged. "I guess."

Leoni had done a couple of psych classes as an undergrad, because she thought they'd help her better understand the motivation of *all* the characters she was going to play once she hit Broadway. So she hadn't used anything she'd learned—like she needed another reminder—and she hadn't expected to end up using it for a gig like this instead. The sisters' fractious relationship was psych 101, and they didn't need an expensive therapist to figure out the problem.

But they also didn't need someone they'd just met to lay out their issues either.

Leoni looked over to where Aspen had constructed some kind of cooking contraption over the fire she'd built so competently, like she had military survival training. "Is that thing from Walmart?"

Aspen dropped to her knees in front of the fire, looking so

offended that Leoni couldn't hold in a spontaneous and overly loud laugh.

"Are you kidding me?" Aspen clutched her hands to her chest. "Your accusation is like a silver bullet to my heart."

Leoni struggled to stop her laugh from dissolving into full-blown giggles. "Willow, you should've told me your sister is a vampire." She didn't add the quip about all the garlic on last night's food and killing Aspen by kissing her.

Willow rolled her eyes and went back to her phone without engaging further.

"Asp made that herself." Flynn grabbed some blankets from the wagon and handed them around. "She's very proud of it, in case you couldn't tell."

"Oh, no, I definitely didn't get that vibe from her reaction." Leoni stood up from the horizontal tree branch she and Willow were perched on. She laid out the blanket Flynn had given her close to the fire and sat down after helping Willow get comfortable on it.

"Ha ha." Aspen gestured toward her creation. "Look at the welding and the hinges. You can't get that level of workwomanship in the mass-produced crap at *Walmart*."

"The only hinge that interests me is the hip hinge in forward fold pose," she whispered to Willow, who glanced up and laughed. Aspen looked even less impressed; she clearly didn't like being the butt of anyone's joke. Leoni wrinkled her nose and nodded like she was appeasing a child. "I believe you."

"Seriously," Aspen said, "come and look at it."

Kelly laughed. "Ooh, you've done it now, Leo. You've offended her sense of craftwomanship. There's no coming back from that."

Leoni pushed herself back up and did her best to stomp with purpose toward Aspen instead of succumbing to her instinct to exaggerate the sway of her hips on her approach. She leaned carefully over the fire and "inspected" the makeshift grill, making noises of approval as if she knew what the hell she was supposed to be appreciating.

Aspen held up a canvas pouch. "*And* it all folds down to fit into this little bag."

Leoni inclined her head. "Wow, that's really cool," she said then pressed her lips together to stop a grin. "You should totally make more and sell them online to *Butches R Us*. I'd get all my butch and masc camping buddies to buy one."

Aspen shoved her hard, and Leoni stumbled to regain her balance, not expecting the rough-housing. She wasn't a feeble flower by any means, but that took her by surprise.

Aspen reached out and grabbed a handful of Leoni's shirt to help steady her. "Oh, shit. Sorry."

Leoni fell sideward into Aspen with the force of her pull, and they both tumbled to the ground.

"Jesus, Aspen," Willow said. "Do you *have* to be so alpha?"

Leoni's hands were on Aspen's chest, their faces were inches apart, and they were in a heap, crotch-to-crotch. God, she felt solid and powerful. But Leoni should move her hands. She should *definitely* move her hands.

But instead, she spent a few more micro-moments staring into Aspen's eyes. Those flecks were so unusual. Leoni hadn't noticed them before, but then she hadn't been this close before. Which she shouldn't be now either. She reluctantly shifted and pushed up from the ground, then she held her hand out to help Aspen up. Aspen grabbed Leoni's forearm and tugged herself upright. It took all of Leoni's strength not to topple over again. She shouldn't have offered. Physics had never been her strong suit.

Leoni brushed herself off and retreated back to the safety of the blanket with Willow, away from Aspen's hypnotic eyes. "It was just an accident, babe," she said and wrapped her arm around Willow's shoulder.

Willow leaned in. "She forgets we're not all as strong as her," she said, loudly enough for everyone to hear.

Leoni squeezed gently, wondering if anyone else caught the wider meaning of Willow's words. Or maybe Leoni was just reading too much into it. In her peripheral vision, Aspen shook her head and went back to preparing her outdoor kitchen.

Oakley went around the group moments later with ice-cold beer. He opened Willow's for her, then extended a metal straw and placed it in the bottle before handing it to her. "For our little princess."

Willow scoffed as she took it, but she didn't remove and discard it. She didn't balk at his term of endearment either. Leoni took her still-capped bottle, wishing she could have a nice straw too since glasses were obviously in short supply. At least it was a twist-off cap, and she wasn't expected to tear it off with her teeth or flick it off with a Zippo like she'd seen Tyler frequently do. Leoni didn't know why she particularly liked that, but she did, and she smiled at the memory. She took out her phone and fired off a quick text to Tyler, hoping she was feeling better. When she slipped her cell back in her shorts' pocket, she glanced across at Aspen, who she never would've met if Tyler hadn't gotten sick. What had started as an "Oh, crap" assignment had turned into an "Oh, my" gig that she was beginning to enjoy immensely...even if it was like being in an upmarket jewelry store where she was only allowed to *look* at the handsome watches.

Aspen and Flynn soon got the pre-prepped food cooking, and more beer flowed as the six of them circled the fire and chatted, mostly about their various work situations. Willow had little to offer, and it was clear she was uncomfortable with that fact, so Leoni avoided adding anything about her fake work to the conversation. Her reticence served a second purpose in clearly frustrating Aspen, whose subtle openings to encourage Leoni to share went unfilled.

"*Actually,*" Willow said, perhaps when she grew tired of not being the center of everyone's attention, "Leo and I have been talking, and we're going to find my passion together."

"Yeah? I'll toast to that." Aspen raised her bottle, and everyone followed suit with words of encouragement.

Leoni didn't miss Willow's fleeting expression of surprise. She must've expected them to shoot her down.

"Do you want to tell us more about where you are with that?" Aspen asked gently.

"No." Willow tucked her legs in and crossed her arms over them. "I don't want to jinx anything."

She took another breath as if she was about to continue then thought better of it. Leoni leaned into her slightly, and Willow looked up. The soft vulnerability in her eyes tore at Leoni's heart, daring her to intervene. Jesus, what was this family doing to her? Keeping her distance professionally had never been so challenging. "It'd be good to talk about it with more people and get their perspectives," she whispered so only Willow could hear.

Willow looked away and shook her head almost imperceptibly, but Leoni saw that Aspen had witnessed it.

"I was lucky," Aspen said. "I knew I liked making things as a kid, but I didn't know anything about architecture until I was fourteen and Zaha Hadid was chosen as the first female Laureate of the Pritzker Architecture Prize. Mom was one of the jurors at the time, and she told me about it. But I didn't do anything with that until I needed to think about going to college. Then I remembered her, so I researched who she was and what she'd done, and that was it. I knew I wanted to do something like that, to be someone like her."

"I didn't know that." Willow took Leoni's hand and intwined their fingers. "I thought you'd wanted to be an architect all your life."

Aspen shook her head. "It was so hard in the first year that I almost quit to do something else."

"And that's where I came in," Flynn said, bringing some levity and breaking the intimacy of the moment. "Once I became Asp's study buddy, she was going nowhere but up."

"Is that true?" Willow asked.

"More or less," Aspen said, though she gave Flynn a shove hard enough for her to spill the beer she was pouring into her mouth. "Having someone to share my struggles with really helped, and

Flynn's passion for architecture and all of her dreams about what we could achieve together lit a fire under my butt."

Aspen wrapped her arm around Flynn's neck and pulled her in for an awkward-looking hug, and in the dusky evening, Leoni could see the fire's flames reflecting in Aspen's slightly watery eyes. She sighed. She was a sucker for a hard woman with a soft heart. Aspen wasn't making it easy to maintain her distance.

Willow squeezed Leoni's arm and leaned close to her ear. "I want that same fire," she whispered. "Will you still help me when this is over?"

How was she supposed to do that when she'd turned her back on her own passion? But she nodded then took a long pull of her beer, which actually tasted better straight from the bottle.

"So you were the one with the big dreams, and Aspen just grabbed onto your coattails to come along for the ride?" Kelly asked, looking at Flynn.

"Uh, no. No, it wasn't like that." Flynn wiped the beer from her chin. "We built each other up. That's what great friends do."

"Have you ever been anything more than friends?" Leoni asked, barely trying to conceal her grin.

"Oh my God, no."

Aspen's instant, and particularly vehement, response made everyone laugh. Except Flynn.

"Excuse me. You could do a lot worse than me." Flynn gestured wildly with her bottle and more beer escaped onto the ground. "You only have to look at Sarah to see that."

Aspen glared at Flynn. "Don't go there."

Game on. "Who's Sarah, Flynn?" Leoni asked then offered Aspen a sweet and innocent smile. The answering resignation in her expression stoked Leoni's mischievousness.

"I'm glad you asked." Flynn batted Aspen's half-hearted shoulder punch away. "Sarah is the woman who stole my best friend's heart and stomped all over it in her Louboutin heels."

Flynn gave Aspen a look Leoni couldn't decode.

"And she's only just starting to emerge from the fog of the broken-hearted." Flynn put her hand on Aspen's shoulder and inclined her head.

Of course Aspen would keep the company of women who could afford shoes like those. There were a few pairs in the costume room back at the office, but she only ever got to wear them for work. What she'd give to actually own a pair of her own. "Somehow I thought you'd be the one breaking all the pretty girls' hearts."

Aspen straightened her back a little and a proud little smile played on her lips briefly before she caught herself. "I don't know why you'd think that, but I'm about fifty-fifty on that score."

Oakley and Kelly chimed in with comments that they had the same impression as Leoni. Clearly, they weren't as close as she'd thought they were, but then she couldn't imagine sharing her love life with a brother, if she had one. "How long ago was this?"

Aspen twisted her empty into the sand and pulled another beer from the cooler she'd been leaning against. "We were together nearly two years, and she left me a little over six months ago."

Flynn scoffed but didn't say anything, though it seemed like she might be desperate to.

"Is there a missing detail you want to add, Flynn?" Leoni had to stop herself from fluttering her eyelashes, remembering at the last second how she was supposed to be presenting. She'd gotten too relaxed, as if she'd known the people around the fire for years, not hours.

Aspen clasped her hand over Flynn's mouth briefly. "No, there isn't," she said.

"What did you do?" Willow asked.

Aspen frowned. "Why would you assume I was the one that did something wrong?"

Willow shrugged. "Educated guess."

"So she did *you* wrong?" Leoni asked, quick to gloss over yet another Willow barb.

Flynn practically growled. "Wrong would be a gross understatement."

Aspen picked at the label on her beer and stared at the fire, and Leoni almost wished she hadn't been so obnoxious about it. But on the other hand, she had a pressing need to know how this Sarah woman had hurt Aspen. Where was the chink in her butch armor?

"Let's just say she didn't believe in monogamy." Aspen glanced across at Leoni and gave her a sad smile.

Ah, a cheater. The worst kind of betrayal. That was something Leoni didn't have to worry about in hook-ups that lasted no longer than forty-eight hours.

"'Didn't believe in monogamy'? The woman lied to you every day of your relationship, and then she robbed you of every cent from your joint savings account, even though you'd been the only one putting anything into it for your—"

Flynn stopped in her tracks when Aspen glared at her, eyes wide and head cocked.

"Mom's told all of us not to have joint accounts with anyone until we're married, and even then, only after Philip has..."

Now Willow joined in with the unfinished sentence game, leaving Leoni to look between her and Aspen and wait for someone to fill in the blanks.

"Oh..." Willow said, then she shook her head slowly. "You were going to get married, and Mom didn't know."

"No one knew," Aspen said before she looked pointedly at Flynn. "Almost no one."

The whole group was struck speechless, and the only sounds were the crackling of the flames and the distant calls of the nocturnal birds just waking up to play. Now Leoni really wished she hadn't pressed Aspen.

"If you want to know if Oakley and I have ever been more than friends, the answer is a resounding no." Kelly's smile softened the force of her conviction slightly, and her intervention allowed everyone to breathe again. "Though we did have a bit of a disastrous love triangle with someone in college."

Flynn coughed like she was choking on her beer, and Aspen patted her back hard.

Leoni really hadn't expected this kind of honesty when she was all but a stranger to them. "I hope you're going to share?"

"That's what Oakley said." Kelly winked at him, and he bumped her shoulder as he laughed with her.

"Do we need the details?" Aspen's expression made it clear that she didn't, though she also looked relieved that the spotlight was no longer trained on her.

"Come on, Aspen, don't be such a prude," Kelly said.

Flynn looked between Aspen and Kelly as if she didn't know which side she was supposed to take. In the end, she didn't say anything.

"Do you remember his name, Oakley? John? Jim?"

"Jason." Oakley wiggled his eyebrows. "And I remember more than his name."

So Oakley was part of the rainbow too. No wonder Willow felt so isolated and had chosen to play pretend with a girlfriend. More than shock them, she clearly just wanted to fit in, and being the only straight child didn't feel special enough.

Willow excused herself, armed with her Kula cloth and Maglite, and disappeared into the darkness of the trees behind their little camping area. She'd been gone only a few seconds before Aspen shuffled across her blanket toward Leoni.

"Thank you," she said quietly.

Leoni frowned. "What for?"

"For being here." Aspen glanced in the direction Willow had wandered off. "It's nice to see my little sister happy."

She watched the progress of Aspen's hand as she ran it through the longer hair on top of her head after she'd removed her ballcap. *What would it be like to kiss her?* Leoni resisted the near-overwhelming urge to wrap her hand around the back of Aspen's neck and pull her in to find out. "Do you think she's happy?" she asked instead. How could the whole family not realize how Willow was the total opposite of that? Were they all so self-absorbed? Aspen didn't seem that way. Oakley, maybe, but Aspen appeared to be the epitome of the good, eldest sister. How could she not understand that Willow still needed her but had no idea how to show it when Leoni had figured it out in just over twenty-four hours?

Aspen nodded. "I've been seeing the occasional light shard pierce the cracks of that attitude armor she's dressed herself in."

Leoni could smell the last vestiges of Aspen's cologne, something with bergamot and worn leather, mixed with her fresh perspiration and the warm evening air. Her predilection for Aspen's type—strong, intelligent, and driven, yet soft and just the right amount of emotional—taunted her, echoing the circumstances that prevented her from edging into Aspen's space. It had stopped her from pressing her lips to Aspen's and discovering how they would be intimate together. Was she gentle or forceful? Did she take her time or couldn't she wait?

The torment reminded her why she was there and *who* she was there for. And the weird desire to protect Willow reared up again and overrode her baser instincts. "That armor's there for a reason, you know?"

"I know," Aspen said.

But did she really? Aspen's smile was too much of a distraction for Leoni to think straight.

"I can't tell you how good it is to hear her talking about figuring out her future though." Aspen moved like she was about to tap Leoni's shoulder with her fist, then she stopped and lowered her hand. "You're obviously good for her."

But I could be even better for you. The look in Aspen's eyes belied the words coming out of her mouth. She was clearly at war with herself. Leoni had seen that look directed her way many times, and there was no mistaking it, no way to misconstrue the hunger.

Leoni eased away from Aspen and thumbed over her shoulder. "I'm going to check on Willow," she said and pushed up to stand.

Wrong sister. Wrong timing. This week was going to be some kind of sweet anguish.

Chapter Twelve

ASPEN FOLLOWED OAKLEY INTO the country club's driveway and glanced in her rearview mirror to make sure Leo followed. Grandpa Tom and Grammy Marge were with her and Willow, and Aspen wouldn't have been surprised if they'd sailed past the entrance to do something else with their day, something less…staid. The golf gene was very much on her maternal Hartwell side, while everyone else tolerated it.

"Willow came home later than we expected," her mom said, leaning forward in the back seat.

Aspen glanced over her shoulder briefly and nodded, surprised her mom had taken so long to broach the topic. "I really thought she was going to camp overnight with us, especially when the sun went down. But when Kelly started playing her guitar, she and Leo were quick to leave." Which had been more than a little disappointing; she'd been looking forward to hearing Leo sing, and now she still didn't know what kind of a voice she had.

"She paddled in the dark? Did you take her back to the car?"

Her mom's accusation was clear, and Aspen gripped the steering wheel tight. How was Willow supposed to grow up when the family treated her like a little girl? "Leo was with her, and they said they were okay on their own. They had headlamps, and we hadn't gone that far from the parking lot." She glanced at Flynn, but no backup was forthcoming even though she'd said that Aspen *shouldn't* accompany them.

Her mom grumbled. "I don't think Leo would deter an attacker, do you?"

She had a point. Leo might be masc, but she was probably

110 pounds at most and didn't cut an imposing figure. She had a very nice one, but not an imposing one. "No one's been murdered around here for over twenty years, Mom."

"Actually, a woman was found dead in the Shou Sugi spa last year," her dad said and tsked. "But the killer was her boyfriend."

Her mom threw her hands up. "How is that better? We don't know anything about Leo, and Willow won't give me her last name, so I can't get Philip to do a background check."

"Mom, you're sounding a little...kooky." Which was unusual. She usually walked the tightrope between paranoia and protection easily enough.

"It's not paranoia; it's reality awareness. And it's kept this family safe for decades."

Aspen chuckled. "Yeah, it has. But I'm sure Leo poses no threat to Willow or the family."

Her mom huffed. "You've got good instincts about people, but I'd still prefer Philip to vet her. Perhaps you could find out for me."

"No way. Willow's already jumped down my throat when I asked a couple of innocent questions. I'm not spying for you, Mom."

"Flynn?"

Flynn gulped. "Uh, sure. I could try." She smiled tightly and avoided Aspen's glare.

Aspen pulled into a parking space and turned to her mom. "Willow isn't one for long-term relationships, Mom. By the time *Flynn* gets you any of Leo's details, the vacation will be over and probably so will they."

"Do you think so?" her mom asked.

She really didn't want to acknowledge the selfish part of her that hoped so. "She's way beyond her usual cut-off point."

"Mm, you're right." Her mom opened her door but didn't get out. "But she's never brought someone to a family event before."

"She could just be tired of being the odd number out when everyone else has someone." Or it could be that this relationship was totally different from all of the vacuous boyfriends Willow had been with before. And that was a good thing, Aspen told herself. If Willow was in a serious relationship, it was a sign she was finally growing up, and wasn't that what everyone wanted?

Seemingly appeased, her mom got out of the car, and everyone headed into the club house and out onto the large patio area overlooking the start of the course. The staff had prepared everything, and six golf carts waited at the bottom of the wide concrete steps, replete with the family's clubs.

Grandpa Bill pulled out the two-dollar coin he used for every family golf tournament. "I've got a good feeling this is the year," he said and handed the coin to Aspen.

"Leo, heads or tails?" Aspen had *accidentally* overheard Willow and Leo talking about the family golf tournament, and Leo had sounded unsure about the whole thing, so Aspen wanted to get her involved from the start.

"For what?" Willow asked, taking Leo's hand.

Aspen smiled at the protective gesture. When Willow was around Leo, there were more and more glimpses of the woman Aspen had always thought her sister would become. "Scramble or foursomes, like always."

Willow shook her head. "Scramble is stupid. We might as well just let the best players of each team play each other, and the rest of us can stay in the clubhouse."

Her little sister had a point, and Aspen wasn't going to argue in favor of their grandpa.

"It's tradition," Grandpa Bill said.

"Which can always be replaced with new traditions." Gramps took the coin from Aspen's fingers and tossed it back to Grandpa Bill. "Foursomes is fairer. And anyways, I love digging around in the sand. Takes me back to my childhood, it does," he said and chuckled.

"You don't know I'm going to be on your team yet," Grammy said and hugged his arm.

Gramps kissed her cheek. "You're always on my team, sweetie."

There was a moment of uneasy silence before Grandpa Bill shoved his coin away. "Fine. Foursomes it is. Do you have the envelopes, honey?" he asked Aspen's mom.

She held them up before laying them on one of the nearby tables in the outdoor dining area. "Jim and I got them ready this morning."

Aspen glanced over at Leo, trying to see what she made of this particular family tradition but quickly looked away when Leo returned her gaze, eyebrow quirked slightly and a knowing smirk on her lips. Either Aspen was being way too obvious, or Leo was way too cocky...though, why wouldn't she be aware of how attractive she was?

When she tuned back in, her mom had emptied the pieces of paper onto the table, Grandma Eleanor was reading them out, and people were shifting into their allotted teams... And Leo came to stand beside Aspen.

"What a coincidence that we're on the same team again," Leo said.

"I had nothing to do with that." The defense was already out of her mouth before Aspen realized what she was saying.

"It's fine. I get it." Leo gave her the butch nod. "You want to make sure I'm good enough for your little sister."

Crap. Aspen had massively misinterpreted Leo's words. Why did figuring out the difference between someone flirting with her and someone just being friendly and fun seem to be getting harder? Of course Willow's girlfriend wouldn't be interested in her. Leo and Willow were in the first flushes of a new relationship when everything else in the world was in soft focus, and every time they looked at each other, they were at the center of a vignetted photograph. "Are you?" she asked, a little harsher than she'd intended.

Leo shrugged. "Your mom doesn't think so, but Tom likes me, and his opinion really matters to Willow." She fiddled with her thumb ring. "So does yours though."

Aspen chuckled, but a twinge of loss tugged at her heart. "It used to, but that's not the case anymore."

Leo began to respond when Grammy whooped loudly and started a slow waddle toward them. "I'm gonna knock the crap outta that li'l white ball."

"You're not on the white team, Momma," Aspen's dad called after her. "You're on blue."

"Pah! Red, white, or blue don't matter," Grammy said. "Our ball is in for the ride of its life. Right, Aspen?"

She put her arm around Grammy and squeezed lightly. "Sure thing, Grammy."

"A little bit of beach time, a dip in the lake... It'll be a golf ball vacay." Grammy cackled.

Aspen exchanged a look with her mom; the cup wouldn't be theirs this year unless Leo was a top LPGA player in disguise.

Once everyone was in their allotted teams, Grandma Eleanor handed out the little colored handkerchiefs she'd sewn to indicate who was on which team. Aspen took hers and shoved it in her back pocket.

"You should be careful which side you put that in," Leo said.

Oakley snickered and covered his mouth. "Naughty."

Aspen frowned. "What're you talking about?" She was right-handed, and she'd stuck it in her right back pocket. Anything else would've been awkward.

"Don't you know your LGBTQ history?" Leo shook her head and tsked, and Oakley joined in, both of them looking like they might dissolve into giggles.

"Bad form, sister. Bad form."

"You've never said anything before." Aspen shoved Oakley's shoulder. "Which pocket do you use?"

Oakley waved his pocket square in the air. "I've got the navy blue, and I'm happy either way, so it doesn't matter which pocket I put *mine* in."

"The colors are for the flag, idiot." Aspen took her red marker from her pocket and looked at Leo. "Grandpa Bill and Grandma Eleanor are super-patriotic, you see? I don't get the joke."

"I'll help you out." Leo grinned widely and pulled her cell from her pocket. After a few moments of tapping and scrolling, she offered it to Aspen.

She took the phone and peered at it. *Flagging?* When she'd taken it in, she looked at the two of them again, sniggering like a pair of teenagers. "Right..." She wasn't about to share her sexual proclivities with her brother or her sister's girlfriend, even to say that neither pocket would work for her with *that* particular pursuit. But Aspen vaguely wished they'd gotten the blue ones. She would've liked to have seen which pocket Leo put *that* one in. *No. No, I wouldn't.* "Thank God our flag doesn't have yellow in it," she said. "Ew, right?"

Leo and Oakley laughed so loud that everyone turned their way.

"What's the joke?" Willow asked, eyes narrowed suspiciously.

"I was just telling Leo about Oakley walking into a tree last night," Aspen said. "If he hadn't been wearing his ball cap, he would've broken his nose. Again."

Oakley held up his hand. "Don't worry, Mom. I was sober when I drove home this morning."

Their mom smiled. "I know you were, with the precious cargo you were carrying."

"Right. To the carts," Grandpa Bill announced dramatically. "And stay in your teams. The tournament has begun. No fraternizing with the competition."

Their group descended the grand steps at various speeds and paired off according to Grandpa Bill's orders.

"I'll drive for us, Maggie," Aspen's mom said.

Leo nudged Aspen and jutted her chin toward Grandpa Bill. "Will he let us borrow his lucky coin?"

"What for?"

Leo motioned toward the carts. "To decide who's driving."

"Those things?" Aspen laughed. "They might be Garias, but they don't hold a candle to your G-Wagen."

"Every vehicle has its merits though, right?" Leo patted the roof of the cart. "We should see what it can do."

Aspen shook her head and got in behind the wheel. "I don't think the club would take kindly to you doing donuts all over their course. But if you're interested in putting *your* SUV through its paces, you should come with me and Oakley when we take Betty and Ruby off-roading."

Leo slid into the passenger seat without argument, and Aspen set off to follow the slow-moving line to the first hole. She hadn't expected her to give up on driving so easily. But she hadn't responded to Aspen's invite either. Did she think it'd be some sort of big sister test to see if she was "good enough" for Willow? "Mom's just being protective of the family, Leo. It's not really about you as a person," Aspen said, bringing them back to the conversation they hadn't finished earlier. She didn't like the notion of Leo believing anyone in the family thought she was less-than.

"Yeah?"

Leo crossed her legs, almost demurely, then immediately uncrossed them and sat with her legs so wide, her knee almost touched Aspen's. It seemed odd, but maybe Leo felt like she was under attack and was just reclaiming her space.

"The family has to be careful with people coming in from the outside," Aspen said. "So Mom has Philip—"

"Philip?"

"He owns a private investigation company in Manhattan." She glanced at Leo to gauge her reaction, but she didn't seem to shift. "He does some digging and checks out people's backgrounds. I only just found out that he did it with Flynn after we started spending time together in college." She drummed her fingers on the steering wheel, trying to shove down the residual anger running through her.

"That couldn't have made you feel good," Leo said, clearly

picking up on it.

"I guess not, but I'm trying not to think about it. I'd known Philip as a friend of the family, but it wasn't until my early twenties that I found out what he did for Mom." Aspen pulled off the road and parked near the first tee. "Stupidly, it hadn't occurred to me that Philip would've dug into Flynn's history. I'm just relieved she didn't interfere, because Flynn's family situation wasn't the best, and if Mom was paranoid, she could've convinced herself that Flynn was trying to get to our money through me."

"Your mom's paranoia aside," Leo said, "it seems like she's got valid concerns that must make it hard for any of you to genuinely connect with outsiders."

"Maybe," she muttered, getting out of the cart. She went around the back to the bags and waited for Leo to join her. "This hole is a par three; I'd go four-iron. Which club would you use?"

Leo pulled a three-wood up slightly, then dropped it back down. She did the same with a number of the other clubs, including a putter. "That's a lot of sticks," she said and shoved her hands in her pockets.

"First-time golfer?"

Leo gave a shy smile and nodded. "Give me sticks and balls this size on a pool table, and it'd be a different matter."

"We could do that tonight if you wanted," Aspen said. "Has Willow showed you the game room?" She brought her sister into the conversation in a bid to expel the instant image of Leo bending over their pool table from her mind.

Leo glanced up at her and seemed to subdue her response. "No," she said a few seconds later, "she hasn't."

"She hasn't, what?" Willow came up alongside Leo and took her hand again.

Why did Willow keep taking Leo's hand but not kiss her? Aspen would be kissing Leo every chance she got if—*No*.

Still, Willow's Insta was bulging with pictures of her and her past boyfriends, and she was always all over them. Maybe she just overcompensated because she was trying to convince herself she was straight, when in fact she was just like her big sister after all.

"You haven't shown me the game room," Leo said. "I'm better—"

"No fraternizing!" Grandpa Bill grasped Willow's upper arm and tugged her away. "They'll try to steal our strategy. Come on, Willow."

Willow rolled her eyes but went willingly. "We'll play tonight," she said before turning away to rejoin her team.

"He's really serious about this," Leo said.

"Sorry about that." Aspen nodded, slightly embarrassed by the whole thing. It had taken Flynn a long time to get used to the way the older members of their family worked, but Leo had been thrown in at the deep end.

Leo pulled a four-iron from her bag and held it aloft. "You should probably show me how to use this thing. I don't want to let the red team down."

"You don't need to worry about that." She jutted her chin toward Grammy. "She, Gramps, and Willow will do their best to sabotage the whole thing."

Leo tapped the grass with the club. "If you don't want giant chunks of grass flying through the air instead of the itty-bitty ball, a few tips would be good."

A thin layer of guilt wrapped around Aspen, and she looked around to see if they were being watched. No one else seemed to be paying any attention, including Willow, who was already huddled with Gramps. But then Aspen locked eyes with Flynn, who tilted her head in clear warning. Aspen shrugged and mouthed, *What?* To which, Flynn shook her head repeatedly.

Aspen ignored her, picked up another club, and moved slightly away from the group to a space with enough room around them for Leo to swing safely. It was in everyone's interest if she spent a few minutes working on Leo's game, especially if they ever wanted to play here again. And being that close to her would be a good way to desensitize Aspen to her presence.

"You're right-handed?" She waited until Leo had confirmed before she continued. "Okay, so grip the club like this."

Leo followed her lead, and her knuckles whitened around the shaft. "Got it."

"Relax your grip a little. You're not trying to choke the thing," Aspen said.

Leo laughed and flexed her fingers. "Sorry."

"No worries." Aspen pushed a tee into the grass and placed the club's head just behind it. "You stand perpendicular to the tee and the direction you want the ball to travel, then you open your legs, so the tee is just forward of the center."

"Okay." Leo stood ahead of Aspen and matched her stance.

Aspen closed her eyes briefly when Leo wiggled her butt from side to side as she was getting comfortable. "It'd be good for you to watch me first."

"Oh, sorry." Leo spun around to face her and flashed a smile. "I'm getting ahead of myself."

Aspen looked at the ground. Leo's front view was equally distracting when her attention was focused on Aspen. "Your arms should hang down pretty straight, like this, so you're not too close or too far away from the ball."

"Yep, got it. Knees bent and stick my butt out." Leo pointed to Aspen's backside.

Overtly, Aspen didn't react, but she couldn't stop the instinctive tensing of her glutes. She dropped her left hand from the club and swung the club back gently, and then she brought it around and over her shoulder. "Think of the swing like you're drawing a circle around your body. Does that make sense?"

Leo nodded. Her intense study made Aspen wish she'd gotten her mom to show Leo how to hit the ball instead. Aspen repeated the motion one-handed a few times and then demonstrated the full two-handed strike. "Now you try it and just keep swinging. Get used to the movement."

Leo took her time getting in the right position, wiggling her ass and shifting her hand on the shaft, while Aspen circled around her slowly, trying hard to concentrate on the fact that she was supposed to be teaching Leo something and not ogling her like some kind of perv.

"You've really never played golf before?" Aspen asked. Leo's form was fluid and natural, like she'd been practicing the action for years.

"Nope, why?" Leo stopped swinging and looked at Aspen. "Do I look good?"

"Uh-huh." *So, so good.* "Okay, so position your club just behind this tee and put all of that together." She inhaled, as if about to strike the ball herself, and got a hit of Leo's cologne, which smelled like something Aspen would wear rather than something that should turn her on. And yet, her body twitched in response. "Exhale as you swing and follow through to strike the ball."

Leo repeated the action, looking for all the world like she was a pro demonstrating perfect form.

"Yo, red team," Flynn shouted. "Grandpa Bill's got his lucky coin out to see who's teeing off first."

Aspen tore her gaze away from Leo and caught Flynn's disapproving look immediately. "On our way."

"You're a good teacher," Leo said as they walked to join the rest of the family.

"You're a quick study. You're gonna be great," Aspen said. "And think about the off-roading invite, yeah? It's a lot of fun."

Leo nodded. "Sure. I'll talk to Willow."

"Great." Aspen rolled her club around and around in her grip. She knew damn well that Willow didn't care for off-roading. That was a good thing, Aspen decided. She'd say that she didn't want to, and Leo wouldn't do it without her. Then Aspen would be off the hook, having extended a poorly thought-out invitation, without having to rescind it for fear of enjoying time with Leo a lot more than she was supposed to.

She let out a deep sigh, almost wishing that her little sister would go back in the closet. Aspen had never had this problem with any of the pretty boys Willow had trotted out to public events the whole family had attended. If she thought about it, she'd never had this problem with anyone Oakley or Flynn had been involved with either, even though they shared a similar taste in women. Sure, she very much appreciated their beauty and appeal, but an out-of-control crush like this? Never.

Aspen just had to get a grip. Getting back in the game after the breakup with Sarah was harder than she'd anticipated, and her eagerness for a new attraction had resulted in her zooming in on Leo, the first interesting woman Aspen had met in a while. The first woman who'd made her think she was over Sarah and ready to move on.

Except moving on to her little sister's new girlfriend was a no-go. The Mancharlson project popped into her head. She'd thought it would be a pain having to work this week, but it could actually turn out to be helpful by keeping her away from some of the other group activities... By keeping her away from Leo.

Still, the week couldn't go by fast enough.

Chapter Thirteen

While they were playing pool, the conversation she'd had with Aspen during the strangest golf game on the planet played over and over in Leoni's mind. *Philip. Private investigation company.* But she hadn't been able to get a moment to herself to call Ginny at the office to make sure everything was definitely in place.

Logically, she knew she didn't have to check anything. Ginny was a savant when it came to the creation of their background stories, fake websites, and social media presence. But equally, she'd never been called upon to deceive whatever high-flying, private detectives the Hartwell family employed. And they'd be world-class. They'd have to be to protect a family this rich and important. Could Ginny really fool someone that good?

She deliberately sank the white ball off her shot on the black ball and forfeited the game; she *had* to talk to Ginny.

"Leo!" Willow pouted and dropped into one of the giant armchairs dotted around the edge of the room, spilling her wine on the floor.

"Sorry, babe." Leoni shrugged and placed her cue on the table. "I need a pee break." She'd heard Flynn say the same thing and figured it'd be better than her usual refrain of "going to the ladies' room." She thought she was doing a pretty decent job of presenting masc, mirroring some of Flynn and Aspen's behavior, especially when what she really wanted to do was sink into her femmeness and soak that same behavior up. The money she owed on her acting training was really paying off with this gig.

Leoni headed to the steps leading up from the basement game room.

"There's a bathroom down here." Aspen pointed to the door on the opposite side of the space.

Leoni inclined her head. "I'd rather go upstairs. My...stuff is up there." Referring to the time of the month seemed a better option than the other obvious one.

"Oh. Right. Of course." Aspen held up her hand and looked everywhere but at Leoni.

Willow groaned loudly. "Well done, Aspen," she said, her words slurring slightly.

Leoni took the opportunity to escape before the sisters went at it again. She took the stairs slowly, a little light-headed from the beer she'd been drinking. A glass or two of wine was Leoni's limit, but *Leo* had to match Aspen and Flynn. And they'd both said they'd need more than a few beers to wash down the bitter taste of defeat, though Leoni thought it was more about flushing away the tension of the day.

At the top of the second flight, she paused at the delicately framed drawings of trees adorning the walls. She hadn't really taken the time to notice them before, so she read the inscriptions on the brass plates. *Aspen. Oakley. Willow.*

"I chose my children's names to convey the strong roots of family I always wanted them to feel."

Leoni turned at the clipped voice of Willow's mom. "That's a beautiful idea, Cate," she said. "Do they all have deeper meanings?"

Cate nodded and came closer. She traced her fingers along Aspen's name. "Aspen represents shielding and protection. It's the tree of heroes."

Of course it is. She wouldn't mind Aspen being her hero. And the way Cate looked at the tree indicated she believed her eldest daughter personified those characteristics. "So that she could protect her brother and sister?"

Cate inclined her head slightly. She didn't shrug. She was far too demure and sophisticated to shrug. But she did whatever action rich and powerful women did in its stead, and Leoni couldn't decipher the emotion behind it. Something though. There was definitely something Cate wasn't prepared to share with her.

Leoni pointed to the brother's tree before she could stop herself. She shouldn't be staying in a situation where the mother could interrogate her, and she really *really* needed to talk to Ginny. "What does that one mean?"

Cate took a handkerchief from her pocket and polished Oakley's plaque. "Endurance and stability. From the oak tree, obviously."

"It's a great name," Leoni said. "Great sunglasses too." She smiled and received a stern look from Cate in return. "And Willow?" she asked, rushing to make up for her ill-advised humor and to end the conversation.

"Mm." Cate moved toward the drawing for her youngest child but didn't touch it or polish the plate. "Elegance and resilience. The ability to grow despite the environment." She smiled tightly as if amused by an inside joke. "I still have hope." She gestured down the hall toward Willow's room. "Has Willow already gone to bed?"

"Nope. She's still downstairs, playing pool. I just came up to use the bathroom."

Cate frowned. "You've bypassed three restrooms..."

Leoni wrinkled her nose. "Female things," she said, hoping *that* would definitely put an end to this excruciating interaction.

"Of course." Cate stepped aside and swept her hand toward Willow's room. "Let me know if you need anything. We have a fully stocked cabinet for such situations."

Leoni gave her the thumbs up. "I'm good. Thank you though." She hurried down the hall, closed the door behind her, and leaned against it with a heavy sigh. *That was strangely uncomfortable.* Cate hadn't been that weird when they'd played golf, but then, everyone else was around them. Maybe that was just about keeping Willow happy. Or quiet. And *that* had been about her digging for information...even though Cate hadn't actually asked her any questions. *Damn it.* She was getting paranoid.

Whatever it was, Leoni didn't have time to think too deeply about it. Right now, she had to call the office. She pushed away from the door, locked herself in the bathroom, and pulled out her cell.

Ginny answered on the second ring. "Leoni? I was just about to leave the office. It's late in New York. Has something happened? Do you need an extraction?"

Despite her anxiety, Leoni chuckled. "Yeah, the shit has hit the fan. Bodies are dropping everywhere. I'm two clicks south of base. Can you send a helicopter?"

Ginny tsked. "Smart aleck. I could just hang up, you know?"

"Sorry, I couldn't resist. Listen, I'm a little worried. The mother employs a PI company, and she looks into everyone who comes into close contact with her family. Is everything in place?"

Ginny huffed. "Oh, ye of little faith. Of course. Just like it always is."

Leoni blew out a long breath. "Okay, but has anyone been sniffing around or calling my cover numbers? Digging around the company website?"

"No," Ginny said. "Your business number is routed here, like always, and I haven't had a single call. This one should be even more simple than usual, because you don't have any social media to update."

Leoni nodded slowly. "Because my company is so successful that I don't need it." She hated to admit it, but she'd been so caught up in the family activities that recollection of her background cover had slipped away a little. A quick brush-up now wouldn't hurt.

"Exactly. And you've got your personal socials locked down, not that you use them all that much. Everything is tighter than a nun's chastity belt." Ginny laughed at her own cleverness. "Okay now?"

"Yeah, I'm good." She dropped her shoulders and tried to shake the tension out through her fingertips like she'd learned in drama school. "Will you let me know if anything changes? If anyone starts digging around?"

"Absolutely," Ginny said. "Now, shouldn't you be sleeping? Or do super-rich people not need rest like normal people?"

Leoni laughed quietly. "It's full-on, for sure." The thought of sharing her attraction to the *other* sister crossed her mind, but she quickly dismissed it. That would be a conversation to share with a friend, and Ginny didn't qualify as that... Other than her mom, she wasn't sure anyone in her life did, even Tyler and Jesse. "I'm going to need a week off to recharge."

"Uh-huh. All that golfing, and luxury spas, and yachting. It must be so tiresome."

"I'm not feeling the empathy, Gin."

"Bye bye, sweetie. I'll see you next week."

Ginny had just hung up when Leoni heard Willow burst into the bedroom.

"Leo? What're you doing in there?" Willow knocked on the bathroom door. "You've been gone *ages*. I got bored."

Clearly, Willow's tipsiness had caused temporary amnesia of what exactly Leoni was supposed to be doing, but there was no need to keep up the charade. "Sorry. I'll be out in a minute." She emerged from the bathroom to find Willow collapsed on top of the bed, legs akimbo, and mouth wide open, snoring like a rhino.

She couldn't say that she wasn't relieved the night was over; the thought of another beer made her nauseous. Leoni closed the bedroom door quietly and quickly dressed in her sleep shorts and tank top. Then she turned her attention to Sleeping Beauty. She pulled the comforter down on the other side of the bed then tried to gently roll Willow over.

Christ, it was like trying to move a dead body. Realizing she didn't have a snowball's chance in hell of shifting her, Leoni decided to fold the blanket over her instead. But if Willow slept like that, with her head to body position looking like something from a horror movie, she'd need a chiropractor in the morning. So Leoni slipped her hand under Willow's neck and lifted slowly, then pulled a pillow from under her head.

Willow's eyes snapped wide open, and Leoni dropped her head back onto the bed. "Holy shit! You scared the crap out of me."

Willow laughed and wrapped her arms around Leoni's neck. "You're so pretty."

Leoni rolled her eyes. "And you're so drunk." She tried to break away, but Willow was curiously strong for a waif.

"You should kiss me." Willow pursed her lips, then she burped and giggled.

Leoni choked down her gag reflex when the noxious mix of wine, shrimp, and garlic snaked up her nostrils uninvited. "*You* should drink some water." She tried to pull away again to get a bottle from the fridge in Willow's walk-in closet, but Willow held fast.

"Seriously. I've been thinking a lot about it today. I want to see if I can be bisexual, at least. Kiss me."

Leoni shook her head. "Come on, Willow. You've had a lot to drink, and I'm not going to be your experiment." She smiled and winked. "And you know that's not the kind of service we provide."

"Why not?" Willow dropped her arms and pouted. "You think I'm ugly, don't you?"

Leoni rolled her neck, glad to be out of Willow's vice-like grasp, and sat on the edge of the bed. "I definitely don't think that. You're beautiful. But I never get involved with clients, and you're not my type."

Willow scoffed. "Type? Who even has a type anymore? Isn't it just a free-for-all?"

Leoni nodded. "For some people, that's true. But everyone's different."

"So what *is* your type? Surely you need to like anyone and everyone in your line of work."

Leoni glanced across the bed at the photo of Aspen and Willow. Aspen looked like she was in her early twenties, but her strong jawline was already evident. As if in judgment, her steely blue eyes seemed to follow Leoni's gaze. *I am* not *putting moves on your sister.* "What and who I like in my personal life has absolutely nothing to do with work. This is just a job, like a vegan flipping burgers at McDonald's."

"So I'm just a piece of meat to you?"

Leoni blew out a breath. Conversing with a drunk Willow was like talking to a child. "I definitely wouldn't use that analogy, no. But this isn't personal, and it doesn't have to be. You're a client I'm providing a service to, that's all."

"But I thought we were going to be friends," Willow whined. She burped again and covered her mouth, then she shuddered. "Ew. I just swallowed my own vomit."

Leoni's gag reflex was once again called into action. "*Please* let me get you some water. I could do with some too." Though dealing with Willow had instantly sobered her up.

Willow nodded and pushed up into a sitting position. "Water, and then you kiss me."

Leoni patted Willow's leg, much like she would if she were comforting her grandmother, and went to grab some water. *Of course there's only one tiny bottle.* She poured half into the glass beside Willow's bed and offered it to her, while she drank the rest of it in two gulps.

Willow sipped at hers and pointed to the space on the bed beside her. "Sit down and show me how to be a lesbian."

Leoni chuckled and sat a little further down the bed than Willow had wanted. "I don't think that's something you can teach. You either *are* or you aren't."

"How am I supposed to know for sure?"

"When you think of being with someone, do you always think of guys or do any other variations slip in there?" She wanted to retract her poor choice of words, but Willow was studying her ceiling intently, clearly considering the question.

After a few moments, she looked back at Leoni. "Always guys."

"Have you *ever* had any kind of crush or feelings for another woman?"

"No." Willow sighed and slapped her hand on the bed. "I think that makes me weird. All of my Insta friends have kissed girls and fooled around."

Leoni sighed. God, she was glad to be out of her twenties, when she was still trying to discover who she really was. "You don't have to compare yourself to anyone, especially people on social media who probably aren't your real friends, anyway... Or are they?"

Willow put her glass on the bedside table then looked down at her hands and clicked her nails. "I haven't met a lot of them, and the ones I have met, it was at events the family attended. See, I told you I didn't have any friends."

Leoni nodded, thinking maybe she didn't either. "Even more reason not to complicate our budding friendship with kissing then, right?" When Willow looked up at her, still with pleading eyes, she pressed on. "Okay. Thinking about movie stars: Tom Holland or Zendaya?"

Willow's eyes lit up. "Tom."

"Shawn Mendes or Dua Lipa?"

"Shawn, but he'd have to shave." Willow wrinkled her nose. "Stubble is itchy when they—"

"Stop." Leoni shook her head. "I don't need details. Just the gut reaction answer is all I'm looking for."

Willow shrugged. "Prude."

She'd never been called *that* before, but it was preferable to going down that road. "Charles LeClerc or Simone Biles?"

Willow wrinkled her nose and frowned. "Who and who now?"

"Not a sports fan?" Leoni waved the question away. "Never mind. I think you *do* know for sure, and you've answered your own question."

Willow stuck out her bottom lip. "Boring."

"It narrows your options, sure, but I don't think that makes it boring."

"So you're really not going to kiss me?"

Willow pouted, but she seemed to have sobered up some, so Leoni wasn't worried she'd have to fight her off again. "I'm really *not* going to kiss you."

Willow sighed. "I bet you'd kiss my sister if she asked you to."

"I wouldn't kiss anyone in this house if they asked me to, Willow. I'm working, and that would be unprofessional." Right at this very moment, it was absolutely true. Pushing Aspen up against the pool table and tasting her was mostly what Leoni had thought about all night, as well as admiring her body as she moved in for shots. But as long as she didn't act on or voice it, she was maintaining important boundaries, *and* she was telling Willow the truth. "Time for sleep?"

Willow sat up then flopped straight back down and pointed to the ensuite. "You go first."

Leoni headed to the bathroom to brush her teeth and take care of her skin regime. When she emerged five minutes later, Willow was under her covers and fast asleep. Leoni went straight to her pile of body-length bean bags and crawled under the blanket, ready for some rest. This family was exhausting her, mentally and physically. As she drifted off to sleep, she revisited Willow's question about kissing Aspen, which led to a very nice movie playing in her head where she got to do exactly that.

Chapter Fourteen

WHETHER IT WAS THE sea air or the fine company in the last couple of days, inspiration had struck as soon as Aspen's head had hit the pillow, and she'd gotten up to take advantage of the muse. Her body ached from yesterday's kayaking, and she'd been planning on spending the day designing the plans for Mancharlson anyway. This way, she could just grab some shut-eye in the morning and recharge. Honestly, she didn't want to miss out on any group activities. Gramps, Grammy, and Dad had done their best to turn the golf tournament into a laugh-fest, and they'd pretty much succeeded. It'd been one of the best yet, but Aspen had to acknowledge part of that was also due to Leo's presence. Not only did she bring out the best in Willow, but she also fit in well with everyone else, like she'd been around for years.

Aspen glanced up when she heard light footsteps on the wooden stairs, but she didn't say a word when Leo wandered through the living room and into the kitchen without seeing her. After all the beer they'd drunk while they were playing pool, Leo probably needed water. And lots of it. Aspen had just finished her second bottle since she'd come down to get some work done, and she'd just been about to get up for some more.

God, Leo had lovely, long legs. Aspen couldn't follow her into the kitchen now, especially since Leo was dressed in shorts and a tank top. There was a limit to the torture Aspen was willing to self-inflict. Damn, she was thirsty though. The bright light from the refrigerator spilled out of the doorway. Maybe Leo was getting a late-night snack. Aspen glanced at her phone. Scratch that: an early-morning snack. She looked down at her design then rubbed her eyes. She hadn't realized how late it was, but pulling the all-nighter had definitely been worth it. If Mancharlson didn't sign off on this design, he wouldn't sign off on anything.

"Oh, hey. I didn't see you there." Leo padded back into the living room and headed straight toward Aspen.

The light from Aspen's drawing lamp filtered over the table she was working on and lit up the floor when Leo had come to a stop. Aspen frowned and studied Leo's bare feet. *Baby pink nail polish?* And it looked like she had regular pedicures too.

"Is something wrong?"

Aspen looked up. "You were wearing water shoes when we went kayaking, so I didn't see your feet."

"Sorry, what was I thinking? I should've shown them to you as soon as we met on Saturday. How rude." Leo smiled.

"Oh, God. Did I say that out loud?"

Leo nodded and laughed quietly. "Now that you've seen mine, you should really show me yours."

"No way. I'm sorry. I don't have a weird foot fetish. I was just surprised." *Which apparently makes me ramble.*

Leo wiggled her toes. "You think shrimping is weird?"

"Shrimping?"

"Yup. Oral appreciation of feet. Why were you surprised?"

"Um, I guess I didn't expect you to be wearing polish." Aspen gestured to Leo's feet and then had to pull her gaze away. She *did* have pretty feet.

"Why not?" Leo put her hand on the chair beside Aspen. "Is it okay to join you, or should I leave you in private to think about toes?"

Aspen pushed the chair out with her foot. "Go ahead. I'm sure I can control myself for now," she said, scrambling for a handhold in the conversation.

Leo sat and put her glass of water on a coaster a good distance away from Aspen's drawing. It was a simple thing, but Aspen always associated little things like that with respect and consideration.

"So you think I shouldn't wear nail polish?" Leo stretched out her leg and looked at her own feet. "I'm masc, not butch," she said and looked at Aspen, clearly waiting for a comeback.

Aspen swallowed, not wanting to look at Leo's cute little bare feet again or the sexy legs they were attached to. Did she have to come down looking the way she did? Surely she'd packed some light sweatpants. "I didn't say that. I just wasn't expecting it." She held up her hand. "And before you ask, I don't know why. And no, I wasn't expecting you to have hairy, hobbit feet either."

Leo laughed again, throwing her head back and exposing her neck. The lines of Leo's body were finer than anything da Vinci ever committed to paper. Aspen looked away quickly and focused on her drawings again. *Coffer. Fenestration. Finial. Cantilever.*

Leo peered under the table. "I take it that you don't wear nail polish?"

Aspen pulled her feet under her chair. "Could we please stop talking about toes?"

Leo arched her eyebrow. "You *are* a closet shrimper." She touched Aspen's arm. "Don't worry, your secret's safe with me. You can suck on people's toes all you like."

"You're impossible." Aspen glanced up to the ceiling and shook her head.

Leo pointed to Aspen's work. "Is this the thing Willow said you were behind with?"

"Yeah, but I've actually just finished."

"What is it?" Leo asked, inclining her head to get a better view. "Sorry, is it okay to look at it?"

"Of course." Aspen swiveled the giant sheet ninety degrees. "It's a retirement village specifically for LGBTQ people. The guy who's commissioned us is a royal pain, but I feel really strongly about the project, so I'm giving it one last try." She sighed. "I really hope he likes this version."

Leo traced the lines of the trees, and Aspen couldn't tear her gaze away from her slender fingers and the way she caressed the paper.

"What didn't he like about the others?"

Aspen shrugged. "All sorts of things. He wasn't exactly sure what he wanted, so he asked us to come up with a concept without any real guidelines. Every time he saw something, he knew he didn't like it, but he didn't know what he *would* like. It's been a challenge, but I think I might've captured his vision even though he hasn't *shared* that vision," she said and laughed.

"I don't really know what I'm looking at, but I think it looks amazing." Leo tapped the drawing. "Will you get to build it too?"

"I don't lay the bricks," Aspen said, "but I work with the contractors to oversee the whole thing and make sure all the specs are met." She looked at Leo and then back at her plan. "I *can* build a house. You know, if you ever need one." Did she add that because she had something to prove? Or just because she wanted Leo to know that she was super-handy? "For you and Willow maybe." Oh, that made it better, for sure.

"Oh, God, no." Leo clasped her hand over her mouth then tapped her finger to her forehead. "That came out wrong."

"Forget it." Aspen waved it away, not wanting to analyze the shot of excitement that rushed through her at the hint that maybe Leo and Willow weren't in it for the long haul.

"It's so cool that this will be for LGBTQ people," Leo said. "I've heard horrible stories about couples being separated as they get older."

"Exactly." Aspen edged forward on her chair. "Like I said, that's why I feel so strongly about being involved. I really want to make it work."

Leo took a small drink. "Sometimes, water tastes like the nectar of the gods," she said.

Aspen tapped her own empty glass. "Especially after all that salty food and beer."

Leo bit her lip and wrinkled her nose. "Do your parents think I'm a boozehound? Did I drink too much?"

Aspen chuckled. "We all did. Is that why you had to get up?" She ignored the last question. Her dad had brought an extra case of beer into the game room, but her mom had given Aspen a stern look when she put their empties into the recycling can.

"My mouth tasted like the inside of a wrestler's underpants, and I've got a headache like that very same wrestler played bouncy ball with my head on the ring floor."

Aspen laughed again and had to try hard to keep it quiet. "Wow, that's very graphic."

Leo waggled her finger in the air. "Maybe, but now you know exactly what I mean, don't you?"

She nodded. "You didn't leave much room for interpretation."

"Which is a good thing, right?" Leo tapped her fingernails on the glass she held. "I think straight-talking is under-rated. What do you think?"

Usually, her answer would be instant. She much preferred to talk to people who didn't play with words and got to the point, people who told the truth, no matter what. She'd learned that lesson the hard way. But she'd never faced a situation like this before, when the afore-mentioned straight-talking would probably mess up her relationship with Willow for good. "Most of the time, I'd agree. But occasionally, it's better for the truth to remain unvoiced, like when people could get hurt." Aspen pushed away from the table, not wanting to see Leo's reaction to her own little nugget of truth. "Refill," she said and grabbed her empty glass.

She went to the kitchen, opened the freezer door, and stuck her head inside since it'd be awkward to put the other heated parts of her body in there. *Stop acting like a horny college student.* Aspen closed the door and topped up her water. *Right. Because telling myself not to feel something works so well.* If it had, she would've been over Sarah months ago.

Aspen peered back into the living room, not sure if she wanted Leo to still be there. Meaning, of course she wanted Leo to still be there. She sucked up a *be-a-responsible-adult* breath and returned to her seat.

"How did your parents meet?" Leo asked, apparently undeterred from her thirst for the truth.

Aspen had answered this question a hundred times, and she knew why most people asked, especially once they'd met her dad's parents. "Because you're wondering how two people from such different backgrounds could've crossed paths, let alone fallen in love?"

"I am." Leo smiled. "Rich folk, poor folk stories only seem to happen in the movies. Or the other way around, like in *Pretty Woman*, which I only know because it's my mom's favorite film. She's a big Richard Gere fan."

"And you're a big Julia Roberts fan because super feminine is your type?" Aspen took a big gulp of water. She shouldn't be interested in who Leo was attracted to. Although if she only liked super femmes, Aspen could stop thinking about them together. Possibly.

"That's not my type." Leo wrinkled her nose but didn't elaborate. "I mean, she looks great in that movie—too thin, obviously—but she's older than my mom."

"Too thin?"

"Mm. It's a bugbear for me. When I used to audition, I got so sick of being told I wasn't skinny enough. Like your weight is directly and conversely related to your acting talent. It's bullshit."

"Why did you stop acting to do...whatever it is you do?" Aspen grinned. She'd decided she liked the mystery of Leo's background. And since her mom had asked her to dig for information, Aspen was even less inclined to ask questions about Leo's life—in the now. But her past was fair game.

"Nicely done." Leo clapped quietly. "You don't want to talk about your parents, so you switched the conversation around to me."

Aspen shook her head. "Not true. It just flowed that way."

Leo arched her eyebrow, and Aspen wanted to crawl back into

the freezer.

"Well, let's get it flowing back to the original question, and then I'll answer yours." Leo winked. "Maybe."

"They met in the post room of Grandma Eleanor's first newspaper. Mom wanted to start at the bottom of the business and work her way up. She didn't want anyone to think she felt entitled to an executive position, even though she had a Harvard business degree. Dad had been working there since he'd left school at fifteen. Ten months later, I was born."

"So they must've been pretty young when they met? Or they just look really good for their age," Leo said.

"Mom was twenty-two, and Dad was nineteen."

Leo wiggled her eyebrows. "Boy toy."

Aspen swallowed. She'd like to be Leo's boi toy. "Is Willow awake too?" Thinking about her sister should be more effective than another visit to the freezer.

Leo smirked as if she might have an idea that she was making Aspen more than a little uncomfortable. "No. Nothing can wake your sister up when she gets to snoring. She sleeps like a baby. A really *good* baby, not the kind that screams and poops all night." She frowned and almost looked serious for a moment. "Strange saying, really. Hardly any babies sleep well, do they?"

Aspen laughed quietly. "Willow's never had trouble sleeping. She was one of those really good babies you're talking about."

Leo smiled softly. "You were around a lot when she was little?"

"Yeah." She picked up her pencil and twisted it around her fingers, hoping that would stop her from wanting to do other things with her hands. Apparently, even talking about her sister wasn't the antidote to her inappropriate crush.

"You sound wistful."

Leo didn't say any more, and she didn't have to. The implication was clear, and it had only taken Leo a few days with the family to realize they were as dysfunctional as any other, regardless of their wealth. Perhaps even more so because of it.

"I miss that kid," Aspen said, unable to stop the slight waver in her voice.

"She hasn't gone anywhere, you know?" Leo wrapped her hand around Aspen's forearm.

She looked down at Leo's fingers, her touch as electric as Aspen had thought it would be, and she had to battle the ridiculously strong urge to place her hand over it. Why was she having such trouble controlling herself? She'd been in the orbit of stunningly attractive women before, many times. What was so different about Leo's gravitational pull?

She sighed and looked up. Leo had moved closer. Within kissing distance. It'd be so easy.

Leo pulled back, breaking eye contact for the first time since they'd met, and cleared her throat. "She's still that same kid, desperate for her big sister's approval *and* her mom's, of course."

Aspen shook her head, the spell broken for now. "Do you really think so?" She wasn't convinced. "I went to college and came back to a totally different sister on my first vacation. It was like she'd been abducted by aliens, and they left one of theirs in her body as an experiment. But I think they liked my Willow too much, and they've never brought her back. That's why this Willow is so pissy. She's been abandoned by her species on a planet full of people busy killing it." She held up her hand. "Sorry, that went dark fast. And sorry for swearing."

Leo widened her eyes and didn't speak, like she was waiting for more, but Aspen had no idea what else she was supposed to say. And they probably shouldn't be talking about Willow anyway.

After the silence had stretched on some more, Leo shook her head and tsked. "You really don't get it, do you?"

"Get what?" Aspen leaned back in her chair and continued to fiddle with her pencil.

"There's no alien being that feels abandoned. *Your Willow* is the one who feels abandoned. You went off to college and didn't look back. You didn't even stay close by in the family business when you graduated. All of that makes it seem like you couldn't wait to get away from the family, from her. You didn't call just to talk to her, did you? And no one checked in with her to see how she felt with her hero gone? Suddenly she was alone, and no one stepped in to fill the gap."

"Oh my god, this is why you don't want to talk about what you do, isn't it? You're a super-shrink and didn't want everyone to know you'd be analyzing their every move." She laughed but even to her ears, it sounded hollow and disingenuous.

Leo's expression and her smile were soft and radiated understanding. "No, I'm not a shrink. I've just had a *lot* of therapy, all of which addressed abandonment issues."

The light from Aspen's lamp reflected in Leo's watery eyes, making Aspen want to pull her into her arms and hold her tight. Leo's shoulders shook slightly as she took a breath that seemed to last forever.

"I'm sorry," Aspen said, successfully overcoming her instinct to comfort Leo. She glanced over her shoulder, seriously considering going to Willow's room to wake her so they could talk about the gaping black hole in their relationship that Leo had just illuminated. How *had* she missed it? How had everyone in the family abdicated responsibility? Except Gramps, Grammy, and Dad, she supposed. But the way they treated Willow just kept her from growing up.

"You don't need to be sorry for what I've gone through. I'm on the other side of it," Leo said, after a while. "But your sister isn't."

"You're right. Thank you." She nodded. But now that Leo had unfastened her armor a little, Aspen wanted to pull off the chainmail altogether. "Can I ask what you've been through that's given you that kind of insight into Willow?"

Leo narrowed her eyes at Aspen, then she looked away and out the window into the blackness of the night. "My dad left when I was six months old." She turned back to face Aspen. "Are you sure you want to hear this? There are no rainbows and unicorns in this tale."

Aspen touched Leo's upper arm briefly. "I'm sure. If you're okay to share."

"Mm." Leo pressed her lips together tightly. "I haven't talked about this with anyone except my therapist, which infers that sharing isn't my thing, I suppose."

Aspen certainly had that impression from the way Leo had avoided talking about herself so far, but she tried not to feel pleased about perhaps being someone special enough to make Leo *want* to share. "You really don't have to."

Leo gave a sad smile, but her eyes brightened. "For some reason, I kind of *want* to, which is a little confusing."

Aspen wasn't confused; she was inordinately conflicted. She hadn't experienced the flickering of a connection like this since Sarah, and if she really compared them both, this blew Sarah out of the water. It was all so...easy and natural. "I think it's good you want to share."

Leo chuckled. "You're one of those soft butches in touch with your feelings, aren't you? I've seen the way you and Flynn are. It must be nice to have that kind of real friendship with someone."

"I can't decide if you're insulting or complimenting me."

"Oh, it's a compliment. I love a woman who's marble on the outside and marshmallow within. Makes them so much easier to handle," she said and winked.

Aspen gulped as quietly as she could manage. Guess that answered her question about the other types of women Leo was attracted to.

Leo laughed. "Relax. I'm just playing with you."

She smiled and nodded. "I knew that." The problem was, she *wanted* Leo to play with her. "But yeah, my friendship with Flynn is something I treasure. You don't have that?"

"Not like that, no." Leo sighed. "I sleep with my friends. Until they get married, that is."

Leo glanced away again, leaving Aspen trying to figure out if avoiding eye contact was something Leo did when she told the truth or when she was feeling vulnerable, something she clearly didn't like to feel. "Playing or not playing?" Aspen asked, opting for straight talk where she could.

"Not playing," she said and finished off her water.

Leo looked back into the house, maybe contemplating whether now would be a good time to escape, without opening her heart to her girlfriend's older sister. Truthfully, Aspen was thinking the same thing. This kind of emotional sharing felt intimate beyond a passing support for her sibling, and it could spill the already-open can of wriggling worms all over the floor.

"Do you know why your dad left?" Aspen's prompt indicated that some part of her had decided the mess was worth making. Leo refocused on Aspen, and her intense stare gave Aspen the opportunity to admire her eyes again. They really did change shades. Did they follow her emotions?

"He never wanted kids," Leo said. "Mom didn't know that when they got together. He told her when she found out she was pregnant, and he wanted her to terminate." She took another deep breath and blew it out slowly.

"You not being born would've been a travesty."

Something undetermined crossed Leo's expression, then she giggled, and Aspen wanted to zip up her own mouth. That was the second thing she'd said out loud without meaning to.

"Is that you straight-talking or not saying the truth in case it hurts me?"

Leo's arched eyebrow indicated she was messing with Aspen again, and she smiled. She was starting to get a handle on how Leo communicated. Though that shouldn't really create the kind of inner delirious happiness it just had. *Because she's not my girlfriend...* "That would be the straight-talk, I promise." She swallowed and added, "Otherwise you wouldn't be here now...making my sister really happy." And not just Willow, but she kept that to herself.

"That's sweet. Thank you."

Again with the locked gaze. Damn it to hell. "And your mom

didn't kick his stupid butt out of the house? Why the heck not?"

Leo sighed and shook her head. "She was in love," she said and smiled softly. "People behave *really* strangely when they're under that particular spell, don't they?"

Aspen grumbled. "I definitely did."

"Sarah?"

Aspen frowned and nodded. She hadn't expected Leo to remember her ex-fiancée's name, let alone say it the gentle way she had.

"How were you spellbound?" Leo asked gently.

"I put up with the cheating. And the lies." Aspen clenched her teeth. Just saying it out loud reinforced how low her self-esteem must've been to tolerate that. "She told me that she'd slept with someone right after our first night together. Said she'd gotten scared about how deeply she'd fallen for me." She slammed her pencil on the table. "How stupid was I to think she wouldn't do it again? And looking back, I know I stuck my head in the sand and ignored the signs. Until I couldn't."

Leo placed her hand on Aspen's forearm again. "I don't understand why people cheat. Why didn't she just stay out of a relationship and play the field without consequence?"

"You sound like the voice of experience." When Leo didn't answer, Aspen said, "She was in it for the money and prestige. She didn't really care about me. She's with someone who looks like she could be her sister now." She shuddered at the thought.

"That's such a weird phenomenon, isn't it? Like you think you're so gorgeous that you find someone who looks just like you." Leo chuckled and removed her hand. "Maybe it's a form of narcissism."

"Are you sure you're not a therapist?" She laughed, hoping the joke would disguise her disappointment at the loss of physical contact.

Leo shook her head. "I told you, you pick up a lot of the jargon when you see one for as long as I did. But I'm really sorry you went through that. You obviously didn't deserve it. Seems like you really loved her."

"I really thought I did." Aspen realized they'd bounced off topic again, but she was enjoying the easy back and forth of the fluid conversation. "Was your mom hoping your dad would change his mind as soon as he saw your gorgeous face?" She coughed. "Your baby face, because all babies are gorgeous, right?"

"Sure." Leo smiled widely. "She probably was, but it didn't work." She fluttered her eyelashes. "Can you believe that?"

She really *really* couldn't. "He must've been the tin man."

Leo laughed. "No heart? You're funny."

"Thought you might like the musical theater reference." Because impressing her little sister's *girlfriend* was top priority, obviously. Why wouldn't it be?

Leo caught her gaze again, and damn, if Aspen didn't want to stay locked in that look all night.

"Anyway, he left, and maybe that would've been okay, except now he's settled down in Florida and is on his third kid. And he's all over Facebook, vying for title of *World's Most Perfect Dad*."

"Wow." Aspen didn't have the words to voice her response adequately. "That must be hard."

"For a long time, I thought it was about me, and that there must be something wrong with me, something fundamentally unlovable. But I hit fuck it on my thirtieth birthday when I didn't hear from him at all, and I guess I had an epiphany of sorts."

Leo shrugged, but the nonchalant action belied the sadness in her eyes, making Aspen long for an acceptable way to hug her in a platonic fashion.

"I let it go. Or at least I thought I had." She glanced away and focused on something Aspen couldn't see. "But maybe that's why I don't have any close friends or long-term relationships, like yours with Flynn, or Oakley and Kelly."

"Are you sure you haven't let that go? You and Willow seem to have something special." Even as she said it, she didn't believe it. More like she was just digging for a reaction. They looked like they had fun together, and they talked a lot, but Aspen still hadn't seen any real display of affection, and they didn't seem to look at each other like they couldn't wait to tear each other's clothes off. Unless, of course, they were both asexual. Willow hadn't shown signs of that with her boyfriends, but again, maybe she'd been overcompensating, acting like she believed she had to for acceptance.

Leo laughed loudly and had to cover her mouth. "Oh, no, this isn't love." She rolled her eyes as if Aspen couldn't pour water out of a boot even with the instructions on the heel. "I don't think that's what Willow is looking for."

Aspen bit her tongue, both to stop the follow-up question of "What *are* you looking for?" and to stop showing the delight at Leo's reaction. "So what was your epiphany?" she asked instead, steering the conversation back to safer waters for both of them.

"It was just the wrong time for him and me. Some parents just don't connect with their kid, but they do with others." She looked at Aspen intensely. "Being here has reinforced that over the past couple of days."

"Huh?" Aspen hadn't expected that. "What do you mean?"

"Your mom and dad. Your mom clearly adores you and your brother, but she seems to struggle with Willow."

Aspen bristled but tried to tamp it down some. "*Everyone* struggles with Willow."

Leo raised both eyebrows. "What about your dad and his parents?"

"And you." Although it seemed like Leo could connect with anyone if she wanted to.

"I'm just listening to her," Leo said. "That's all she really wants: her family to see her for who she is and not rue who she isn't."

Aspen picked up her pencil again and rolled it between her fingers. "You know, my mom pays a therapist $500 a week, and as far as I'm aware, he hasn't gotten to the root of her relationship with Willow. You really could make a killing if you ever need a fallback profession, other than hitting Broadway."

"I'm doing okay, thanks."

The twinkle in Leo's eyes hinted at the challenge that Aspen should take another run at finding out what her profession was. But Aspen wasn't falling for it. She didn't want the veil torn down to discover some tiny man puppeteering a giant-sized head. She cringed internally. What's with all the *Wizard of Oz* references? She'd never even seen the movie. "You really think that's the problem? Willow thinks my mom doesn't love her?"

Leo shrugged and tugged at her ponytail as if it was bothering her. "She hasn't said that, and I might be way off-base. But she's the under-achieving black sheep of the family. At least, looking in from the outside, that's how it seems." She frowned and gave her hair another pull before she yanked out the hairband and let it down fully.

Leo's long locks cascaded over her bare shoulders, reaching her breasts: the breasts Aspen had been trying not to stare at, even though her tank top stretched taut over them, dragging Aspen's attention their way like a siren's call did to a sailor. With her hair released from the cruel captivity of a ball cap *and* a rubber band, Leo was even more beautiful. Could that even be possible?

Fuck. How was she supposed to ignore her attraction now? Aspen was doomed to crash onto the rocks and smash up her heart. Again.

Chapter Fifteen

LEONI'S EYES FLICKERED OPEN and then closed again. The banging in her head was worse than she'd thought it would be, but why was it getting louder?

"Leo! Wake up. It's Mom!"

Leoni squinted against the bright sun slicing through the half-closed blinds, sure its heat might sear her eyeballs.

"Get in. Quick." Willow looked down at Leoni and threw her comforter back.

Barely conscious, Leoni dragged herself out of her bed mountain, but as she rose, her foot was still wrapped in the blanket, and she fell headlong across the floor. "Ow..."

"Is everything all right in there?" Willow's mom asked through the door.

"Mom! Just wait." Willow jumped off the bed and helped untangle the trap from around Leoni's foot. "Jesus, how did you tie yourself up like this?"

Leoni rubbed her head and shrugged, but she had a feeling her late-night conversation with Aspen had something to do with it. The less sexual release she got, the more she tossed and turned in bed. Her inner voice laughed hysterically. *Yeah, of course it's only about the sex.*

"Leo!" Willow whispered. "Get up."

They grabbed her pillows and blanket and stuffed them in Willow's closet, then jumped onto the bed. They sat up against the headrest, and Leoni pulled the comforter up to cover as much of her as possible.

"Okay, Mom. You can come in."

The bedroom door opened, and Cate came in holding a tray loaded up with goodies. "I thought you might like breakfast in bed?"

There was a hopeful note in her voice that had been missing when she'd regaled Leoni with the family tree thing.

"What do you *really* want?" Willow asked.

"You're so sharp." Cate smiled as she edged through the doorway to place the tray on the nearby dresser. "I *really* wanted to apologize to Leo. I think I might've come across a little...sinister last night."

"Mom, what did you do?"

Leoni shook her head. "No, not sinister." She was *something*, but that wasn't it. "It was interesting to find out how you chose your children's names. I don't think many parents put so much thought into it." She chuckled. "I have no idea why my mom called me Leoni. I think she just liked the sound of it."

"It's a lovely name that's mostly associated with lions, meaning strength and power. Most parents hope that their children will be strong enough to face the harshness of the world." Cate gave a slight rueful smile. "Do you have siblings?"

"No," Leoni said, choosing not to acknowledge the growing brood of half-siblings her dad was rearing. "I'm an only child." She stopped, realizing she'd been about to give more details about her single mom. Leoni was already concerned about the Hartwell family's PI digging into her background, so she really shouldn't be furnishing Cate with additional information to help with that endeavor.

Willow grumbled. "That must be nice."

Cate winced as if her daughter's words had flown through the air like daggers and sliced at her soul. Leoni thought briefly about saying something, but she was being paid to help Willow, not her mom.

Cate backed out of the room. "Well, again, I'm sorry if I was strange. I should stay away from the gin; it takes me down some odd roads."

Now it made sense. The dark lord of spirits had been at the helm. "You were fine, honestly."

Cate smiled and closed the door behind her softly.

Willow huffed dismissively. "I'm sorry about her."

"Don't be. All parents are weird in one way or another." She got out of bed and brought the breakfast tray back, settling it on the bottom of the bed before she got back in. She took a sip of orange juice, and it tasted like cold, heavenly nectar, so she drank half the glass. Then she picked up a Danish and shuffled around on Willow's bed to face her. "Can I ask you something though?"

Willow narrowed her eyes. "You can ask. I just might not answer," she said and bit down on a croissant.

"Your mom's super cool about Aspen and Oakley being queer, and she didn't bat an eye at us two in bed together, so why did you want a fake butch-slash-masc girlfriend instead of a femme?"

Willow's jaw twitched, and her eyes darted all over the room before she finally settled her gaze on Leoni. "You really meant what you said about us being friends after you go home?"

Leoni recognized the subtle change in Willow's demeanor and nodded. "I really do." She thought about what she'd shared with Aspen last night—which had been far too much of her truth—and that maybe she wasn't as put together as she'd thought judging by her lack of relationships. "It turns out I don't have many real connections either, so I could do with a friend too."

Willow nibbled at her top lip and picked at her breakfast. "Let me think about it."

"Of course." Leoni could relate to Willow's unwillingness to talk about her family stuff. God only knew why she'd confessed so much of *her* real life to Aspen last night, especially about her dad, whom she hadn't told anyone about, except to say that he was dead. Which he was, in a way. They were dead to each other, apparently. Maybe she hadn't let go of those feelings of being unlovable after all, because she still wasn't letting herself get into a relationship where she might be loved rather than simply lusted after. Aspen probably thought she was a total loser now...but what did that really matter when they couldn't happen anyway? What Aspen thought was irrelevant.

Unless, once Leoni and Willow were friends, Aspen might be interested in exploring their connection. She allowed herself a smile at the wisp of that possibility.

"Okay," Willow said, "I'll tell you why I wanted someone...sort of like you but more butch." She shrugged. "Sorry, but you seem more like me than Aspen."

Leoni laughed. "When all this is done, you'll see the real me. But you're absolutely right." She touched her face. "Every time I leave this room without a full face of makeup, I feel more naked than I would if I went out there in just panties and a bra."

Willow's eyes sparkled, and she grasped Leoni's hands. "I knew it!" She flicked Leoni's ponytail over her shoulder. "I bet this is killing you."

"Urgh, you have *no* idea. I mean, you *do* your hair, don't you?" She pulled the band out and her hair fell across her shoulders and down her back, then she pulled some strands around her cheeks. "It frames your face and highlights your eyes. Hair ties are fine when you don't want to set your hair on fire while you're cooking, but what's the point of having long hair if you tie it up and shove it under a ball cap the whole time? You may as well cut it off." She gestured to her ball cap on the dresser. "When I get home, I'm going to have a ceremonial burning of that." She squeezed Willow's hands. "But I might keep those cargo shorts for bumming around the house. They're so much freer than yoga pants."

"You're funny." Willow ran her fingers through Leoni's hair. "And your hair is so beautiful. You *have* to tell me what you use to get it this soft." She dropped her fingers and wrinkled her nose. "I'm sorry about last night, by the way."

"Wow, two apologies from two Hartwell women in less than ten minutes," Leoni said. "Is there something we can get your sister to apologize for, and then I can complete the set?"

"Mm." Willow's smile fell away. "She'd have to actually do something wrong for that to happen."

"So how does that play into your 'let's be a lesbian' plan?"

Willow sighed deeply and sank back onto the bed. "It was all just a stupid bid for attention, which I'm never going to get. I thought that if I brought someone like Aspen or Flynn home, my mom would like them, and then she'd see me... And maybe even like me. Flynn's the other daughter Mom wanted. Not me. I'm just not good enough. I never have been, and I never will be. I'm too much like my dad, and I don't think Mom likes that. She's driven and motivated in ways I'm not, just like Dad."

"But she clearly loves him," Leoni said and rubbed Willow's forearm gently. "Why do you think she wouldn't love you if you remind her of him?"

Willow looked up at the ceiling and frowned. "I don't know. I suppose that doesn't make sense. But Aspen has built her own business from scratch with Flynn, and Oakley has worked his way up to run the magazine arm of the company, and I've done nothing but spend the family money."

The gulf in achievement couldn't be missed. Even without her mom's apparent distance, it'd be easy for Willow to feel bad when she looked at how their lives were working out. "Have you had a chance to think about what your passion might be?" She expected the answer to be no. It'd only been two days, and those days had been packed with activities. It wasn't like Willow'd had the space or time to meditate on it.

"I have actually. I took a first aid course back when I tried college, and I helped a sea turtle one time in San Diego."

The two didn't seem that related, but Leoni would run with it. "How did you help a sea turtle with your first aid course? Did he need a Band-Aid?"

Willow grinned. "No, silly. I was scuba diving La Jolla canyon–"

"Wow, I bet that was cool," Leoni said. "There's something so majestic about everything under water, don't you think?" She sighed deeply. "I've always wanted to scuba dive." But she'd never really had the money or the opportunity. It was slightly hard to sympathize with Willow when she started a story like that, as if deep-sea diving was as regular as throwing a ball against a wall.

"Really?" Willow patted Leoni's leg excitedly. "We can totally do that this week if you wanted to."

Leoni placed her hand over Willow's. "Shut up. Are you kidding?"

Willow shook her head. "We've got a boat at the Three Mile Harbor and all the gear. You're going to love it. I'll talk to Dad and organize it when we get up."

"That'd be amazing." She grinned. This job was surprising her in good ways. "But, back to your story."

"Oh, right, yeah. So I saw a green sea turtle struggling to swim. You're not supposed to go too close, and it's illegal to touch them, but something didn't seem right." Willow sighed, shaking her head slightly, as if she were reliving the moment. "Then she looked up and started making her way toward me."

It was so clear from Willow's words to her expression to the sudden calmness that *this* could be her passion.

"I'll never forget that look in her eyes." Willow glanced at her. "It sounds lame, doesn't it?"

"Not at all. It sounds beautiful." Leoni smiled.

"She just looked like she was hopeful... And she was asking me to help her."

"Was anyone else down there with you?" Leoni asked.

"Yeah, Kelly was in the water too. Oakley and Aspen had just gone back up, and Flynn doesn't like getting wet, so she was on the boat, like always. We've got underwater radios, so I called Kelly over. By the time she had gotten to me, the sea turtle had swum right up to my nose." She let out a deep breath.

"That must've been magical," Leoni said. "All those animal-slash-human rescue videos I see on Insta always amaze me. But you've lived one. I'm so envious."

Willow widened her eyes. "Really?"

"Really. That's such a huge deal." Leoni smiled, submerged in the beauty of Willow's experience. "What did you do when she was that close?"

"I could see fishing wire wrapped around and around her front flipper, like a hundred times. So Kelly and I took out our diving knives and sliced it all off, a little piece at a time, and put the line in our debris bags so it couldn't cause any more damage. It took us nearly thirty minutes, and when we'd finished, she swam around us a few times before she took off... I hadn't really thought about that memory in the couple of years since it happened. But when I got to thinking about things I was passionate about, that was the first thing that came to mind. Closely followed by the first aid course."

They sat for a couple of minutes in silence, with Willow sipping her espresso and Leoni finishing off her OJ. There was so much more to Willow than she was showing her family, and she was a completely different person from the one Leoni thought she was when they first met a couple of days ago. Getting Willow to think about her possible career trajectory had sparked a similar quest in her own mind, but she'd shoved it down deep, figuring it might be something to consider when she got home. She'd stopped committing to her own dream and had settled for second best. Better to know and accept that than keep chasing something that only a tiny percentage of people ever managed though, right? And her situation was vastly different from Willow's, someone who had the financial stability to literally do anything she dreamed of. She talked of Oakley as if he'd done something great by working his way up the company hierarchy, but Leoni bet he was still living in an apartment the family owned. Theirs was a different world, one where they didn't have to make the really hard choices.

Aspen's achievement, however, *was* something for Willow to admire, just as Leoni did. She put the brakes on that bullet train before it could leave the station; their early morning conversation had left a lasting impression, and it wasn't one she should be dwelling on right now. "Okay, so what do you create if you put sea turtles and first aid courses together? Nursing? Veterinary medicine? Doctor? Animal rescue?"

"*That* part I've still got to work out, but I don't want to be a doctor," Willow said. "It's the nurses who spend the most time with patients."

"Huh." Leoni shook her head. "You're a conundrum, kiddo, I'll give you that."

Willow frowned. "What do you mean?"

"Friends are honest with each other, right?" Leoni waited until Willow nodded, even though she narrowed her eyes, like she was expecting an attack. "You seemed pretty self-absorbed when I first met you, and I think you've decided it's preferable for people to see you that way than to show them who you really are. Which, going by the sea turtle story and seeing you around your gramps, is actually a very kind and thoughtful young woman."

Willow scoffed. "I don't want anyone thinking I'm soft. People take advantage of you and try to exploit you."

Leoni placed her juice glass back on the tray then put her hand on Willow's knee. She was starting to realize that being filthy rich had its drawbacks when it came to perceptions and connections. "I can see how you might think that generally, but I don't get it in relation to your family... If you really think about it, does it even make sense to you?"

Willow rolled her eyes. "This friend thing is making my brain hurt." She frowned and leaned closer to Leoni. "When you fell over, did you hit your face on something?"

Everything had happened so fast, Leoni couldn't really recall anything before tugging up Willow's comforter to cover herself. Up to that point, she'd still been half-asleep. Maybe more than half. "I don't know, why?"

Willow tentatively touched Leoni's right cheek. "Does that hurt?" she asked, pressing it.

Leoni jerked back and would've fallen off the bed backward if it hadn't been for Willow grabbing her arm.

"Careful!" When Willow had pulled Leoni upright, she laughed. "That's a yes?"

"Yes!" Leoni got off the bed and hurried to the bathroom to inspect her face in the mirror. "Oh, crap." Now that she thought back, she remembered mashing her face against the base of Willow's bed when she fell. Serious swelling was already starting to show.

Willow came to the door. "Are you okay?"

"Perfect." Leoni shook her head. "I need ice to get the swelling down. Maybe it won't bruise," she said, more in hope than anything else, because she didn't have the makeup to cover it up, and Willow's complexion was too light to borrow anything she might have. She pressed the area under her eye lightly and had to bite her tongue to stop from cursing. God, had she broken something in her face?

Willow put her hand to her mouth. "You're going to have a black eye for the Fourth of July party."

Leoni frowned. "I'm more worried that I've got a fractured cheek."

"Don't worry." Willow retreated into her bedroom and grabbed her phone. "I'll make an emergency appointment with our concierge doctor. She'll check you out and give you an X-ray—and we'll cover the cost, obviously."

Leoni tried to smile, but it hurt. Funny how it seemed to be more painful now that she'd seen the damage. Still, she was grateful that a big chunk of her money from this gig wouldn't have to disappear into hospital fees. "Thank you." A *concierge* doctor though? What the hell was that? Something only super-rich people had, she guessed.

She sighed, went back into the bedroom, and dropped into Willow's armchair. The only time she'd had a black eye was when someone had smacked her in the face with a piñata stick at her fifth birthday party. "How are we supposed to explain this to everyone?"

Someone answered Willow's call, and she held a finger to her mouth before running through what had happened with the person on the other end of the line. "We'll tell everyone the truth, with the minor adjustment that you tripped over my shoes rather than the makeshift bed you shouldn't be sleeping in, because we're supposed to be sleeping together." She looked over at Leoni's bed arrangement. "You should sleep in the bed with me from tonight," she said and winked. "I promise you'll be safe."

Leoni chuckled, then held her face. "You chose Tom Holland over Zendaya—I *know* I'd be safe, but I'm good on the dog shelf. Those bean bags are really comfortable."

Willow went to the door after pulling on some yoga pants. "I'll go and get you some ice and tell Mom what happened. You should get dressed. Dr. Silva will be here in forty-five minutes."

Willow swept out of the room, and Leoni got up to put on some clothes. The last time she'd gone to an ER, she'd waited five hours to be seen, and it was ten hours before she'd been treated. Money might not be able to buy love or happiness, but it could pretty much buy anything else.

Chapter Sixteen

"Do you want me to drive her to the hospital? It's no trouble." Aspen didn't need to glance at Flynn to know there was heat coming her way, but she didn't care. If Leo had a head injury, she should be in a hospital.

Grandpa Bill laughed. "Certainly not. The local hospital is for local people who have limited healthcare choices."

Aspen caught Leo's eyebrow quirk, despite it being lightning fast. "He's not being elitist. Grandpa Bill and Grandma Eleanor actually fund the free clinic that's attached to the public hospital. They have for decades."

Leo frowned and held up her hands. "I just like that he doesn't want to clog up the system with something this minor." She touched her cheek as if it were nothing, then grimaced like it was definitely something.

Aspen walked over to Leo and looked a little closer at her face. "It doesn't look minor to me. Your eye's so swollen, I bet you can barely see out of it."

Leo tapped the opposite side of her head. "I've still got a good one."

Her expression belied her nonchalance. There was fear behind her eyes, and it was clear she *was* concerned about her face. Aspen didn't know if Leo was butching it up, but she really didn't have to. Especially after their mutually vulnerable conversation last night. "It's okay to be a little scared, you know," she whispered so no one else could hear.

Leo pressed her lips together tightly and nodded. "Honestly, I'm fine. Willow says Dr. Silva is the best there is, so I've got nothing to worry about, right?" She held the ice compress to her face and winced again. "It adds to my butch cred."

Aspen turned to Willow. "How did this happen again?" She didn't succeed in keeping the accusation from her tone, but even she wasn't sure what she was implying. She certainly didn't think Willow had hit Leo. It just seemed like a strange thing to happen, and Aspen liked everything to be logical and explainable.

Willow narrowed her eyes. "Why? Have you forgotten what I told you three minutes ago?"

Flynn came alongside Aspen and nudged her shoulder. "Come on, dude. We were on our way out."

The gate intercom buzzed, and their mom answered it to give the doctor access.

"Willow," their mom said, "take Leo to the library, and I'll bring Dr. Silva in."

Willow glared at Aspen one last time before she linked her arm through Leo's and guided her away. Their mom opened the front doors, and Aspen waited with her on the front steps for the doctor's fully loaded Range Rover to pull up.

"Is there something you're not telling me?" her mom asked.

"What do you mean?" She'd always been terrible at hiding things from her mom as a kid. Why hadn't that changed now that she was fully grown?

"Leo," her mom said, as if that should be enough for the truth faucet to open.

Aspen gestured back into the house. "I didn't do that to her, if that's what you're asking."

Her mom laughed lightly. "I know *that*. You wouldn't even kill a mosquito when you were a child. I'm talking about the looks you two are exchanging."

Aspen inclined her head. "We talked last night after I'd finished the drawings, that's all. Willow seems to be quite attached to her, so I'm making the effort to get to know her."

"Willow does seem to be different around her. Less spiky."

"Yeah, I think so too." Aspen thought about what Leo had said last night about Willow just wanting the family to see her. Maybe the spikiness was just for protection against huge family expectations.

"But they're not very physically demonstrative. Especially for a young couple who should still be in that honeymoon period." Her mom held out her phone. "Look at your sister's Instagram. They've been going out for two months, but there isn't a single photo of them together."

Aspen looked at the screen as her mom scrolled through Willow's feed. "I thought she kept that hidden from you."

Her mom scoffed. "As if I'd let that stop me from keeping an eye on my own daughter."

"Maybe Leo is an unusually private person." She was definitely unusual in plenty of other ways that were messing with Aspen's head. "Maybe their relationship isn't...you know." She really didn't want to discuss her sister's sex life with her mom. She didn't want to discuss that with anyone, especially since Aspen's dreams were still peppered with Leo's presence. Thinking about her that way wasn't helpful to anyone.

"Sexual? Why wouldn't they be having sex?"

"Mom!" Jesus, was the doctor *walking* the half-mile driveway?

Her mom rolled her eyes. "Don't be such a teenager, Aspen."

Finally, the doc's car rolled into view around the bend and pulled up in front of them. *Oh, thank god.*

"I still think it's strange," her mom said, as the doctor and her associate got out of the car. "And the conversation about you and Leo isn't over."

"There is no me and Leo, Mom. You're seeing something that isn't there."

"Don't gaslight me, Aspen." Her mom arched her eyebrows. "I know what I'm seeing." Then she turned and gave Dr. Silva a huge smile. "Welcome, Dr. S. Thank you for coming so quickly."

"Of course." Dr. Silva smiled. "Someone's had a little accident?"

"Yes." Her mom made her way back inside the house. "She's

waiting in the library."

Jannick, Dr. Silva's associate, unloaded a portable X-ray machine from the rear of the vehicle, and Aspen helped him up the steps and through the doorway with it. Then she followed them all to the library.

Flynn jogged up to Aspen. "Come on, let's leave them to it. I'm sure the doctor doesn't need an even bigger audience."

"I'm helping get this through the house." She heard how lame she sounded before she'd even finished the sentence, but she continued anyway.

"It's okay, Aspen," Jannick said. "I've got this."

She clenched her jaw and dropped her hand. She hadn't actually been providing any worthwhile assistance, other than to guide Jannick to the library, but he'd been in there for enough medical emergencies and call-outs not to need her guidance.

Leo was seated on one of the reading couches with Willow beside her, holding her hand. When their mom looked back at Aspen, she flicked her gaze to their hands, hoping her mom would see and then lay off her.

"Asp, seriously. All the good donuts will be gone if we don't go soon. The whole town's out to celebrate the shop reopening, and they're eating my cinnamon and coffee ice cream right now."

Aspen glanced at Leo, who caught the look and smiled. Why didn't she want to leave her? Leo was in safe hands, it wasn't anything life-threatening, and Aspen bore no responsibility for it, and yet, the thought of going out to enjoy herself seemed wrong somehow. Which was irrational, obviously.

"Will you bring a box back?" Leo asked. "After everything Willow's told me about them, I don't want to miss out either."

"See. Everyone wants Dreadnought donuts." Flynn shoved Aspen's shoulder lightly. "Let's go."

Oakley hollered something inaudible from deep in the house, but the word *donut* was unmissable.

"Bring back plenty for everyone," Grandpa Bill said, without looking at her.

He sat on another sofa close by, watching the proceedings as intently as he did his medical dramas. Maybe *he'd* done this to Leo so he could watch the doc in action. She laughed at herself for thinking that, however briefly, and turned to leave without another risky glance at Leo, since her mom seemed to be watching her every move.

"Okay." She pulled Betty's keys from her pocket and dangled them in front of Flynn's face. "Let's go."

Oakley and Kelly piled into the back of the Bronco, yammering about donuts and ice cream as if the shop's return was the second coming. Flynn stayed silent and just eyeballed her from the passenger seat.

Aspen turned the music up loud in the back speakers. "What?" she whispered to Flynn.

"Did something happen last night?"

Aspen closed the electric gate behind them and headed into town. "Last night? We played pool. Everyone went to bed. I got up and finished the amended Mancharlson proposal—"

"Which, again, is a-maz-ing, and I think he's going to love it," Flynn said. "But that's not going to get you off the hook."

"What hook?"

"The one in your mouth that Leo seems to have cast without realizing it."

Aspen shushed her too loudly, and Kelly leaned forward.

"What's that about Leo?" Kelly asked.

Aspen glanced into the backseat. "Flynn was just wondering if Leo would still be able to scuba dive."

"Hopefully she hasn't broken anything," Kelly said. "It'd be a shame if she messed up her perfect face."

Flynn swiveled around in her seat and frowned. "You think she's perfect too?"

Crap. Maybe no one would catch it...

Kelly narrowed her eyes and leaned further into the front. "Who *else* thinks she's perfect?"

Oakley kicked the back of Aspen's seat. "I get the appeal, but it's not me. That means it's got to be one of you two."

Aspen glanced at Flynn, whose expression pleaded with her to take responsibility. She couldn't expect Flynn to cover for her, or it might risk her chance with Kelly. And *that* relationship had a shot at coming to fruition. "I may've mentioned that I thought she had perfect symmetry. You know, like I appreciate the curves and lines of a beautiful building. It was just a passing comment." She stopped talking. Her rambling was a giveaway around people who knew her as well as these three.

"Did you just compare a woman to a building?" Oakley laughed and pushed his knees harder into Aspen's seat. "Man, that's hilarious. How on earth do you ever get laid with lines like that?"

"It wasn't a line," Aspen said. "And I'm not comparing Leo to anything. I just made a comment, that's all." In her rearview mirror, she saw Oakley and Kelly exchange a knowing look, then she glared at Flynn and mouthed, "Thanks."

"You really think she has a perfect face?" Flynn asked.

Kelly leaned forward again. "Don't you?"

Flynn shrugged. "I haven't really paid her that much attention."

Aspen stifled a smirk. All of Flynn's attention had been directed toward Kelly, but she still hadn't seen it. "Flynn has a type, and Leo isn't it." She ignored Flynn's panicked expression and looked at the sunlight dappling the road through the trees on both sides of the street. It was a beautiful day, but it couldn't distract her from thinking about how Leo was doing back home.

Kelly nodded. "Of course. I forgot."

"You can be forgiven for that." Oakley slapped Flynn's shoulder. "It's been so long since we've seen her with someone, how are we supposed to remember she has a type?"

Flynn shoved his hand away. "Screw you, Romeo. Just because you'll sleep with anyone with nice eyes. I'm more selective."

"Being pan is the most natural thing in the world," he said. "Why limit yourself to one flavor of ice cream when you can have them all?" He pointed to an empty spot ahead. "Speaking of which, you should grab that."

Aspen pulled into a road-side space a few hundred yards from the donut shop. It looked like the line snaked down the street almost the same distance in the opposite direction. Everyone got out, and conversation stopped until they got to the last person and slipped in behind them. A couple of the shop's staff were making their way toward them, handing out menus and taking orders, and Flynn tapped her repeatedly on the upper arm.

"Cinnamon and coffee ice cream," she sing-songed.

Aspen shrugged her off and laughed. "I don't think I've ever seen someone over the age of twelve get as excited about dessert as you do."

Kelly put her arm around Flynn's shoulder. "She can't help her sweet tooth."

Oakley grinned. "If only she could find a sweet girl." He motioned to the cute brunette from the donut shop about to reach them. "What about this beauty? She's *definitely* your type."

Aspen suppressed a smile at Flynn's obvious discomfort with everything about the current situation. Before her Kelly obsession kicked in, Oakley would've been one hundred percent correct about Flynn's attraction to the woman about to take their order, but now, Flynn probably wouldn't look twice.

"Hi there! Welcome to Dreadnought's," the waitress said brightly. "Are you taking out or eating in?"

"Takeout, please," Aspen said.

She smiled and handed each of them a menu from the ones tucked under her right arm. "You can scan the QR code for our app and order from your phone, or I can take your order right here."

Aspen looked at her name badge and smiled. "We'll order with you, Lottie." She loved technology—couldn't do without it—but she also loved the mini-interactions she got at places like this.

It took a while to get everyone's order plus all the different donuts they needed to take home. But Lottie smiled the whole way through it, even when Oakley dithered and changed his mind four times in between outrageous bouts of flirting. It got her attention though, and she accepted his number when he offered it along with payment for the food.

When Lottie was a reasonable distance away, Oakley lightly shoved Flynn's shoulder. "Snooze, you lose, Flynnster."

Flynn shrugged. "I didn't even try."

"If she had, you wouldn't have stood a chance," Kelly said and touched Flynn's cheek.

Aspen stepped closer and pulled Flynn in for a half-bro hug, knowing she'd need the physical support because her legs would've gone cartoon-style rubbery.

Oakley scoffed then looked serious. "Why *didn't* you try?"

Flynn opened her mouth but words didn't follow. Aspen couldn't say that Lottie wasn't Flynn's type, because she was very similar to Kelly in most ways.

"Maybe because she's too classy to hit on someone when they're just doing their job," Kelly said.

Flynn leaned into Aspen a little harder.

"Exactly, Kelly," Aspen said. "My buddy's got more game than you."

Oakley laughed. "Is that why we haven't seen her with anyone for the past couple of years? Because she's got so many options, it's too hard to choose."

Aspen punched him in the chest, hard enough to make him realize he should back off. He looked like he was about to say more when his fleeting expression indicated he'd gotten the message. Problem was, she'd have to explain herself the moment they were alone.

"So. Scuba diving," Kelly said. "If Leo hasn't broken anything, she should be able to get her mask on okay, right?"

"I guess that depends on how tender it is." Aspen blew out a breath. She'd stopped the uncomfortable conversation for Flynn only to take her place under the spotlight. "I hope she can do it. Willow said it was something she was really excited for."

"As excited for it as you are for buildings and women's symmetry?" Oakley asked.

Lottie returned, carrying a tray of tiny ice cream cups, so Aspen didn't respond.

"I thought you might like these while you wait." Lottie looked directly at Oakley and gave him the tray. "There are some special flavors in there. That one is just for you." She pointed at one that had a slip of paper beneath it and winked at him.

"Thank you, Lottie," he said. "That's so thoughtful. I can't wait to taste the special."

Lottie smiled and batted her eyelashes, and everyone waited until she'd retreated once again before they gagged and laughed.

"*I can't wait to taste the special.*" Aspen shook her head.

"Jealousy is *not* a good color on *any* of you," he said then grinned widely and stuffed Lottie's message into his shorts' pocket.

They all grabbed a taster cup and dug in, then fell silent again aside from the murmurs of appreciation around the taste explosions.

"God, I've missed this place," Flynn said.

"You've missed your mouth too." Kelly dragged her finger under Flynn's mouth to capture some escaping ice cream.

When she licked her finger, Aspen could practically see Flynn's brain explode. Flynn's eyes half-closed, and she let out a long, throaty sigh before she coughed and covered her mouth.

Puddle alert. Aspen clamped her teeth together to stop from dissolving into laughter. It was almost too painful to watch. When she looked away from Flynn, Oakley was staring at her. He looked down his nose, smiling and shaking his head. The penny had clearly dropped. Now Aspen would have to convince him to keep Flynn's secret, at least until the party. He grinned widely. *Damn it.* This was going to cost her. The last time she'd asked him to keep something quiet, she'd had to use chopsticks to eat all her food for a week. She shrugged. At least her secret crush on Leo was still safe. For now.

Chapter Seventeen

"So, young Leo," Willow's gramps said, pointing to her face. "Did you do that to yourself so you could escape this circus? You can tell me."

His wife and Willow giggled. "Gramps, you're so bad," Willow said.

Leoni smiled—which didn't hurt at all after the lidocaine injection—and shook her head. "No, it was your granddaughter actually. She's got a mean right hook."

"Leo!" Willow covered her mouth but giggled beneath her hand.

Her grands laughed, then they pushed up from their chairs. "Time for a little light snack. We won't be eating for hours if we've got to wait for Bill to catch dinner." He winked at Leoni, and they headed out of the library, chuckling.

After all the fuss and every single Hartwell family member crowding around her for the past couple of hours, along with the concierge doctor and her associate, Leoni was glad of the silence and room to breathe.

Willow let out a deep sigh. "I wish that I could tell my dad and grands what's really going on with you, and why I've been forced to do it."

Leoni didn't bother to take issue with Willow's choice of words. No one had *forced* her to do anything, least of all fake a queer relationship when she was straighter than a highway in the middle of Nebraska. "Maybe you should. Your grands have a great sense of humor. Seems like they'd probably get a kick out of it and would enjoy playing along. It might not be a good idea to tell your dad though. It'll put him in a weird po—"

"No." Willow's eyes widened. "I can't tell anyone. No one needs to know anything about it. I just need to get through the week and achieve my goal."

"About that..." Leoni wrinkled her nose and edged closer to Willow. "Now that we're officially building a real friendship, can we maybe talk about the goal thing?"

"Again with the talky-friend thing?" Willow rolled her eyes and flopped back on her couch. "Maybe I've had the right idea all along about not having friends. All you seem to do is make me think too hard. Aren't we just supposed to paint each other's nails, gossip, and...run the world?"

Leoni let out a relieved laugh and shook her head. "Good save. I was about to say that the fifties called, and they want their ideals back."

"It was funny though, right?"

"Yeah, that was very funny actually." Leoni frowned slightly. "Your family is missing out on who you really are, you know?"

Willow gave her a shy smile then looked away and seemed to be studying the wall of books like she was searching for a first edition. Leoni waited, giving her the silence she clearly needed.

"Do you really think so?"

"I really do." Leoni took a deep breath, wondering about the sanity of sharing the details of her own life so freely with the two sisters, but there was something about being around a family where there seemed to be so much thwarted love that it could dissolve into a Shakespearean tragedy at any moment. Something that made her re-evaluate her own situation. Something that made her want to go beyond the call of duty and actually help them. "The Willow you've shown me... I would've loved to have had you as a little sister when I was growing up." She ignored the burning behind her eyes and tried to swallow the ball of emotion that seemed intent on stopping her breathing.

Willow, however, did no such thing. She jumped up from her

seat and jumped *on* Leoni, bouncing all the air from her lungs while also making her burst into laughter. She wrapped her arms around Leoni and squeezed so tight, Leoni thought she might crack a rib or two. A droplet of salty liquid found its way onto her lip, and she returned Willow's embrace with similar feeling. "Christ, this is like an episode of Oprah."

Willow emerged from the hug. "The only reason I get that ancient reference is because we're in media, and I've met Oprah at our charity events."

"That woman is a legend. *Everyone* should know who she is."

Willow shifted from Leoni's lap but left her legs draped over her. "Did you mean that? Or did it just feel like it might be a nice thing to say?"

Leoni frowned and rapped Willow's shin lightly. "I'm not going to say something like that without meaning it. And just so you know, I hardly *ever* say things like that." Fact was, she couldn't really remember the last time.

Willow gave another shy smile. "I suppose I should let you talk about the 'goal thing' then. What diamond of wisdom are you going to drop on me today, guru?"

"*Pearl* of wisdom."

Willow adopted a haughty expression. "Diamonds are better than pearls, and your advice has been far superior to anyone else's before you." She frowned. "Mostly because they tried to *tell* me what to do rather than try to help me figure it out, like you're doing."

Leoni couldn't work out why Willow's mom would take a different parenting approach to her youngest daughter, but again, she reminded herself that she was here on Willow's request, so her needs took priority, even if they crossed her professional boundaries. But this whole gig had been different from the start, so she was just being flexible and adapting. *And* blurring the lines. But it wasn't like Willow would be filling in a Google review when she left. "So you said that your goal for the end of the week was to get your mom to *see* you, right? That hasn't changed?"

Willow shook her head. "I don't know that it's going to happen, but she does seem to like you. Her coming in this morning with breakfast and an apology is unheard of."

Since Willow had told her the sea turtle story, Leoni had run it over and over in her mind. Willow's plan revolving around her mom's acceptance of Leoni was severely flawed and a long shot. Relying on the charms of someone else to get her mom to notice her missed the mark. She just had to convince Willow of that. "What if you change tack on *how* you get her to see you?"

Willow narrowed her eyes. "You don't think it's going to work, do you? A week isn't enough time. Ooh, I know." She bounced in her seat and jiggled Leoni along with her. "What if you stay for longer? Or come back for Aspen's birthday celebrations next month?"

"Your sister's birthday is next month?" As soon as it left her mouth, she knew she'd given away more than she wanted to.

Willow widened her eyes and leaned back on the sofa, grinning. "You like her, don't you?"

Leoni shrugged and pulled at the bill of her ball cap. "Sure. I like all your family." Not a lie; she just *really* liked Aspen.

Willow shook her head slowly. "Nope. I think you like my sister in a very different way from the rest of my family. You never did tell me anything about your type."

"That's because I was trying to be professional." She picked at the seam of the couch then stopped immediately, realizing it was probably a family heirloom worth more than her car.

"But now we're supposed to be friends, and friends share." Willow wiggled her eyebrows and looked smug. "You know all about my preferences. Tell me yours." She poked Leoni's waist. "Convince me that strong, successful, butch women aren't your catnip."

Leoni rolled her eyes and looked over Willow's shoulder at the closed door, praying for an interruption. "Aren't you supposed to be getting ready for the family fishing trip?"

"Subtle, but I've got time." Willow laughed lightly then offered her trademark pout. "I don't want to be in a one-sided friendship."

"It's not one-sided. It's just fresh. And I haven't had much time to tell you anything about me." She pulled her ponytail over her shoulder and sighed. "Sharing isn't my strong suit, I'm sorry."

Willow huffed. "It's not mine either, but I've talked to you more openly than I have to anyone in a long time."

Leoni grasped Willow's shins and wiggled her legs. "Okay, pouty-face. I'll give it a try. And then we talk about your goal. What do you want to know?"

"Do you like guys? Girls? Enbies?" Willow inclined her head. "Ooh, are you pan like my brother?"

"I told you just after we met. Strictly women...and yes, women exactly like your sister," Leoni said and wrinkled her nose.

"Ha! I knew it." Willow smiled brightly, but that soon faded, and she frowned. "I'm sorry you can't do anything about it."

Leoni shrugged. "It's not a problem. Honestly. I'm here for you, remember?"

"So you'd come to Aspen's birthday party next month to help me keep working on Mom?"

"If you really want that, then yes, of course I would," Leoni said. "But that brings us back around to a different way to achieve your goal." She smiled, and Willow groaned.

"Fine. But let me grab some coffee before you tell me all about your clever plan."

Willow swung her legs from Leoni's lap and headed out of the library, leaving Leoni alone with her thoughts. Ruth wouldn't be impressed if she found out that Willow and Leoni were forming a friendship *or* that Leoni had kind of fallen for Aspen. Leoni would have to be made of stone not to lust after her—she was sure Ruth wouldn't fire her for *that*—and if she'd been able to limit it to a physical attraction, she would've been golden. She could've gone home on Saturday with a story to tell the rest of the team, and Ruth would've been so happy, she would have made good on the big fat bonus she'd dangled in front of Leoni's nose to fill in last-minute. She was sure that Willow would add a tip for her service and let Ruth know how successful the week had been.

But then Willow's fridge was out of water when she woke, spitting feathers and dehydrated, and that stock faux pas had led to last night's chat. And *that* had led to finding out more about Aspen, specifically more about how she was such an open and kind person, and how soft and fluffy she was under that tough-looking exterior. *That* kind of combo, apparently, was Leoni's undoing.

The whole family was encouraging her to color outside the lines without even realizing it, and it was like they kept spiking her drinks with truth serum, which led to Leoni sharing her personal life instead of sticking to the script and the carefully curated background Ginny had invented.

Willow returned with a tray of coffee cups and cookies and a big smile on her face. And why did that make Leoni's heart swell? She'd had enough therapy to know this family was beginning to fill in the holes in her soul she'd been covering over with single-serve relationships and duct tape. And while part of her was screaming that she shouldn't allow herself to get too attached, she decided it was time to stop listening and start making real connections.

Willow placed the goodies on the table beside their couch and handed Leoni a cup. "I've thought of something else I want to talk about."

Leoni readied herself for another too-personal probe. "What's that?"

Willow resumed her position on the sofa with her legs on Leoni's lap and cradled her cup. "When you first talked to me about finding my passion, I asked you if this job was yours."

Leoni frowned, hardly able to believe that Willow had remembered that part of the conversation. But then, Willow had been shielding at the time and convincingly portraying the immature, rich kid everyone took her for. "And I said it wasn't."

"Yes." Willow sipped her coffee and murmured appreciatively.

"We have this shipped in direct from the Wallenford Estate in Jamaica; do you like it?"

"Oh my god," Leoni said after she'd tasted it. "I think my tongue just had a mini orgasm."

Willow clasped her hand over her mouth and giggled. "I didn't think it was *that* good. Remind me to give you a barrel of beans to take home with you."

"A barrel? I only have a carryon."

Willow swatted her shoulder. "No, silly. They're cute, tiny wooden barrels. It'll fit in your hand luggage, no problem."

"Thanks. I'll keep it for special occasions." Leoni could only imagine how much coffee like that cost, but if Willow was happy to gift her some, it would be impolite to turn it down.

"Or I could just send you a barrel after a couple of weeks."

Leoni didn't know how to respond to Willow's generosity, so she laughed it off. "Anyway, you were saying..."

"I don't think I'll ever be able to drink this without thinking of what you just said." Willow took another sip and smiled. "Right. You said this job wasn't your passion, but you didn't say what was. And then you told Aspen that you'd studied musical theater in college. Was that true?"

Leoni nodded. "I can't believe I told her the truth, but yes."

"Is theater your passion?"

Leoni disguised her immediate unwillingness to answer with another long drink of her coffee. Opening up was hard, and she wasn't sure she was ready to discuss her broken dreams with Willow. She was thinking of baby steps rather than giant leaps. "I thought you'd said we could get back to me delivering diamonds?"

Willow looked at Leoni, her expression serious. "Please just say yes or no, and then I'll leave it alone." She held up a finger. "For now."

Leoni sighed. "Yes."

Willow grinned, looking intensely pleased with herself. "Great. Hit me with the wisdom."

Leoni smiled at how comfortable Willow seemed to be around her. This was only the fourth day, but it'd been like watching an accelerated time-lapse video of a butterfly emerging from its chrysalis. Once again, she was hit with the intense notion that she had to help the rest of the family see it too. "Okay, animals or people?"

"Animals or people what? I thought we'd finished with all the questions about who I was attracted to," she said and giggled.

Leoni laughed so hard, she almost spilled her coffee. "Sorry, I should've been more specific. Would you rather *work* with animals or people?"

"Oh." Willow nodded slowly. "I see where this is going. My instant reaction is animals. I think." She bit her bottom lip and looked up at the ceiling. "Yes. Animals. And we're the cause of most of their problems anyway, so it seems right to do something about it...doesn't it?"

"Absolutely." It was easy to give Willow the approval she craved when she made a lot of sense. Leoni pulled out her phone and googled *jobs with animals*. "Top three options are veterinary work, pet care, and wildlife conservation."

"Ooh, ooh." Willow bounced in her chair. "The last one."

"Given your turtle experience, that makes sense." She googled WWF, the only wildlife organization she was really aware of. "Wow. Program manager in Africa..."

"Really?" Willow's eyes widened. "I'd need to go back to college though, right? Study zoology or marine biology."

Leoni nodded. "Yeah, but this could be your calling. What's a little study time to follow your passion?"

"I'd love to go to college for something like that." Willow sighed deeply. "I don't know why I didn't think of it before." She gave Leoni a wide smile and squeezed her hand. "Thank you."

She shrugged and glanced away, a little overwhelmed by Willow's genuine gratitude. "It's nothing."

Willow pulled her legs off Leoni's lap and knelt closer. She took both of Leoni's hands and held them to her chest. "It's not nothing, Leo. I've spent too much time floating around doing nothing real with my life. I'm nearly thirty!"

Leoni chuckled. "It's all downhill from there. I must be practically ancient to you."

Willow swatted her thigh. "You know what I mean. Time can just disappear, month after month, year after year, and then one day, you wake up, and the chance to chase your dreams is long gone."

Leoni shook her head. "I thought I was the one dropping diamonds of wisdom?" She had seven years on Willow, and she was still "floating" and making excuses not to get back to her real passion. It was sobering to think she hadn't tried hard enough, that she'd never had the guts to pack up and head to New York, to really try to make it happen.

The library door swung open, and Aspen came in. Leoni sighed. *From dream career to dream woman.*

Though neither were within reach.

"Hey, I just wanted to check on the patient." Aspen held out a light pink box. "And bring you something guaranteed to make you feel better."

Leoni smiled. "That's thoughtful, thank you." She raised her cup. "Will it go with the best-tasting coffee in the world?"

Aspen opened the box and tipped it slightly to reveal its contents. "These babies go with *everything*, don't they, sis?" She pointed to a pink icing-topped cronut the size of Willow's head. "I got your favorite, with homemade raspberry jam and creamy vanilla chocolate chip ganache."

Willow narrowed her eyes. "My favorite from when I was nine?"

Aspen's shoulders sagged slightly. "It doesn't matter. There're plenty of others to choose from."

"No." Willow got up from the couch and picked it out of the box. "That one's perfect. I just..."

Come on, Willow, say it. Meet her halfway.

Willow nibbled on her top lip. "I can't believe you remembered."

Aspen winked. "Of course I do. I used to take you to Dreadnought's every Saturday morning all through summer for years." She looked at Leoni and shook her head. "You should've seen the mess she used to get into. Cream on her nose and her cheeks, and *every* finger was a sticky mess."

Willow giggled. "I did *not*. Don't believe her, Leo." She took a napkin from Aspen's other hand and sank back on the sofa. "Stop looking at me. Both of you!"

Leoni turned her back, and Aspen put the box on the table closest and sat on the adjacent sofa.

Aspen motioned to Leoni's cheek. "What did the doc say? Is anything broken?"

"Thankfully not. The X-ray didn't show any fractures at all. I've got to ice it for fifteen minutes three times a day. Actually, I should do that now." Leoni grasped the arm of the sofa to get up.

Aspen waved her back down and jumped up. "I'll get it. We've got some compresses with special cotton sleeves, so the cold won't burn your skin."

Aspen glanced at Willow, who was chin-deep in her cronut and making all sorts of noises Leoni didn't want to hear, and she suspected her sister wouldn't either. She and Aspen exchanged a look, and heat rushed up Leoni's spine. She wouldn't mind eliciting those sounds from Aspen one bit.

Aspen began to back out of the room awkwardly. The back of her heel must've caught on the edge of a rug, because she stumbled backward into a bookcase, and several books fell on her head and around her.

Willow laughed. "It's good that they're not Grandpa Bill's first editions."

"Aw, crap." Aspen squatted to the floor, rubbing her head and picking up books.

Leoni got up and joined Aspen on the rug. "Do we need to call your family doctor back?" She laughed lightly and looked for physical damage without touching her.

Aspen shook her head. "I'm fine. I've had worse knocks than that." She took the books from Leoni's hands, and their fingers touched.

Leoni pulled away reluctantly but quickly, and Aspen turned away to reshelve the books. She sat back down beside Willow and chose a tasty-looking pastry. Better she fill her mouth than imagine doing *other* things with it, like kissing Aspen's forehead better before moving down to her lips. One of those pesky books was bound to have grazed Aspen's gorgeous mouth.

Aspen pointed to the door when she'd finished clearing up. "I'll go get that ice pack for you—and maybe one for me too," she said and grinned.

Leoni was reminded of something Willow had said that morning to her mom. She waited until Aspen had left before she asked, "Do you really wish you were an only child?"

Willow clicked her nails. "No. I just wish... I don't know. She's the golden child, and she gets everything she wants."

"But hasn't she worked for those things?" Leoni held up her cronut in defense when Willow glared at her. "Hold on. Before you bite my head off, I'm not on anyone's side. It just seems like Aspen works hard to create the life she wants. There's nothing stopping you from doing the same thing now that you've found your passion, is there?"

Willow blew out a long breath and rolled her eyes again. "Are we back to my goal?"

"We are, yeah. And we've only got a few minutes before Aspen gets back." Leoni smiled. "Now that you've got an idea of what you want to do, I think we should start some serious research over the next couple of days. Then you should announce your new plans to everyone at your Fourth of July party."

"And you think that's going to make Mom see me?"

Despite Willow's expression falling slightly into sadness, Leoni had to bite her lip to stop from laughing.

"What?"

Leoni wiped the cream from Willow's nose with a napkin. "Aspen was right. You *do* get messy with those things."

"It's the only way to fully appreciate them." Willow touched her face and then licked her fingers before using a napkin to clean up. She looked up at Leoni, her eyes uncertain. "Are you sure about making a big announcement?"

Leoni nodded. "I think it's a better way to get your mom to see you, that's for sure. You want her to see *you*, not the person you're with." She took Willow's free hand and squeezed. "And I think we should talk to Aspen too. She might be able to help."

Willow's lip curled slightly. "I don't think she'll want to."

Leoni shrugged. "She might surprise you, and I'll be there with you every step of the way, I promise."

Willow wrinkled her nose. "Okay. If you think it's a good idea."

"I think it's a great idea, mostly so you start living life for yourself and not for the approval of other people. Once you're doing something you love, you'll care less about external validation."

"Like you do?" Willow asked.

Leoni inclined her head. She wasn't seeking the approval of others—she'd given up on getting that from her father a while back—but she couldn't really say she was living life for herself either. Otherwise, she'd be in a cheap apartment in New York right now trying to carve out her dream career. "Like I'm trying to do, yeah."

Willow put her napkin on the table and then took Leoni's hands again. "You promise you'll help me? Even after the end of this week?"

Leoni gave Willow a warm smile. "I promise. You'll have to break up with me so we can do the cliché lesbian thing of being best friends after, *obviously*, otherwise your family might get freaked out."

"Aspen isn't friends with her exes, especially not Sarah."

Leoni bit her tongue and tried to shove the green-eyed goblin back down to where it belonged, which was nowhere in this particular scenario, because she had no right to be jealous of anyone when it came to Aspen. "So Sarah isn't still hanging around? She doesn't live a few mansions down the road or anything?"

"God, no. She's in New York, and she models all around the world. There was nowhere near enough excitement around here for her liking. She's a massive drama queen."

New York wasn't far enough. Neither was Australia. The moon would be about right. "Will she be at Friday's party?"

"She could be. Grandpa Bill and Grandma Eleanor are good friends with her grandparents. They live in Southampton," she said, as if that provided Leoni with all the pertinent information she needed.

"Which means?"

"Old money." Willow grimaced. "And conservative." She pushed up from the couch. "I have to get ready for the fishing trip. Are you sure you don't want to go?"

Leoni shook her head. "I don't want to see giant hooks in the mouths of fat fishes, thanks. So gross."

"I'm not a fan either." Willow shrugged. "But it's one of this week's *family* traditions. I'll see you later tonight," she said and left the library.

Leoni sat back to enjoy the rest of her delicious cronut and coffee. It was eighty degrees and a bluebird sky, and she was in a beachfront property. Her afternoon and evening involved catching some rays in between dips in the sea. What could be better?

Having a certain sister join me and apply my sun lotion. But that was as likely as her cutting off all her hair and never wearing heels again.

Chapter Eighteen

"I'm sorry, Mom," Aspen said. "I did tell you that I'd have to do some work this week. This is a big job, and it's important to us." She glanced at Flynn. "Right, buddy?"

Flynn nodded quickly. "Yep. Big, important job."

Aspen frowned, and Flynn shrugged almost imperceptibly. She was so bad at being anything other than one hundred percent honest.

"I know you did, honey," her mom said. "I was just hoping you wouldn't have to miss out on any of the family traditions. And your grandad is unnaturally excited about taking out his new boat for its maiden voyage. He'll be disappointed you won't be there."

"I *am* sorry, Mom. But this project isn't just about the money for the firm. I'm invested emotionally."

Her mom's expression softened, and she caressed Aspen's cheek. "I understand, and I love that. Do you know how proud I am of you?"

"Mom..."

Her mom took Flynn's hand too. "I'm so proud of both of you. Okay, time to get ready. We're leaving at two. Don't be late, Flynn, or the captain will have us in the brig."

"I'll be ready," Flynn said and smiled.

"And we'll bring some mahi-mahi home for you, if you're lucky," her mom said and left the kitchen.

Aspen headed for the lounge to check over her drawing one final time, but Flynn stopped her in the hallway.

"What are you doing, Asp?"

"I want to be fully prepared," she said. "It's been a few hours since I finished the plan, so I want to take a fresh look at it now that I've had some distance. Check I haven't missed anything."

"You haven't," Flynn said. "*We* haven't. It's perfect. But that isn't what I meant. What are you doing staying here with Leo?"

Aspen frowned. "I'm not staying here with Leo. Mancharlson's email said that he'd call if he had any questions, and if he calls while I'm on the fishing boat, I won't want any distractions. I'll need the plan at hand."

"Your grandad's new 'fishing boat' is a Legacy Superyacht. You could use one of the staterooms *if* he calls, which he probably won't, because, like I said: perfect."

Aspen could've used the actual office that was on board if she'd wanted, but... "I'm giving you and Kelly some space too. If I'm not there, we can't get into our little bubble, and then you can actually try talking to her."

Flynn's eyes widened, and she shook her head. "I can't do that. I need my wingman, or I'll make a total fool of myself. You saw how I was earlier. If you hadn't held me up, I would've been a melted puddle on the ground."

Aspen chuckled. "Think of it as exposure therapy. You've got to put yourself in that situation repeatedly, so you can handle it when she says yes to a date with you."

"You think she will?"

"I think she'd be crazy not to."

Flynn jutted her chin. "And this doesn't have anything at all to do with your sister's hot girlfriend staying behind too?"

"Definitely not. But the doc did say that she should take it easy, and someone should be around to make sure she's okay."

"Shouldn't that be Willow's job?"

"I don't know what to tell you. Willow never misses a chance to go out on the ocean; she's always loved the water." Aspen thought of all the times she'd taken her little sister swimming once she'd taught her how, and warmth ran through her. It was nice to have that kind of reaction instead of the usual semi-dread. "She really takes her birth sign seriously."

"More seriously than the health of her girlfriend, apparently."

Aspen shrugged. "It's not like Leo's got a concussion, Flynn. She's just bruised her face."

"What are you two scheming about?" Oakley asked as he came downstairs into the hallway, looking supremely smug. "How to ask Kelly on a date?"

Flynn flapped at Aspen's arm. "You told him?" she whispered before he reached them.

"No. Play it cool," Aspen said, then she looked over Flynn's shoulder to her brother. "What're you talking about?"

He came up behind Flynn and wrapped his arm around her shoulder. "I'm talking about this little one having a massive crush on my best friend."

Aspen laughed. "Yeah, right. They've known each other nearly twenty years, and suddenly Flynn starts crushing? Doesn't make much sense, little brother."

"Pah! Have you never seen a friends-to-lovers rom-com?" he asked and dropped his arm from Flynn's shoulders.

Flynn kissed her teeth. "That's just movie stuff."

"Yeah." Aspen punched Oakley's arm. "Come on, little bro. We could say the same to you. You've been friends with Kelly for even longer. Maybe you're going to fall madly in love with her by the end of the year."

Oakley gagged. "Ew, that's *so* gross."

"Is it?" Aspen chuckled. "Why? Look at the people you've dated. Some of them could be Kelly's siblings."

Oakley shook his head. "I don't have a type. I like all types."

"Exactly." Aspen tapped her head lightly. "So why *wouldn't* you suddenly decide you like Kelly?"

"You probably shouldn't put things like that in his head," Flynn said.

Oakley looked between the two of them and then pulled Flynn around to face him. "Look at me and tell me, honestly, that you're not crushing on my best friend." When Flynn didn't answer immediately, he let her go and huffed. "I knew it! You've been super freaky around her for a while now, but you've been on another level this week."

Aspen grabbed his wrist. "Oaks, you can't tell her."

He frowned. "Are you kidding? I can't keep a secret from Kelly. We tell each other everything—and I mean, *everything*." He wiggled his eyebrows then gave an exaggerated wink.

Flynn covered her mouth. "Aw, crap. This is such a bad idea."

Aspen tugged Oakley's arm when he tried to pull away. "I'm serious, brother. You've got to let Flynn tell her at the party."

His eyes lit up, and he inclined his head. "Oh, that'd be so romantic," he said. "You're really going to risk telling her?"

"Do you know something?" Flynn grasped Oakley's shoulder. "She hates me, doesn't she?" She dropped her hand and sank against the wall. "This is hopeless. I told you I was out of her league."

"Out of whose league?" Kelly asked as she came out of the living room.

"Cara Delevingne," Aspen said without hesitation, while Flynn pressed herself further against the wall in the apparent hope that it would absorb her. "She might be at the party on Friday. These two both like her, but Flynn thinks Cara's too good for her."

"We'll have more in common," Oakley said. "We're both pan."

"You'll both be out of luck," Kelly said. "Cara's been with an old school friend for a few years now." She smiled at Flynn. "And she isn't out of your league at all."

"An old school friend?" Aspen asked. "They took a while to get together. I wonder if they always had a thing for each other?"

Kelly shrugged. "I don't know. Maybe now is just their time." She tapped her watch. "It's nearly two. Is everyone ready?"

"Yeah. I just need to grab my bag from my room," Flynn said and darted upstairs.

"I'll meet you outside," Oakley said. "I just need to talk to Aspen about something."

"Sure. I'm going to grab some water for the drive," Kelly said. "Do you want some?"

Oakley nodded then waited until she was out of earshot. "The party is three days away. That's way too long to keep a secret from anyone, let alone my bestie." He gave her a lop-sided grin. "Unless..."

Here comes the shakedown. "What do you want?"

"I don't know yet." He put his finger to his lips. "I'm going to have to think about it *very* carefully. It's a big, big ask, isn't it?"

She nodded slowly. There was no way she'd be able to keep anything like this from Flynn. "Huge."

"Ginormous."

Aspen gave him a hard shove. "Just think about it and get back to me. And keep your mouth shut in the meantime, okay?"

He mimed zipping his lips together. "Sealed like Fort Knox," he said and sauntered down the hallway toward the front door.

Aspen blew out a long breath and shook her head. This was turning out to be a complicated week. She went into the living room, sat in front of her drawing, and placed her cell on the table. She traced the lines of the trees in much the same way as Leo had in the early hours of this morning when they'd shared precious time alone. Then she leaned back in her chair and laced her fingers behind her neck. *What am I doing?*

Footsteps thundered down the stairs, and Flynn shouted her goodbye. Doors closed, and there was plenty of yammering and more shouted goodbyes before Aspen was left in peaceful silence.

She studied every inch of her drawing. Flynn was right; it was as perfect as she could get it. It checked all Mancub's boxes and even created some he wouldn't have realized he needed until he saw this iteration of the design. And yeah, she could easily have gone on the fishing trip and used her grandad's fancy yacht-office with its own satellite for cell and Wi-Fi, but when she'd discovered Leo wasn't going on the trip, the opportunity to spend some more time with her overpowered her family obligations. Not that she'd admit it out loud to anyone, of course.

She rubbed hard at her forehead. This always happened when she connected strongly with someone. Being around them became her primary concern. She thought about how she'd almost flunked her first year in college after getting obsessed with the football team's cheerleading captain, and how she'd neglected work when she and Sarah first met. Both of those had turned out badly, but this one seemed worse somehow because the relationship wouldn't get the chance to start, let alone end. It was an obsession without an obvious outlet. The not knowing how it might turn out felt like a special kind of torture, as did the plague of what ifs and musings about multiverses, wondering if she'd met Leo before her sister in any of them.

She pushed away from the table and shoved her cell in her pocket. *Talking* to Leo wasn't illegal, and Aspen had nothing else to do but wait for Mancub's call. She could control herself, and Leo probably wasn't interested anyway, since Aspen couldn't be any more different from Willow.

She stepped out of the cool house, and the afternoon heat wrapped around her like a warm blanket. She inhaled deeply, and the sea air rushed in like a balm to her soul. She pushed her sunglasses back and squinted to take in the gorgeous, clear blue sky before she dipped her foot into the pool, vaguely considering taking a swim. Deciding against that, Aspen pulled her foot out and walked the length of the pool out onto the deck that overlooked their private stretch of beach. The only dot of color on the almost-white sand was Leo laid out on one of their wooden cabanas, her tan skin contrasting against the dark blue bikini top and beach shorts she wore.

Aspen hesitated at the gate and glanced over her shoulder toward the house. Safety beckoned, not just from the harmful rays of the sun since she'd neglected to apply lotion, but also from the dangerous situation she was currently intent on embracing. *I'm not a lovestruck teenager.* She pushed open the gate and headed toward Leo.

As Aspen got closer, she could see that Leo had rolled the waistband of her shorts over and over and tucked the shorts' legs under themselves, revealing way too much of her skin for Aspen *not* to snapshot the mental image. Doing so immediately made her feel like a pervy voyeur, and she tore her gaze away to focus on the beauty of the ocean instead of the beauty lying a few feet away.

"Do you mind if I join you?" Aspen tossed her towel onto the adjacent cabana and untied the drapes for a little shade.

Leo looked up from under her ball cap and smiled. "I don't think you have to ask permission for that on your own personal patch of paradise, do you?"

"It's only polite." She sat on the edge of the bed. "How are you feeling?"

Leo motioned to the water. "Excessively relaxed and very much soothed." She touched her cheek briefly. "The painkillers and the ice have conspired to take care of this for now."

"That's good news," Aspen said. "I was afraid we were going to have to take you to a plastic surgeon."

Leo arched her eyebrow. "Worried about me losing my rakish good looks?"

Aspen nodded. "Something like that. Once you cross the threshold of any Hartwell family home, your well-being is everyone's concern."

"Is that why you haven't gone on the fishing trip? You drew the short straw and had to stay to keep an eye on me?"

"Not at all. I stayed to put the finishing touches to my drawing."

"Really?" Leo didn't sound convinced. "It looked pretty finished last night, and Flynn said you'd sent it off to your client early this morning."

Damn Flynn for not keeping her trap shut about anything. "We did, but Mancharlson might call for final amendments, and I don't want to be out on the boat when he does."

"I think the only reason he'd call would be to thank you for turning his vision into reality."

Aspen puffed out her chest and grinned. "You think so?"

"I do," Leo said and relaxed back onto her bed.

Aspen kicked off her sliders and pulled the split mattress up into a sitting position.

"Don't you like the sun?" Leo asked.

"I didn't put protection on." Aspen got comfortable and made sure she was shaded. "I just came out for a quick break."

Leo sat up and pulled a bottle of sun lotion from underneath her lounger. "Do you want me to put some on for you?"

"God, no—I mean, no, thanks. I'm going to do some laps in a minute."

Leo replaced the bottle, quietly laughing. "I've always wondered why people have pools when they're so close to the ocean. What *is* that about?"

Aspen shrugged. "Some people don't like the feel of the sand on their wet feet. Some people just like the *sound* of the ocean but are too scared to go in it. And you can control the temperature of the pool. The Atlantic can get pretty chilly."

Leo turned onto her side to face Aspen. "Which one of those applies to you?"

"None," she said. "*Obviously*."

"Okay." Leo chuckled.

"Are you looking forward to the party?" Aspen asked, overly desperate to continue their conversation.

"Sure, it sounds like a blast." Her expression turned more serious. "Are *you*?"

"What do you mean? Why wouldn't I be?"

"Willow mentioned that your ex-fiancée might be there."

Aspen clenched her jaw. "Did she?"

Leo nodded. "Are you expected to play nice at high society get-togethers, even with someone like her?"

Aspen couldn't stop a small smile. She quite liked the dismissive way Leo referred to her ex, as if there was an edge of protectiveness to it. "I am, unfortunately, especially since my parents don't know the full story. As far as they're concerned, the relationship ran its course and ended amicably."

"There are a lot of secrets in this family," Leo said. "Kind of makes me glad it's just me and Mom." Her gaze flickered slightly, as if she thought she might've spoken out of turn. "Why haven't you told your parents what really happened?"

"It's not worth the trouble it would cause. The two families have been friends for generations, and I don't want to drive a wedge into that. We're over. No one else needs to suffer because of it. Does that make sense?"

"I guess." Leo picked at the edge of her beach towel. "Families and politics. This is a different world from the one I'm used to."

Aspen frowned. "But you clearly exist in it. I still don't know what you do for a living, but you don't drive a G-Wagen if you bus tables."

Leo looked away. "It isn't a world I was *born* into."

"Oh, of course. Sorry."

Leo smiled, her confidence apparently returning quickly. "Sorry I wasn't born with a silver spoon like you? You don't need to apologize. Especially after the way you've made your own way, without your family's money...which is reflected in *your* ride. How old *is* your truck?"

Aspen let out a sigh of relief, glad she hadn't offended Leo. "I hope you're not disparaging Betty. She's in mint condition considering she's a first model Raptor from 2010. It was the last expensive gift I accepted from Mom and Dad. Now Mom makes me something every year instead. I don't know if you saw the long, leather pouch on the table last night?"

"Yeah, I thought it probably held your mechanical pencils and architect bits."

Aspen shook her head. "Nope. Mom said that she couldn't *not* celebrate one of the best days of her life, so she took up pyrography."

Leo chuckled. "Pie-what?"

"Pyrography. It's burning wood with a red-hot pen, basically. Every year, she makes me a cute little wooden disc." She smiled. "She's pretty good at it now. The first ones were pretty basic, just writing, but now she can create really intricate animals. But it wouldn't matter if all she did was write on them with a Sharpie, because she's still *making* me something instead of just buying it. And that means so much more because it's coming from her heart and her time."

"Is that just for you?"

Aspen laughed. "You've been with Willow for a couple of months now, what do you think? She still likes her things, just like Oakley. It's a me and Mom thing, which makes it even more special. That little pouch goes everywhere with me."

"It's good that she chose wood as her medium and not rocks."

"Exactly. It's a lot easier to carry around."

"It's usually kids making things for their parents," Leo said. "I love that your mom's subverted that expectation."

"It is pretty cool, isn't it?" Aspen nodded back toward the house. "I can show you them later if you're interested?"

"I'd really like that." Leo's smile was dazzling and genuine. "So back to your family drama. If your ex comes from money too, why steal yours?"

"Because she could." Aspen shrugged. "I think she might be an undiagnosed sociopath. She took a group of her closest friends to Vegas, stayed in the penthouse suite at the Bellagio, and blew all the money in one night in the casino. I kind of hate that place now."

A flicker of something crossed Leo's expression. "There's more to Vegas than all that." She inclined her head. "Actually, I take that back. It's the circles of hell, numbers two to four. You must've been planning a helluva wedding."

Aspen nodded. "Vera Wang dresses don't come cheap."

"I can imagine. And I bet you would've looked absolutely beautiful in one."

"It wasn't–" She stopped herself and chuckled at Leo's wide smile. "Funny. I was going with a Ralph Lauren tux. Obviously."

"*Obviously*." Leo nodded like she was appeasing a child. "I'm sure you would've looked *very* suave."

Aspen swallowed hard and tried to ignore the flirtatious dip of Leo's gaze. "What do you plan to wear for your wedding? Will you wear your hair down or will you get a ball cap to match your outfit?"

"Now who's being funny?"

Aspen shrugged. "Just making conversation before you go back in the sea."

"How do you know I've been in the sea?" Leo asked, arching her eyebrow in apparent amusement.

Busted. "Because you're wet," she said, motioning to Leo's legs, which she now noticed were bone-dry. Leo's eyebrows arched higher, and she pressed her lips together, clearly trying not to laugh.

"I am?" Leo's lips twitched as she inspected her arms, which were also already dry.

Aspen spotted a patch of wetness on Leo's towel under her bent leg. "Your towel. Your *towel* is wet. *That's* what I meant."

"Uh-huh. So you weren't watching from the house before you came out to join me then?"

Aspen dropped her shoulders. "I wasn't *watching*. I just looked out the window to see what the waves were doing, and you were in the water." She dropped her head back against the sunbed. She should've led with that explanation, but Leo got her unbelievably flustered. "You didn't answer the question," she finally said, hoping to return the conversation to safer waters.

Leo touched the ball cap shading her eyes. "You want to know if I'd wear my hair up or down?"

She nodded. "I already assumed you'd wear a suit."

Leo held her amused expression. "I don't know how I'd wear my hair, because I haven't spent much time thinking about my wedding."

Something crossed Leo's face too fast for Aspen to interpret before Leo looked back at the ocean. *I barely know her. Of course I can't understand her every nuanced expression.*

"I've never met anyone who's made me think about settling down, let alone getting married." Leo turned back and wiggled her eyebrows. "But Vera Wang? Nothing but the best for your lady, huh?"

"But she's not my lady anymore." Aspen raised her eyebrow when the words had settled *without* the usual weight in her gut to accompany them. She really *was* over Sarah. Her effervescence from the epiphany immediately fizzled out when she *also* realized she was developing a new attachment to another woman, unavailable in a totally different way, and which would inevitably hurt in an entirely different way too.

So she should probably leave. Right now. Go back to the house and pound out a hundred laps to dispel some of this undirected sexual energy. Sit back at the table and wait for Mancub's phone call. Eat another couple of massive donuts and pretend they were her feelings.

Something, *anything* to take her out of Leo's magnetic orbit.

But her ass remained glued to the cabana, and she didn't try all that hard to pull it away.

Chapter Nineteen

"I DIDN'T REALIZE THEY were going to be back so late." Leoni sat on the kitchen stool and got comfortable.

Aspen looked up from the fridge and smiled. "That's sweet."

Leoni frowned. "What is?"

"That you're missing Willow so much."

Leoni chuckled but quickly stopped, reminding herself that she *wasn't* on a date with Aspen, and that, yes, she *should* probably be missing her girlfriend. "We're not joined at the hip. But, yeah, I like being around her." *That* didn't sound very convincing. *Must try harder.*

"I can see that. Time apart is good, so you can miss someone and look forward to seeing them again." Aspen placed a variety of salad stuff on the counter. "Do you wish you'd gone with them?"

"To watch helpless fish hang from torture hooks in immense pain?" Leoni arched her eyebrow. "What do you think?"

Aspen laughed and looked happy with Leoni's response. "Sounds like a no."

"Ten points to you." Plus, it would've meant missing out on this alone time with Aspen, which she'd really enjoyed so far. She might've enjoyed the time on the beach even more if Aspen had stripped down to more suitable sunbathing attire, but that delight was denied. The shorts Aspen wore rode halfway up her thigh, giving Leoni tantalizing glimpses of her strong legs, but the upper half of her body remained a mystery.

Which was a good thing, of course. Perving on her client's big sister was bad enough, but actively seeking out interactions like this and encouraging her to get naked so Leoni could apply sun lotion was behavior she wouldn't be sharing in her debrief.

But she still didn't retreat to the refuge of Willow's room and away from the heavenly temptation.

Aspen held out a knife. "Cucumber or lettuce?"

Leoni took the knife, and her fingers accidentally brushed Aspen's. They locked eyes for a moment too long, then Leoni made an awkward grab for the cucumber on the countertop. "I'll handle this. Slices or chunks?"

"Whichever you prefer." Aspen crouched behind the island and came back up with a salad bowl, which she placed between them.

It'd take more than that to keep me away from you...under different circumstances. Leoni began to cut the vegetable and nearly sliced off the end of her finger with the knife. "Wow, that's sharp."

Aspen grabbed Leoni's hand. "Have you cut yourself?" she asked, her eyes flashing with concern.

Leoni didn't pull away. Aspen's strong hand wrapped around hers felt way too perfect to end the sensation prematurely. Damn, why couldn't she behave herself? "Nope." She wiggled her fingers. "No damage."

Aspen gazed at Leoni, then finally released her hand. She indicated the rest of the knife set, which was magnetized to a wall-mounted slab. "They were a gift from a famous chef."

"But you don't know which one?" Leoni asked, turning the wooden handle over in her hand.

Aspen shook her head. "Sorry."

"I've never seen such a pretty blade. It looks like agate."

Aspen pointed to Leoni's cucumber. "Less admiring, more chopping," she said and grinned.

Leoni resumed her slicing and added it to the bowl once Aspen had thrown in the lettuce. "I'll take the tomatoes now."

"Then you'll probably get even more excited when I give you a serrated knife for them." Aspen pulled a short-handled knife from the wall and turned back.

She seemed to hesitate before she placed it on the countertop instead of offering it directly to Leoni.

"Afraid you're going to slice my fingers off?" Leoni asked.

"Something like that." Aspen gave a shy smile but didn't look up. "Are you okay to do the rest of the salad while I prep the chicken?"

"Sure." She watched Aspen bend over to get the meat from the bottom shelf of the fridge and sighed. Maybe it would've been safer to have just gone fishing. She snapped her gaze away when Aspen glanced over her shoulder and hoped she hadn't been caught out. Aspen's lips twitched slightly, indicating that she *had* noticed Leoni ogling her tight butt.

"Would you like a beer?" Aspen narrowed her eyes slightly, as if she could sense that really wasn't Leoni's drink. "Or there's a Sancerre in here that'll pair nicely with the meal."

Thank God. She really couldn't handle more of the horrendous bloating caused by all the beer-drinking this week.

"Wine, it is," Aspen said and smiled widely before Leoni had responded.

She looked down at her chopping board and focused on creating perfectly sliced rounds of tomato. The alternative focus was proving far too alluring. Aspen popped the cork and poured two glasses. Leoni half-closed her eyes and fluttered her eyelids when she tasted the wine. "Wow." She licked her lips and sighed deeply. "That tastes like God has crushed the grapes with Her very own feet."

Aspen laughed. "Your metaphors are very colorful."

Leoni wrinkled her nose. "In a good way?"

Aspen pulled a variety of jars from a drawer and began to combine them in a small bowl. "For sure. I even wrote the 'wrestler's underpants' one from last night in my journal."

Leoni raised her eyebrow. "You keep a diary?"

"Nope," Aspen said and grinned. "I keep a journal."

"I apologize." Leoni put her knife down and slapped her own wrist. "I hope you'll forgive my enormous faux pas."

Aspen pressed her lips together tightly and shook her head slightly. "I don't know about that. My forgiveness isn't easily won."

Leoni nibbled the inside of her cheek. This was all so wrong. How had innocently preparing a meal become an opportunity for shameless flirtation? She really shouldn't play along. "I'll do *anything* to garner your forgiveness, kind prince," she said, affecting an English accent straight from *Downton Abbey*.

Aspen burst in to laughter. "'Kind prince'?"

"Oh, I'm sorry— Kind *princess*. Is that better?" she asked, barely able to contain her own amusement but still slightly disappointed that Aspen had picked up on her moniker instead of the "*anything*" part of her sentence.

Aspen inclined her head. "Oh, them's fighting words, kid."

"Who're you calling 'kid'? We're practically the same age."

Aspen stopped mixing her meat rub. "We are? I thought you were closer to Willow's age."

Torn between being flattered that Aspen thought she was six years younger than she was and insulted because that also implied she wasn't mature, Leoni waved her knife in Aspen's direction. "I'm thirty-one *actually*."

Aspen grinned and held up her hands. "Then it's *my* turn to apologize. Call it quits?"

"For now," she said, though the last thing she wanted to do was that. Leoni took another sip of the delicious wine, and they continued to chop and mix quietly.

"Why were you so surprised that I have a journal?" Aspen asked as she stirred olive oil into her bowl of herbs and spices.

"I don't know," Leoni said honestly. "I suppose I shouldn't be. You're clearly very artistic, with your job *and* in the kitchen." She pointed to the special concoction Aspen was rubbing onto the chicken breasts and tried not to imagine Aspen's large hands rubbing massage oil onto her skin and working her muscles.

"Mm." Aspen put the meat into a glass dish and placed it in the oven. "Speaking of being artistic, do you want to know what else

I've written in my journal about you?"

She knew what she *wanted* Aspen to be writing about—the same thing Leoni had been dreaming about every night since she'd gotten here—but she simply shrugged. "Only if you want to tell me."

"Your musical theater degree." Aspen picked up her glass and came around the island to sit beside Leoni. "You said that you sometimes wish you were using it. That stuck with me."

"Why?" she asked, stunned that Aspen had remembered that tiny detail from a passing conversation.

Aspen took a deep breath and glanced across the room as if she wasn't sure she should continue.

"It's okay," Leoni said. "Say what you're thinking." God, how she wished *she* could.

"You seemed quite sad when you said it, like you regret not following your dream." Aspen touched Leoni's forearm gently. "Are you sure that's okay to say?"

Leoni looked down at Aspen's hand, the simple touch setting her on fire, and nodded. "It's fine." She closed her eyes briefly and fought back the sudden onset of low-level grief. Yet again, one of the sisters had levered herself into her psyche. Let her in or slam the vault door closed? "It's true. Even though I keep telling myself I'm happy with what I'm doing, I sometimes wish that I'd had the courage to pursue my acting career. And I wear so many masks for work, I'm a little scared that I don't really know who I am anymore." *Way too honest.* She hopped off the stool. "Bathroom break," she said, as breezy as she could manage, and practically ran out of the kitchen.

She closed and locked the door behind her and leaned against the sink, breathing shallow gulps of air as she stared at her reflection in the mirror. "What the heck do you think you're doing?" she whispered. Aspen didn't know her, didn't know who or what she was, and if she did, Leoni was pretty certain that she wouldn't be showing as much interest as she had been. So what was the point of letting her in? Why was Leoni allowing her vulnerabilities to bubble to the surface? Talking to Willow was one thing—they were beginning to build a friendship—but Aspen was in the dark about everything, and that's the way it needed to stay.

Wasn't it? How *would* Aspen react if Leoni and Willow told her what was really going on, and why Willow had done it?

Leoni turned on the faucet and splashed cold water on her face. Willow's secret wasn't hers to tell just because she was attracted to her big sister. It wasn't. But that didn't mean she couldn't enjoy this connection while it lasted. It'd felt good to say those words out loud. And though she hadn't hung around to gauge Aspen's reaction, there certainly didn't seem to be any judgment in her eyes. *Because she doesn't know the whole story.* Which she didn't need to. But wouldn't it be nice to talk through her career with someone else for once, instead of running the same damn laps around her head?

She smiled at the soft knock on the bathroom door. Aspen cared enough to follow her. That was a new, and most welcome, experience.

"Leo? Are you okay in there?"

Leoni dried her hands and placed them against the solid wooden door, where she imagined Aspen's face would be on the other side of it. "Yeah, I'm fine." She glanced back at herself in the mirror. "I just wanted to see how my cheek was doing." Thankfully, the purple-green bruising of earlier seemed to already have faded slightly. A visit into town for some concealer, and no one would be able to tell the difference.

"Uh-huh. Might be a good idea to pop another cold compress on it while the chicken cooks... I'll go get one out of the freezer. Come join me when you're ready."

"Okay," Leoni said, again trying to infuse some enthusiasm into her words. She waited until the sound of Aspen's bare feet on the floor receded before she took another look at her reflection. She tugged at the bill of her ball cap and silently reiterated her promise to douse it in lighter fuel and set fire to it in her backyard as soon as she was home.

But first, she had to get through the rest of this gig.

She padded back into the kitchen and retook her seat. Aspen was ready and waiting with the ice pack in her hand, and she gently pressed it to Leoni's face. Leoni let her hold it there for a moment before reaching up to keep it in place herself. Once again, their fingers touched, and even with, or perhaps because of, the emotions flying around, Leoni imagined Aspen's fingers in other places all over her body. But her thoughts weren't of breathless declarations of lust and desperate grasps at each other's bodies. Instead, the touches were tender and slow, exploring rather than conquering, mapping rather than unseeing.

The oven timer beeped, and Aspen tended to her creation. Leoni enjoyed the simple act of watching her move about the kitchen, and her wandering mind watched Aspen making breakfast for them...on more than two mornings in a row, which was all she'd ever managed with anyone else.

Aspen returned to her seat. She picked up the wine bottle but stopped shy of topping up Leoni's glass. "I probably shouldn't be forcing alcohol on you after your painkillers earlier."

"You're probably right. I'd totally forgotten." Leoni pushed her drink away. "Better remove the temptation."

Aspen glanced at her briefly then pulled away the wine. "I'm sorry I upset you. I didn't mean to pry."

Leoni arched her eyebrow. "Yes, you did—mean to pry, not upset me. That would be mean, and you don't seem mean."

Aspen smiled widely. "No one's ever called me that. Nosey, yes, but not mean." She shrugged. "I guess I've always liked the deep and meaningful conversations more than shallow chit-chat."

"And I've always been the other way around."

"Because you prefer to keep people at a distance?"

Leoni shook her head. "There you go again."

"Sorry. I'll shut up." Aspen sat up straighter on her stool, increasing the distance between them slightly.

"It's okay, I'm only teasing." Leoni touched Aspen's arm. "But you're right. Like I said last night, I didn't think I was worthy of anyone's attention for the longest time."

"Is that why you didn't stick with the theater?" Aspen asked. "Standing up on stage is probably one of the best ways to demand attention."

Leoni inclined her head. "I guess I hadn't thought of it from that angle before. I did try for a few years in LA, but then I kind of fell into my current work and soon got used to a steady paycheck. When you've been as poor as I have, not living from hand-to-mouth can be quite seductive." She wagged a finger when Aspen's expression changed to one of pity. "Stop that. I don't want or need your sympathy." She looked away for a moment and sighed deeply. "Sorry. That came out a lot harsher than I intended. I get my stubborn pride from my mom. She never liked handouts and pity."

"It's okay," Aspen said softly. "What else do you get from your mom?"

"Wow, I don't think I've ever been asked this many personal questions."

"Not even from people who wanted to sleep with you?" Aspen's eyes widened as she clearly realized the implication of her question. "I didn't mean *I* wanted to sleep with you. Obviously. I just mean... The people that've wanted to..." She puffed out her cheeks and ran her hand through her hair. "Please put me out of my misery and tell me you know what I mean."

Under different circumstances, that would've been out of the question. There was little more amusing than watching an otherwise strong and confident woman flustered and tongue-tied. "*Obviously* you don't want to sleep with me," she said, unable to resist. "And there's never much talking when it comes to the people I briefly share a bed with."

Aspen frowned and looked like she might explode with embarrassment.

"I get my wicked sense of humor from my mom," Leoni said and smiled sweetly.

"Finally," Aspen slapped her hands on her thighs, "you throw the dog a bone."

"And I'm very careful with my money, like she is." Leoni gestured to the grandeur surrounding them. "Even if I was uber-rich, I don't think I could ever bring myself to buy a house like this. This kind of expression of wealth is overwhelming." She bit her lip, thinking she might've spoken out of turn. It wasn't something she would've said to Willow but given that Aspen had ostensibly eschewed her family's wealth, perhaps it'd be okay.

Aspen looked guilty. "Then it's probably a good thing that we don't have this vacation in Grandpa Bill and Grandma Eleanor's place in Southampton."

"Mm, old money," Leoni said, remembering that was where the family of Aspen's ex lived. "I can only imagine what that place is like. So does your family celebrate here for your benefit?"

Aspen shook her head. "No. This is Grammy and Gramps' house. Their side of the family lived in the Hamptons long before it became a billionaire's bolt hole. Their actual house was demolished, and this was rebuilt in its place a little while after Mom and Dad married. It was probably the first thing Dad did once he had access to the Hartwell family fortune."

"Is that why your mom has the rule about no joint bank accounts until you're married?" Leoni wiggled her eyebrows and smiled.

"Low blow." Aspen clutched her heart. "But no, I don't think so. Mom's never been worried about Dad's spending."

Wouldn't that be nice? She didn't voice the thought. Aspen wasn't like either of her parents in that way. "I guess I'm secretive like my mom too," she said, returning to Aspen's original question and to the topic that had made her rush out to the bathroom for refuge. "I don't like to talk about what I do for a living because it's not something I'm particularly proud of."

"You're a stockbroker, aren't you?"

Leoni laughed lightly and shook her head. "Oh no, I definitely couldn't lower myself to that level."

The oven timer went off again. Aspen slipped from her stool and grinned. "Saved by the bell."

After taking the chicken out of the oven, she passed Leoni a bottle of water without being asked. Leoni smiled at the simplicity and thoughtfulness of the gesture. What would it be like to date someone like Aspen? To really be taken care of and nurtured?

Aspen popped the chicken back on the top shelf. "Two more minutes until a taste explosion."

Leoni chuckled. "That's some claim. I hope your cooking can back it up."

Aspen rubbed her hands together. "I'm supremely confident it will." She was about to sit down again when her cell phone rang. She checked the screen. "I'm sorry, I have to take this. It's the retirement village client."

The enthusiasm in Aspen's voice swept Leoni up in the moment, and she edged off her seat as Aspen went to the far end of the kitchen to answer. Lots of "Yes, I understand," "No problem," and "Of course" didn't tell Leoni much, and Aspen's limited body language gave her nothing either. Leoni found herself creeping closer and closer to the window, strangely invested in the outcome. Just because she'd seen the final drawing and gotten caught up in Aspen's emotional tie-in? Or because of something else she didn't want to voice?

"Yes, sir. Absolutely." Aspen turned as she ended the call and jumped back slightly when she nearly ran straight into Leoni.

Then Leoni was wrapped in Aspen's arms, and she was spinning around and around, lifted from the floor like she weighed nothing.

"We've got it!" Aspen shouted. "We've got it." She lowered Leoni to her feet and stared deeply into her eyes without releasing her.

Leoni could barely breathe, but it wasn't because of the tight grip Aspen still held her in. Aspen's lips were so close. Her eyes so joyous. Her body, so strong, pressed against Leoni's.

Three inches separated Leoni from what her heart yelled at her to do. A finger's length between their lips and the promise of a firebrand kiss, of something extraordinary. An invisible connection fizzed and popped in the tiny space, drawing them together like opposing magnetic forces.

And then Aspen blinked repeatedly like she was waking from an enticing and too intense dream. "Willow," she whispered and released Leoni from her powerful embrace. "I can't..."

She backed away slowly at first, before she turned and rushed out of the kitchen. The oven timer sounded again, reinforcing the end of the moment of possibility, and Leoni sank into one of the couches by the window, her heart thundering against her chest and her lips tingling with the anticipation of Aspen's kiss.

A kiss that could never be.

Chapter Twenty

Aspen took two oxygen tanks from Flynn and loaded them onto the boat. When she came back for the rest, she glanced up at the dock, where Oakley, Kelly, and Willow were getting Leo fitted up with a wetsuit and flippers. Why it took all three of them, Aspen didn't know, but it gave her the opportunity to talk to Flynn alone. When the family had gotten back from the fishing trip—just after the phone call from Mancharlson and the near-kiss with Leo— Aspen had focused on the excitement of securing the project, and that's all they'd talked about over dinner. Aspen was desperate to talk to Flynn about the whole Leo situation. "How'd it go with Kelly yesterday?" she asked.

"I've been dying to tell you." Flynn's wide grin lit up her face. "It was amazing! She helped me cast lines, or whatever it is Grandpa Bill called it, and we caught a huge mahi-mahi together." She put her hands to her chest and looked up the gangway with a dopey expression. "She was so kind and patient with me."

Aspen shook Flynn's shoulders. "That's fantastic."

Flynn nodded like a bobblehead on a bumpy road. "And because she was teaching me stuff, she had to get close. A *lot*." She wiggled her eyebrows and grinned.

"And you didn't go weak at the knees and faint on her?"

"The first thing, yes. *Obviously*. But I managed to stay conscious." Flynn jumped on board and put her arm around Aspen's shoulders. "I'm crazy for her. I don't know what I'm going to do if she turns me down on Friday."

Aspen nudged Flynn's ribs. "Don't even *think* like that, let alone say it out loud. You've got to be positive and confident. People are attracted to that."

"Okay. Positive and confident," Flynn said. "I'll channel you."

Aspen shook her head. "No need. Just be the Flynn you are at work. Be the Flynn you are with other women."

Flynn dropped her arm from Aspen's shoulders and sat on the boat railing. "No can do. I told you, she's not like other women, and I want to be the best version of me for her."

"Then you don't have to do much, buddy." Aspen sat beside her. "You're an amazing person, and Kelly can see that. And I think there's been some signs that she feels the same."

Flynn frowned. "Really? When?"

"In the donut line. Before we left for kayaking. She's been throwing out some vibes too."

Flynn smiled and puffed her chest. "Do you think it's really going to happen?"

"I really do."

Flynn turned, her expression serious. "What's your brother making you do to keep our secret?"

Aspen waved the question away. "It doesn't matter what it is as long as he keeps his mouth shut. I'll do anything for you. You know that, right?"

Flynn pulled Aspen into an awkward, sitting half-hug. "I love you, Asp."

"I love you too."

They sat in silence for a minute, and Flynn stared along the dock toward Kelly. Aspen stared too, but her gaze fell on Leo as she went inside the shop to put on a wetsuit. Even from this distance, her enthusiasm was obvious. Willow looked happier than she'd seen her in a long time too, which made the warm glow of watching Leo ebb away into an ice bath. If Aspen didn't get a grip on her attraction, she was going to destroy that happiness along with the hope of rebuilding her relationship with Willow completely.

"I need to tell you something," Aspen said quietly. She felt so bad about the thoughts running through her head that she wasn't sure she wanted to voice them, but she'd shared everything with Flynn and vice versa for nearly twenty years. Why stop now?

Flynn turned her back to Kelly and the dock. "Is this about Leo?"

She nodded. Of course Flynn would already know. She'd warned Aspen off from the moment Leo had gotten out of her G-wagen last Saturday. But Aspen hadn't listened or, more accurately, she hadn't been able to stop herself from being pulled into Leo's mesmeric orbit.

Flynn rubbed her forehead with the heel of her hand. "Something happened while we were all out fishing, didn't it? Is that why Leo stayed in Willow's room all night? She was quiet in the car on the way here."

Aspen gave Flynn a quick rundown on the day from their late-night conversation over Aspen's drawing to going out to the beach and to the moment she returned to the kitchen after the near-kiss to find Leo had gone. "The thing is, she didn't pull away either. Like, maybe she feels it too. This is torture. Spending all this time together, getting to know her, watching her with Willow, and seeing Willow the happiest I've seen her since she was a kid." She doubled over and held her head in her hands. "I don't know what to do."

Flynn grumbled. "Yeah. You do know."

Aspen sat up and sighed. "I do."

"It's just three more days. Then she'll drive out of here on Saturday morning, and you won't have to see them together."

"Until Thanksgiving." Aspen closed her eyes at the futility of the situation.

"That's only for a long weekend, and there are a lot more people at that. All your grandparents' and parents' friends and close colleagues will dilute Leo's potency. And it's at Grandpa Bill and Grandma Eleanor's place, so there's more room to lose yourself. You'll probably only end up seeing them at the big dinner."

"Christmas. Birthdays. Easter." Aspen blew out a long breath. "It'll be never-ending."

Flynn patted Aspen's back. "But there'll be plenty of time in between all those events for you to meet someone else, especially now that you're over Sarah." She smiled and raised her eyebrow. "And if she and Willow don't work out..."

"I couldn't do that. Just like I wouldn't pursue any of your exes. There's a code."

Flynn shook her head. "Not for lesbians, there isn't."

"Really?" Aspen gestured toward Kelly, who was still waiting at the entrance to the shop. "So if Kelly turns you down on Friday, you wouldn't mind if I made a move?"

Flynn frowned. "That'd be different. I'm in love with Kelly, and I have been for years, probably since I met her. Willow isn't in love."

"You know that for sure, do you? Look how different she's been with Leo compared to all her short-term boyfriends. I haven't seen her smile this much since she was nine years old."

Flynn inclined her head. "I guess." She grasped Aspen's shoulder and squeezed. "I'm sorry, Asp. This sucks."

"It sucks the big one." Aspen heard footsteps thundering on the wooden gangway and looked up to see the four of them rushing toward the boat. Leo's wetsuit hugged her in places that Aspen wanted to touch, and her massive smile made Aspen smile in return. Behind Leo, Willow was actually running too, and her enthusiasm and glee seemed to match her girlfriend's. And that made Aspen so happy. Leo was obviously good for both of them, but Willow had gotten there first. So Aspen just had to suck it up and get over her. *No problem.*

Once they'd all boarded and stowed their gear, Aspen guided the boat out of the harbor, and she headed toward Shinnecock Inlet. They could've just driven there and parked close by, but last night, Willow had told Aspen how much Leo wanted to scuba dive, so she wanted to give her the full experience.

She'd just gotten halfway into Gardiner's Bay when Leo and Willow joined her at the helm. "Do you want to steer?" Aspen asked, hoping that if she acted like nothing had happened between them, she could convince herself to pass it off as nothing too.

Leo pointed to Gardiner's Island on the right and then Plum Island on the left up ahead of the boat. "Not when there's humungous land masses still in view."

Aspen chuckled. "You drive a giant G-wagen; you can't be worried about your motor skills."

"You'd be surprised," Leo said, her expression guarded. "But we didn't come up for that." She took Willow's hand and pulled her forward slightly.

Oh, crap. Had Leo told Willow what happened last night? Did she want Aspen to take responsibility and tell Willow it was all her? Why couldn't she have done this on dry land? But Aspen raised her eyebrow when she took in Willow's demeanor, like she was making herself smaller somehow, and she seemed to be lacking her usual resting-mean face. There was no sign of rage that Aspen had almost kissed her girlfriend either. "What's going on?"

Willow looked at her then back at Leo, almost as if she wanted her to rescue the situation. *What* situation?

"I...need your help," Willow finally said.

"Phew." Aspen blew out a breath and dropped into the captain's seat. "You scared me."

Leo frowned and gave her a warning look out of Willow's eyeline. *Message received: keep mouth shut.*

"You looked worried," Aspen said. "That's why I thought something was wrong. What can I help you with?"

Willow sat in a seat beside her. "I've found my passion."

Aspen stayed focused on Willow, though she wanted to look up at Leo, thinking that she'd found her passion too but couldn't do a damn thing about it. "What do you mean?" She'd heard so many ridiculous plans and schemes, none of which had developed into anything solid.

Willow took Leo's hand and smiled up at her. "Leo's been helping me figure out what I want to do with my life, and I know what that is now." She turned back to Aspen. "But I think I might need your knowledge."

Aspen blinked and bit back her immediate thought that Willow should be having this conversation with Gramps, who always backed her every whim. *But* Willow hadn't gone to him this time, so she deserved to be heard. And Aspen didn't want to throw up a roadblock to the progress they'd been making on their relationship. "Okay. What do you need to know?"

"I want to surprise Mom at the party on Friday," Willow said, "but I've got to do some planning first."

Aspen's high hopes sank like a stone. This was already starting to sound like another scheme. She glanced at Leo, whose expression seemed to implore Aspen to keep an open mind. Obviously, Aspen wasn't doing so well on her poker face, because Leo had picked up on her skepticism. "Planning is good," she said and nodded.

Willow shifted in her seat and gave Aspen a cautious smile. "I want to study marine biology, but there are so many colleges that offer it as a science major, and I don't know where to start."

Aspen cut the engine to focus all of her attention on her sister. "You want to do what?"

Willow jumped up out of her seat. "I told you this was a bad idea."

"Hey now." Leo grasped Willow's wrist and halted her escape. "It was just a question."

Willow spun around and glared at Aspen. "No, it wasn't. She isn't taking me seriously."

"What's happening?" Oakley called up from the lower deck.

Aspen leaned around the canopy. "It's nothing bad. I just need a minute."

"Do you want me to take over?"

"Nope. We'll be on our way soon enough," Aspen said. "Just relax."

Oakley shrugged. "Okay. *That* I can do." He turned and flopped back onto a sunbed beside Kelly.

Flynn started to get up from her chair, but Aspen shook her head and gave her the thumbs up. She turned back to Willow and put her hands on Willow's shoulders. "I *am* taking you seriously. You just surprised me, that's all. You've never mentioned wanting to go back to school." She smiled. "I think it's really exciting news, and I'd love to help you."

"Yay! That's amazing." Willow gave a big smile.

"We can go back now and get started if you like," Leo said.

Willow pulled Leo closer. "No way. You really wanted to do this, and I want to make it happen."

Aspen wished she was still sitting down. The self-involved flake that she'd seen her sister develop into was crumbling away with every second she spent with Leo. Aspen couldn't recall an instance where Willow had actively chosen to do something that someone else wanted to do over her own priorities. "How about we do both? Oakley can get us around to the diving area while we go to the lower deck and get some ideas on paper."

Willow frowned. "But I've brought my iPad."

"It's a figure of speech," Aspen said.

They headed down to the lower deck, and Aspen promoted Oakley to captain.

"Do you need help with anything?" Flynn asked.

"Nope, we've got it." Aspen gestured to their surroundings. "Just enjoy the ride."

Flynn's grin couldn't have gotten any bigger when she clearly realized that left her alone with Kelly. Willow led the way into the living room, and Aspen grabbed three bottles of water from the fridge before she joined them at the table. As she sat down, she remembered some of Leo's words at her drawing table on Monday night. "Your Willow *is the one who feels abandoned. You went off to college and didn't look back... like you couldn't wait to get away from the family, from her.*" Now seemed like as good a time as any to begin disabusing Willow of that notion. It should've been too private a conversation to have in front of someone she'd only met five days ago, but it was Leo's insights that had led Aspen here.

Aspen touched Willow's arm to get her attention. "Before we get started, I need to tell you something."

Leo's eyes widened slightly, but she stayed silent. They obviously needed to have a conversation so Aspen could explain she had no intention of telling Willow about it or pursuing Leo in any way.

"I need to tell you that I love you," Aspen said and immediately began to second-guess her decision to do this in front of Leo.

Willow frowned. "What?"

"Mm," Leo pushed back in her chair, "I should go."

Willow placed her hand over Leo's. "Please don't."

"If you're sure," Leo said.

Willow nodded, and guilt yanked on Aspen's heart hard. Her little sister *was* still there, and she needed love. And Leo was giving it to her, even though she'd said it wasn't that. But Aspen had been all but absent for the past fifteen years, too busy with ambitions to forge her own path to notice that her little sister had lost her way. "I've gotten caught up in my own life—getting my degree, starting a business, making it successful—and I've neglected you because of it. I never meant to. I never should've lost sight of my little sister. But I did. And I'm so sorry for that."

Tears edged Willow's eyes, and her chin trembled slightly. "You still love me?"

God, what have I done? She reached across the table for Willow's other hand and squeezed it. "Of course I do. I'm sorry for making you feel like I don't."

"But you never come home anymore. The only time I see you is at this vacation and family events that Mom won't let you miss."

Aspen nodded. "I know. And that's wrong. I'll change it, I promise." She smiled and wiped away the falling tear from Willow's cheek. "I'll visit you in college. And you can come stay with me on breaks."

"I'll stick with it this time," Willow said through the tears that were falling freely. "I really want to do this, and I'll make you proud."

Aspen stood and pulled Willow into a tight hug. "I know you will." She opened her eyes and looked down at Leo, who was smiling back at her. But there was something behind her expression, a sadness that seemed out of place. What was she thinking? Did she feel the same connection Aspen did? Was she wondering what could've been if she'd met Aspen instead of Willow?

Aspen closed her eyes again and concentrated on holding her little sister, who had begun to sob in her arms. They were on track to rebuild their relationship, and that was all down to the woman who had also somehow positioned herself between them. But Willow didn't know that, and she could never know that. Aspen just had to be the big sister and ignore her own wanting heart.

Chapter Twenty-One

LEONI PULLED THE COMFORTER up to her chest and closed her eyes. It had been a wonderful day, and the scuba diving experience had surpassed anything she'd thought it could be. The still peacefulness deep under the ocean had been almost spiritual. It was a church Leoni could see herself worshipping at regularly, *if* she didn't live in the middle of a desert. And there was the small matter of funding a hobby like that.

"Is something wrong, Leo?" Willow asked. "I thought you'd be buzzing."

"I am. It was so beautiful, I guess I've been struck a little dumb by it all." *Shit.* This was clearly the downside of letting someone get close. It made it harder to hide what she was thinking and feeling.

Willow sighed deeply as she got into her bed. "I know what you mean. It really is amazing to be that close to something so beautiful."

"I can see why you want to be a marine biologist. I didn't realize scallops had eyes. That blue was so vibrant." She gestured to Willow's and said, "Like yours," but she was thinking of Aspen's eyes and of how close they'd been to each other in the water. Especially when the fin on Leoni's right foot began to rub, and she thought her toenail was being ripped off. Aspen had been the one who'd spotted she was in trouble and had come to her rescue. Leoni's toenails were actually fine, but Aspen checked on her periodically for the rest of their dive, and once again, Leoni enjoyed the feeling of being looked after.

"I don't think I'm going to get much sleep tonight." Willow switched on the bedside lamps and the fairy lights running around the ceiling.

"Too excited?" Leoni asked, glad for the change of topic. She hadn't had time to analyze what she was feeling, and she didn't particularly want to explore it with Willow. She'd be happier taking this friendship thing a little slower. These last five days with both sisters had whipped her up into a tornado of new emotions and vulnerabilities, and she needed some quiet time to figure out an exit strategy, before the storm inevitably and unceremoniously dumped her on her ass when it ended.

"Yeah." Willow sat up and created a pillow tower behind her, indicating this was only the beginning of the conversation. "I want to thank you again for all your help this week. You've changed my life."

Leoni laughed gently, a little taken aback by the sincerity in Willow's tone. It wasn't a throwaway, casual line at all, and Willow's soft smile pulled at Leoni's heartstrings. "You're a bright woman. You would've figured it out soon enough."

Willow shook her head. "I'm not sure that's true—the figuring out part, not the bright part. That *is* true." She smiled again. "You came into my life and pushed me to see things with a different perspective. To see lots of things with fresh eyes, I guess." She drew her knees up to her chest and hugged them. "I just couldn't see anything changing, but in less than a week, you've focused my career path, repaired my relationship with Aspen, and become a close friend. It's huge, Leo. I can't tell you how much I appreciate what you've done...and what you've already come to mean to me."

Leoni tugged her scrunchie off and shook out her hair, avoiding the intense eye contact Willow was throwing her way. So much for hitting pause on the emotion-swirling. "It's been an intense few days," she said. "I've shared more about myself with you and your sister than I have with anyone else in years." It wasn't years. It was *ever*. She'd opened up quicker than an oyster being shucked, but the pearl of who she was inside hadn't been stolen. It'd been left in place and nurtured.

Willow raised her eyebrow. "Like yesterday, when everyone else went on the fishing trip?"

Leoni nodded, though she'd almost shared far more than words when they'd been alone. She couldn't decide if she felt guilty about not telling her new *close* friend about it.

"But you'd like more than friendship with Aspen, wouldn't you?"

Leoni smiled, unable to stop herself from picturing Aspen in her wetsuit, peeled halfway down and exposing her strong shoulders and arms. But that image morphed into Aspen preparing their dinner last night, and a ridiculously fuzzy warmth spread through her like a reverse and far more pleasant shiver. "I wouldn't say no if it was offered."

Willow threw back her comforter and flopped full-length onto her front. She steepled her fingers under her chin. "What if we could make that happen?"

Leoni chuckled at the child-like glee in Willow's expression. "And how are *we* going to do that?"

"I don't think it's going to be that hard, honestly," Willow said. "I was going to tell everyone we'd broken up and decided to be friends anyway. After that, it's just about putting you two in the same room and letting fate take its course."

"Fate?" Sure, there was an undeniable connection, but *fate* might be pushing it.

"Yes. Fate. Don't be so closed off."

Leoni laughed. "That's all I'd ever been until I got here! But you two..."

"See? Fate." Willow grinned.

"You're going to be a scientist," Leoni said. "You're not supposed to believe in things that can't be tested and proven."

"You've changed my life, and we can change yours—if you let things take their course."

Leoni smiled and inclined her head. "So you're saying that me coming into your lives is some kind of destiny? And the Universe gave Tyler COVID—"

"Who's Tyler?"

"The very hot butch woman who was supposed to be here with you for the week."

"Oh, right."

"So the Universe gave her COVID and somehow convinced my boss to send me, a high femme, in her place just so I could alter the course of your life?"

Willow nodded. "And yours."

At least in the moment, her life *was* changed. "And mine." Leoni shrugged. "Maybe you're on to something."

Willow wiggled her eyebrows and looked smug. "So you agree we should put the new plan into motion?"

"I'm going back to Vegas on Saturday, and you'll be heading off to college. That doesn't put me in Aspen's orbit." Leoni had to battle hard not to be caught up in the excitement of Willow's whirlwind. It sounded almost viable, but she had to be realistic.

"You heard Aspen today. She's going to make more of an effort to see me, so we make sure you're visiting at the same time."

Leoni smiled. "That sounds great." She didn't want to ruin Willow's mood by pointing out the realities of her own life. There was really no way Leoni could hope to visit Willow more than twice a year. She couldn't take that many vacation days, and she couldn't afford to spend her hard-earned cash on endless flights. Aspen and Willow had gotten her thinking about her own career, and she intended to think about it some more when she got home, but really, how likely was it for her to make it to Broadway now? Hadn't she left it too late?

There was a quick knock on Willow's door before it swung open, and Aspen burst in with a huge smile on her face. "I've got great news," she said. "I put out some feelers, and an old college buddy just—" Her gaze traveled to Leoni tucked into her makeshift bed in the corner of the room, and she frowned. "What's going on? Have you two had a fight?"

Leo said no more or less at the same time as Willow said yes.

Aspen's frown deepened, and she closed the door behind her quietly. "It's not a good sign if you can't even agree on whether you've been fighting or not."

Willow looked at Leoni, clearly panicked. "We're not fighting, are we?"

Leoni pulled the comforter high up around her shoulders. "Nope."

Aspen motioned between the two sleeping arrangements. "So you haven't been sharing a bed this whole time?"

Leoni sighed and wanted the beanbags to absorb her into them. She wanted no part of this potential mess, so she stayed quiet and waited for Willow to answer in case their answers didn't match once again.

"It's complicated," Willow said. "You wouldn't understand."

Aspen glanced at Leoni, then she walked across the room and sat on the edge of Willow's bed. Leoni sighed. Aspen had clearly taken their Monday night conversation to heart and was intent on repairing her relationship with her sister, and she probably saw this as another step on that pathway. It would've been sweet and endearing, heart-warming even, if it didn't mean that she was about to discover their deception. And even though it was Willow's duplicity and Leoni was simply providing a service, somehow Leoni had wanted to be the one to tell Aspen about it, to absolve her of any guilt or judgment. But it was in Willow's hands now, and there was nothing she could do to control the situation.

Aspen gave Willow a gentle smile. "Try me, little sis."

Leoni curled her toes when she saw the relief in Willow's eyes. It was obvious she *wanted* to tell Aspen what was really going on. Leoni fought against the instinct to remind Willow that only a few days ago, she hadn't wanted to tell anyone about her elaborate web of lies, even her treasured Gramps and Grammy, but the last shred of professionalism she'd been hanging onto reminded *her* that wasn't her place. And a lot had changed in that short time. But how much easier would it be to stick to their plan of splitting quietly and becoming friends? Then no one would get hurt. *No one meaning me.*

Willow bit her lip and looked across at Leoni. "Do I tell her?"

Leoni sighed. *Please don't put this on me*, she wanted to yell. Everything had gotten so complicated. She was supposed to be Willow's friend now too, so her advice should be in Willow's best interests, not Leoni's selfish ones.

"Tell me what?" Aspen glanced at Leoni, searching for clues.

Damn it. Doing the right thing sucked the big one. "I think you want your old relationship with your sister back, so you already know the answer, Wills."

Willow suddenly grinned. "Wills?"

Leoni shrugged. "Just trying it out."

"I like it!"

Aspen cleared her throat. "Whatever it is, you can tell me."

Willow's grin fell away, and she looked like a puppy desperate to be loved. "You have to promise not to get mad at me."

"Okay," Aspen said slowly.

Willow pushed up into a sitting position and crossed her arms. "Promise?"

Aspen made the motion across her heart. "I promise."

Leoni shook her head, not believing it was one Aspen would be able to keep once she heard the truth.

"Leo isn't my girlfriend." Willow gave a theatrical sigh. "Oh God, that felt good to say out loud." She patted her bed. "No offense, Leo."

"None taken," Leoni muttered, more interested in Aspen's reaction, which, if her expression was anything to go by, looked like relief and not a small amount of joy. Maybe Leoni's pessimism had been misplaced.

"Why are you pretending that she is?" Aspen asked.

"That's a long story," Willow said and smiled, clearly thinking her confession was going well so far.

Aspen raised her eyebrow and gave the hint of a smile. "I have time."

"Okay," Willow said, and then she launched into the long and winding tale of how the family's neglect had "literally forced" her into a last-ditch attempt to be seen by their mom.

The way Willow told it made it almost seem like a reasonable progression and a logical step to hoodwink the family, but the look on Aspen's face indicated she didn't see it in quite the same light.

"So you're not queer at all?" Aspen asked. "And that's why you've only been holding hands with Leo, and why you aren't even sharing the same bed?"

"Not even a little bit gay," Willow said and looked as rueful about that as she had when Leoni had tested the theory, "which was a bit disappointing actually."

"And you two are just friends?"

Leoni huddled deeper into the comforter at the hopeful note in Aspen's voice. Could she dare to share Willow's optimism that this might actually work out for all three of them?

"We are now," Willow said brightly.

Aspen's eyes narrowed. "What does that mean?"

Willow shrugged. "We got off to a bit of a rough start on Saturday because Leo wasn't who I ordered."

And I'm back to being take-out. More worryingly than that, though, was Aspen's darkening expression.

"Who you 'ordered'?"

Even from her vantage point across the room, Leoni could clearly see Aspen's jaw clenching repeatedly.

"Uh-huh," Willow said, still somehow blissfully unaware of the gathering storm cloud over Aspen's head. "From a company called Perfect Fit." She smiled widely. "And she's been exactly that. Look how well she's fitted into our family."

Aspen's nose flared. "Let me get this straight: you didn't know her until five days ago. You've let a complete stranger into the house without any background checks, and you paid for the privilege?"

Willow scratched absently at her ear. "The *company* did the background check, silly."

"And who did the background check on the company?"

Willow wrinkled her nose. "There was no need for that. They came highly recommended from a number of families."

Aspen scoffed. "I bet they did. How much?"

Willow laughed lightly. "Oh, you don't want to know that. You couldn't afford her, that's for sure."

Leoni closed her eyes and took a deep breath that felt anything but cleansing. Willow's explanation made it all sound so *dirty*.

"This is insane." Aspen shook her head. "I could get on board with you feeling neglected and unseen by me and Mom. I don't really understand why you thought a girlfriend would fix that, but I get that you've been trying lots of things to see what stuck. But hiring a prostitute and inviting her into our *home—*"

Willow pouted. "You promised not to get mad."

"Hey now," Leoni said, "I'm not a sex worker. We don't even allow kissing, which is why—"

"Be quiet, *Leo*, or whatever your name is," Aspen said, her lip curling in obvious disgust, then she refocused on Willow. "When I made that promise, I had no idea you could've done something so careless and," she gave Leoni's another disdainful look, "distasteful."

"You're overreacting," Willow said. "And there's no need to be so mean to Leo. She's just doing her job."

Aspen raised her eyebrows. "Mean? If you think *I'm* being mean, let's go tell Mom and see what her reaction is." She pushed off the bed and headed to the door.

"If you tell Mom about Leo, I'll tell her about your engagement to Sarah and how she ran off with all your money."

Oh, crap. Leoni hadn't anticipated Willow resorting to blackmail. She was too busy worrying about how she was supposed to tell Ruth everything had gone to hell when she had to come back early.

Aspen stopped dead, her hand grasping the doorknob, and then she turned slowly. "Are you serious?"

Willow nodded. "I'm going to tell Mom everything on Friday

before the party. I want her to know, but I want to tell her on my terms. She shouldn't hear it from my big sister snitching on me."

Aspen glared across at Leoni. "That doesn't mean *she* has to stay."

Leoni held up her hands. "Don't worry. I can leave first thing in the morning."

"No, you won't." Willow slammed her hand onto her bed. "Leo is my friend, and she's done more for me in five days than anyone in this family has done for me in the past ten years. I want her here, and I need her here. She stays, and that's non-negotiable."

Aspen clenched her jaw and shook her head. "Fine. Just keep her out of my way." She grasped the door handle again.

"What was the great news from your old college buddy?" Willow asked.

Aspen's shoulders dropped. "She works at Stony Brook, and she's offered to give you a tour of the facilities tomorrow. It's one of the top-five best colleges to study marine biology, and it's only an hour away." She glanced briefly at Leoni. "*She* should stay here."

Willow jutted her chin. "No. She comes with, or I don't go."

Leoni fiddled with a strand of her hair. "It's okay, Wills. I'll just stay in your room. I can say that I don't feel well."

Aspen huffed. "Because it's so much easier to lie, right?"

Leoni swallowed and looked away, unable to bear the rejection in Aspen's eyes.

"I want you to come with me," Willow said. "I wouldn't even be thinking about college if it wasn't for you. I'd really like your support."

"Fine. But she rides in the back and keeps quiet."

"She's not a dog, Aspen. You should bring Flynn. She can ride in the front with you, and we'll ride in the back."

Aspen sighed deeply and pulled open the door. "Whatever. Just be ready to leave at nine."

Aspen pulled the door closed behind her but stopped short of slamming it. She may as well have. She could have stuck Leoni's heart in the doorjamb and slammed the door shut. That couldn't pain her more than the look in Aspen's eyes. Hurt, betrayal, sorrow. It was all there. And it was only there because of Leoni.

She pulled the comforter over her head and sank into its darkness, wishing she'd never taken this damn job in the first place.

Chapter Twenty-Two

ASPEN SMASHED THE AVOCADO far more forcefully than she needed to, but her rage required an outlet. Better this than busting her hands open on the punching bag downstairs, since slinging weights for two hours had done nothing. What the hell had she been thinking? Of course Leo, or whatever her name *really* was, was too good to be true. Because she was *acting*. Playing a part just like she'd learned to in musical theater school. Except that was probably a lie too. *Everything* had been a lie, and Aspen had fallen for it, just like she'd fallen for Sarah and all the other wrong women before her.

Her mom was right: it was hard to find someone who had genuine feelings for them, because most everyone else just saw dollar signs instead of the person. Her mom had been lucky with her dad, although he was prone to being a spendthrift, but Aspen and her siblings stood no chance of ever finding a real connection based on their personalities. Unless they swam in their own uber-rich pool... Aspen had tried that with Sarah and still drowned.

She slammed the fork down and took a breath. This was stupid, and Willow was right: she *was* overreacting. Leo hadn't come into the house looking to seduce Aspen, clearly, but she *had* almost kissed her. And it'd been Aspen who had pulled away and not let it happen. *Damn it*. Where was Flynn? She was usually on her second cup of coffee by now. Aspen needed her counsel.

Her mom came into the kitchen and gave her a quizzical look. "I can hear you in the library, honey." She peered into the bowl Aspen was working with. "What did the avocado do to you to deserve *that*?"

Aspen shrugged. "It's called smashed avocado, Mom."

Her mom pressed her lips together tightly and gave Aspen the *mom face*. "Don't be facetious, darling."

"Sorry." The seeded sourdough popped up in the toaster. Aspen smeared the avocado onto the two slices and topped it with the poached eggs, then she dropped onto a stool to dig in.

Her mom poured a cup of coffee then sat beside Aspen. "Has something happened with your retirement village project?"

"No." She brightened at the thought, if only for a moment. "That's perfect. The client can't wait to get started. He's submitted the plans for final approval, and once they're in place, we can break ground."

Her mom sipped her coffee, looking over her cup at Aspen. She tried to ignore the scrutiny and shoveled a forkful of food into her mouth.

Her mom put her hand on Aspen's forearm. "You'll give yourself indigestion. Are you in a hurry?"

Aspen glanced at her watch. "Not really. Willow isn't even up yet." She couldn't bring herself to refer to Leo.

"Are you all doing something together again today?"

Aspen swallowed and looked at her mom. She was mad at Willow and Leo for lying, and now they'd dragged her into it. "Yeah, the four of us are going to a matinee in New York."

"Oakley and Kelly aren't going with you?" her mom asked.

Aspen shook her head and didn't offer a reason, wishing she'd just made coffee and gone back to her room. She hated lying, especially to her mom, and there was no way she wanted to involve her brother and Kelly in the deception. She was still undecided as to whether she'd tell Flynn what was going on.

"It's nice to see you two getting along so well again."

"Uh-huh." Aspen stuffed another big forkful into her mouth. That *had* been nice, and it was another thing Leo had been responsible for, along with igniting Willow's motivation to do something with her life. But it had all been a lie, and Leo was just keeping herself busy while she played everyone bar Willow. And maybe she'd been lying to her too. How could their friendship be real when it had started out as a business transaction?

"Aspen, I feel like I'm having a conversation with a teenager."

Aspen shrugged. "Hot food, Mom. Eggs get cold quick, and then I can't eat them. And I worked out hard this morning."

"Mm. I heard that too. You were clanging those weights around like church bells," her mom said. "So if it isn't a work problem that's making you like this, what is it?"

Aspen frowned. "Like what? I'm just eating breakfast after a tough workout. What's the big deal?"

Her mom pursed her lips. "That's what I'm trying to find out if you'd stop obfuscating. Why would you actively spend time with Leo if it's hard for you?"

Aspen dropped her fork to her plate. "Why do you think it's hard for me?" It'd been hard because she'd wanted it so much. Now it was going to be hard because Leo's lies were still papercut-fresh, and proximity would be like squeezing lemon juice onto them.

Her mom shook her head slowly. "I *know* you. You're an extension of my heart."

Aspen pushed her plate away and turned in her seat to look at her mom. "Like you've seen, Willow and I are working on our relationship. Leo is her girlfriend, so that means she's going to be around. It doesn't matter how I feel about Leo, whether I like her or not." Though she strangely harbored both of those emotions right now.

"But you do like her, don't you?" her mom asked. "There's a fizz in the air between the two of you."

Flynn and Kelly burst into the kitchen from the outer door, both of them bleeding sweat, and Flynn gasping for breath.

Aspen was always happy to see Flynn, but her timing couldn't have been any better right now. "Have you been *running*?"

Flynn bent over double and looked like she was trying to answer but couldn't quite gather the oxygen required to breathe, let alone talk.

Kelly grinned and rubbed Flynn's back. "She said she was thinking of training for the New York half-marathon next March, so I offered to assess her fitness and build a running program for her." She shrugged. "It's safe to say that we've got a long way to go. It's good we're starting now."

Aspen struggled to contain her stunned laughter and simply nodded.

Flynn managed to straighten up. "I was thinking of raising money for PFLAG," she said, looking at Aspen. "Remember?"

"I do." She didn't. "You wanted me to do it with you, but I remember telling you that I only run if I'm running away from someone or toward something," she said, parroting Flynn's excuse for not running with Aspen on the rare occasion she did.

Her mom frowned. "I thought you enjoyed running?"

Aspen shook her head. "Not since I got that cyst in the back of my knee." That part *was* true. "Anyway," she said and tapped her watch, "we should both shower and get ready." She put her arm around Flynn's shoulder, and they headed out of the kitchen.

"Get ready for what?" Kelly asked. "Oakley was stoked for some off-roading."

Aspen stopped at the door. Zipping around the dunes all day in Betty would have to wait. "We're going to see a Broadway show, but Willow said she could only get four tickets," she said, hating the tangled web she was being forced to weave. "You should go ask her." She rushed out of the kitchen and pulled her phone from her pocket to text Willow as they went upstairs. They hadn't liaised on an excuse, and Aspen had just said the first thing that had come into her head. Willow would have to take care of the fallout.

"You know this is messed up, don't you?" Flynn asked when they got to the top of the stairs.

"About as messed up as pretending to be a budding marathon runner, yeah, I do know."

Flynn kissed her teeth. "I'm going to tell Kelly how *I* feel. You can't say the same."

"It doesn't matter about those feelings anymore," Aspen said. "And none of this is my fault. I'd rather Leo went home and Willow come clean, but this is Willow's crapshoot, and I'm letting her handle it."

"Okay, okay." Flynn put her hand on Aspen's shoulder. "I'm sorry it's worked out like this."

"Thanks, buddy." Aspen headed toward her room. "Maybe a shower will wash away the malaise." She cleaned up and changed without putting too much thought into any of it, just wanting to be on autopilot for a while. But everything came flooding back when she went outside to her truck, and Willow and Leo were already there waiting in the back seat. Flynn jumped in the passenger seat moments later, and they headed out toward the university.

After a couple of miles of total silence, Aspen met Willow's eyes in the rearview. "Did you handle Kelly and Oakley?"

"Yes."

Aspen blew out a breath. Two steps backward then. She would've thought agreeing to keep Willow's secret might've won her a few sister points.

"What did you tell them?" Flynn asked.

"That we were going on a triple date with two of Leo's friends after the show, and they'd just cramp your style."

Flynn spun around in her seat. "You said what?"

Willow frowned. "I think you heard me just fine. What's the problem?"

Aspen nudged Flynn's shoulder and shook her head slightly.

"Nothing," Flynn said and faced the road again.

Aspen cranked up the stereo, and she and Flynn spent the rest of the journey murdering every song that came on the radio. If it hadn't been for the occasional glare from Willow and lost look from Leo, Aspen could almost have forgotten what was going on.

She drove onto the campus, and Jess met them in the parking lot.

"It's been too long." Jess flung her arms around Aspen and

Flynn and smiled widely. "And you must be little Willow. Aspen talked about you *all* the time in college. You sounded like a perfect little angel."

Willow glanced at Aspen and gave her a small smile. Maybe there was still hope to salvage their relationship even after this mess.

"My wife's a professor at the Dental Medicine college. We're going to swing by and pick her up, then we can go on the unofficial tour." Jess winked. "First though, I need to drop you three off at the East Side Dining facility."

"They can't come around with us?" Willow asked.

Jess shook her head. "It's best that it's just you. We don't want to draw too much attention to ourselves. All of this has to be a little under the radar." She tapped her nose. "The college doesn't want everyone knowing that they allow the occasional old family favor, if you know what I mean."

Willow nodded then she moved closer to Aspen. "Thank you," she whispered. "I know you don't like using the family name for anything, but especially for something like this."

"I'll do whatever it takes to help you," Aspen said. "I'm sorry I didn't help you find your true north before."

Willow wrapped her arm around Aspen's waist. "You're helping me now, and that's all that matters."

Jess motioned for them all to follow her, and she led them to the cafeteria.

"Nice building," Aspen said, appreciating the mainly glass construction and the curving roof reaching for the sky. It seemed like a nice metaphor for what her little sister was trying to do.

"I think you'd like the West Side Dining building more," Jess said, "but it's on Circle. This place is closer and has more options in case we're gone longer than expected." She touched Willow's arm. "There's lots to see, and we might get caught up in it."

Aspen, Flynn, and Leo took a table, and Jess put her arm through Willow's. "Right then, little angel. Let's take a look at your future."

Willow's eyes brightened, and she smiled widely. God, it was good to see her so free and happy. But then Aspen caught Leo's gaze, and her own smile fell away at the reminder of the intruder. "Have fun," she said and watched them walk out of the food court, already laughing and deep in conversation.

"Iron Waffles? Yes, please. Coffee?" Flynn asked, but she was out of her chair and heading away without waiting for a response.

"We should talk," Leo said.

"No, we shouldn't. There's nothing to talk about." Aspen took her phone out and scrolled through her emails, hoping Leo would just leave her alone. The sleepless night she'd had, the conversations with her mom and Flynn, and her own swirling thoughts had done nothing to help Aspen figure out how she felt about the whole situation. Some distance and alone time would be the only way she could work through everything that had happened over the past six days. Right now, her heart and mind were like the lotto machine, with all her emotions bouncing balls inside it. Leo had just pulled anger, and Aspen had no idea which one would come out next.

"I wanted to tell you, but it wasn't my place."

"I need some air." Aspen pushed up from the table and headed for the door, unable to bear being so close to Leo. She was confusing *everything*.

She emerged from the cool air-conditioned building and turned her face up to the clear blue sky. The heat of the sun spread across her face, chest, and arms, and she drew in a long breath through her nose. Two more days, and then she'd be back to work, with this vacation a fading memory. She heard footsteps come up behind her and assumed it would be Flynn.

"Just go back inside and keep her company. I can't be anywhere near her right now."

"Can we please just talk about it?"

Aspen's shoulders sagged, and she turned to face Leo, steadying herself for her reaction to Leo's proximity. Beyond the anger, her beauty was still undeniable, as was the way she made Aspen *feel*. But she had to get over that. "What would be the point? You'll be gone in two days, and we'll never see each other again... Unless I wanted to pay you to spend time with me, of course. Would I get to choose your name? Can it be whatever I want it to be?"

Leo flinched a little, and her expression spoke of an intense sadness. But that wasn't Aspen's problem or her responsibility.

"My name is Leoni," she said. "We just shortened it. And Willow and I have become good friends, so you probably will see me again. That's one of the reasons we should talk."

"There's more than one?" Of course there was. Their connection... If it had even been real. "Ah, is it about you conning my parents and my whole family? Do you actually feel remorse about that?"

Leo sighed. "It's not a con. I'm not trying to extort money, and it's not a scam. Your sister was tired of being in your shadow, and she had no idea how to get out from under it to make your mom see her. But more than that, she wanted *you* to see her again. She's still a kid, really, and she acted out, that's all."

Aspen shoved her hands in her pockets and shrugged. "You were still being paid as part of this whole deception. How am I supposed to trust you after that?"

"Because it's just a job, Aspen. Next week, I'll be some other client's way of getting a nagging parent off their back or proving a point to a shitty colleague."

"So that's your job? You become the girlfriend for *anyone* who pays enough, and you lie about your life for a living." She took a deep breath. She *had* to know. "Was *any* of it real?" she asked, gesturing between the two of them. "Did I imagine it? Or did you play me just for fun so you and Willow could have a good laugh about me falling for you?" She closed her eyes and clamped her mouth shut. Too much. She'd said too much.

Leo touched Aspen's forearm and took a step closer. "It was real. It *is* real. These jobs don't change who I am on the inside or what I feel for someone. I avoided answering questions about what I do for a living, and I only lied about my relationship with Willow. Everything else was all me. My parents, my history, my college dreams. All me."

Damn, Aspen wanted to believe her. And what reason would Leo have to lie? But that wasn't the point. Aspen didn't know *what* the point was, and she needed time away from Leo to figure it out. She shook her head. "How am I supposed to believe any of that?"

Leo took Aspen's face in her hands gently. "Believe this," she said and pressed her lips to Aspen's.

For a blissful moment, the feeling of Leo's mouth on hers, her warmth, the buzz zipping through her like an electrical current... Everything was just as perfect as she'd imagined it would be over and over every night and day since Leo had walked into her life, and all of it conspired to wipe her mind clean of the complications.

But it was only a moment. She took Leo's shoulders and pulled back.

Leo looked at Aspen and smiled. "Tell me that didn't feel as real to you as it did to me."

Aspen backed away slowly. Of course it felt real. Of course it was perfect. But it didn't blow up the wall of lies between them. "Tell Flynn I'll wait in the car," she said and walked away.

She didn't look back. She couldn't. The look in Leo's eyes would dissolve her resilience if she saw it again. She reminded herself she was here to support Willow. Just Willow, and not her "for-hire girlfriend." And then the realization hit her. Even if she could get past the lies and convince herself to believe that, moving forward, Leo would be honest, it didn't change the fact that Leo was still a body for hire. That was the career she'd chosen over trying to pursue her acting dreams.

How could Aspen be with someone who spent their days and nights being other people's pretend partner?

She couldn't. Her mind and heart might currently be in complete conflict and confusion, but that was one thing Aspen knew for certain. She wouldn't be anyone's second best. Not again.

Chapter Twenty-Three

THE CINNAMON ROLL WAFFLE beat Leoni before she was halfway through, and she used the last of her coffee to wash it down. Her appetite had left along with Aspen, but when she'd returned to the table, Flynn had already loaded it with three different kinds of waffle and looked so happy that Leoni couldn't bring herself to disappoint her.

"Are you sure I shouldn't have gone after her?" She couldn't quite believe that Flynn hadn't followed Aspen to her truck either, but what did Leoni know about handling Aspen when she was upset? Or angry, and that one scared her a little, though the veneer of rage was thin, and her pain was easily visible behind it.

"Trust me, I'm sure," Flynn said after she'd finished her mouthful of waffle. "Aspen doesn't get angry often, but when she does, it's best to leave her alone to calm down." She shrugged. "Whenever she's dealing with strong emotions, whatever they are, she likes to do it solo."

Leoni didn't know if that surprised her or not. When she and Aspen had engaged in deep conversation, it'd been Leoni who struggled to share, not Aspen. But that wasn't in the heat of the moment, she supposed. "How long does it usually take her to calm down?"

Flynn gave a wry smile. "I won't be expecting any conversation on the way back to the beach house. When she gets like this, she becomes the epitome of the strong, silent type."

"Do you think she'll ever forgive me?" Leoni was going home in two days and could simply put this job to the back of her mind, but somehow she knew that wasn't going to be possible, not least because she and Willow were friends now, and that meant making the effort to stay in touch. How was Leoni supposed to talk to Willow without asking how her hot sister was doing—and if she was seeing anyone? Someone who didn't lie to her about who she was.

Flynn inclined her head and frowned. "Remember who you're talking to, Leo. I'm not going to answer questions like that. Aspen is my best friend, and I'm not going to do or say anything that might risk that friendship or worse, hurt her." She stabbed at a piece of waffle. "She's only just gotten over Sarah, and that was hard on her. Really hard."

Leoni nodded. "I really like her, Flynn. We've got a connection, and that's something I've never had before. I don't want to just give up and let it go."

Flynn stared at Leoni as if she were studying her or looking for something very particular. "Then don't," she said after a long period of silence.

Leoni swallowed, and hope fired up in her heart. That was enough, and she wouldn't push Flynn further. Those two words gave her enough to hang onto, and she had two more days to convince Aspen to give her a chance.

Willow burst in through a side door and rushed over to the table, grinning widely. Aspen's friend Jess followed at a more sedate pace, but her smile told a story too.

"I have *got* to come here." Willow sat down beside Leo and grabbed her hands. "This place is a-maz-ing!" She did a double-take and frowned. "Where's Aspen?"

"She's waiting in the truck," Flynn said.

Willow rolled her eyes at Leoni. "Is she still mad at us?"

Leoni shrugged. "I think she's mostly mad at me."

"That's not fair. *I'm* the one who brought you here," Willow said.

"But I'm the one she's fallen for." Leoni half-smiled. She'd thought Aspen felt the same but hadn't expected to feel so bereft when Aspen said those perfect words. It was worse that she could believe it'd been some game Leoni and Willow had played, although that *had* been Leoni's cover-up plan. But her feelings for Aspen had been genuine from the get-go.

"Has Aspen gone exploring?" Jess asked when she reached the table.

"She's in her truck sulking," Willow said. "But that is *not* going to ruin this day." She jumped back out of her seat and hugged Jess. "Thank you so much for showing me around and for introducing me to the dean."

Jess looked vaguely confused about Aspen's absence but didn't comment. "Oh, okay. Well, tell her not to be a stranger." She put her hand on Flynn's shoulder, and Flynn got up to hug her. "Or you. Now that you both know where I've landed *and* Willow will be studying here, I'm going to expect dinner every couple of months."

"You got it," Flynn said and pushed her chair under the table. She slipped the untouched waffle into a takeout box. "Asp might want this."

Willow wrinkled her nose. "I bet she won't. She doesn't eat cold food that should be hot."

Flynn shrugged. "Then I'll eat it. I'm not wasting a tuxedo strawberry waffle."

"Can you find your own way back to the parking lot?" Jess asked and gestured to a food stall. "I'm starving, and those wings are calling my name."

"No problem." Flynn gave her another hug, and they headed back to the truck.

Willow hooked her arm into Leoni's, and Flynn walked ahead of them. "I'm not waiting to tell Mom until tomorrow. I'm too excited."

Leoni smiled and pulled Willow in tighter. "I'm so happy for you, Wills. You're really making it happen."

"Thanks to you."

"And your sister. Sounds like she's pulled some strings for you."

Willow nodded. "It might be our family name that got me in the front door, but it's going to be my hard work that will make her proud."

Leoni looked across the parking lot to see Aspen leaning against the hood of her truck, a perfect picture for a sapphic calendar. The light sheen of sweat on her chest glistened like diamonds in the sun, and her T-shirt pulled taut across her shoulders, hinting at her strength. Leoni sighed loudly. Had she really blown her chance to discover the joy that lay beneath Aspen's clothes?

Willow bumped her shoulder. "Subtle."

"Do I need to be?"

"I guess not." Willow giggled. "Wouldn't it be funny if you ended up as my sister-in-law *and* my best friend?"

Leoni nearly choked on a sharp intake of breath. "I think you're getting ahead of yourself. Aspen doesn't even want to *talk* to me, so I don't think a marriage proposal is imminent." And even if Aspen *was* talking to her, Leoni wouldn't want *that* to be the topic of conversation.

"She'll come to her senses eventually," Willow said. "You've just got to be patient."

Now she had to add patience to the perseverance Flynn advised. She wasn't known for either of those things, but if the past week had shown her anything, it was that she was still growing as a human being and more than capable of change.

By the time they got to the truck, Flynn was munching on the waffle she'd brought.

"Told you she wouldn't eat it," Willow said.

"I got a quesadilla from a food truck." Aspen moved to indicate the empty wrapping stuck in the truck grill. "How'd it go?"

"Fantastic! I spoke to the dean and told her my SAT score, and we talked about why I want to study marine biology. She said that my SATs are more than acceptable for the course requirement, so I just need to get home to spend the rest of the day writing my personal statement. If she likes what I write, I could join the college in September and get started!"

Aspen wrinkled her nose and tapped her watch. "Mom won't

be expecting us back until late."

"Don't worry about that," Willow said. "I'm going to tell her where we've really been all morning, and why."

Aspen raised her eyebrows. "You're coming clean today?"

"Yep. Then everyone can enjoy tomorrow's big party."

Aspen glanced at Leoni, and she shrank at the cold look in Aspen's eyes.

"Mom will want *her* to leave when you tell her the real story," Aspen said.

"Then I won't stay either." Willow crossed her arms. "It's time for a lot of things to change at home."

Leoni focused her gaze on the tarmac, wishing it would crack open and let her disappear into it. "There's no need for that, Wills. We can see each other anytime. I don't have to stay."

Willow huffed. "Oh my God. I want you to stay: the fireworks are beautiful, and Gramps and Grammy sing. They really like you, and you know I do, so that's that."

Leoni bit her lip to suppress an inappropriate smile. She was used to bossing butches around, not being on the receiving end of a fiery femme giving orders. She kind of liked it, though she was fully aware that the novelty would soon wear off. That fuzzy unfamiliar feeling wrapped around her heart again and dared her to settle into it.

Aspen grumbled, tore the food wrapping from her truck, and got in. "Let's go."

Those were the last two words she said for the entire drive home, while Willow babbled excitedly and regaled them with every second of her tour. When Aspen pulled up in the driveway, Willow grabbed Leoni's hand and tugged her out of her side of the car and held on as she ran toward the house.

"Mom!" she yelled after pushing the door open and rushing in.

"Willow? What's wrong? Has something happened?"

Cate's questions got increasingly louder as she came from whichever room she'd been relaxing in. When she eventually got into the hallway, her face was red, and she looked panicked.

Willow took her mom's hand. "I need to talk to you," she said and dragged them both to the library.

"You're scaring me, Willow. Is everything all right? Where's your sister?"

"Everything is more than all right, Mom. And Aspen and Flynn are on their way in." Willow closed the door behind them. She sat her mom on one couch, and then she sat on the opposite one, pulling Leoni down with her.

Cate seemed to be focusing on Willow's hands, as if searching for something, and Leoni realized what she was looking for. "We're not getting engaged," she said, hoping to put her mind at ease.

Cate sighed. "Oh. I see. So what is it that has you so worked up, Willow?"

"Before I start, you've got to promise that you won't interrupt me. You need to hear the whole story before you say anything, okay?"

Cate nodded. Leoni looked at the library door and wished she was on the other side of it, then Willow squeezed her hand, reminding Leoni why she was there.

Willow took a deep breath, and then she slowly and quite eloquently laid everything out: how she'd been feeling for the past ten years, how she saw her place in the family, how invisible she thought she was, and finally, what she'd done about it all this week, starting with commissioning Leoni as a pretend girlfriend and ending with the news that, subject to a successful application essay, she would be studying at Stony Brook from September so that she could follow her passion.

Cate struggled to keep quiet, that much was obvious, and she went through a whole gamut of visible emotions. Her eyes teared up, and her chest heaved as she clearly tried to stop herself from sobbing. Leoni hadn't expected that reaction, but she was glad to see it, for Willow's sake.

When Willow had finished, her mom edged forward on her seat and took Willow's hands in hers. "I don't have enough years left to apologize for making you feel that way." A single tear fell, and Willow wiped it away gently.

Leoni stared at a bookshelf. She wanted to support Willow, but this was such an incredibly intimate moment that she really felt she shouldn't still be there. "I should leave you to this."

"Just let me do one thing before you go," Willow said. "Mom, none of this is Leo's fault. She was just doing her job. I want her to stay for the party, and I don't want you to be mad at her, okay?"

"I'm not mad." Cate focused her gaze on Leoni and smiled. "I know who you are, Leoni York, and I know you work for Perfect Fit." She held up her hand when Willow opened her mouth to protest. "I'm sorry, darling, but this is precisely why I like Philip to complete background checks on everyone coming into this family's orbit. She could've been anyone, Willow."

"I understand." Willow nodded. "I thought it was worth the risk, but I promise I won't do anything like it again."

Leoni tugged at her ponytail. So Ginny's skills weren't so infallible after all. It wasn't surprising that they were exposed as amateur when faced with the resources of a family worth billions. "How long have you known?"

"Since Monday evening," Cate said. "It took a little longer than I would have liked, which is testament to your company's IT expert, but very little stops Philip from discovering the truth."

Even though she said it so lightly, Leoni could imagine the same line coming from the mouth of a Bond villain. "For what it's worth, I'm sorry I deceived you all."

Cate nodded. "But if you hadn't, I wouldn't be thanking you for helping us find our way back to each other." She held out her hand.

Leoni stood and shook it, then she began to back away to the door. "I'll leave you to it."

"Thank you, Leoni. And please say that you'll stay for tomorrow's party."

"I will. Thank you for the invitation." She closed the door behind her and rested her head against it momentarily. If only Aspen could be as forgiving as her mom...

Chapter Twenty-Four

ASPEN RELAXED INTO THE sun lounger and looked out to the horizon. She'd miss the peaceful quiet of this view when she went back to continue work on the retirement village project. That thought brought excitement with it, and she couldn't wait to get started. Usually, being away from work for a week made her a little antsy, and she hadn't expected this vacation to be any different, but it had confounded those expectations. If it hadn't been for the drawing she'd had to rework, Aspen probably wouldn't have thought about work at all.

Leoni's presence had made that difference. When she was around, she became Aspen's sole focus of attention. And that had been torture because Leoni was her sister's girlfriend.

Except she wasn't.

And she never had been. Leoni was a girlfriend-for-hire, providing an unusual, but apparently very lucrative, service. Maybe it wasn't that unusual. Aspen had heard of escort services, obviously, but she'd never actually come across anyone who worked for one, and she'd definitely never considered *using* one, no matter how desperate her crappy love life got. So now that Leoni *wasn't* in a relationship with her sister, and Aspen couldn't shake the feeling that their connection *was* very real, where did that leave them?

Aside from dinner last night and lunch today, she hadn't seen much of Willow. Aspen was still reeling from the laidback way her mom had handled the whole situation, having gone from mild paranoia to acceptance in the space of a couple of days. It seemed like everyone in the family acted differently when it came to Leoni. She couldn't deny that she was stoked to see Willow so motivated, and she was looking forward to seeing the first draft of her personal statement, which Willow wanted her to check over. And she was grateful that the upward tick in their relationship had continued despite the Leoni bombshell.

Leoni. It suited her. Leo was a cute name, but now that Aspen knew she was *Leoni*, there was no way she'd shorten it again. And after her mom had seemingly swept the whole fiasco away like sand on the deck, it appeared that Aspen might have to get used to seeing Leoni around after tonight's party.

She still didn't know how she felt about that, but she probably didn't need to concern herself with it too much. Willow was going to college and, after the current project in LA, Aspen would go home to San Francisco, occasionally traveling for projects across the country, and maybe one day, even farther than that. Thanksgiving, Christmas, and the Fourth of July were still likely the only times Aspen would have to see her.

No, she needed to get Leoni out of her head, at least for now, because tonight was all about Flynn. Aspen pulled her phone from her pocket to text her, then she turned at the sound of the house gate swinging open. Flynn waved and jogged over.

Aspen chuckled. "I'm impressed you're keeping up with this running thing."

Flynn flopped full-length onto the adjacent bed and groaned heavily. "It's killing me. *Everything* hurts. Everything." She grinned. "But on the flip side, I'm getting a lot of Kelly's time. And it seems like she might be enjoying it as much as I am."

"The pain's worth it then?"

"You bet." Flynn motioned to the barge 150 yards to the left of the beach house. "And when those fireworks go off tonight, I'm going to put it all out there and see what happens."

Aspen held out her fist and Flynn bumped it. "You've got this, buddy. And I'll be here for you, whatever happens."

"Thanks." Flynn turned to face Aspen. "How are you feeling

about the whole Willow and Leo thing, now that it's out in the open?"

Aspen sighed and rolled to her side. "I don't know. I need some distance and time to think on it. You know how I am."

Flynn nodded. "Sounds like your mom took it better than you have."

Aspen inclined her head. "Right? I talked to her about it a little over breakfast. She said the *not knowing* is almost always worse than the actual knowledge. Once Philip had dug up everything there was to know about Leoni York and followed the money back to Willow, Mom knew the truth of what was happening. She said she'd just relaxed and waited for the fallout."

"I bet she didn't expect Willow to come to her and confess everything though."

"Nope. She said that surprised her, but in a very good way." Aspen picked at a splinter of wood on the sun lounger. "I think that her guilt over how she'd made Willow feel overrode any anger she might've had at the deception."

"And the danger," Flynn said. "Your family has to be so careful about new people. I'd still like to know what Philip found out about me and mine."

Aspen shook her head. "Whatever it was, it didn't worry Mom."

"But it could've. My mom..." Flynn swallowed hard. "Your family could've stopped us from being friends. We wouldn't have the company. We wouldn't have this bromance."

"No one could've stopped this." Aspen punched Flynn's shoulder lightly. "But it's ancient history, isn't it? Mom knows what she's doing, I guess. Anyway, what's your plan for tonight? Do you have some fancy speech prepared, given that you tend to get a bit tongue-tied around her?"

Flynn grinned widely. "I'm just going to speak from the heart and see what comes out. Spending the time alone with Kelly on the boat and then running together these past couple of mornings has made it easier."

"Do you think she'll be mad when you tell her that was just a ruse to get her alone?"

Flynn puffed out her chest. "Nope. It might've started as a ruse, but I'm gonna see it through now. We're going to run the New York half-marathon together, no matter what, and if it goes well, we're going to train for others all around the country and raise money for PFLAG, like I told you the other day. We've got big plans."

"That's quite the commitment from Kelly," Aspen said. "It's looking like tonight will be a shoo-in."

Flynn swung her legs from the bed and sat on the side. "I hope so. She's the one for me, I know it."

Aspen smiled, though the notion of there being "the one" was heart-breaking. How easy would it be to miss that person? To pass them in the street and never discover what could've been. To live on different continents with paths that never crossed. Seven billion people in the world, and the average person meets eighty thousand in a lifetime. The odds of finding "the one" were phenomenally stacked against everyone.

Then what if you found "the one" and dismissed them because of circumstance?

"Where are you going to do it?" Aspen asked, nudging herself from her musings.

Flynn turned around and motioned to the giant marquees and the bandstand that had been erected along the beach. "Nowhere near any of that. I'm going to suggest that we take a walk along the shore. We can get away from the crowd but still see the firework display. I picked up one of those mini, foldable picnic blankets from the Eastport General Store."

"I love their scones. Is that where the ones in the kitchen appeared from a couple of days ago?"

Flynn nodded and smiled. "Kelly mentioned they were her favorite treat a while back."

"Sneaky. You must've gone out early that day."

"I did it before the golf. Everyone was too busy getting ready to notice me disappearing for a half hour."

Aspen looked at her watch. "Speaking of getting ready, I guess we should get to it. I know how long it takes you to fix your hair."

Flynn shoved Aspen's shoulder. "Nearly as long as it takes you to do your makeup."

They made their way back to the house. At the top of the stairs before they parted for their separate rooms, Flynn grasped Aspen's shoulder. "I know you need to work through stuff alone, but I'm always here if you want to talk anything through."

Aspen nodded. "I know."

"Don't take so long processing that by the time you've finished, you can't do anything about the thing you've spent so long thinking about."

Aspen frowned. "Is that your convoluted way of telling me to think faster?"

Flynn shrugged and backed away, holding her hands up. "I can't tell you how to think or what to think. No one can. But it should be about the way you *feel* too. Don't forget that."

Aspen waved her away and turned to go to her room. That was always her problem: she couldn't separate her heart from her head, and she could never forget the way she felt. Just like it had taken her months to get over her feelings for Sarah because she couldn't *forget* her. Aspen thought that she'd loved Sarah, but they'd never shared conversations that resonated as deeply and as intimately as sex. They'd never talked like she and Leoni had. Was she really going to let Leoni's job get in the way of what could develop between them?

***

Aspen straightened her tie and took one last look in the mirror before heading downstairs to the party that had kicked off two hours ago. She gave the pool a wide berth; it was already packed with kids dive-bombing and playing what looked like a highly competitive game of dodgeball. After taking so long to get ready, she didn't want to have to head back for a change of clothes now. She collected a bottle of beer from the pool bar and snagged a couple of hors d'oeuvres from one of the many buffet tables, then she began the rounds expected of her as a member of the hosting family.

While she shook hands, kissed wives, and talked about a mixture of topics from her latest build to the stock exchange to the dire state of the country's politics, Aspen kept a subtle eye out for Willow. She saw Kelly, Flynn, Oakley, and another person on the dance floor, which had been built on the beach in front of the main stage. As she made her way through the attendees and got closer to them, she recognized the other woman from the line at Dreadnoughts who'd given Oakley her number. Good. That would keep him busy and less focused on what Kelly and Flynn were up to. He still hadn't cashed in his chip for keeping Flynn's secret, but she knew that didn't mean he'd decided to let it go. It just meant he was *really* thinking about how epic a prize he could claim.

On a large table under the far marquee, Aspen finally spotted Willow, along with their mom and dad, Leoni, Gramps, and Grammy. At the edge of the dance floor, Grandpa Bill and Grandma Eleanor were slow dancing to their own beat, staring into each other's eyes, oblivious to the high-energy track pumping from the speakers.

"Hey." Aspen pulled out a chair between Willow and their mom.

"You look handsome," their mom said and straightened the knot of Aspen's tie. "I love this color on you."

"Thanks, Mom."

Willow grabbed Aspen's forearm. "What did you think? Is it terrible? Should I start again?" She stuck out her bottom lip. "I've spent nearly thirty hours on it if you don't count sleep, which I don't because I barely closed my eyes all night."

"Whoa." Aspen placed her hand over Willow's and ignored

Leoni behind her. "Relax, little sister."

Willow took a deep breath and let it out slowly. "Okay, I'm calm. Is it bad?"

Aspen shook her head and smiled. "It's fantastic. You're incredibly honest about what you've been doing these—"

"You mean, what I *haven't* been doing?"

Aspen squeezed Willow's hand. "What you've been doing since you left high school. You haven't tried to sugarcoat the past few years or make excuses, and that's what makes this work, makes it feel real. You own up to feeling lost, and you've shown exactly why your desire to study marine biology is different from anything else you've tried to do. Your passion for the ocean shines through all of it."

Willow blinked rapidly and looked up at the sky, as if she was trying to fight off tears. "So it's good?"

"It's *great*. And the way you talk about the moment it clicked for you," Aspen looked over Willow's shoulder at Leoni, "when you were talking about it with your...friend, that's really powerful. I like the analogy about finally finding a direction to swim instead of just treading the water of life too."

Willow gave her a tentative-looking smile. "Are you sure about that bit? I thought it might be a bit too cheesy or cliché."

Aspen shrugged. "What if it is? It's not contrived, and that's the main thing. It feels like you. It feels genuine. It feels like the epiphany you've been waiting for instead of just trying another thing that doesn't light your fire." She glanced at Leoni again and pushed down the hint of jealousy that she'd been the one to help Willow find her passion. But Aspen had abdicated responsibility for her little sister, so she was also grateful. Leoni's answering smile took Aspen's breath, and she forced herself to look away.

"Can we read it?" their mom asked.

Aspen frowned. "You didn't send it to Mom and Dad?"

"Of course she didn't, Aspen," their dad said. "Little Willow has always thought you hung the moon."

Willow rolled her eyes as if Aspen had asked her if the world was flat. "I wanted you to be the first one in the family to read it."

Aspen saw Leoni look away and noted Willow's deliberate choice of words. Leoni had obviously been the first to read it and had probably helped her draft it, since she'd also been MIA with Willow since yesterday afternoon. But their dad's words hit home too and reinforced her vow to do better by her sister. "I love you, little sis. You're going to be amazing at this, I can feel it."

"Me too." Willow threw her arms around Aspen's neck and hugged her tight. "Please talk to Leoni," she whispered so only Aspen could hear. "I think you two would make the cutest couple."

Aspen shook her head. "I don't think so, Willow."

"Please. For me."

"That's not fair."

Willow giggled and released her. "So you'll talk to her?"

Aspen sighed, knowing she had no choice. Maybe it'd be for the best anyway. One final talk to clear the air and move on. "Yes," she said. "I'll talk to her right now." She grabbed her beer and stood. "I'm going to take a walk along the beach. Would you like to join me, Leoni?"

"Good luck," their mom said quietly.

Aspen shook her head. Was she the only one who was uncomfortable with this whole situation?

"I'd love to," Leoni said and joined her.

They navigated the crowd, although Aspen had to stop to talk to several people. As they passed the dance floor, Flynn caught her gaze and pressed her hands together in prayer. Aspen didn't know whether the gesture was related to Leoni or Kelly, but she gave Flynn the thumbs-up. Judging by how close Kelly was dancing to Flynn, Aspen had a feeling everything would go well for them tonight. They eventually made it to the other side of the marquees, and she checked her watch. The fireworks would begin in fifteen minutes. She hoped Flynn would choose to walk along the beach in the opposite direction. She didn't want to get in the way of true love, especially when she was in the process of wrecking the possibility of it for herself.

They walked in silence until the bass of the music was only a distant vibration. The first quarter of the moon was bright in the clear sky, and it bounced off the darkening ocean now that the sun had fully set. Leoni walked alongside Aspen, but she kept a respectful distance between them. Her pull was as strong as the moon's draw to the ocean, and Aspen battled not to tentatively reach out to take her hand. What would Leoni's hand feel like in hers? Would they try over and under before settling into an awkward hold that was uncomfortable for both of them? Or would it fit perfectly, naturally, easily?

It would remain a mystery.

"I need you to know that everything I told you about my mom, my dad, and me was completely true," Leoni said. "I've got a folder in Willow's room with a complete backstory for Leo King, insanely successful divorce lawyer from Chicago. Educated at Yale. Followed parents into family business. One brother, also in law. There's a very impressive website, a LinkedIn presence, and the whole nine yards my company created, one I'm supposed to use." She gestured into the air, and Aspen stuck her hands in her pockets to keep herself from reaching out. "But I didn't use any of it. I couldn't even bring myself to lie about my job. The truth just bled out of me from the moment I stepped foot on your property, and I couldn't do a damn thing about it. I got close to your sister, and I got close to you. And I broke every one of the company's rules. The only lie was that Willow and I were together. Everything I felt, everything *you* felt was real, and I wish I'd kissed you in the kitchen and told you the truth right then, like I wanted to. But I was on a job, and Willow had paid for me to pretend to be her girlfriend until *she* decided it was over. Not me."

The first aerial shell exploded into the air, and Leoni jumped and stumbled. Aspen caught her, and Leoni's scent hit her nostrils. Leoni pressed her hands against Aspen's chest and looked up into her eyes, her expression soft and wanting. All Aspen had to do was dip her head and claim Leoni's full lips.

Instead, she steadied Leoni and took a step back. A chain of comets fired into the air, their long tails crackling and fizzing in the night sky. The oohs and ahhs of appreciation of their partygoers floated toward them on the sea breeze, and Aspen glanced back to see everyone's attention focused on the barges and what would come next. Beyond the party, she also saw two silhouetted figures walking in the opposite direction and recognized Flynn's unique gait. She smiled and crossed her fingers, then turned back to Leoni and prayed for steel to run through her heart instead of blood. "I appreciate your honesty, but none of that really matters. Beyond you just doing your job and being paid to lie, you're a body for hire to the rich and shameless. And I can't risk my heart on someone who spends their time pretending to have feelings for other people, pretending to be someone else."

Aspen took a deep breath to gather the courage to continue in the face of Leoni's reaction. The wisp of hope that had gathered in her eyes had been chased away by Aspen's words, and all that remained was a profoundly deep sadness and the hint of tears to come. "You said yourself that you're losing who you are because you've been wearing so many masks. I can't go through that with you. I won't, not after I've just pieced my life back together after Sarah took a sledgehammer to it."

Leoni's body began to shake, and Aspen grasped the inner fabric of her pockets to keep from pulling Leoni into her arms. "I think you're an amazing person, and in another life, some other universe where we were in a different situation, I would love to have seen where this could've gone. But not this one, not like this." She swallowed against the rising choke of her own throat and closed her eyes to focus on the blackness of her eyelids instead of the dimming light in Leoni's eyes. "It'd break my heart. I hope you can understand that."

Aspen took another two steps backward for fear she really

wasn't strong enough to see this through, to do what had to be done and stick to it instead of folding Leoni into an embrace and promising her the world.

The fireworks continued to pop, fizz, and explode over the ocean in a dazzling display of color and light, but here, the color of Aspen's life drained from her body and ebbed away into the gently lapping waves before her.

"I'm so, so sorry," Leoni whispered, then she turned and ran along the sand until she reached the far side entrance to the back of the beach house, avoiding everyone.

Aspen sank to the ground, hugged her legs to her chest, and let the sob finally escape her throat. The water danced around her feet, soaking her shoes, but she didn't move. Perhaps the waves could wash away the crushing sorrow that wound around her heart like a Virginia creeper, invading and smothering it.

Or perhaps she'd just have to live with the pain all over again. But this would be different. She already knew this would be an incomparable agony, a torment that would make her split with Sarah feel like a kindergarten breakup. Aspen touched her mouth, the ghost of Leoni's lips still fresh and crisp from yesterday. She'd never had a kiss like it.

And she never would again.

Chapter Twenty-Five

Leoni came out of the bathroom to find Willow hugging Leoni's luggage to her chest. "Are you holding that hostage?"

"If I say yes, will it make you stay?"

Leoni chuckled and shook her head. "They'll go into the company closet for other people, and I'm hoping I never have to wear any of them ever again." She inclined her head. "Although like I said, I might steal the cargo shorts just to bum around the apartment in."

Willow put the bag beside her and stuck out her bottom lip. "I can't believe you're leaving. This week has gone by so fast."

Leoni sat on the bed and put her arm around Willow. "But look at what you've achieved too. You'll keep me posted about your college application, won't you?" To say she was slightly invested would be an epic understatement. After everything that had happened here, there was no way she could just push Willow out of her head like she usually did with clients after a job. Although part of her wished she could do that with Aspen, she knew that wouldn't be happening either.

"Every step of the way." Willow leaned her head onto Leoni's chest. "I'm going to miss you," she said quietly.

Leoni smiled. "You're the first person other than my mom to say that."

Willow sat up and looked at her with a serious expression. "You're the first person I've said it to in a long time." She glanced away and busied herself with pushing her cuticles down with her nails. "I still think all of this was fate, even though everything hasn't worked out the way I hoped it would."

Leoni studied her own short nails. She couldn't wait to get back to the salon and have acrylics reapplied.

"Leoni?"

She folded her hands together and sighed. "You're probably right. We were being greedy and over-ambitious hoping that we could figure out *both* our lives in one week."

Willow placed her hand over Leoni's. "Your life is great though. You get to travel all over the country, meeting new people."

"Most of the work is on the West Coast. We only really go anywhere else for stellar files, like yours. There are companies like us all over the States, and we tend to stick to our own territory."

Willow nudged her. "Is that your way of telling me that I won't see you all that often?"

"It wasn't, but..." Leoni shrugged. "I don't get a lot of vacation time, so we're going to have to make use of FaceTime."

"That sounds like you're crying off Aspen's birthday next month."

Leoni nodded. "Even if I could come, it wouldn't be a good idea. We're both hurting, and we need some distance and time away from each other." She closed her eyes briefly and saw the pain in Aspen's expression last night. She didn't want to ever see that look again.

"Thanksgiving?" Willow asked. "That's nearly a half-year away. That'll be plenty of time to recover, won't it?"

Leoni chuckled. "Spoken like someone who's never had their heart..." She couldn't finish the sentence. If hers wasn't broken, it had a hairline fracture at the very least.

"Do you...*love* my sister?"

Willow's frown reflected the ridiculous notion of her question, and Leoni laughed.

"I really like her, but it's a bit too cliché to suggest I might be in love with her after a week." Love was such a strong word, often bandied around too easily with little thought for the profundity of the emotion. "I've never loved anyone except my mom and—"

"That's a very different kind of love." Willow laughed, and Leoni joined her.

"It really should be, but people can be weird."

Willow chewed on her bottom lip and squeezed Leoni's hands. "I think it won't be that long before I tell you that I love you."

That unfamiliar flood of warmth raced through her again. That was going to take some getting used to. "We've talked about this, Wills. No hot lesbian action for you."

Willow giggled and tapped Leoni's thigh. "You know what I mean. As a friend. As part of my family."

Leoni's heart heaved tight against her chest, and she had to concentrate to breathe properly. Her family was her mom. There had only ever been the two of them, but Willow was offering an instant expansion pack, as freely and simply as Leoni had heard love *should* be given. "I don't know what to say to that."

"You don't have to say anything." Willow checked her watch, then she stood and pulled Leoni up with her. "Time to go... It doesn't feel like enough, but thank you again for everything you've given me this week. You've helped me find my true passion, and I can't wait to start living instead of just aimlessly cruising."

"You do love your water metaphors, kiddo. Just make sure you tell my boss how amazing I've been when you get her follow-up email." She huffed out a breath and shook her head. It seemed so strange to talk about the business transaction that had led to one of the best weeks of her life. This was exactly why Ruth told her employees never to mix business with pleasure. Separation was a painful pleasure only because it wasn't forever.

"I promise to give you a great review," she said and laughed. "But there won't be enough stars to show how fantastic you've been. I'm sure Tyler couldn't have done a better job."

Leoni wrinkled her nose. "She might've been more professional though."

Willow pulled her into a hug. "I didn't need professional. I needed you, exactly as you are."

"Wow, you're determined to make me cry." She pulled out of

the hug and grabbed her carryall.

Willow took Leoni's hand, and they headed downstairs. The whole family was waiting in the living room, and they got up to say their goodbyes. Aspen stood behind everyone, with her hands stuffed in her pockets and an unreadable expression.

Willow's gramps wrapped his arms around her so tight that Leoni thought he might crush her ribs.

"Well played, Leoni," he whispered. "I wish I'd been in on the fun."

"Me too," she said. "I think you would've caused all kinds of chaos."

He released her and then gently pinched her cheek. "I don't know what you're made of, but you've worked some magic this week on my Willow, and I can't thank you enough for that."

"Pretty sure I'm just flesh and blood." Leoni laughed.

Cate rubbed Leoni's upper arm, and her husband smiled beside her. "Don't be a stranger, Leoni," she said. "Now that we've done a background check on you, you're welcome here anytime."

Leoni suppressed a smile at her attempt at a wink. There were some things that elegant women just couldn't do convincingly. "Willow has invited me for Thanksgiving," she said. "I don't know if I'll be working, but if I'm not, would that be okay?"

Willow bounced up and down beside her. "Please, Mom."

"We'd love to have you."

Leoni looked over at Aspen, but she couldn't gauge her reaction to the invitation. "I'll be here if I can." She hadn't wanted to burst Willow's bubble about being here for that holiday. Thanksgiving was one of their busiest times, and Leoni had worked every one of them since she'd been at Perfect Fit. The likelihood of her being free was minimal.

When Flynn and Kelly took their turn to say goodbye, Leoni motioned to their clasped hands. "Is this a new development?"

Kelly raised their joined hands and grinned. "You're not the only one who's been keeping a secret from everyone this week. Flynn finally got around to asking me out."

"Finally?" Leoni asked and saw Aspen's expression brighten.

Kelly nodded. "I've been hinting for a while now, and she's caught up with the program."

Flynn looked like she'd won the Powerball lotto. Her grin was so wide, the rest of her features were barely visible.

"I'm happy for you. You're really cute together."

The grandparents on Willow's mom's side were as perfunctory as they'd been all week with their farewell, and Oakley hugged her briefly. "Bring the G-Wagen in November, and we'll do some off-roading."

"Sure." She didn't have the heart to tell him that she'd likely never ride in that beast of a truck again and happily so. Her Volkswagen GTI was more than enough car for her to handle.

Everyone but Aspen slipped away into the living room. She stepped forward and held out her hand. "Good luck with everything."

Leoni looked down at Aspen's hand then shook it after a long moment. It felt as perfunctory as Bill's handshake, but Aspen's eyes gave her away. Leoni didn't want to make it any more awkward than it was, so she gestured to the front door. "I better get going. I hope your retirement village project goes well. I'm sure it'll be amazing with you at the helm." She didn't wait for a response and turned for the door, bag in hand and Willow rushing after her.

"Maybe she'll be different at Thanksgiving," Willow said after Leoni had put her holdall in the back seat.

"Don't worry about any of that." Leoni gave Willow one final, long hug, then held her at arm's length. "You need to focus all of your energy and time on your new career. Okay?"

Willow nodded, and she began to cry. Leoni opened the door and climbed behind the wheel. She was already running slightly late with all the farewell fanfare, and if she embraced Willow now, they'd both end up sobbing. "Let me know when the college contacts you to beg you to attend."

Willow wiped at her tears. "I will."

Leoni closed the door and headed down the driveway. In the rearview mirror, she could see Willow waving. Movement caught her eye on a first-floor window, and when she took another look, Aspen stood there, with her hands pressed against the glass. She swallowed hard and focused on the road ahead. Aspen had made it clear there could be nothing between them, and Leoni accepted that. She set off on the ninety-minute journey to the airport, praying for the flight to be on time. She just wanted to get home to her apartment and be surrounded by familiar things. And she needed her mom too.

Hope is the thing with feathers that perches in the soul and sings the tune without words and never stops at all... The Emily Dickinson quote popped into her head unbidden. Could she hope for two paradoxical things at the same time? Could Leoni hope that Aspen might change her mind while also hoping to forget all about her?

She shook the thought away. The last thing she really wanted to do was forget *anything* about sweet, gentle, and sexy Aspen. There was pleasure in that pain somewhere, in the memories of their time together. But right now, all Leoni could think about was the lost opportunity of what could have been.

And that stung like nothing before it ever had.

Chapter Twenty-Six

Aspen didn't feel like being sociable, but this would be their last few hours together until her birthday next month. Usually, that prospect didn't bother her too much. Flynn was almost always close by, and Oakley and Kelly were perfect in small doses.

So what was different about this week, aside from the obvious interloper, whom Aspen had just watched drive away as she stood in the window like some tragic romantic hero? Except there was nothing heroic about letting Leoni slip through her fingers.

Tired of trying to parse out her emotions, she headed downstairs and joined Flynn, Oakley, and Kelly poolside just as Kelly handed Oakley money. "What were you betting on this time?" she asked.

Oakley shoved the dollars in his pocket and waved as if it was nothing.

"You." Flynn crossed her arms and gave him the stink-eye.

Oakley rolled his eyes. "Snitch."

"I'm learning from you," Flynn said.

Aspen took the empty seat between Flynn and Oakley. "What did I miss? Whatever you're learning from my little brother, you should ditch immediately."

Kelly shook her head. "Oakley told me about Flynn's plan to ask me out last night, and Flynn isn't happy about it."

Flynn scowled. "He could've ruined *everything*. Kelly knew for *two* days."

Aspen shrugged. "So I don't owe you anything for *not* keeping Flynn's secret then. That's one piece of good news." She lightly punched Flynn's shoulder. "It didn't ruin anything, buddy. You two look super happy."

Flynn grinned and shifted her chair even closer to Kelly. "We are."

"I *had* to tell her," Oakley said. "She knows when I'm keeping something from her, and she thought it was something bad. She practically interrogated it out of me."

Kelly nodded. "That's true. And I couldn't have been happier when I found out what it was."

Oakley tapped loudly on the table. "Tell them what else is true."

Kelly smiled. "I was planning the same thing."

"You were *not!*" Flynn said.

"I was tired of waiting for you to make the first move." Kelly kissed Flynn's knuckles. "I'm glad he told me. I would never have wanted to miss out on your sweet proposal."

"A wedding already?" Aspen raised her eyebrows. "I thought you just asked her out."

Flynn shook her head. "Not *that* kind of proposal." She looked at Kelly and gave her a shy smile. "Not yet anyway."

Aspen frowned as she recalled the reason for her brother's bet. "Exactly why were you betting on me?"

"Don't worry about it," Oakley said. "It's probably too raw for you to appreciate right now."

Aspen clenched her jaw, sure that he was probably right, but perversely, she still wanted to know. "Just tell me."

Oakley rubbed his hand across his beard and sighed. "We were betting on whether or not you'd let Leoni leave."

Kelly shrugged. "Sorry, Aspen. I'm an old romantic. I didn't think you'd let her go so easily."

"And I knew you would." Oakley looked far too pleased with himself and then glanced away when she glared at him. "Sorry, sis. I did say I thought it'd be too raw."

"Do you want to talk about it?" Kelly asked.

Aspen shook her head. "Not with everyone." She glanced at Flynn. "Maybe just you."

Flynn's surprise was clear when she narrowed her eyes.

"Already? Are you sure?"

Kelly and Oakley stood and picked up their coffee cups.

"We'll leave you to it."

Aspen pushed up from her chair. "No, you guys stay here. I could do with a walk." She grabbed a couple of bottles of water from the outdoor bar fridge as they headed toward the outer gate. She kicked off her shoes to go barefoot and didn't say anything as they walked across the sand to the shore. She looked to the left, where she and Leoni had walked last night, and then decided to go in the opposite direction.

"Was it Sarah?" Flynn asked when Aspen still hadn't spoken.

Aspen squatted and scooped up a handful of fine sand. "Partly." She opened her fist and spread her fingers, allowing the sand to escape. Had she let Leoni go as easily, as if it were so simple to let the sands of time move on?

"Meaning?" Flynn asked gently. "Are you not really over her?"

Aspen shook her head. "That's not it. I'm definitely over Sarah. A photo of her with someone new popped up on my feed, and I didn't feel anything except maybe sorry for the girlfriend, who doesn't know the road ahead."

Flynn blew out a breath. "Thank the Lord for small mercies. I didn't want to take a hit out on the woman to get her out of your head once and for all."

Aspen laughed. "Do people even do that?"

"People will do anything for enough money."

Aspen's shoulders sagged. Flynn had hit on the problem without even realizing it. "Luckily, there's no need for that. I *am* over her, but she's left some wounds, and Leoni picked at them, though she had no idea she was doing it."

"All wounds heal eventually. If you told Leoni what she was doing wrong, I think she cares enough to fix it or stop it or do whatever it was she needs to do."

Aspen stopped walking and looked out at the still ocean, so clear and blue like the sky above them. Endless calm stretched all the way to the horizon. She hadn't experienced that kind of peace in her heart for a long time, but when she'd been with Leoni, her mind had stilled, and her heart had dared to hope that she could find it again. "It wasn't that easy... I don't understand how she could help Willow find her passion but dismiss her own dreams."

"What?"

"She wanted to be a stage actor, but instead she decided to use her talent to fool people into thinking she's whoever the high-paying client wants her to be."

Flynn grasped Aspen's arm and pulled her around to face her. "That's the problem? You're angry with her because of her job?"

Aspen shrugged. "I didn't think I was angry, but maybe I am, yeah."

Flynn sighed deeply. "I'm going to lay some truths down for you now, so you remember that you asked to talk to me, and you know I've got opinions. Okay?"

Aspen nodded, though her stomach dropped.

"You don't understand what it is to be poor. You made a choice not to live off your parents' money, but if our company failed tomorrow, you could move in here or pick any one of the dozens of homes your parents own across the world. You don't know what it is to *have* to do something whether you want to or not. You've never had to work to eat. You've never *not* been able to clothe yourself or decide if you're going to spend your last five dollars on food or gas. You're judging her on unfair standards. She had dreams, just like you, but she didn't have the support to make them happen, not fully. Live a mile in her heels and then see if you're so quick to judge."

Aspen remained silent and absorbed Flynn's words slowly, giving them the time and space they deserved. Flynn knew exactly what she was talking about. She'd been in that position, where her mom had chosen to buy lipstick for herself instead of food for Flynn. Leoni had been raised by a single mom, and she'd said outright that she hadn't been born into any kind of money. So

Aspen couldn't, and wouldn't, judge Leoni for choosing security over her dreams. But still…

"You're right. I'm not in a position to judge her, and I won't. But it's more than that. I can't get past her job, and her job won't change. She's still a high-paid escort for hire to anyone who can afford her. And she said that she usually sticks to a script instead of the story of her life, but what if that wasn't true either? Every time she disappeared on a job for a week, this exact thing could be happening all over again. What if she pretends to be someone's girlfriend and then falls for them? How am I supposed to trust her?"

Flynn inclined her head. "That's exactly what it comes down to: trust. If you can't bring yourself to offer Leoni a clean slate and not bring the baggage you've picked up from your relationship with Sarah into it, then you shouldn't. She deserves more than that. And so do you." She hung her arm around Aspen's shoulders. "You might be over Sarah, but that doesn't mean you're ready for a new relationship."

Flynn's declaration hit like a gut punch. "What if I'm never ready?" Aspen asked. "What if Sarah broke something inside me, and I can't get past it? Can't repair it?"

Flynn shook her head. "I don't believe that. You might have a lot of work to do, and you might need a therapist to help you with that, but if you want to move beyond something, you have the power to do it. You don't have to leave it in Sarah's hands." She tugged on Aspen's neck. "And you've got people around you who love you and will support you through it. You know that."

"I do." Aspen turned into Flynn and hugged her. "I love you, buddy."

Flynn slapped her hard on the back. "I love you too. And I'll always be here for you, whatever you need."

Aspen sighed deeply. She knew that. She'd always known that since they'd forged their friendship in the early years of college. Trust had always been an issue for the Hartwell family, but Aspen had never thought it would be a problem for her. So it was something she'd work on, just like Flynn suggested, no matter how long it took.

But the one thing she *needed* was something Flynn couldn't give her—something she didn't *want* Flynn to give her—and apparently, it was something she couldn't have without doing a shit-ton of work on herself. A special kind of love. A love that lifted two people higher than they could go alone. But what if, after all that work, she never met another person who made her feel as free as Leoni did?

Chapter Twenty-Seven

LEONI TOSSED THE HOLDALL in her closet and closed the door on it. For now, she didn't want to think about masc clothes, or work, or the Hartwell family. Well, that wasn't strictly true. She was happy to think about Willow but, after that, none of them. She had no doubt her subconscious would work against her while she slept, and she'd be plagued with dreams of the *other* sister, but while she was awake, she was a grown woman perfectly in control of her thoughts.

She shucked off her clothes and took a quick shower, then she crawled into bed with a bowl of popcorn and flicked the TV on in search of a horror movie. No rom-coms, and no romantic movies masquerading as action or sci-fi movies. She wanted a solid, slasher film. Two hours of impossibly high-pitched screaming, arcing blood splatter, and shouting at the college girls *not* to go outside in just their bra and panties.

In between all of those things, Leoni texted Tyler and found out she was feeling much better and would be back at work the following week. Moments after that, Jesse messaged to see if Leoni wanted *company*, the offer of which came with a devil emoji, as if it wasn't clear what she was offering. Leoni lifted the spare pillow to her nose and inhaled. The faint woody scent of Jesse did nothing for her. Just over a week ago, she'd mounted Jesse with wild abandon and rode her hard, with joy and no trace of complicated emotions. Where had *that* Leoni gone, and would she be coming back? *Not tonight*. The text could've been the answer to her question too, but she reminded herself that she wasn't supposed to be thinking about any of that right now. Slasher movie and screaming. Drown out the deep and meaningful stuff crying out for attention.

She hit pause and almost called her mom but then thought better of that too. Her sadness was tingling just below the surface of her skin. One word from her mom, and she'd dissolve into gut-wrenching, teenage-type sobbing. She told herself that she was in her thirties and that kind of behavior was beneath her. The breath that caught in her throat threatened to reveal otherwise, so she pressed play and turned up the volume. The screaming could give her brain something else to bitch about.

When Leoni woke to the bright sun streaming through her blinds, she drew in a long breath through her nose. Well, she *tried* to do that but stopped immediately when a piece of last night's popcorn tried to zoom up her nasal passage and into her brain. She snorted the offending chunk out and opened her eyes to discover several other pieces of popcorn in places they shouldn't be.

She stretched out like a cat. Willow's six-foot beanbags had been surprisingly comfortable, but nothing beat Leoni's firm, cool mattress for comfort. And nothing beat waking up alone either. She ignored the spiky little niggle that said she didn't know what she was talking about, and wouldn't the strong, athletic body of Aspen beside her be glorious to snuggle into on a lazy Sunday morning?

She saw the baseball cap she'd tossed onto her dresser and smiled, deciding that she'd video the ceremonial burning and send it to Willow. She couldn't wait to wash her hair and not truss it up. She'd gotten used to hiding her long locks under that damn cotton cage but letting it free would feel like a mini revolt after the past week.

Leoni grabbed her phone from the bedside table and checked her local nail salon. She had no one else to please and nothing to do all day, so she could spend it getting back in touch with herself. Shower. Makeup. *Real* clothes. New nails. And maybe a glass of wine with lunch at a nice place in town.

There was already a message from Willow, telling her how weird it was to wake up alone and how much she missed her. Leoni returned the sentiment, though she didn't want to overthink being alone. *This* was her life. It was a life she liked, and a week in the Hamptons had been an indulgent reality break, nothing more. She resisted the temptation to ask about Aspen and just told Willow about her plans for the day instead.

Sounds like heaven. Gramps and Grammy have asked me if I want to live with them while I'm in college. What do you think?

Leoni smiled. She'd been used to giving her opinion about clothes and makeup to the other women she worked with, but now she had an actual friend who valued her thoughts on deeper things. *I think it's a great idea.* She didn't know what the campus accommodation was like at Stony Brook, but she had no doubt it wouldn't be up to Willow's standards.

You'll have a place to stay when you visit me...

I'll let you know when I have vacation time.

Promise?

I promise. Shower time. Talk later x

Leoni allowed herself one last stretch, an almost lethal decision that nearly led to her snuggling back into bed for a little nap, then she threw back the covers and got up to start her day. *Alone.*

At the salon, after stopping herself from sharing the events of the week with her nail technician, Leoni texted Tyler to see if she was free for lunch. Apparently, she needed to ease back into the relatively solitary life she'd left behind a mere week ago.

I think Jesse's free.

Leoni sighed. She didn't want to talk to Jesse. She'd known Tyler the longest, and if she was going to talk to anyone, it had to be her. *I want a conversation, not a booty call.*

Got it. Text me the name of the place. I can be there by 2:30

Leoni got to the café at two, and the waiter gave her a table by the window, where she could watch the world go by. All she saw were couples, all kinds and all seemingly obsessed with each other. It was the opposite of when you bought a new car, and then all you saw on the road was the exact same model, as if no other vehicles existed. Now she was seeing only what she wasn't part of.

She'd just sipped the last of her wine when she spotted Tyler on the sidewalk heading toward her. The usual thrum of excitement was absent as she watched Tyler get closer. Even her outfit of faded jeans and sheer black T-shirt, pulled taut over the muscles she spent hours building, stirred nothing.

What was wrong with her? Maybe she should've invited Jesse instead. After their impromptu sex party a week ago, seeing her would be a perfect way to test her emerging theory that Aspen had broken her.

Maybe not broken. That seemed extreme, since they'd done nothing more than kiss once. Leoni was just a little bent out of shape, and she needed to nestle back into her mold. That was all, and it would take time because she'd never experienced anything like it before.

Tyler came into the café and wrapped her in a strong hug. "I was expecting a baseball cap, cargo shorts, and a plaid shirt." She dropped onto the seat opposite Leoni. "I can't decide if I'm disappointed or not."

Leoni played with a strand of her hair and enjoyed the softness of it between her fingers. "I played the part. I'm not keeping the accoutrements," she said and told Tyler of the baseball cap's fate.

"Has Ruth approved the destruction of her property?" Tyler grinned. "She'll take it out of your commission."

"I don't care." Leoni flicked her hair over her shoulder. "It had to be done." Perhaps the cap could be the symbolic beginning of letting go of Aspen too.

"What was Willow Hartwell like?" Tyler asked after the waiter came to the table and took her order for a beer, and Leoni ordered a coffee.

"She was everything you'd expect her to be, based on her Insta, and I thought she was going to be an absolute nightmare. She was *not* impressed that she didn't get you."

"What was that about?"

Leoni shook her head. "It was complicated. You were supposed to be butch competition for her sister, and she wanted her mom to take more notice of her."

Tyler grumbled. "Poor little rich girl not getting enough attention. Could she have been any more of a cliché?"

Leoni bristled at the dismissive description. The waiter returning with their drinks and a food menu gave her time to curb her reaction and not jump to Willow's defense. She ordered a brie and cranberry toastie and took no notice of Tyler's request.

"Like I said, it was complicated. She was just lost. And floating." Leoni chuckled at the watery reference. Willow would've been impressed.

Tyler curled her lip and huffed. "I'd like to be lost and floating in billions of dollars. What a hardship that'd be."

Leoni didn't appreciate the aggressive edge to Tyler's tone but tried to tamp down her desire to protect Willow's reputation. "They live in another world, that's for sure." One she'd been invited into. As family. Even with the stabbing loss of what could have been with Aspen, Leoni had gained something so very precious.

"Tell me about the week." Tyler leaned forward on her elbows. "Tell me everything."

Over their food, Leoni regaled Tyler with details of the weird family golf tournament that had been more serious than the Ryder Cup, the insane kayak polo, the amazing scuba diving experience, and the Fourth of July party and hour-long fireworks display on their own mile-long stretch of private beach, though she'd watched that through watery eyes on the floor of Willow's bedroom. She didn't tell Tyler everything, like she thought she might. She'd wondered if the Hartwell sisters had opened up her emotional floodgates, making it easy for her to share with everyone close to her. But clearly, there was a difference between close *proximity* and close *emotionally*.

"I wish I'd gotten to drive that G-Wagen," Tyler said. "Damn COVID."

Leoni shrugged. She doubted many would say that COVID had done them any favors, but in this instance, she could.

"Was the kid any less lost after spending all that money with Ruth?"

Leoni smiled. "Actually, yeah. She's going to college in September to study marine biology."

Tyler gave a bitter-sounding laugh. "Must be nice to decide you have a new dream and have all that money behind you to follow it through."

Leoni nodded. "No doubt," she said and drifted away from the conversation. She'd convinced herself that her dream was out of reach until she'd built up the reserves to pursue it. But as the years passed and her savings grew, adulting and practicalities took precedence, and she'd allowed her dream to fade. Instead of following her heart, she'd settled into a comfortable life with very little meaning in any aspect of it. No real friends. No one to share anything with. No ambitions or goals to work toward. She was coasting just as much as Willow had been, and her life was ticking away one second at a time, one fake romance after another. But helping Willow had been one of the most rewarding things she'd done in a long, long while, probably since finishing college.

So maybe it *was* time to revisit her own dream. She pulled out her phone and checked her savings account, still optimistically called Dream Pot, which she'd been feeding monthly from her Perfect Fit gigs but had stopped keeping an eye on a couple of years ago. The healthy balance caused a sharp intake of breath. She had over fifty percent more than her target of two years' worth of living expenses.

She put some money on the table and got up. "Thanks for coming, Tyler, but I've got to go."

She had the money, and she had the dream. The only thing holding her back was herself. How high could she fly if she opened her wings and let the wind take her where it may?

Chapter Twenty-Eight

"You want an office in New York?" Aspen sank deeper into the booth and stretched out her legs. "Have we taken on a gorilla client I don't know about?"

Flynn rolled her eyes. "Don't be weird. You know I wouldn't take on a new client without consulting you, no matter how much the contract might be worth."

"We have to concentrate on the Mancharlson project right now. We don't need any distractions now that we've finally landed something this big."

"We've been in the business nearly ten years." Flynn tapped the table repeatedly. "Covering both coasts is what we always talked about."

"That was before remote working became such a big thing. Now we don't really need one office, let alone two." That wasn't strictly true. Neither of them had the apartment space to run a business from, and Aspen would hate the lack of separation anyway.

"Okay, so let's relocate to the East Coast and just have one office."

"The retirement village is here in LA, Flynn."

"This one is, but he's talking about developing one in or close to every major city with a high LGBTQ population. New York has the highest population in the States. He's already mentioned it."

"He's talked about Chicago and San Francisco too." Aspen took a long slug of her beer. "Is this sudden rush because of Kelly?"

"There's no rush. Who said anything about rushing? I'm just putting it out there."

"Look, buddy, I'm happy for you, I really am. But you and Kelly have only just started dating. Do you really want to upend our whole business just so you can be close to her?"

Flynn took a deep breath and sighed. "Yes, I do. Life's too short to be wasting time traveling from coast to coast, snatching a couple of days here and there. And it's too expensive to do it every weekend. I don't see any other way."

"Let me get this straight," Aspen said. "You want to risk our business of ten years to be close to your girlfriend of two weeks?"

"Don't be so dramatic." Flynn shook her head. "You've just said that remote working is easier than it's ever been."

Aspen sighed. "Look, I don't want to put the brakes on your heart, and I don't want to jinx anything, but what if you and Kelly don't work out?"

Flynn's answering grin was unexpected. "You couldn't jinx us even if you tried, which obviously, I know you wouldn't. Kelly and I are forever. I know that all the way to my bones."

Aspen said nothing and finished her beer. She'd never seen Flynn so sure of anything in her life, and she was always confident in everything she did. Aspen supposed that Flynn and Kelly had been dancing around each other for long enough that it wasn't just about the official amount of time they'd been dating. And sometimes people just knew they'd found *the one*. She swallowed hard and blinked away images of Leoni from her mind—images that Willow had been at great pains to share with her via social media. Finding out that Leoni was a high femme had done nothing to help her increasing sense of losing someone special.

Which was why she couldn't possibly stand in Flynn's way now. "So you're buying me dinner to butter me up. Is that about right?"

Flynn grinned wider and nodded. "That's about right. Is it working?"

Aspen shrugged. "It's all going to come down to the quality of the T-bone. If you've brought me to a classy joint, whose chef knows how to cook steak properly, your chances are pretty good.

If not..." She held up her hands. "I guess we're staying put."

Flynn laughed. "Their chef is a local legend. Movie stars eat here. Do you really think I'd leave something as important as your steak to chance?" She waved to get the attention of waitstaff, and they ordered their food and more beer. "How's the therapy going?"

"It's going." Aspen picked at the label on her empty bottle. "The thing she seems most eager for me to learn is to leave the past where it is. Otherwise I can't begin to live in the moment...or some crap like that."

Another waiter returned with their beer as Flynn laughed. "If that's how seriously you're taking it, you're probably not going to be moving forward quickly."

Aspen clinked her bottle to Flynn's and smiled. "I'm kidding. I just didn't expect it to be quite this hard." She pulled her wallet from her pocket and took out a card to show Flynn.

"'The more anger toward the past you carry in your heart, the less capable you are of loving in the present.' Fortune cookie?"

Aspen placed it on the table beside her beer when Flynn handed it back. "No, butt-face. It's a quote from some clever relationship specialist, apparently."

"Seems like they wrote that especially for you."

Aspen traced her fingers over the words. "It kind of feels that way. I think that's probably why she gave it to me. She pulled a drawer out from her desk with about thirty compartments full of cards like this."

"One for every day?"

"Or one for every emotional condition." Aspen laughed, but it was reflex rather than genuine humor. "It only took her a second to decide I needed this one."

"How many ridiculously priced sessions do you think it's going to take before you feel like you'll be able to leave your anger in the past and live in the moment?"

"I'm going twice a week, so maybe...1,560? I should be fixed by the time 2040 rolls around." Aspen held her bottle in the air.

"I'm not drinking to that morbid prediction." Flynn pushed Aspen's beer away. "You're not someone who's afraid of hard work. I think you can do better than that."

"Hard work on *myself* is very different from any other hard work I've ever done."

Flynn shrugged. "Better that than just turning up to every session and avoiding the tough stuff." She grinned again. "And the payoff will be worth it. When you can trust again, you'll be open to finding someone who deserves you. If you work quick, you might be in one piece again at your birthday party, ready for all the eligible rich bachelorettes who'll be there."

Aspen groaned. "That didn't work out so well last time, did it?"

"That woman is a particularly twisted individual." Flynn curled her lip. "Your mom won't invite her, will she?"

"You know the grands are close to the Duncan family, and as far as most people know, we split amicably."

"And you haven't specifically told your mom *not* to invite her?"

Aspen shook her head. "Come on, Flynn, you know the drill. The party's *for* me, but it's not *my* party. If it were up to me, I wouldn't have one at all."

"Killjoy. You can't deny us all the opportunity to celebrate you being brought into existence."

"You sound like Mom."

The waitstaff brought their meals, and Aspen wafted the divine smell of grilled steak upward.

"And while we're on the subject, this dinner is doubling up as your birthday gift," Flynn said, waving her fork in the air.

"That's fine with me. You know how I feel about birthday gifts too."

Flynn shook her head. "One day, someone's going to change your mind about that. You're denying a lot of people the joy of gift-giving. There's no way I could forego getting gifts for Kelly. Heck, I want to get her something every day just for being alive and in my life."

"So you want to *buy* her love?" Aspen sliced into her steak and sighed happily when the knife slipped through it like it was butter.

"No. I already *have* her love. I just want to show her how much I love her."

"Aren't you supposed to do that with actions?"

Flynn stabbed at Aspen's plate. "Shut up and eat your food before it gets cold. You can't talk about something you're not hip-deep in the middle of."

Aspen put a piece of steak in her mouth, and it practically melted. She tried hard to concentrate on that, on being *in the moment*, instead of thinking about Flynn's words and how right she was...and instead of thinking about Leoni and how she might've been someone Aspen could easily have loved.

For now though, just this moment was guaranteed, and her friendship with Flynn was definitely something to celebrate and treasure.

"Even if this steak had been as leathery as the face of a sixty-year-old surf bum, I wouldn't stand in your way with New York." She picked up her beer and held it aloft again. "Whatever it takes, we'll make it work, I promise."

Flynn grinned widely. "Now that's something I can drink to."

She nudged her bottle to Aspen's, and they drank to an uncertain yet somehow certain future.

Move forward and live in the moment... And maybe one day, Aspen would be able to do exactly what her therapist's card advocated: love in the present.

Chapter Twenty-Nine

THREE WEEKS OF PRECISE planning, countless conversations with her old college buddy, Samantha, a remarkably easy resignation from Perfect Fit, and Leoni was on her way to New York to follow her dream. Still, she wished she'd taken the window seat instead of thinking that her mom might like it. Then she wouldn't be in the middle of her mom's animated conversation with the vaguely attractive older guy with good hair and bad breath.

"So this is your first time in New York?" the man asked, his sewer-breath diving up her nose like a cloud of noxious gas.

"First time on a plane!" Her mom clapped her hands together. "Thanks to my beautiful daughter."

"That's nice." He smiled widely at Leoni, but it looked fake, and he quickly turned his gaze back to her mom. "What're your plans when you get there?"

Her mom patted Leoni's knee. "First, we have to get Leoni settled into her new apartment. Then there'll be lots of shopping and sightseeing."

"So you're moving there?" Sewer-breath asked her mom.

"Not me. At least, not yet," she said and winked at Leoni. "Not until she's a famous actress."

"You're an actress?" he asked, glancing briefly at Leoni. "She obviously got her good looks and talent from you. I wouldn't have been surprised if you'd said you were the actress. Or model."

He wiggled his eyebrows, making them look like a giant hairy worm was crawling across his forehead. Leoni looked at her mom. She couldn't possibly be falling for this crap, could she?

Her mom waved the sickly sweet line away. "Oh no, my

daughter is the one with all the talent. I couldn't act my way out of a paper bag." She took Leoni's hand. "And she has the voice of an angel."

Sewer-breath offered Leoni's mom a card. "If you're at a loose end and want dinner one evening, or if you want to see the *real* New York, give me a call."

Leoni raised her eyebrows. This guy moved fast.

Her mom didn't take the card. "I only go for dinner with *single* men."

Sewer-breath frowned and jerked his arm back. "I...I'm single."

Her mom chuckled. "I noticed you as we boarded, you being such a handsome man and all, and I thought, wouldn't it be nice if he ended up sitting next to us? But when you handed your passport over, I saw a wedding ring." She gestured to his hands, which he shifted out of sight. "And now it's suspiciously absent."

His head twitched, and he grumbled. "So why talk to me at all?"

Her mom laughed. "I never miss an opportunity to tell anyone about my smart, amazingly talented daughter, and you were a captive audience. Why would I assume you were only talking to me to get me into bed?"

"Goddamn woman." Sewer-breath turned on his butt cheek and faced into the aisle.

"Whatever comes out of his ass for the next few hours can't smell worse than his god-awful breath," Leoni whispered.

Her mom giggled. "Now that he's dealt with, I can enjoy the window seat." She almost pressed her nose to the glass and took some photos on her phone. "It looks like you could almost take a walk on those fluffy clouds."

Leoni leaned in to see. "Hopefully the sky will clear so you can see the landscape. Seeing the country from up here is something else."

Her mom relaxed back into her chair and took Leoni's hand. "Thank you again for bringing me with you for this."

"Thank you for wanting to come. I know how hard it is for you to get vacation time."

"I would've quit if they hadn't given it to me," her mom said. "I couldn't miss my baby doing this." She smiled and squeezed Leoni's hand. "I'm so happy that you're finally following your dream. You were wasted with that girlfriend company."

"Thanks, Mom," Leoni said.

"Although, wouldn't it have been weird if you'd ended up in a real-life, lesbian, no-sex version of *Pretty Woman*? After how many times you've watched it with me, it would've been like we'd somehow manifested it into being."

Leoni laughed. "I did think of that when I had to get a whole new wardrobe for the week." She shook her head, remembering Aspen standing at the window of the house, watching her leave. "But the sister of my super-rich girlfriend didn't chase after me when I left."

"Her loss," her mom said and rubbed Leoni's forearm.

She smiled at the predictable mom response, but she knew she'd lost something too. The *not knowing* how good something could've been somehow seemed worse than losing it after she'd had it.

"It'll be lovely to see Samantha again after all these years. I'm glad you'll be staying with her for a while."

Leoni shook off the melancholy of her last gig and focused on the excitement of her new future. "Yeah, it will. I haven't visited her since she first got the ensemble job in *Wicked* a couple of years ago. And her apartment building is really nice. I got lucky that her old roommate just got her big break in Hollywood."

"You two were so close when you were in college," her mom said. "I thought for sure that you'd move with her to New York."

Leoni shrugged. Samantha came from a far more financially secure background than she had, and her parents had helped support her living costs for three years before she secured her first regular show. But she wasn't about to tell her mom that and make her feel bad. She'd spent way too much of Leoni's childhood apologizing for their lack of money, especially when the checks never came through from Leoni's dad. "I guess I just wasn't ready to take the risk."

"Mm." Her mom cupped Leoni's face. "And I suppose it had nothing at all to do with you wanting to support me." She smiled and kissed Leoni's forehead. "I've appreciated everything you've done for me, baby, but you'll never know how proud I am of you for taking the risk now. Next time I come visit, it'll be to see you headlining a Broadway show."

Leoni chuckled. "I love your confidence, Mom, but I think you'll be visiting me long before that happens. It'll take me a while to earn a reputation off-Broadway before I get a whiff of anything big. And I'm okay with that."

Sewer-breath vacated his seat, muttering something under his breath Leoni didn't catch. "He was such a dick."

Her mom nodded. "I have to fend off men like him all the time."

Leoni smiled. "That's because you look like a model."

Her mom swatted Leoni's shoulder. "Smart ass."

"Can I ask you something?"

Her mom narrowed her eyes. "Probably."

Leoni swiveled sideways in her seat. "Did what happened with Dad stop you from trusting other guys?"

Her mom pulled in a long breath and sighed heavily. "It did for a long time, yes. And it especially hurt when he married another woman and started a new family. I didn't trust another man for a few years after your father, but it's not good for you to hold on to that kind of toxic thought process." She shrugged. "It wasn't hurting anyone but me. Your father was certainly living his life to the max."

"Without *us*," Leoni said, then wished she hadn't because her mom's eyes teared up almost instantly.

"I'm so sorry for what he did to you, baby. I know you haven't let yourself get close to anyone because you're worried they'll leave like he did."

Leoni frowned. "You knew that?"

Her mom nodded. "I don't have to be a trained therapist to see that. You don't even have close friendships. Samantha was your last close friend and that was ten years ago." She caressed Leoni's cheek. "But something's changed, hasn't it?"

Leoni smiled. She might not have been close to anyone else, but her mom could still read her like a book. "Yeah, it has."

"Is that why you're asking about your father?"

"Partly. Aspen said that she wouldn't be able to trust that anything I said was true, that I might fall for another client just as easily as I did for her—"

"But now you don't have that job." Her mom grinned as if she had the solution to all of Leoni's problems, but it wasn't that simple at all.

"I don't think that makes any difference. If the trust isn't there, it doesn't matter what my job is, because I'd always meet new people I could fall for, theoretically."

"I suppose you're right," her mom said.

"So my question was more around how long it takes to stop letting your past relationships rule your future ones. None of your guys have lasted much longer than a couple of years, and I just wondered if that was still because of Dad."

Her mom shook her head. "I really don't think it is. I just haven't found anyone I *want* to be around for longer than that. Those affairs just ran their course. They weren't bad guys. I can assure you that not every guy on the planet is like that buttwipe," she said, indicating the empty seat beside Leoni. "They just weren't the guy for me long-term."

"You haven't given up?"

"Ooh, no. As long as I've got a pulse, I'll still be open to finding that someone special. It just doesn't dictate my life like it used to." She smiled and patted Leoni's knee. "And while you were young, you've got to remember that I wasn't just looking for someone special for me. They had to be good enough to be around you too."

Leoni laid her head on her mom's shoulder. "I probably haven't told you enough how much I love you. And I definitely haven't thanked you enough for being such an awesome mom."

"That's the easy part when I was blessed with such a wonderful daughter." She rested her head on Leoni's. "But thank you. That's lovely to hear."

They sat like that for a while. Leoni's mind whirred with questions and possibilities, the most prominent one being, could she and Aspen have a future someday?

"In response to your question about the past ruling your future, that's different for all of us. No one experiences life the same way as any single other person. We all have our baggage, and trauma, and childhood, and each piece of that contributes to how we deal with everything life throws at us. So if you were hoping for a solid answer on how long you might have to wait for your *Pretty Woman* moment, I can't give it to you, I'm afraid."

Leoni closed her eyes against the threatening tears. Her makeup was supposed to be waterproof, but she didn't actually want to put it to the test. "I guess I'm trying to decide if I should let go of hope. Willow is desperate for me to get together with her sister, and she wants me to come to Aspen's birthday party next week. But I don't know what to do. I'd said I couldn't, because I wouldn't be able to get vacation time. Now I don't have a job, so that's not a problem, *and* I'll only be ninety minutes away by car. Willow nearly jumped through the screen at me when I told her I was moving. I don't want to upset Aspen though, and if there is any chance of us ever getting together, I don't want to ruin that by turning up and ruining her party." She blew out her cheeks. "What am I supposed to do?"

Her mom chuckled. "Oh, love, I can't tell you that. I couldn't tell you that when you were a kid, and I'm not about to start now. You're still in Aspen's orbit because you and Willow are friends, so if it's meant to happen, it will. If two people are meant to be together and *want* to be together, I don't think there's a force in the world that can stop it."

"You believe in *the one*?"

"I believe in the one and the many," her mom said and laughed. "And while I'm waiting for the one, I'll busy myself with the many. You could do the same."

Leoni shook her head. "I don't seem to be interested in that anymore." She thought of the goodbyes she'd had with Tyler and then with Jesse, who'd surprisingly made it clear she would happily follow Leoni to New York. But Leoni had felt nothing other than a distant fondness for the one night they'd shared.

"Well, it's only been a few weeks. The fire's still burning bright. If it doesn't fade to embers after months and months, then you have to decide whether to move on or move in."

Leoni narrowed her eyes. "Move in?"

"Yes, move in," her mom said. "Visit Aspen and see how the land lies. See how close she is to putting her past where it belongs. Life's short, baby. You have to make your own fate if you want something bad enough."

"Mm, I get it." Leoni thought of all the moments she'd shared with Aspen, the conversations, the looks, the fun they'd had, the *almost* kiss, and then the *half* kiss. It all held so much promise and had made her feel emotions she'd thought had been buried under the rubble of her father's abandonment, never to see the light of day, let alone the light of love.

Was that what this was? Could she really have begun to fall in love in just a week? When were you supposed to *know*? And how did your heart tell you? Did it send your head a memo when Cupid's arrow hit the love instead of the lust target?

She had so many questions, and the only way to answer them was to see Aspen again. Whether that was in a week or a year though, she couldn't control. What she *did* have the power to do, however, was be patient and wait. Her mom's fire analogy seemed logical too. And while she waited, she had a new career to build. And all the world was her stage.

Chapter Thirty

ASPEN PICKED WILLOW UP and twirled her around and around, and she giggled just like she used to when she was a little girl. The sound wrapped around Aspen's heart and poured warmth into it. She'd really believed she'd lost Willow for good. She tried to shut out her mind's interjection that she would've had it not been for the intervention of a complete stranger—a stranger who embedded themselves into their lives as naturally and as easily as if she'd been there all along.

"I'm in! I'm in!" Willow yelled between high-pitched squeals of delight.

"This is the best birthday present you've ever given me," Aspen said as she set Willow down.

"What's all the noise about?" Flynn looked down on them from the balcony, shaking her head. "I thought you weren't telling her in case it didn't pan out."

Willow's head snapped back. "Tell me what?"

Aspen clapped. "Nice one, Flynn. Willow just showed me her acceptance email. She's going to college in September."

"That's what I meant," Flynn said and retreated back inside.

Willow sat down beside the pool and dipped her feet in the water. "She's a terrible liar."

Aspen shrugged. "Makes her a really good friend... Let's talk college and the best birthday gift ever."

"Me going to college can't be your gift. It's not your birthday until tomorrow," Willow said. "Let's talk about your secret."

"Only if you promise not to tell anyone." Aspen blew out a breath and joined Willow poolside. "Flynn hasn't talked to Kelly about it yet, but she wants to open a New York office for the business so they can be together properly. The long-distance relationship thing is proving too hard for them both."

Willow wrinkled her nose. "That's nice for them, but why would Flynn think I'd get so excited about that?" She frowned and then her eyes lit up. "Unless it meant that you'd be spending more time up here. Is that what it means?"

Aspen splashed her feet in the water. "It doesn't mean anything yet. We've got to figure out finances and clients and see if it's even viable, especially with the retirement village we're working on. That's going to take eighteen months, possibly more."

"But you wouldn't have to be in LA the whole time, would you?" Willow pouted. "It's not like you're actually building it."

Aspen chuckled. "That's true, but we have to do site visits and check that everything is being built to spec at various stages throughout the process."

"You like traveling," Willow said. "And Flynn would do half the work, wouldn't she? Isn't that what having a partner in business means?"

She nodded. "That's one of the benefits, yeah."

Willow grinned. "Do you know who else just moved to New York for work?"

Aspen shrugged. "Nope."

"Guess."

Aspen rolled her eyes. "You know I don't like guessing."

Willow nudged her shoulder. "I know that, but I also know that you used to humor me and guess anyway."

Aspen sighed. "That was when you were a kid."

Willow wiggled on the spot and gave Aspen her cutest grin. "I'm still a kid."

"A kid who's going to be a world-renowned marine biologist and conservationist."

Her kid sister was growing up and had chosen a career outside the family business, just like she had. She couldn't be more proud.

"Guess," Willow said and crossed her arms.

"Miley Cyrus?"

"Be serious."

Aspen held up her hands. "You didn't say the guesses had to be serious."

Willow swatted Aspen's shoulder. "Of course they do. Only realistic guesses, please."

"Then you're going to have to be more specific," Aspen said and smiled. "Is this person moving to the Hamptons?"

"No."

"Where in New York then?"

"Queens."

Aspen chuckled. "You know someone who's moving to Queens?"

"Why? What's wrong with Queens?"

"Nothing at all. It's just a little different from the places your usual friends are from."

"I didn't say she was my friend."

"Ah." Aspen tapped Willow's nose gently. "A she? And she's not your friend."

"A she, yes, but I didn't say she *wasn't* my friend." Willow smiled widely. "Actually, she *is* a friend and will probably become my best friend in the whole world, like Flynn is your bestie and Kelly is Oakley's bestie."

Aspen frowned. There was only one person Willow had gotten this excited about, but she was supposed to be in Las Vegas. "Leoni?" she asked quietly, barely able to say her name out loud. A flood of emotions assailed her, and she couldn't decide which to focus on.

Willow clapped and whooped. "Yay, you got it!"

Aspen nibbled the inside of her cheek, searching for something to say, some way to respond. Was Leoni finally following her dream or had she just moved offices with her escort company? "Why?"

Willow shoved her so hard, she nearly fell in the pool. "That's all you've got to say? I thought you'd be excited."

Aspen shook her head. "It's complicated. You know I'm getting therapy to sort myself out after Sarah."

"You've had, like, four weeks, haven't you? You should be fixed by now."

Aspen laughed lightly. "I *have* done a lot of work in nine sessions, but I'm not a broken vase that just needs to be put back together. And Leoni's job was a massive obstacle for me."

Willow's eyes sparkled mischievously. "You should ask her to come to your birthday party tomorrow."

"It's Saturday night," Aspen said. "That's really short notice, and I'm sure she's already busy with a client or something." She shuddered at the unpleasant thought.

"Mm, I suppose she *could* be busy...*auditioning* or going out for drinks with her theater pals." Willow wiggled her eyebrows and pressed her lips together tightly, like she was desperately trying to keep something inside.

"Wait. What?" Aspen's breath caught at the possibility. "Leoni's moved to New York to follow her theater dream?"

Willow nodded and broke out into a huge smile. "She was stuck just like I was. I told her it was fate that we met. Now we're both doing what we were always supposed to be."

Aspen's world tilted on its axis slightly. "Fate?"

"Yep, and now you're thinking of moving your office to New York too." Willow pointed to the sky. "Fate. The stars are aligning for all of us. It's a huge country, Aspen. What are the odds that we all end up in the same state purely by chance?"

"Whoa, I didn't say we were moving. I said we were thinking of having a *second* office."

"That would be a silly expense," Willow said. "You're a small firm and only need one office. Even I can see that."

Aspen's heart hammered against her ribs. It could've been fear or excitement. Maybe even both. She'd dreamed of all the different scenarios that would mean her getting together with Leoni, but she'd never thought any of them could actually happen. And after only a month. Was she ready for Leoni? *Could* she be ready for Leoni?

She stopped the barreling thought-train. After the way they'd parted, Leoni might not be interested anymore. It was clear that she and Willow had forged a wonderful friendship, and maybe Leoni would tolerate Aspen's proximity for that reason only.

A firm shove from Willow brought her back into their conversation. "Are you okay? You look like you're having a stroke."

Aspen frowned. "That's dark. And unlikely. It's good that you're going to look after animals and not people."

"Whatever. Are you inviting Leoni or not?"

Aspen looked up into the bright, clear sky and squinted against the intensity of the sun. Why did inviting Leoni back into her life make her feel like Icarus? She had no wings to lose, but her heart was still vulnerable. "Does she even *want* to come?"

Willow pulled her phone from her skirt pocket. "Let me ask her."

"She's probably too busy to get back to you." Aspen looked away from the flurry of Willow's thumbs on her cell screen and allowed herself a small smile. No matter what happened, she was so happy that Leoni had decided to follow her dream. It seemed only right after helping Willow find and follow hers.

Willow sighed heavily. "Oh my god."

"What's wrong?"

"Leoni wants to know if *you* want her to come or if I've bullied you into asking her." Willow stared at Aspen when she said nothing. "So? You do want her to come, don't you?"

"If she's not doing anything more important, then yeah, I'd like her to come." Aspen clamped her teeth together so she couldn't rescind the invitation. Her therapist's voice echoed in her head: *Live in the moment.*

Willow rolled her eyes. "What could be more important that your birthday party?"

"Attending an audition."

"Good point." Willow focused on her phone again. "I'll make sure she doesn't have to skip something like that."

Another age seemed to pass before Willow made an encouraging sound.

"No auditions. No hot dates. No other plans." Willow popped her phone back in her pocket. "Leoni is coming tomorrow!" She jumped up and danced on the spot. "I can't wait to see her. I'm going to tell Gramps!"

Willow skipped off, leaving Aspen to contemplate her feelings. Maybe, though, she shouldn't be overthinking it. She'd spent the last month wishing everything had been different, wishing that she'd never met Sarah, wishing that her heart had been open to Leoni the first time around. Aspen wasn't fully healed, no, but she *was* determined not to mess up the second chance she'd been given.

No more wishing. Wishing wouldn't make anything happen. If Aspen really wanted to see what a future with Leoni held, she had to take the risk and open up. And if she opened her heart, maybe love could rush in.

Chapter Thirty-One

Leoni waited behind the curtain, her heart still flip-flopping over whether or not this was really a good idea. It was one thing to be a last-minute invitation to Aspen's birthday party, but it was another thing altogether to gatecrash the stage. "Are you sure about this?"

"I'm not sure, no." Willow clasped Leoni's hands and held them to her chest, then she grinned widely. "I'm absolutely positive."

Leoni blew out a long breath and shook her head. "I think I'm shooting too high. I should never have suggested something so grand."

Willow laughed. "Nonsense. Love is all about grand gestures. That's what all the books and movies say, isn't it?"

Leoni thought once more about the ending of her mom's favorite movie. That wasn't a particularly grand gesture, and that guy had all the money in the world. She was trying to win the woman *with* all the money in the world by doing something Aspen might not even like. "But this is neither of those things. This is real life, and I could be about to mess everything up. For good, this time."

Willow grasped her shoulders and shook her not so lightly. "Stop second-guessing yourself. This is going to be one of those moments you'll retell a thousand times." She wiggled her eyebrows. "And I can't wait to tell the story to your kids."

Leoni nearly choked on fresh air. "Whoa, slow your roll. We're not even talking yet."

"You'll be more than talking by the end of tonight." Willow gave a mischievous grin.

Leoni laughed, despite herself. "If I'd known how much fun a best friend could be, I might've done this a long time ago."

Willow arched her eyebrow. "It wouldn't have been the same. How many times do I have to keep telling you this was fate. Perfect timing. The Universe at play."

"You're way too much of a modern-day hippie for your age," Leoni said.

Willow shrugged. "It's Gramps' and Grammy's influence."

Leoni checked her watch for the fiftieth time in the past ten minutes she'd been standing there, partially sunken in the sand in five-inch heels. "Why does time go so slow sometimes? Shouldn't your mom be getting up on the stage by now to give her speech?"

"Relax. Everything's going to be fine. More than fine. You're going to be flawless."

Leoni swallowed hard. "I haven't performed in front of an audience for years. I don't think flawless will be the adjective you'll use at the end of all this."

"Your guitarist and backing singer will help you with that."

Leoni wrung her hands. She'd conveniently pushed *that* little nugget to the back of her mind. She planned to go on stage and totally ignore the fact that an eleven-time Grammy award-winner would be playing with her. "The things your uber-rich family can afford blow my mind."

Willow drew her into a hug. "She's doing this for free. Brandi's a family friend."

Heart palpitations kicked in, and Leoni was sure the damn thing was about to burst out of her chest and make a run for it. "Oh my God, I think that makes it worse."

"You look like a million dollars, by the way."

"You're a billionaire, so I don't know if that's a compliment or an insult."

"Silly. It's definitely a compliment." Willow giggled. "Aspen is going to *die* when she sees you looking like that. Your dress is beautiful."

"She better not after all this effort." Leoni looked down briefly before snapping her gaze back up. "Samantha practically poured me into it. Are you sure it looks good?"

Willow shook her head slowly and whistled, though it only came out as a weird wind sound. "Good doesn't begin to describe it. You look so hot, I could almost think about having you for myself. *Almost*." She peeked through the curtain then jumped back and tapped Leoni's shoulder repeatedly. "Mom's coming! Mom's coming!"

Cate came around the corner of the small marquee they were huddled under. She smiled and took Leoni's hands in hers. "You look stunning. I can't wait to see Aspen's face when you come out and sing for her."

Leoni nibbled her lower lip, not quite sure how to respond. The way the Hartwell family had welcomed her into their lives was still overwhelming. Cate's transformation from ice-queen matriarch to nurturing mom-of-her-new-best-friend had been particularly unexpected. Leoni and Willow had Zoomed almost every day in the five weeks since she'd last been here, and Cate had video-bombed a third of those to say hi. That had risen to every time they'd chatted in the last week as they planned this surprise in the hope that Aspen would actually invite her. Leoni would've hated all the effort to have gone to waste if Aspen hadn't extended an invitation, mostly for her own selfish reasons, but also because Cate and Willow were almost as excited about it as she was.

Cate cupped Leoni's cheek gently. "Don't worry, honey. I know my daughter, and she's going to love this. I promise." She smiled and elegantly ascended the steps to the rear of the stage.

Leoni and Willow parted the curtain a little more so they could watch Cate, and so Leoni could search for Aspen. She didn't have to look for long before the sight of Aspen almost stole her breath. She looked incredibly handsome in a tailored tux, complete with a crisp-looking white shirt and dark bow tie. Her hair was swept back, exposing the undercut around the sides, and the way she wore *all* of it made Leoni swoon. Was this a dream? Because

Aspen couldn't possibly be real. She simply *had* to be the very fabric of Leoni's fantasies. Unconsciously, she licked her lips and released a low sound of the sincerest appreciation.

Willow nudged her lightly. "Shush. Save that for the bedroom."

"But...*look*." Leoni waved her hand. "Forget that. All you see is your big sister. Just..." She let out a deep sigh. "Oh. My. God."

Willow rolled her eyes. "Whatever."

The band stopped playing and left the other side of the stage to warm applause, then a hush fell over the gathering. Leoni noticed Jim and Oakley join Aspen, and they sandwiched her in a tight embrace. She would've expected a slight tug of envy at the fatherly display, but all she felt was joy that Aspen had that kind of connection with her dad.

"I won't keep you long," Cate said, "but, as you know, I always have to say a few words at my handsome daughter's birthday parties."

Aspen blushed adorably and smiled, and Leoni wished she was beside her, holding her hand.

"Most of you here will also know that Aspen refused any more birthday gifts when she was twenty," Cate said. "But there was no way I could stop celebrating one of the four most important days in my life. If you're trying to work out the other three, I'll save you the trouble: they're the birth of my other two beautiful children and my wedding day."

The crowd made a collective "ah" of tender appreciation, and Willow gave a happy sigh.

"Anyway, every year since Aspen's command, I've been trying to master the art of pyrography, and Aspen now has a growing—and very amateur—collection of little trinket discs that I've lovingly created, even though they're quite terrible."

"They're gorgeous, Mom," Aspen called out. "But every year, they get better," she said and grinned.

"Well, this year, there isn't one." Cate held out her empty hands. Aspen frowned slightly, and the crowd gave a sad-sounding sigh.

"But I think I've got an even better gift for you this year. And this one isn't just from me. My gorgeous daughter Willow has been absolutely instrumental in making this happen."

Aspen frowned again and began to look around, but Jim put his arm around her shoulder and gestured for her to keep her focus on the stage.

"This year, we're blessed with good fortune and good timing, because our wonderful and extremely talented friend Brandi Carlile has been able to join us." Cate turned to the opposite side of the stage and held out her arms.

Brandi swaggered up the steps from the other side of the stage, semi-acoustic guitar slung over her shoulder, looking sparkly in a sky-blue trouser suit and navy shirt. Ear-shattering applause and hollering erupted. When Leoni spotted Aspen's grin growing even wider, she would've bounced on the spot if it hadn't been for her outfit only being conducive to the minimal amount of movement required for seductively sashaying... Which was something she was desperate to do now in Aspen's direction.

"But Brandi isn't your birthday surprise."

Cate turned to look in their direction now. Leoni's heart tried to escape through her throat this time, and she swallowed hard.

"Tonight, we have a *very* special guest." Cate smiled then turned back to face Aspen and her friends and family. "I'd like to introduce someone who's going to set this stage alight. And you'll want to remember her name, because she's going to do exactly the same thing on Broadway. Ladies, gentlemen, and gentle folks, please welcome to the stage...Leoni York!"

Leoni's years of training kicked in, and a kind of weightlessness allowed her to glide up the stairs on auto pilot. Cate exited the stage, and Brandi sat atop a bar stool, ready to accompany her. Despite the thousands of snowy-white bulbs adorning the area where the crowd gathered, everything darkened and vignetted so that only Aspen was in crisp focus in the center of Leoni's vision. She heard Brandi count her in, then she played the opening bars of "Starting Over." Leoni looked at Aspen as she sang her version of the song, changing it here and there to tailor it more to the future that lay ahead of them—if Aspen wanted it.

Distantly, she registered the vocal approval of the crowd, but all she saw was Aspen's gorgeous face and the raw emotion clear in her eyes, even when those eyes began to glisten with tears. Leoni released all of her dreams and hopes into the words, infusing them with the passion and promise of a thousand forevers. They *would* start over, and it didn't matter where they were or where they went, as long as they were together.

Leoni finished the song and tuned back in to the deafening applause of the crowd. Aspen ran toward the stage and jumped up onto it. She swept Leoni up in her arms and kissed her. Once again, everything else disappeared around her, and the only thing, the only person in her awareness was Aspen. Handsome, sexy Aspen, who held Leoni aloft in her strong arms and shared the possibilities of their union in a tender and all-consuming kiss. Every second leading to this moment, all the competing complications and emotions snowballed around them, and Leoni had the sensation of tumbling inside that snowball like they were careening down the mountainside in an avalanche of love and hope.

Aspen lowered her to the floor slowly and pulled away, only enough that the slightest wisp of air could slip between their lips. "You are the most amazing woman I've ever met."

Leoni ran her fingernail over Aspen's lower lip and enjoyed the carnal reaction in her half-lidded eyes, which was accompanied by a deep, primal growl. "Any chance we could take this away from your adoring crowd?"

Aspen blinked as if she were just realizing they weren't actually alone. "I think they're *your* adoring crowd now."

Aspen turned and bowed to their audience, then she went to Brandi, and they bro-hugged. Leoni hung back, more than a little over-awed by being in the presence of such a hugely talented woman, but Aspen held out her hand, and Leoni took it.

Connected this way, maybe Leoni could do anything, including stringing a sentence together that wasn't a babbled fan-girl stream of nonsense.

"It took me a while to convince my wife to take a chance on me too," Brandi said.

Leoni frowned. "Really?"

Brandi shook her head. "No, not at all," she said and laughed. "Just keep singing to this one, and she'll never let you go."

"Thanks for coming, B," Aspen said, "but I've got to leave my own party early."

Brandi chuckled and motioned to her band coming up the stage steps. "Don't worry, we'll keep this rabble entertained. You go see about starting over," she said and winked.

Leoni looked away, suddenly bashful.

Aspen touched her arm lightly. "Your heels are absolutely beautiful, but I'm in a hurry to get you inside and alone. Any chance I can take them from you while we walk?"

Leoni's heart raced at the thought of finally being alone with Aspen, and she nodded.

Aspen got to her knees and, without taking her eyes from Leoni's, gently removed her shoes. She hooked the straps over her fingers and held out her hand. "Shall we?"

They hadn't gotten down the stage steps before Brandi and her band kicked off with "The Joke." Aspen led Leoni along the edge of the crowd, nodding and giving her thanks to well-wishers. They were almost back to the house gate when a stunning blond stepped out of the crowd, putting herself in between them and the almost perfect getaway. Leoni felt Aspen tense beside her, and she immediately understood who the interloper was.

"I thought you might never get over me. It's so wonderful to see you back on the horse, Aspen." She turned her gaze to Leoni and slowly looked her up and down. "Or should I say the donkey?"

"I'd rather be a donkey than a one-trick pony," Leoni said before Aspen could respond. "Have a lovely evening." She guided Aspen around Sarah and continued to the house without looking back.

"I'm sorry about that," Aspen said as she opened the gate, "but the way you dealt with her was kind of hot."

Leoni tugged on one end of Aspen's bow tie and pulled it open. "If you think that's hot, what's about to happen will set you on fire."

Aspen sighed deeply. "I have no doubt about that." She scooped Leoni up into her arms and carried her inside and upstairs to her room.

Leoni could still hear the music and smiled. "Looks like you're going to be able to make as much noise as you want."

Aspen set Leoni down, placed Leoni's shoes on a nearby chair, and took a step back. "I should apologize first."

Leoni slipped Aspen's tie free of her collar and tossed it aside, then she opened the first couple of buttons on Aspen's shirt. "There's going to be plenty of time for that and *all* the talking we need to do tomorrow." She slipped her hands inside Aspen's jacket, pushed it over her shoulders, and let it fall to the ground. "But right now, I just want to feel you." She pressed her hands against Aspen's strong chest. "And taste you." She ran her tongue along Aspen's bottom lip and sucked it into her mouth when Aspen let out a breathy sigh. "I need you to take me to bed and show me how much you want me."

Aspen trailed her fingers along the single strap of Leoni's dress. "This looks expensive. If you don't want me to rip you out of it, I'm going to need instructions."

Leoni turned slowly, pushed her butt into Aspen's crotch, and touched the top of her dress. "Hidden zipper."

Aspen's hot fingers seared through the material as she took her time drawing the zipper down to Leoni's waist. She pulled the strap over Leoni's shoulder and kissed her neck, then she pulled Leoni into her and peeled the dress over Leoni's breasts. Leoni ground her butt firmly into Aspen's hard body behind her and watched Aspen's tanned, strong hands moving downward over her chest and stomach.

Aspen turned her around into a hard and heavy kiss, crushing their lips together hungrily. Leoni pushed her tongue into Aspen's mouth, desperate to taste her, claim her. Aspen pulled back and gave her a wicked smile, then she slowly dropped to her knees, pulling the rest of Leoni's dress down as she dug her fingers into Leoni's ass.

When she kissed Leoni's heat through her lace panties, Leoni grasped Aspen's hair and yanked her back slightly, shaking her head. "As much as I love the sight of you down there... Not yet." She grabbed Aspen's shirt and guided her back to her feet, then ripped the shirt open. The buttons didn't pop off like they did in the movies, but the effect was still the same: Aspen's chest and stomach were exposed. Leoni saw Aspen had ink on her upper abs, leading up to her chest, and she touched her nails to the script. "What does sui juris mean?"

"It's Latin for 'of her own right.' I take it to mean I am my own. It's about independence."

"It's beautiful." Leoni moved closer and kissed each of the flowers beneath the writing as she dragged her nails across Aspen's shoulders, taking her shirt off. She pushed Aspen back onto the bed and remained standing while she unbuckled Aspen's belt and threaded it from the loops of her trousers. Then she tossed it aside and hitched her dress up so that she could climb on top of Aspen and straddle her.

Aspen put her hands on Leoni's hips and pulled her down onto her crotch. "I've wanted you like this from the moment I first saw you."

Leoni laughed lightly. "Should I have worn cargo pants and a plaid shirt instead?"

"God, no. This dress..." Aspen shook her head slowly, and the way her eyes raked over Leoni's body was clear evidence of her appreciation. "This dress is perfection." She slipped her fingers into Leoni's hair. "And your hair is..." Her eyes half-lidded. "Your hair is gorgeous."

Leoni traced the outline of the crescent moon nestled low between Aspen's small breasts. "You don't prefer the baseball cap?"

"That thing should be—"

"Burned?" Leoni smiled. "Already done." She inched back along Aspen's thighs and dipped her head so that her hair fell onto Aspen's chest, then she dragged it lightly down over her stomach.

Aspen moaned. "Jesus, that's sexy."

Leoni lifted her head and repeated the same movement, even more slowly.

"I can't take this." Aspen flipped Leoni onto her back and lay between her legs, pressed hard against her.

"Impatient much?" Leoni arched up and kissed her soft lips. Aspen responded, and the intense passion of it took Leoni's breath.

"I've waited long enough."

Leoni dug her nails into Aspen's back. "And whose fault is that?"

"My shoulders are broad enough to take the blame, if you need to assign it to someone." Aspen claimed Leoni's mouth again before she could respond, and she ground against her, slow and firm.

"I need you inside me," Leoni said when Aspen finally came up for air. Her patience was lacking too. Finally being this close to Aspen, teetering on the edge of finding out if the reality of being together blew the fantasy into the next realm, was almost too much to bear. She hadn't known whether or not this would happen so fast, but now that she was here, Leoni couldn't wait any longer to be filled with everything Aspen had to offer her.

Aspen gave her a cocky grin. "You *need* me?"

"*Need*," she whispered, arching her back and pushing out her breasts.

That did the trick. Aspen fell against her, biting and nibbling her neck as she continued to push rhythmically against Leoni's sex. Leoni wrapped her legs around Aspen's waist, minimizing the distance between them and wanting their clothes to disintegrate into nothing so that they could be skin to skin at last.

Aspen dug her fingers into Leoni's ass again, making her gasp into Aspen's mouth, and Leoni unwrapped her legs and pushed her panties down. Aspen helped, tearing them off with little care as to the delicate material.

"Up or down?" Aspen asked, yanking at the soft satin of Leoni's dress.

"Up," Leoni said and raised her arms so that Aspen could tug the dress from her body. Her bra was similarly dealt with, and then she lay totally naked under Aspen's gaze.

Aspen shook her head. "Is this really happening?"

She cupped Aspen's jaw and ran her thumb across her cheek. "Yes," she whispered. "Now, please, for the love of all that's unholy, *fuck* me."

Aspen shifted off Leoni to her side and pressed the heel of her hand against Leoni's pussy. "Fuck, you're on fire."

"Another thing you're to blame for." Leoni grasped the back of Aspen's neck and pulled her in for another long and deep kiss. She grabbed Aspen's wrist with her other hand, trying to guide Aspen to give her what she so desperately craved.

"Now who's being impatient?" Aspen whispered.

"Both of us."

Aspen slipped her fingers inside Leoni, and Leoni gave a guttural growl, a sound she didn't recognize as her own. She tightened around Aspen, drawing her in deeper, and pushed her hips up from the bed, eager to meet Aspen's powerful thrusts.

"Harder." Leoni moaned and lost herself in Aspen's perfect rhythm. She cursed and cried out, not caring that someone out there at the party might hear her.

Aspen circled one of Leoni's nipples with her tongue, before she took it into her mouth and sucked, syncing to the tempo of her fingers. She slipped her arm under Leoni's body and pulled her closer, and Leoni rose and fell, pushing against her in perfect time. Her breathing became more rapid, and her curses more regular as Aspen took her higher.

"Oh, God, baby," Leoni cried out as the sensation of complete weightlessness overtook her whole body, and the entirety of her feelings and emotions coalesced deep within her. The intensity of it all continued to rise inexorably to the precipice of her pleasure. "Now," she whispered.

With one last deep thrust, Leoni tumbled into the center of her storm, pulsing and throbbing around Aspen's presence inside her. She rode out the long wave of ecstasy, and tremors coursed through her body, firing every nerve ending simultaneously into a desire so profound that it almost brought tears to her eyes.

She squeezed herself hard around Aspen and wrapped her hand around Aspen's bicep. She looked deep into Aspen's eyes and saw everything she'd never believed she deserved, waiting there for her to claim it as hers. And somehow, she knew that no matter what came next, she simply had to have Aspen alongside her to share it, good or bad. The word that people used so flippantly, to apply to food, TV programs, and cars took on its true meaning when Leoni stared further into Aspen's beautiful blue eyes. Leoni could almost see love take physical shape between them, reaching out, wrapping around their hearts, and binding them together with unbreakable vines.

Could she say it though? Could she give voice to the feeling that had invaded her blood and was pumping around her body, now as necessary to her existence as oxygen? She swallowed and took a shallow breath. What was a heart for if not to fill it with that feeling and share it with the one who put it there? "I love you," she whispered, her heart thudding against her ribs, fearful of what rejection might come.

Aspen's expression softened immeasurably, as if all tension in her body had slipped away. "I love *you*."

And instantly that feeling became fire, nurturing and feeding her very soul, as if it had always been there. The vines around her heart softened and fixed in place, becoming one with her being, with her love for Aspen.

The explosion of emotion caused Leoni to giggle, and she flipped onto her side. She slipped her hand over Aspen's crotch. "I've got an idea," she said and wiggled her eyebrows. "Your family likes tradition, so I want to start a birthday one just for you."

Aspen jutted her chin and smiled mischievously. "What kind of tradition?"

"My mom's grandad was half-Irish, and she said he used to give her the same number of birthday bumps as her age."

Aspen frowned. "What exactly does a birthday bump entail?"

"Someone takes your arms, and another person takes your legs, and they throw you—"

"That doesn't sound like a tradition I'd like." Aspen chuckled and shook her head.

Leoni tapped Aspen's stomach. "If you'd let me finish?"

Aspen held up her hand. "Go ahead."

"They throw you up in the air and bump your butt on the floor," Leoni said. "But since I don't want to share you—at all—I'm thinking birthday orgasms."

Aspen raised her eyebrows. "And I'm thinking you might've forgotten that I'm *thirty-five*. I don't think I've had that many orgasms in a *year* before."

"That's barely more than one every two weeks!" Leoni wrinkled her nose. "That's definitely got to change."

Aspen took Leoni's hand and kissed her fingertips. "And I'm *very* good with that prospect, but I still think you might be aiming too high for one day."

Leoni pulled her hand free, opened Aspen's trousers, and slipped inside. She moaned lightly when her fingers glided easily between Aspen's hot, wet lips. "A girl's got to try," she whispered and circled Aspen's rock-hard clit.

"Oh, Jesus." Aspen dropped her head back onto her pillow and exhaled.

Leoni sighed deeply at Aspen's simple surrender and the way her body moved under Leoni's hand. She might not hit her target, but boy, she was going to enjoy the challenge.

Chapter Thirty-Two

THE SUNLIGHT STREAMING IN through the half-closed blinds warmed Aspen's face as she began to stir. That alone would've been enough to make her smile, but when she became aware of the beautiful woman wrapped tightly in her arms, she grinned wide enough and long enough for her cheeks to hurt. She buried her nose in Leoni's gorgeous long hair and inhaled deeply.

"I'm beginning to think you might have a hair fetish," Leoni whispered.

Aspen suppressed a smug chuckle at the hoarseness of Leoni's voice. "Sounds like all that screaming's made your throat raw."

"And whose fault is that?"

Aspen laughed lightly and nuzzled into Leoni's neck. "I had no idea you were such a blamey-pants."

Leoni twisted in Aspen's arms to face her. "There are a *lot* of things you don't know about me—and might not like."

Aspen traced a finger across Leoni's cheek, pushing away a wisp of hair to tuck it behind her ear. "I doubt that."

"I get gassy after chocolate," Leoni said and raised her eyebrows as if that could be a deal-breaker.

Aspen shrugged. "I get gassy if I drink too much soda."

Leoni ran her finger down the center of Aspen's chest and stopped at the top of her tattoo. "I sleepwalk. I wake up holding all kinds of crap from my bedside table, thinking it's a vital piece to a time-travel machine."

Aspen laughed. "That's very specific. Do you have aspirations to become a time-traveler?"

Leoni's expression became quite serious. "Every time I read a book about it, yeah, I do."

"I think I can cope with that." Aspen trailed her hand over Leoni's hip. "And you didn't do it last night."

"That's because I was exhausted from giving you so many orgasms." Leoni flashed a wicked grin.

Aspen slipped her hand over Leoni's hip and squeezed her butt cheek firmly. "I can't take the blame for that too. The new tradition was your idea, and I told you it was ambitious."

Leoni giggled adorably. "But I had a lot of fun trying."

"You were like a little orgasm vampire." Aspen sighed and jiggled her hips. She was deliciously sore. "I think you might've sucked me dry, and I won't be able to come for a month."

Leoni rolled on top of Aspen and pressed her breasts against Aspen's chest. "We'll see about that." Then she inched her way lower down the bed with a trail of kisses until she pulled Aspen into her mouth again.

"Oh, fu..." She didn't complete the word or the thought. Once Leoni's lips were wrapped around her clit, there was nothing in her awareness other than that out-of-this-world sensation. She relaxed back onto the bed, put her hands behind her head, and closed her eyes. Leoni played with Aspen's breasts as she kept a perfect rhythm with her tongue. The extra stimulation quickened Aspen's ascent, and she pinned herself to the bed, so all she could feel was Leoni's expert touch. The buzz of ecstatic electricity built to a crescendo before Aspen crashed through her thinly held barrier of control, and she tumbled into the pleasure, experiencing a sense of instant joy that rippled through every muscle.

Leoni raised her head only after she'd milked Aspen of every last shudder and pulse of delight, and she had to pull away, unable to take any more.

Leoni looked exceptionally pleased with herself. "You were saying about not being able to come for me?" She climbed halfway up Aspen's body and rested her wet chin on Aspen's stomach.

Aspen swallowed, her mouth dry. "I was wrong."

Leoni traced her fingernail over Aspen's tattoo, more languidly than she had last night, and she looked thoughtful.

"Is something wrong?" Aspen couldn't imagine what that might be after the exceptional night they'd shared, but clearly something had slipped into Leoni's mind and was bothering her.

"Nothing's wrong," she said. "It's just... This is very intense."

Aspen wanted more but Leoni's expectant look told her she needed a response first. She played with a wisp of Leoni's hair, the soft silkiness of it tickling her fingers. "That's a good thing, isn't it?"

"I don't know," Leoni said. "This is all new territory. I haven't felt anything like this before. Have you?"

Aspen smiled, a little smug now. She liked the idea of being a first *something* for Leoni. "I guess you have to tell me what it feels like for you, so I can answer that question."

Leoni tapped Aspen's stomach gently. "This isn't the time to fish for compliments."

She tilted her head. "Are you *sure*? 'Cause it kind of feels like it is." When Leoni arched her eyebrow, Aspen melted.

"I've already told you how I feel about you." Leoni dropped her gaze to Aspen's chest as if her tattoo required a closer study.

Aspen swallowed. Leoni *had* said the words but, if the way she'd almost crushed Aspen's hand was anything to go by, *I love you* had come after a particularly intense orgasm, and that wasn't always the most truthful time for anyone. "You meant what you said last night?"

Leoni frowned and looked up. "Of course I did. They're not words I'd ever say lightly."

Aspen nodded slowly. Their family situations had been so different, and Leoni had explained what she'd been through, but Aspen hadn't really grasped the depth of those effects until now, when the vulnerability was so real in Leoni's eyes.

Leoni's expression darkened, and she suddenly pushed up from Aspen and sat back on her heels. "Did *you* not mean it?"

Aspen sat up and grasped Leoni's hands. "Oh, I *definitely*

meant it." She kissed Leoni's knuckles and looked into her eyes, hoping Leoni could see the way she felt. "I love you, Leoni. I don't know what witchcraft it is either, and it *is* intense in a way I've never experienced."

Leoni was silent for a while. "You've been in love before," she said quietly. "You've said it to other women and meant it. How is this different?"

"You're right, I have. And I did mean it. But what I felt wasn't *this*." Aspen caressed Leoni's cheek. "I'm not good with words, so I don't know that I can put what's in my heart into a sentence that's powerful enough to really do justice to it." She pulled Leoni closer and kissed her forehead. "But I can spend years *showing* you...if you'll let me."

"Smooth," Leoni said and gave a half-smile. "I know there are no guarantees or certainties, and I'm not asking for any. I'm just a little scared by how much I feel already, y'know?"

Aspen nodded. "It's the same for me, I promise." She thought briefly about Sarah, about the football team's cheerleading captain, and about the couple of women in between. She *had* loved them, and with Sarah especially, she'd thought it might last— Hell, that's why she'd proposed. But now, it was clear they'd just been the support act for the headliner.

"So the grand gesture last night wasn't too much?" Leoni asked.

Aspen grinned. "Are you kidding? Do you have any idea how many times I've dreamed about a beautiful woman with a voice as gorgeous as yours singing just for me?"

"You have not!"

"I have! That's why I wanted to hear you sing when we were camping." Aspen slipped her hand around Leoni's neck and kissed her deeply. "You have an amazing voice, and the reality blew the fantasy into another universe." She pulled back slightly. "Willow told me you've moved to New York to try to get into the theater. Is that true?"

Leoni frowned. "You sound doubtful."

Aspen ran her fingers down Leoni's arm and tilted her head slightly. "My sister's been known to bend the truth a little to get what she wants. I wasn't sure if she was telling me what I wanted to hear, so that I'd invite you last night."

Leoni narrowed her eyes. "I think we should talk about that."

Aspen's chest tightened momentarily until she consciously repeated *Live in the moment* in her mind. "Which part isn't true? The move or the theater?" After last night, after finally experiencing what they could be together, what compromises and concessions was she prepared to make?

"They're both true," Leoni said. "But what if I hadn't left my job? What if I was still just a 'body for hire to the rich and shameless?' Would that still be a problem?"

Aspen sighed and flopped back on the bed. "I know where you're going with this," she said, "and it was the thing I wanted to apologize to you for last night."

Leoni gave a tight smile. "I'm all ears."

"I wasn't being fair," Aspen said. "Flynn pointed out that people do what they have to so they can get by, and I didn't have the right to judge you for your job."

Leoni nodded slowly. "I appreciate that, but that's not all it's about, is it? You said that you couldn't risk your heart on someone who pretends to be someone else, who pretends to have feelings for other people, but my new job doesn't change that." She shrugged. "That's what acting is too, except I'll actually be kissing and touching those people in front of hundreds of other people. I'm still a 'body for hire,' aren't I?"

Aspen scrubbed her hand over her head. "Crap. I hadn't looked at it like that."

Leoni's eyes widened as she edged away slightly. "So now what?"

She didn't miss the look of panic in Leoni's eyes as she grasped at the bedsheet and pulled it across her. Aspen sat back up and placed her hands on Leoni's covered thighs. "It doesn't change a thing. I've been getting therapy a couple times a week since you left, and I've been working on my trust issues and on the anger from my relationship with Sarah. I'm learning to let it all go so I can love in the present."

"Learning?" Leoni asked.

Aspen nodded and chuckled. "I'm a work in progress."

"Aren't we all?" Leoni laughed lightly and relaxed her white-knuckled grip on the sheet.

"I've recognized that I've got trust issues, and I'll overcome them. I see now that it doesn't matter what you do for a living. Meeting new people is part of any career, and you could fall for anyone. I've just got to make sure that you know how much I love you and that I give you everything you need, and then you won't have to look elsewhere."

Leoni arched her eyebrow. "Is that how it works?"

Aspen nodded. "I hope so." She motioned to the bedsheet. "You don't need that, I promise."

Leoni let the barrier fall away. "It was a pretty poor replacement for the walls you've broken down already," she said and smiled.

"You don't need those either." Aspen took Leoni's hand and placed it over her own heart. "And neither do I." She sighed deeply. "I *know* this is different. I *feel* it. So will you bear with me while I carve the best version of myself for you?"

"I will." Leoni pressed her lips to Aspen's, sealing the deal. She pulled back and giggled, clutching her stomach as it growled.

Aspen laughed. "Someone's hungry." She held up her hand when Leoni opened her mouth to talk. "I know, I know. That's my fault too for using up all your energy all night."

"Do you think it's safe to go downstairs, or will there be a welcoming committee?"

Aspen shook her head. "How is it you know my family so well after only spending a week with them?"

"I've been talking to Willow a lot over the past month, so I've been learning all about you," Leoni said and winked. "You can quiz me if you like."

"Maybe later," Aspen said when Leoni's stomach growled again, this time much louder. "We need to feed you."

Leoni swung her legs off the bed. "Mm, I didn't bring an overnight bag…"

Aspen jumped off the other side and pulled out a pair of sweats from a drawer and a plaid shirt from her closet. "For old time's sake." She offered Leoni the clothes and grinned.

Leoni came closer, smiling mischievously. "Only if you dress me."

"Happy to." Aspen slowly covered Leoni with her shirt and pulled it closed before buttoning it from the bottom up. When she'd finished, she stepped back and let out an appreciative sigh. Leoni looked like Aspen's wet dream with the shirt almost halfway down her thighs. "Maybe you don't need the sweats," she whispered.

Leoni arched her eyebrow and lifted her leg, toe pointing downward like a ballet dancer. "Your family is downstairs; I need the sweats."

Aspen rolled her eyes. "Fine." She got to her knees and slipped them on, taking her sweet time to pull the waistband over Leoni's perfect little butt.

Leoni ran her hand through Aspen's hair and tugged her head back slightly. "You look good down there."

Aspen gave her a wicked smile. "*You* look good from *down* here."

Leoni's stomach grumbled again. "Another time?"

Aspen got to her feet and held out her hand. "Definitely."

Leoni's small hand felt perfect and warm in Aspen's as they headed downstairs.

They stopped at the kitchen door, and Leoni gestured to the counter, where Aspen's half-eaten birthday cake sat. "Looks like you missed out last night."

"Hardly. Last night was better than all the cake in the world, or anything else you can think of." Aspen tugged Leoni in for a hard kiss. "Hey, everyone," she said as they entered the kitchen. Just as Leoni had predicted, most of the family were gathered for breakfast. They were spared anything overly embarrassing. Flynn's eyebrow quirked, and she grinned, but everyone else smiled normally and greeted them both as if they'd been coming down together to the family post-party breakfasts for years. Aspen hadn't clocked that Willow was missing until she emerged from the pantry.

"Yes, yes, yes!" she yelled and practically tossed the tray of eggs onto the kitchen counter before she ran across the marble floor and jumped into Aspen's arms.

"Happy Sunday to you too," Aspen said, returning Willow's tight embrace.

Willow let go of Aspen's neck and flung her other arm around Leoni. "I'm so happy I could burst!"

Aspen smiled. Willow had never been interested in her previous relationships, let alone been this invested. "I'm glad you approve."

Willow released them both and gave Aspen a light shove. "I'm glad you got out of your own way." She positioned herself between them and wrapped her arms around their waists. "Can I make you breakfast to celebrate?"

Aspen laughed. "I don't know. Can you? Since when do you cook?"

"Grammy's been teaching me." Willow pulled them to the bar stools, and they sat down while she went around the other side of the counter.

"She's going to be cooking some of our meals every week now that she lives here," Grammy said from across the room. "And when she goes on her expeditions, she'll need to cook too. She's getting ready to be self-sufficient, aren't you, peanut?"

"I am." Willow stood a little straighter and sort of wiggled on the spot. "Omelet?"

Leoni clutched her still-growling stomach. "I need *all* the eggs."

"Perfect." Willow began to crack eggs into a bowl she'd pulled from under the counter. "Has Aspen told you she's moving to New

York soon too?"

"No," Leoni said and gave Aspen a side glance.

Aspen slipped off her stool as almost everyone around the main table made some sort of *"What?"* exclamation. "Orange juice?"

Leoni nodded, apparently unaffected by Willow's statement. "We haven't had much time to do a lot of talking," she whispered to Willow, who giggled as she beat the eggs.

"Flynn can explain," Aspen said after she'd filled two glasses and sat back down beside Leoni. "But nothing's set in stone yet."

Flynn grinned. "I wanted to wait until we'd gotten everything in place, but..." She held Kelly's hand, and her eyes lit up. "All this travel isn't working for us, and I can't stand being so far away from you all the time. So I asked Aspen if she'd think about opening a second office in Manhattan, or maybe closing the San Francisco one and moving everything to the East Coast. So we're just working out the logistics around our existing client base."

"Oh my God, baby, that's amazing." Kelly beamed, then she gave Flynn's arm a light tug. "How did I not realize you were keeping a secret from me?"

Flynn shrugged. "Apparently I can keep the good ones."

"That's wonderful news," their mom said. "It'll be fabulous to have you both so close to home again."

"*If* everything works out," Aspen said, though now that she and Leoni were a thing, she couldn't see herself wanting to do the kind of traveling Flynn and Kelly had been doing either. Flynn gave her a look that implied she'd read her mind. "What do you think? Would you want me closer?"

Leoni frowned. "Do you really need to ask?"

Aspen shrugged. "I don't know how you see us working. I didn't want to assume."

Leoni laughed lightly. "I have no idea either, but we'll figure it out. And we'll make it work." She picked up a fork and pulled Aspen's birthday cake toward her.

"Cake for breakfast?" Aspen smiled. "What about the omelet?"

"I'll have room, don't worry. I can eat cake and chocolate *any* time of the day. Didn't you know it goes in a different part of the stomach?" Leoni waved her fork in the air after she'd munched on a piece of cake. "It's just another thing you don't know about me."

Aspen moved in for a kiss and tasted the sweetness on Leoni's lips. "That's okay. I've got a lifetime to learn everything there is to know. And I can't wait."

Epilogue

Two years later

Leoni gently touched the ebony black wig on her head as she checked herself in the mirror for the final time before curtain up. Everything was perfect: costume, hair, makeup. She looked up at the handwritten message from Aspen, which she'd pinned to the top right of her mirror beneath the bright bulbs.

Butterflies in your stomach just mean you're about to fly. You were made for this x

She kissed her fingertips, then pressed them to the paper. Aspen would be out in the audience. Willow had come back early from a college expedition especially to see the show, and Leoni's mom, Flynn and Kelly, and the rest of the Hartwell family would be there too. And every one of them would be cheering her on in her first lead role performance on Broadway. While she'd been prepared to work in Off Broadway shows forever so long as she could tread the boards, this right here was everything she'd dreamed about as a young girl, everything she'd hoped she could achieve as she worked her way through college.

There was a light knock on her dressing room door, startling her a little. "Come in," she called.

Aspen peeked around the corner with a huge smile. "Victor said it was okay... Do you mind?"

Leoni jumped up from her chair, yanked the door open, and pulled Aspen in by her tie. "You look good enough to eat," she said, admiring the way Aspen filled out her navy suit. "I'm really going to enjoy undressing you later."

Aspen grinned and wrapped her arms around Leoni's waist. "I can't wait for that—*obviously*—but I didn't mean to distract you. You're ready to blow them away and give them the best Elphaba they've ever seen?"

Leoni inclined her head. "I think you're forgetting Cynthia Erivo."

"I think *you're* forgetting how amazing you are."

Leoni cupped Aspen's cheek. She didn't believe it, but she loved that Aspen did. "I wish I could kiss you right now, but Katie would kill me if I smudged my makeup, and I don't want to be on the sharp end of her Northern English tongue."

"You better not want to be on the end of anyone's tongue other than mine," Aspen said and winked.

Leoni placed her hand on Aspen's crotch and squeezed gently. "That's one thing you'll never have to worry about."

Aspen's eyes half-lidded, and she moaned quietly. "You're making me wish your standby could take your place." She caught Leoni's wrist and moved away from her touch. "But you have an audience to wow and a reputation to seal with the most memorable opening performance of your life."

Leoni scoffed. "No pressure then."

Aspen kissed Leoni's hand. "See you out there, superstar," she said and closed the door behind her.

Moments later, the intercom in her dressing room alerted her to get into position. Leoni hummed her scales as she slowly walked to her entrance, then she began to mutter, "Imagine an imaginary menagerie manager managing an imaginary menagerie," over and over. Victor motioned her over, and she climbed the steps to stand in the wing, waiting to rush on stage onto the courtyard of Shiz University.

Suddenly her poise abandoned her, and her pulse pounded in her ears so loud that she could barely hear Samantha delivering her speech, trying to explain how she could possibly have been friends with the wicked witch. Leoni placed her hand on her stomach to steady her quickening breaths and tried to ignore the heavy knock of her heart against her ribs like a battering ram. She closed her eyes and pictured Aspen's note. *You were made for this.* God, she hoped so, or she was about to make a total ass of herself in front of over sixteen-hundred people.

Leoni swallowed against her Sahara-dry mouth and drew in a long breath through her lips for sixty seconds before she released it slowly. Her heart calmed to a gentler tap, and her legs stiffened like steel beneath her. She *was* ready, and she *would* deliver the performance of her life. There was her cue, and Leoni ran on stage and into the bright burning lights of the Gershwin Theatre.

Nearly three hours later, she stood alongside the rest of the *Wicked* cast for their fifth curtain call. Every single member of the audience was on their feet, but Leoni only had eyes for the group of people in the center of rows one to three. Aspen's love shone like the sun, and Leoni bet her hands were sore from her non-stop clapping. Leoni's mom was in tears, her makeup completely ruined. She'd stopped clapping after the third call, and her hands were clamped to her face. Willow's joy was clear too, and she switched between clapping and bouncing up and down. Flynn and Kelly, plus the rest of the family and grandparents smiled and gave their appreciative applause.

Leoni blew them all kisses as the main drape finally went down, then she was enveloped in a tight embrace from Samantha, and the cast congratulated each other.

"You were spectacular." Samantha clasped Leoni's hands. "I had goosebumps when you sang 'No One Mourns the Wicked.'"

Leoni shook her head, a little dumbstruck. "I don't have the words," she whispered, her throat choked with the emotion of it all.

Samantha draped her arm over Leoni's shoulder as they made their way off stage. "Let's lubricate you with some celebratory champagne and see if we can change that."

Leoni opened her dressing room door and entered backward as she continued to respond to the amazing feedback from the rest of the cast. She closed the door quietly, rested her head against it, and closed her eyes. *I did it.*

"I've got a feeling there's a Tony Award coming your way."

Leoni turned around quickly at the sound of Aspen's voice, but she could barely see her over the gigantic bouquet of stargazer lilies she held in front of her. "Baby!"

Aspen placed the flowers on Leoni's dressing table just in time to catch Leoni in her arms.

Leoni pressed her lips to Aspen's and kissed her passionately. If she hadn't already been off the ground, the kiss would've defied gravity and lifted her up anyway. She pulled back breathlessly and laughed when she saw her shimmering green lipstick had transferred to Aspen's lips, as had some of her green-face makeup.

Aspen let Leoni down to her feet again and looked in the mirror. "Tell no one of this," she said and grinned, before she grabbed a tissue to wipe at her lips and chin.

Katie burst into the dressing room with her clean-up kit and shook her head when she saw Leoni wasn't alone. "Kisses ain't skincare. You need to do one so I can take the green shit off her missus's face." She held the door open and pointed while giving Aspen her stern *I take no crap* look.

Aspen gave Leoni one last kiss and retreated quickly before Katie was forced to physically kick her out, which she was more than able to do, despite her diminutive stature.

"Alreyt, chuck. Sit yersen down, and let's get this muck off yer face."

Leoni complied, and her normal skin color was soon uncovered. After Katie had been kind enough to quickly apply some light makeup and lipstick, Leoni got out of her costume and slipped into the navy satin charmeuse halter gown and gold shoes she'd treated herself to when she'd gotten this part. She adjusted the gold necklace holding the dress up, smoothed the A-line silhouette over her waist and hips, and checked herself out in the full-length mirror. "You'll do," she said and swept out of her dressing room to join the after-party on the fourth floor of the main building.

When the elevator doors opened, Leoni saw Aspen waiting just to the side with two glasses of champagne in her hands. Her mouth dropped slightly open, and her eyes gave away her desire in the most perfect way. Two years in, and the fire still burned bright in that, and every other, department.

Aspen strutted toward her, shaking her head. Leoni gave her a full twirl. "That's beautiful, but I can't see a way in."

She ran her finger down Aspen's tie. "Left side concealed zipper," she whispered into Aspen's ear, "but I'll be keeping it on while you're on your back wearing just this tie."

Aspen gulped and offered Leoni a glass. "I'll drink to that."

Just as they toasted, Leoni's mom rushed up and pulled her into a hug. "I'm *so* proud of you, honey."

"Thanks, Mom."

More hugs followed from Willow and the rest of the Hartwell family, and Leoni sighed happily, floating on a cloud of family love, the likes of which she couldn't have dreamed any more than a leading role on Broadway.

Samantha somehow made her way through to Leoni and clinked her glass to Leoni's. "This moment was all we talked about when we were in college. Can you believe it's finally happening?"

Leoni shook her head. "Not quite. It still feels like it might be a dream I'm about to wake up from."

Samantha pinched Leoni's arm. "See? It's totally real."

"Ouch." Leoni slapped Samantha's hand away.

"Leoni, you amazing creature."

She turned toward her director and gave him a hug. "Victor, thank you. Thank you for believing in me." She pulled away slightly and peered into his eyes. "Did I do okay?"

His raucous laugh filled the room. "*Okay?* Sweetie, you were divine." He motioned to the woman by his side. "Which is why Harper Quinn of *Playbill* would very much like to interview you," he glanced at Aspen, "*if* you can tear yourself away from your hunky companion."

Aspen blushed adorably, and Leoni kissed her cheek. "Do you mind?"

She shook her head. "I'll be here." She slipped her hand around Leoni's neck and drew her in for a deep, passionate kiss. "I'll always be here."

As Leoni pulled away, she took a few seconds to gaze into Aspen's soulful eyes and knew, without a shadow of doubt, that Aspen really would always be there. It had taken them both a little while to settle into their rhythm, but Aspen had overcome her trust issues, and Leoni had let her fear of abandonment go. Surrounded by the intensity of love from Aspen, Leoni's mom, Willow, and the rest of their family now, Leoni could barely recall how lonely life had been before she'd landed the sister act job. And she could never have imagined that would result in a handsome partner, a wonderful best friend, and a loving extended family.

The past no longer held either of them in its fevered grip and, just like Aspen's therapist had advised, they were living and loving in the present. And damn, their present life was better than any of those romantic movies her mom loved so much, and their happy ending was just beginning.

~ THE END ~

Thank you for reading *The Sister Act*. If you enjoyed Leoni and Aspen each discovering the love of their life, it would be amazing if you could pop a review on Amazon for me! If you haven't read any of my other books, maybe you'd like to try my number one US bestseller *Sanctuary* (the first in the Windy City Romance series).

And if you'd like to keep up to date with my new projects (and Ally McGuire's), sign up for the Wifey Romance newsletter, which I share with the love of my life, and get a free co-write short story (rebrand.ly/WifeyRomance). See you there!

Other Great Butterworth Books

Unwritten by Helena Harte
No strings is fun 'til it unravels.
Available from Amazon (ASIN B0DGQFFHYB)

Heart of the Storm by Ally McGuire
Sometimes a storm is just what you need to clear the skies ahead.
Available on Amazon (ASIN B0CYTSQXWW)

Change in Time by RJ Nyx
Book Two in The Extractor Series: Working in the past is hell on your future.
Available on Amazon (ASIN B0DWG24C66)

Racing Hearts by Sydney Lear
Life in the fast lane is great...until you lose control.
Available from Amazon (ASIN B0DZP9X3G2)

Driving Me Barking by JP Preston
Sometimes to find yourself, you have to lose your imaginary friends first.
Available on Amazon (ASIN B0DWG1LLXN)

Escape in Time by RJ Nyx
Book One in The Extractor Series: Working in the past is hell on your future.
Available on Amazon (ASIN B0DSJFDZ7R)

Ship of Dreams by Brey Willows
Two rival captains, one deadly mission, and secrets that could set the skies ablaze.
Available on Amazon (ASIN B0DRW1X75N)

Chucking Putty at the Queen by Simon Smalley
A heartbreaking, humorous, and courageous exploration of what it takes to be ones authentic self.
Available from Amazon (ASIN B0DGGBV22W)

The Promise by Addison M Conley
When the world keeps pulling you under, who do you reach for?
Available on Amazon (ASIN B0DDY9FH6Z)

Back to Back by Jo Fletcher
."When Fred and Ruby's worlds collide, can love rise from the rubble?"
Available on Amazon (ASIN B0D6M499K2)

Sanctuary by Helena Harte
Passions ignite and possibilities unfold. Welcome to the Windy City Romance series.
Available from Amazon (ASIN B0D4B42RRW)

Brave Enough to Love by Valden Bush
In a dance between truth and sacrifice, can they rewrite the rules of love?
Available on Amazon (ASIN B0CQP8PMVB)

Dead Ringer by Robyn Nyx
Three bodies. One killer. No motive?
Available on Amazon (ASIN B0CPQ8HFK7)

Medea by JJ Taylor
Who will Medea become in her battle for freedom?
Available from Amazon (ASIN B0CK2FB7GW)

Virgin Flight by E.V. Bancroft
In the battle between duty and desire, can love win?
Available from Amazon (ASIN B0CKJWQZ45)

Fragments of the Heart by Ally McGuire
Love can be the greatest expedition of all.
Available on Amazon (ASIN B0CHBPHR6M)

Here You Are by Jo Fletcher
.Can they unlock their hearts to find the true happiness they both deserve?
Available on Amazon (ASIN B0CBN935ZB)

Stunted Heart by Helena Harte
A stunt rider who lives in the fast lane. An ER doctor who can't take chances. A passion that could turn their worlds upside down.
Available on Amazon (ASIN B0C78GSWBV)

Dark Haven by Brey Willows
Even vampires get tired of playing with their food...
Available on Amazon (ASIN B0C5P1HJXC)

An Art to Love by Helena Harte
Second chances are an art form.
Available on Amazon (ASIN B0B1CD8Y42)

Let Love Be Enough by Robyn Nyx
When a killer sets her sights on her target, is there any stopping her?
Available on Amazon (ASIN B09YMMZ8XC)

Dead Pretty by Robyn Nyx
An FBI agent, a TV star, and a serial killer. Love hurts.
Available on Amazon (ASIN B09QRSKBVP)

Nero by Valden Bush
Banished and abandoned. Will destiny reunite her with the love of her life?
Available from Amazon (ASIN B0BHJKHK6S)

Warm Pearls and Paper Cranes by E.V. Bancroft
A family torn apart by secrets. The only way forward is love.
Available from Amazon (ASIN B09DTBCQ92)

Judge Me, Judge Me Not by James Merrick
One man's battle against the world and himself to find it's never too late to find, and use, your voice.
Available from Amazon (ASIN B09CLK91N5)

Music City Dreamers by Robyn Nyx
Music brings lovers together. In Music City, it can tear them apart.
Available on Amazon (ASIN B0994XVDGR)

Scripted Love by Helena Harte
What good is a romance writer who doesn't believe in happy ever after?
Available on Amazon (ASIN B0993QFLNN)

Call to Me by Helena Harte
Sometimes the call you least expect is the one you need the most.
Available on Amazon (ASIN B08D9SR15H)

What's Your Story?

Global Wordsmiths, CIC, provides an all-encompassing service for all writers, ranging from basic proofreading and cover design to development editing, typesetting, and eBook services. A major part of our work is charity and community focused, delivering writing projects to under-served and under-represented groups across Nottinghamshire, giving voice to the voiceless and visibility to the unseen.

To learn more about what we offer, visit: www.globalwords.co.uk

A selection of books by Global Words Press:
Desire, Love, Identity: with the National Justice Museum
Aventuras en México: Farmilo Primary School
Times Past: with The Workhouse, National Trust
Young at Heart with AGE UK
In Different Shoes: Stories of Trans Lives

Self-published authors working with Global Wordsmiths:

Max Beeken
Maggie McIntyre
John Parsons
Dani Lovelady Ryan
Kit Stone